T0165594

Praise for Aliya S. King and *Platinum*

"Fast-paced. . . . An entertaining mix of sex, betrayals, high drama, and tragedy [that] will keep the pages turning."

—*Publishers Weekly*

"The unbeatable combination of sex, drugs, and hip-hop makes for entertaining reading, and readers won't want to put this down. . . . The ending will blow you away."

—*Romantic Times*

"*Platinum* is a great choice for a beach read because of the pace of the story, but it has something most beach reads lack: good writing. . . . A noteworthy debut."

—*Clutch Magazine*

"A quick and exciting read full of glamour, intense drama, and characters loosely based on people we all love to stalk via gossip magazines and blogs."

—Global Grind

"An entertaining, fast-paced read that not only leaves you on the edge of your seat but provides a full serving of drama, plot twists, and realism. . . . Well-crafted."

—APOOO BookClub

"Engrossing."

—AllHipHop

"Stellar. . . . Captivating. . . . *Platinum* will take you on a rollercoaster ride."

—The Fresh Xpress

"A juicy ride through love in the hip-hop fast lane. The plot twists will make you wince and squirm, especially when you try to imagine the real-life characters who may have suffered such indignities!"

—Erica Kennedy, *New York Times* bestselling author of *Bling*

PLAT

INUM

Aliya S. King

A Touchstone Book
Published by Simon & Schuster
New York   London   Toronto   Sydney

Touchstone
A Division of Simon & Schuster, Inc.
1230 Avenue of the Americas
New York, NY 10020

First Touchstone trade paperback edition May 2011

TOUCHSTONE and colophon are registered trademarks of Simon & Schuster, Inc.

For information about special discounts for bulk purchases, please contact Simon &
Schuster Special Sales at 1-866-506-1949 or business@simonandschuster.com.

The Simon & Schuster Speakers Bureau can bring authors to your live event. For more
information or to book an event contact the Simon & Schuster Speakers Bureau at 1-866-
248-3049 or visit our website at www.simonspeakers.com.

Designed by Akasha Archer

Manufactured in the United States of America

1   3   5   7   9   10   8   6   4   2

Library of Congress has cataloged the hardcover edition as follows:

King, Aliya S.
Platinum / by Aliya King.
p. cm.
1. African American women—Fiction. 2. Sound recording industry—Fiction.
3. New York (N.Y.)—Fiction. 4. Urban Fiction. I. Title.
PS3611.I5713P57 2010
813'.6—dc22
2010003780

ISBN 978-1-4391-6025-1
ISBN 978-1-4391-6026-8 (pbk)
ISBN 978-1-4391-6500-3 (ebook)

Dedication

This book is dedicated to three people (and one collective group of friends in my head) who inspire me to write every day:

Dr. Gerald Davis: my professor of African American literature at Rutgers University. In 1990, I wrote in a paper that I hoped to one day write a novel that he would teach in his class. He wrote in the margins: "I'd *leap* at the chance!" My heart swelled. Someone believed it was possible! He made *me* believe it was possible.

Dr. Gerald Davis passed away in 1997.

Mrs. Lillie Gist: My English teacher for both ninth and twelfth grade at Clifford Scott High School in East Orange, New Jersey. When I returned as a teacher, she became my confidante. When I left to pursue a writing career, she was my biggest cheerleader. The tiny clips I sent her from small magazines thrilled her. I can't even imagine how proud she'd be to hold this book in her hands.

Mrs. Gist passed away in 2006. I'm still heartbroken.

And, Mrs. Rita Z. King. She gave me my first job as a writer for *The Fifth Ward Quarterly* (circulation: 250). She was my first editor. And I learned from her not only the basics of writing but the tenacity and determination it takes to follow your dreams.

I walked with her to the mailbox as she sent off pitches to *Reader's Digest* and *Essence*. We crossed our fingers and dreamed of seeing her name in print on the walk home. I read the rejection letters that were sent back, all worded very nicely, that she collected in her bureau.

Every time I get a story accepted, I feel like I'm sharing the byline with my mom.

Thankfully, Mrs. Rita King is very much alive and kicking. She works out every morning at 5:30 A.M. Drinks water and eats oatmeal and stays away from sweets. She'll outlive us all. This woman takes no tea for the fever.

Finally, this book is dedicated to my dear readers at aliyasking.com. The ones who always comment, (Hey Katura!) and the ones who lurk and never say a word. Knowing you log on and read what I have to say is inspiring. I'm humbled by your support, and I love you all for being a part of my online world. I won't run away again. I promise.

PLATINUM

one

BETH DIPPED HER HEAD AND SLID HER SHADES FROM HER FOREHEAD to the bridge of her nose. It was out of habit, not necessity. There wouldn't be any photographers in the parking lot of her gynecologist's office at seven a.m. on a Saturday.

She'd only been photographed alone once, last summer, when she went to Riker's Island after Z punched out a cop at a concert at Madison Square Garden. The paparazzi caught her speeding up to the courthouse to post bail, her dirty blond hair covering her eyes and tears streaming down her face.

In the doctor's office, Beth kept her eyes straight ahead, grabbed a clipboard, scanned it quickly, and signed it. She returned the paperwork to the receptionist, who gave her a look of half boredom and half disdain. Beth wondered if the look was especially for her. Or if every patient got the same look.

It could have been that she recognized the name Beth Saddlebrook and wondered what it was like to be married to someone like Z. Or she could have noticed that she marked off "specific problem" instead of "general wellness checkup" as the reason for her visit.

She sat in one of Dr. Hamilton's examining rooms, her long legs dangling over the side of the vinyl-covered table. A nurse came in to ask preliminary questions. Beth told her she thought she might have a yeast infection, something she knew was not true. The next nurse gave her a cup for a urine sample and then took a vial of blood. They'd test it for whatever they could right in the office and Dr. Hamilton would look over the results before she came in. She'd be able to tell Beth what she really needed to know.

Sweat dripped down the small of Beth's broad back. She was built like a linebacker—and sweated like one. She wasn't fat. But her mother always said she came out of the womb as solid as a concrete wall.

The central air in the doctor's office made the examination room feel like the inside of a meat locker. But the beads of sweat on her forehead kept popping up. It was as if her body didn't believe it had escaped from the thick, muggy August heat.

Dr. Hamilton didn't do the courtesy knock. She opened the door with such force that it banged against the wall and slammed shut before she was facing Beth.

"You have trichomoniasis," she said, and then folded her arms tight across her chest. Like Beth, Dr. Hamilton was one of those white girls from West Virginia who could neck-swivel better than most black girls from Jersey. And like most white women with roots in the South, she had a no-nonsense demeanor that belied her ethnicity. She had been Beth's first and only gynecologist. She'd known her since Beth was twelve.

Beth pretended to be shocked and confused, raising a hand to her mouth and looking around the tiny room as if the explanation for her latest malady could be found in the glass container of cotton balls or the box of disposable gloves.

"You haven't had enough, Beth?" Dr. Hamilton's eyes bored holes into the top of her head. "Will you leave him before or after he gives you HIV?"

Beth flipped up her head to the ceiling and then leveled it at Dr. Hamilton.

"My period is late," she said. "I thought I should come in because—"

Dr. Hamilton let out a loud rush of breath—a snort that had tinges of a scream. She turned her back on Beth and went to the door.

"Yeah, you're pregnant too. Get undressed. I'll be back to examine you."

Beth carefully took off her tracksuit. Beth's closet was lined with her uniform: tracksuits in vinyl, cotton, and velour. She knew a Juicy sweat suit wasn't exactly the height of couture. Especially among the other wives in the New Jersey enclave she lived in, also known as Rappers Row because so many artists lived there. But Beth couldn't compete with those women anyway. They bought new bags every three months, something Beth couldn't understand. If it was still functional, why would you buy a new pocketbook? Because it was *seasonal*? And Beth couldn't fathom wearing stilettos, skirts, or dresses any more than she could fathom buying a new purse just because the season had changed. Beth had enough money to walk into Gucci and leave it completely empty. She was sent dresses and sumptuous leather boots by designers every week. They were all dutifully boxed up and sent to her friends back home in West Virginia. Tracksuits were good enough for her. They were easy and comfortable and hid her body well.

Beth was from Miracle Run, a mining town in West Virginia. Halfway between Ragtown and Bula, Miracle Run didn't quite live up to its name. No miracles. And nowhere to run. Nothing but dirt, rattlers, and of course coal; a thin layer of dust hung in the air at all times, clogging your ears, your brain, and your way of thinking.

Now, in Dr. Hamilton's office, Beth was many years and five hundred miles away from Miracle Run. She lived in a McMansion purchased with the profits of her husband's tour dates and royalties. She had a staff of people running her massive house, just three doors away from Reverend Run. But she still felt like she needed to protect herself from dirt. In her life, it was everywhere. She knew women like Kimora Simmons snickered at her. But she wore her jumpsuits anyway. And Timberlands too.

Beth closed her eyes tight and stripped off her bra and panties, stuffing them inside the folds of her tracksuit. On *Oprah* she'd once heard that almost all women were fussy about the way they arranged their clothing before a gynecological exam. No one ever left panties on the outside of that sad little bundle of clothing. Even though they were about to have their legs splayed and their orifices probed, somehow visible underwear would make them feel even more vulnerable. Beth pulled the gown over her body and scooted her butt down low to the edge of the table so Dr. Hamilton wouldn't have to tell her to. She stared at the ceiling, calculating. *If I'm pregnant, the baby was conceived in early July. Had to be like the first of the month, 'cause that was the same day Z came back from Anguilla.*

She listened closely to see if she could hear Dr. Hamilton out in the hall. When she was sure she heard nothing, she hopped up, went into the pocket of her track pants, and took out a crumpled sheet of paper. She positioned herself back on the table just as Dr. Hamilton did a courtesy one-knock and came back in.

"You've had seventeen urinary tract infections," said Dr. Hamilton, sitting on the wheeled stool and rolling herself up to Beth. She put Beth's feet in the stirrups and snapped on a pair of gloves.

"That's genetic," Beth said, bracing herself for the doctor's touch.

Dr. Hamilton didn't even pretend she was paying attention. "You've had gonorrhea, syphilis, and you may have HPV, which is the virus that causes cervical cancer. You've had seven yeast infections in the past two years because your husband refuses to get treated for it so he can stop passing it back to you."

Dr. Hamilton did not tell Beth that she was going to put her hand inside her. Without warning, her left hand was deep inside Beth, probing. Her right hand was pressing into Beth's abdomen. Usually Dr. Hamilton was quiet during the actual examination, her head cocked to one side as if she could hear Beth's body speaking to her. But this time she talked straight through like she was giving a lecture.

"You come in here with things I can treat," she said, her fingers on Beth's cervix. "And then you come in here with things I can't.

Like herpes. Which, by the way, you will have forever, as I'm sure you know."

Dr. Hamilton removed her fingers from Beth, peeled her gloves off, and let out a deep sigh. Beth pushed herself up to a sitting position, trying to keep the gown from slipping off.

"I'm not sure if I can continue to treat you," said Dr. Hamilton, looking over Beth's file. "If you won't take any measures to protect yourself and stay healthy, I really don't want any part of—"

"How far along am I?" Beth asked.

Dr. Hamilton rubbed one hand over her face, put her clipboard down on the counter behind her, and gave Beth a wan smile.

"About eight weeks."

Beth grimaced. "Eight? Are you sure? We didn't start trying until six weeks ago, which means the baby was conceived when? Like around the first? It couldn't be mid-July, right?" Beth's eyes swept the office for a calendar. "It would have to be around the first of the month—" Beth had her mouth running so fast, trying to get confirmation that she'd conceived during the right time, that she forgot about the paper in her hand until Dr. Hamilton took it away from her.

"What is this?" Dr. Hamilton glanced at the paper and then her face flushed. "A Chinese birth prediction chart? What the—" She rolled her eyes. "Do I really need to refer you to a psychiatrist?"

"That chart was buried in China seven thousand years ago and it's ninety percent accurate," Beth said, reaching for the paper. "I tried it with my mother and me and all my brothers and it came out right every time."

Dr. Hamilton's shoulders slumped. She leaned against the door to the room and clutched the clipboard to her chest.

"You have four healthy boys," she said in a soft voice. "Beautiful boys. I delivered every one of them."

They exchanged a brief look. In her third pregnancy, Beth had been pregnant with twins. Only one survived. Z blamed Dr. Hamilton. Beth did not.

"You cannot continue to subject yourself to that man's disease-ridden flesh because he wants a little girl. You just can't."

Beth smoothed her hands across her hair, calculating her due date in her head. She *felt* it this time. She'd never *felt* like she was having a girl. But this time was different. Beth had read *How to Choose the Sex of Your Baby* by some guy named Shettles. He said that boy sperms were faster and more aggressive, so if penetration was deep, the boy sperms had a head start. If you just did it missionary style, there was a better chance for the girls to make it.

She'd done everything in the book. She didn't actually have the whole book. She'd never read a whole book. But she had a photocopied packet of all the important stuff that she'd gotten from her best friend, Kipenzi. Kipenzi didn't believe a word of it but thought it was entertaining.

For the past six months, she'd only let Z have sex on top of her. No doggie style, ever. He whined, begged, and complained regularly. On one occasion, when he was drunk, he grabbed her shoulders, forced her onto her stomach, and then put one hand underneath her to lift her up. She fought her way out of bed and ran into the room of their oldest son, Zander, and slept on the floor.

Seventeen-year-old Zander found his father passed out in front of the door to his brother Zakee's room, naked and with vomit on his chest and in his three-inch afro. Zander dragged his father to the master bedroom before one of the other kids saw him there and freaked out.

She'd had sex with Z every day in the five days of her ovulation cycle, which meant she had to drive an hour from home to Electric Lady Studios in the Village every day for a quickie on the couch in the studio lounge. She'd kept him away from caffeinated beverages (the caffeine gave those pesky boy sperms an extra boost), and she'd douched with water and vinegar right before they'd had sex. (According to Shettles, the more acidic the woman's body, the better chances for having a girl.)

Kipenzi had highlighted one line from the excerpt. Something about the chances of having a girl being increased if the woman did not have an orgasm. In the margins of the pages, Kipenzi had written "How do you stop yourself from coming?" That was one tip Beth didn't have to worry about. She'd had three orgasms in her life. And only one of them was during sex with Z. (She'd had sex with only two other men in her entire life, both experiences that she actively tried to wipe from her memory.)

"Bethie?"

Hearing the doctor call her by her nickname, the name her mother used to call her, made her head snap up. For a half second she thought it was her mother calling her name, and her brain rushed with an overload of things she would tell her. *I have four boys, Mommy. Just like you.*

"I'm going to give you a prescription for the trich. Here's some information about it," Dr. Hamilton said, pressing some brochures into her hand. "Are you taking prenatals?"

Beth nodded. She'd been taking a prenatal vitamin every morning since she was fifteen and Dr. Hamilton told her she was pregnant with Zander.

"I'm going to refer you to Dr. Browning. He's just joined this practice and he's great. I want you to—"

Beth reached out and grabbed Dr. Hamilton's shoulder. "No."

Dr. Hamilton kept her eyes on her paperwork. "I really think he might be a better—"

"No."

The doctor looked into Beth's face. It was the same round, pasty face that had come into her office in Miracle Run almost fifteen years ago. At fifteen, Beth had already reached her full height, nearly six feet tall. Her mother had brought her in after finding her on the living room couch with Z.

"Caught her with that little nigger from New York City down here visiting family," Beth's mother said, her fat cheek packed with tobacco. "Need to know if she's been fucking. So I can put her ass out directly."

Beth's mother told her to do a full pelvic exam. The young girl screamed bloody murder, bucking and jumping every time the doctor tried to put the speculum inside her.

When Dr. Hamilton told the mother that Beth was pregnant, the woman pulled her hand back as far as it would go and smacked Beth so hard that she rolled off the table and landed on the floor. Her gown came off and she was naked, crying and trying to scamper under the table to avoid her mother's blows. Dr. Hamilton had to pull the woman off Beth and have her escorted from the office. The doctor had never allowed her back in.

But she continued to see Beth through the pregnancy and delivered her son, Zander, with her boyfriend Z standing right next to Beth, cheering Beth on and crying at the same time. Then Dr. Hamilton moved her offices to New Jersey, escaping coal mine country for her own reasons. She thought she'd never see Beth again.

But two years later in came Beth, pregnant for the second time. She was living in Queens with Z, in an apartment in Fresh Meadows. She rode out to Dr. Hamilton's Englewood office in a new Acura, driven by Z's manager. A year later she was pregnant with twins and being chauffeured to the office in a Lincoln Navigator.

Now she drove herself, in one of seven late-model luxury cars, and left the boys with their father or the nanny. Dr. Hamilton had watched Beth grow up. As with all her patients, in some morbid way she was also watching her die. But Beth seemed to be looking for a shortcut.

Dr. Hamilton took Beth's hand off her shoulder and scribbled something on her clipboard.

"Your due date is early May," she said. "Make an appointment with the receptionist for two weeks from today."

Beth nodded and exhaled. Early May. That sounded right. It had to be. She kept her hands folded in her lap until the door closed and then reached for her underwear and began to get dressed. There was a knock and she froze. She grabbed the jacket to her tracksuit and held it up to her body. Dr. Hamilton kept her body outside the door and let her face peek through.

"What if it's another boy?" she asked. Her eyebrows were creased.

"It won't be. The law of averages is on my side," Beth said.

"And if it's a boy?"

"Z wants a girl so bad that I think he can will it to happen," Beth said. "A boy is not an option. We have four already. Are you sure about eight weeks? I'm thinking more like six."

"Eight weeks. Maybe more. Look. It could be a boy," said Dr. Hamilton. "God is just fucking with you at this point. You have to decide if you want to keep creating new life. Or save your own."

Dr. Hamilton closed the door and Beth pulled her legs through her pants and knotted them. She took out the elastic holding her hair back, smoothed her hair down with both hands, and then replaced the band. While she reapplied lip balm and lotion she thought about what Dr. Hamilton said.

She knew the doctor thought she was a fool. Not for trying to have a girl. But for trying to have one with Z.

How exactly do you explain to a doctor that your husband is your hero? How do you explain what it feels like to see a little black boy with dusty hair talk shit to the white man who managed the general store when your own father was scared to ask his boss for a switch to the day shift? How do you fix your mouth to explain that the memory of seeing Z crack a bottle over the back of Leon Tucker's head for poking Beth with a stick made you swell with pride years later?

And what about her boys? Z gave her a reason to take them and run at least once a month. But then what? Then she would become her own mother. What if she couldn't handle single motherhood? Her mother had left her father and taken all the kids. A year later, the state had all the boys and Beth was pregnant.

Beth Saddlebrook had no confidence that she could raise her boys on her own. If nothing else, Z was their father. And in some ways, he was her father too.

Of course there were other women. Of course there was drama. Z was a dog. And as such, he was the leader of their pack. Four boys and a skittish den mother who kept coming up pregnant instead of remembering to replace her NuvaRing. It didn't make sense. And Beth knew that.

She ambled out of the doctor's office, her slew-foot gait making her seem nine months pregnant when she wasn't even showing. She left a twenty-dollar bill on the counter and gestured to the nurse to make sure she saw it. Beth pressed a button on her cell phone and waited. She put the earpiece into her ear and took the stairs to the lobby instead of the elevator so she wouldn't lose the call.

"Who dis?"

"Boo, it's Beth. Where's Z?"

"He's in the basement. In the booth. I'ma tell him to hit you right back."

"No. I need to talk to him now."

"Beth, he don't like it when I give him calls in the booth."

"Boo, it's an emergency."

"Hold on."

"This is Dylan, who is this?"

Beth rolled her eyes. "It's me, Dylan. Put my husband on the phone."

"Beth, can I please have him call you right back? I've been trying to get him to do these drops for three hours."

"I'll hold."

Dylan, the other white girl in Z's life, the one who always knew where he was, inhaled and then exhaled hard through her nose.

"Fine. Hold on, please."

Beth was two miles away, pulling onto the parkway, when her husband finally picked up.

"Who is this?"

"Baby. It's me."

"What's going on? You a'ight? I'm working I can't talk."

Z had a marble-mouth, rapid-fire delivery that made it nearly impossible for some people to understand him. Sometimes Beth wondered how he managed to sell millions of records when he could barely speak clearly.

"I just left the doctor. I'm pregnant."

"Get the fuck out of here! God is good, baby. You know that? God is good."

"I know. It's just like your grandmother said. Four boys and then a girl."

There was a silence on the other line.

"You know it's a girl? How you know already?"

"I don't know for sure. But Z, I feel it this time."

"Yo. You know my grandmother was a powerful woman. She said I wouldn't have nothing I really wanted till I had a baby girl. You heard her say that."

"I know," Beth said, "I remember. But Z, I mean, even if—"

"Don't even play like that, mama. Don't fucking play like that. My grandmother predicted my mother's death. She predicted everything that ever happened in my life, so don't even fucking act like you don't know. Last thing she told me was that my daughter would save my life. I don't even know what the fuck she meant. But we gotta have a baby girl, Beth."

Beth kept her hands tight on the steering wheel. She heard Z inhale something.

"What was that?"

"A Newport, baby, just a cigarette, calm down."

Beth took one hand off the steering wheel just long enough to bite at the cuticle of her thumbnail.

"Are you sure? It's just a cigarette?"

"Don't ride me, Beth."

"I'm sorry, Z! I'm sorry. Calm down."

"I can't talk now. See you at the house."

"I love you, baby."

"Beth, I love you too. Sorry I yelled. You feel okay? You need Boo to get you something?"

"Are you coming home tonight?"

"Yes, baby, I'm coming straight home to kiss both my baby girls."

Beth looked up into her rearview mirror to see the grin spreading across her face. She told her husband she loved him and continued home.

He didn't come home for three days.

FACT: THERE WERE OTHER WOMEN. BETH KNEW THIS. HAD ALWAYS known it. And she'd turned a blind eye for years. He didn't *love* them. He didn't *need* them. He just fucked them. Sex was always a necessary evil for Beth. She'd lost her virginity at twelve to a beer buddy of her father's who thought she was sixteen. Sex was what you did to calm your husband down, keep him home, or apologize. It was not for pleasuring yourself.

So he fucked other women. Fine. Beth just didn't like blatant disrespect. One night in a hotel? Fine. Two nights and now the kids need an explanation? Not cool.

On the third night without her husband in bed with her, Beth turned off *Frasier* and pulled out her laptop. Her fingers flew over the keyboard, taking her to all the gossip sites she scoured. Theybf .com had a huge photo of her best friend, platinum-certified R&B singer Kipenzi, pulling her underwear out of her butt outside a CVS. Beth winced, knowing her friend would be mortified.

She scrolled through all the headlines, looking for her husband's name. When she reached a story she'd read earlier that evening, she clicked out and went to mediatakeout ("You'll never believe who has HERPES and IS SPREADING IT ON PURPOSE!!!!!!!" screamed the headline), then she went to perezhilton and finally concreteloop.

There, in the upper-right-hand corner of concreteloop, were three rotating pictures, highlighting the top stories on the site. A photo came up, under the title *"Coupled Up!"* And there was Z.

Beth clicked on the picture, enlarging it. She peered closely at her computer screen. Z was at a nightclub, wearing clothes Beth had never seen before. He'd often have Boo or Dylan buy him new clothes to avoid coming home. In the picture, he had his hand running through his thick afro while he leaned over to talk to a woman. The woman was standing on tiptoe, her hand cupping his ear. His mouth was wide with laughter.

Beth pulled up her knees and settled the computer on her lap. She brought the screen closer, practically to her nose, as if she could see down to the pixels and understand exactly why her husband was bold enough to be photographed at a club with another woman two days after she told him she was pregnant for the fifth time.

The woman was small and thin with creamy, cocoa brown skin. A long sheet of hair hung down her shoulders. One wide brown eye was visible above her hand. She had on fake eyelashes and tons of mascara.

From her profile, she seemed plain. This worried Beth. When she saw him hugged up with the cute ones, she never worried. They weren't really interested in Z, just wanted to get their pictures on the gossip sites. Z was known to go a week without showering or brushing his teeth, just because. It was the plain ones, like this chick, that would hold their breath and deal with his stench just to get pregnant.

Z usually tired of his groupies before Beth could even catch one. But this one—this one she kept seeing around. Her picture was up in the studio; there were paparazzi shots of them at parties, premieres. Boo told Beth he'd been sleeping in the studio for three nights, overwhelmed by creativity and recording like mad. It was a lie. Beth knew he was with this woman.

And as always, Z was creeping with a black girl.

Beth tried to convince herself that it didn't matter. But it did. She wondered if he was missing something from her. Is that why he cheated? He loved to run his hands in her stick-straight, naturally blond hair. He was constantly staring into her eyes and commenting on how beautiful they were—the color of some marble he had when he was seven. In bed, he'd hold her hand and point out the contrast of their skin. *Damn, you pale as hell,* he would say, smiling. He said it like it was a compliment. Like it was some worthy feat she'd accomplished down in the Miracle Run coal mines.

So why did he *always* cheat with black girls? Did he want to run his fingers through their nappy, kinky hair? Did he like to intertwine his hands through fingers that looked like his? What was it? Beth peered harder into her laptop and jumped when she heard her phone ring. She pressed talk immediately, not taking her eyes off her laptop.

"Yeah?"

"Beth, I'm so tired."

"Kipenzi, you okay?"

"No."

Beth moved her laptop to the bed and sat up straight.

"What's wrong? Where's Jake?"

"Jake's in the studio. Beth, I don't want to sing anymore."

"Is this about the pictures online?"

Kipenzi groaned. "Pictures? From where?"

"Never mind. Are you okay?"

"I'm over it, Beth," Kipenzi said. "I'm really over it. My feet hurt. My throat hurts. I just want to sleep."

"You need a vacation," Beth said.

"No, I need a retirement plan."

"Sleep on it, Kipenzi," Beth said. "Call me first thing in the morning. I'll bet you'll feel different."

Kipenzi hung up and Beth refreshed her Internet connection and did a final lap across all the gossip sites, ending at mediatakeout. ("DOES she have HEMMERRHOIDS!?!? You will NEVER BELIEVE who was caught DIGGING UP HER BUTT at a pharmacy. NASTY!!!! Click here for exclusive photos!!!!!!!") Beth closed her laptop, slid it into the drawer of her nightstand, and turned to her side, holding her belly as she slept.

two

"MS. HILL, IT'S NOW TEN FORTY-FIVE."

The bundle wrapped in Leron custom bed linens didn't move. Ian cleared his throat. And then cleared it again. In seven years, he'd never had to wake his employer. At six a.m. each morning, she packed fresh mint leaves in a tiny teapot her boyfriend Jake had made for her. She was usually wrapped in a thick robe and reading the *New York Times* over a cup when he came into the apartment. So when Ian came in, the smell of mint was usually wafting through the penthouse in Trump Tower. But this morning there was no smell at all.

"Ms. Hill?"

Ian's heart flipped over once. And then he forced himself to remain composed. If something was wrong, if she was . . .

Ian thought of his binders. Lined up on a shelf in Kipenzi's office were ten black binders with her company logo on the spine. Each one contained vital information that was indispensable to a different aspect of Kipenzi's life. There was the travel binder, which listed all the resorts Kipenzi loved, the hotels she hated, and the numbers to all the private jet companies she used. There was the personnel binder: a collection of all the hairstylists, manicurists, waxers, and stylists that Kipenzi used in seven major American cities. When her personal stylists were unavailable, it was Ian's responsibility to fly in one of the women or men on the carefully numbered list. There was a hair weave binder, with samples of yaki and remy hair glued down. In that binder, there were contact numbers for dealers who dealt directly with swamis in India who sold the hair their faithful cut off out of religious devotion.

There was a tenth binder, one Ian had never used. Over mint tea one morning six years ago, Kipenzi had told him everything she wanted him to do in the case of her death. Ian had taken copious notes, nodding solemnly. He spent the rest of the afternoon typing, printing, and hole-punching her notes and organizing the binder with binder tabs labeled Music, Guests, Poems, Funeral Parlors, Pallbearers.

Ian knew that if he needed that binder, he'd have to take a shot of vodka from the bar in her screening room first.

He leaned in close and stared at the bundle. Ian let out a silent sigh of relief when he saw the bundle gently rise and then fall. She was breathing.

"Ms. Hill, if you need to sleep in today—"

"I'm awake."

Kipenzi's voice was so clear that Ian was startled. He expected her voice to be thick and groggy. Ian took a step back to the bedroom door, in case she wasn't properly dressed.

"Oh. I—it's close to eleven and I thought—"

Kipenzi yanked the linens off her head and sat up straight in one jagged motion. Her hair, a web of long, tight spiral curls, was a fuzzy nest, some of the ringlets covering her heart-shaped face.

"Ian. I'm done."

"Excuse me?"

"*Terminado, fini, acabado.* Done."

"Done with sleeping?"

"No. Done with everything."

Ian raised one eyebrow and waited for Kipenzi to speak. She tried to blow a piece of hair out of her face. It rose slightly and then fell back over her nose.

"I'm done with this hair, first of all," Kipenzi said. She lifted a curl and then let it drop to her shoulder.

Ian turned to leave the room. "I'll have Samantha summoned for the afternoon to tend to your hair."

Kipenzi growled: a sound Ian had never heard come out of her mouth.

"I don't want someone to do *this* hair. I want every track, bead, sewn-in, glued-in lace front out of my head immediately. I want *my* hair—the strands that naturally grow out of my scalp—to be styled. Can you handle that, Ian?"

Ian kept his back to his client. "Is there anything else I can get for you, Ms. Hill?"

"Do you even understand how draining it is to drag around this fake hair everywhere I go?" Kipenzi asked. "It's itchy. It feels wrong on my neck. Makes me break out. I feel like I'm trapped in a Halloween costume."

Ian nodded without turning around. "Anything else?"

"I need you to call Melinda and tell her that I'm done recording for Musictown."

Ian turned around. "Excuse me?"

"Now I have your attention," Kipenzi said. "Sit down, please."

Ian eased over to a lilac settee near the floor-to-ceiling windows overlooking the Hudson River. He sat down, crossed one leg over the other, and clasped his hands together.

"I do not want to sing professionally anymore," Kipenzi said. "Ever. Not another concert. Not another studio session. No more tours, no more albums. Nothing. I'm done."

Ian nodded slowly.

"I don't want to watch my weight. I want to eat carbs on a daily basis. I want to gain weight in winter and lose it in summer. I want to walk through Central Park, with my dog, and not be disturbed. I do not want security to trail me everywhere I go."

"I can see how—"

"Ian. Can you please not interrupt me? This is, like, an existential crisis for me and I'm finally verbalizing how my life is, like, totally fucked up. So if you could just let me get this out, I'd really appreciate it."

Ian closed his eyes for three seconds as an apology.

"I do not want to get dressed up every time I leave the house. I don't want to wear stilettos. I want to wear jeans. And Converse sneakers. High-tops. I always liked that look. And white tank tops. I don't want to wear foundation, mascara, fake eyelashes, and lipstick. I hate lipstick. It feels foreign on my lips and I always end up smudging it."

Kipenzi stopped speaking and stared at Ian. He opened his mouth to speak and then stopped.

"You can say something now."

"What can I do to help you?"

"Who is in my apartment right now?"

"Your diction tutor is in the kitchen. You're supposed to go over the tapes you recorded."

"Fuck that. I'm done with that. I'll keep my southern accent. I like saying *y'all*. It's cute. It's who I am. I'm southern, dammit."

"You're auditioning for a role, so—"

"I know why I wanted her *yesterday*. But this is today. A new day. I don't want anyone to train my accent out of me. I'm done with that. Who else is here?"

"Mali, Josephine Bennett's assistant. She has sketches for the bridal dress you are modeling in her show during Fashion Week."

"Not going. Sorry. Next."

"Mrs. Bennett will be quite disappointed."

"I'll send her some flowers. Next."

"Your trainer. He's going over the menu with the chef. This is an all-protein week."

"Fuck that. I want a cinnamon roll from Au Bon Pain. Can you please get Elizabeth to get me one?"

"They don't carry them anymore."

"What?" Kipenzi placed her hands on either side of her body on the bed and gave Ian a dramatic wide-eyed look of desperation. "Since when?"

"It's been a while. The mayor banned trans fats. The folks at Au Bon Pain couldn't make them taste the same with any other kind of fat. So they just took them off the menu."

Kipenzi swung her feet over the side of her bed, planted them on the floor, and then rested her chin in her hands.

"Can you tell Elizabeth to get the recipe and use trans fat and make me a cinnamon roll?"

"Yes."

"And can you call Melinda and tell her I quit?"

"No. I can't do that."

"Why not?"

"Ms. Hill, are you not feeling well this morning?"

Kipenzi stood up and stretched. Then she clasped her hands behind her back and put one of her feet into both hands. She pulled her leg up and up and up until it was fully extended over her head in a move called a six o'clock because her legs were perfectly vertical like the hands of a clock at that hour. She released her leg and then gave Ian a wide smile.

"I feel wonderful. I feel relaxed."

"You also have some designers waiting in your office for you. They had staggered appointments from eight a.m. to ten thirty to show you their ideas for the redesign of your office."

Kipenzi twisted her lips to the side. "What time is it?"

"It's eleven."

"And they waited all this time?"

"Of course. I told them you were running behind schedule."

"And because I'm Kipenzi Joy Hill, they are waiting for me." Kipenzi gave Ian jazz hands. "'Cause I'm a *stah*!"

Ian ran his hands over his hair and raised his eyebrows.

"Oh God, Ian. Stay with me. I'm not crazy, okay?"

"Okay."

"I just don't want to deal with this business anymore. I've been working since before I could walk. Did you know that?"

"Yes, I did."

"I was on *Family Matters*. I played a baby whose father was dating Aunt Rachel."

"You've told me several times."

"Ian, how long does the typical American work before retiring?"

"You can receive Social Security benefits beginning at age sixty-two. Assuming you start working at twenty-one, that would be forty-four years."

Kipenzi's mouth dropped. "That's insane."

Ian let his head dip to one side and shrugged his shoulders. "It is difficult for the common man."

"What about early retirement?"

"Depends on the company you work for. They can offer you a package."

"Great. So my company is giving me an early retirement. I offered. I accepted. Beginning today."

"And the people who work for you?"

"I'll still need you, Ian. But everyone else can go kick rocks."

"A bit harsh, no?"

"Yes. Very harsh. That's exactly how I'm feeling this morning. *Harsh*."

"With all due respect, Ms. Hill. You have a staff that depends on you to feed their families."

Kipenzi closed her eyes for a moment and then ran her hands across her hair. "I understand that. I do. But I have to do what's right for me right now. I don't know if I've *ever* done that, Ian. I don't think I've ever made a decision that was based on what was best for me."

"Understood. Should I dismiss everyone downstairs?"

Kipenzi walked into her closet and began to look around. "Yes, please. And can you get Elizabeth to get me a pair of pink high-top Converses?"

"Should I reschedule the designers?"

Kipenzi turned around. "You know what? I think I will meet with them. I'd like to see their idea of what would make a good office for a *stah* like me."

"Maybe you should wait."

"No, no, no, don't start, Ian. I'm just different. Don't you ever wake up and just feel different?"

Kipenzi didn't wait for a response. She found a pair of jeans in a built-in drawer at the back of her cedar-lined closet. She put on a T-shirt, a souvenir from her last tour that was hanging up as a decoration.

"Shall we?" she said to Ian.

"Would you like me to get you a pair of slippers?" Ian asked, gesturing to her bare feet.

"How often are the floors in this apartment cleaned, Ian?"

"Twice a day."

"I think my feet will be just fine."

Ian put his hand on his hip and Kipenzi slipped her arm inside.

"Front staircase or rear?"

"Front," Kipenzi said, smoothing back her hair with one hand. "Just because I'm retiring doesn't mean I don't like to make an entrance."

Ian gave Kipenzi a look. That line was written in one of her binders, but he wasn't sure which one. Maybe it was one of the inspirational quotes she liked to collect for interviews. He dismissed the creepy feeling the quote gave him and then led his client down the spiral staircase into her new life as a retiree.

KIPENZI NODDED HER HEAD UP AND DOWN, ALTHOUGH SHE COULDN'T hear a word the designer was saying to her. The woman had on bright red lipstick. It was applied too thick, like she'd done it with her fist while driving around midtown Manhattan, looking for a parking spot.

Physically, Kipenzi Joy Hill was in the living room of her apartment, expertly designed by Sills Huniford in all white, cream, and shades of beige. *Natural*, the designer had said to her. We'll use *natural* for the window treatments. "Is that the same color as *flesh?*" Kipenzi had asked her. The decorator had just smiled. She didn't get it.

Mentally, she was everywhere but her living room. She was three years old, sitting next to Bill Cosby, waiting for a scene to begin in which she was playing Rudy's best friend at a sleepover. She was seven, belting out "The Greatest Love of All" on *Star Search* and getting a perfect four stars from Ed McMahon seven weeks in a row. She was fifteen, losing her virginity to her boyfriend in the back of his tour bus. Her group, Love and Happiness, was opening for his. He teased her about being his opening act. Now he was releasing singles on his myspace page while Kipenzi was selling out arenas as a solo artist.

"How long have you been doing this?" Kipenzi asked the designer, who was holding up a large piece of foam core with sketches on it. The designer slowly lowered the paper, as if she'd known all along that Kipenzi wasn't really paying attention to her.

"I gave you a copy of my resume. I have over twenty years of experience."

"Right. What do you think of a SpongeBob theme in here?"

"SpongeBob." The designer looked around the living room as if she expected someone to pop out and clue her in on the practical joke.

"Yes, SpongeBob SquarePants. You know, that little yellow—"

"Right. I know SpongeBob."

"I'm thinking bright yellow on the walls. And the office can be an exact replica of his little pineapple under the sea."

"I'm not sure if I know what that would consist of . . ."

"I know he has a television that looks like it's inside of a diver's helmet. That's pretty cute." Kipenzi looked up at the ceiling. "And

I know he has bamboo wallpaper. That would be fun. We could get Pierre Deux to make us a custom roll."

The designer blinked a few times and then smiled. She had a bit of red lipstick on her front teeth. "I think that could be very kitschy and cool!" she blurted.

Kipenzi's heart sank. Her worst fears were true. Her life was a joke. This woman, lipstick on her teeth and all, was a professional. She'd graduated from Parsons. Owned her own firm. Came highly recommended. And yet she was willing to sit here and agree to convert her client's study into an ode to a cartoon character. She wouldn't dream of telling Kipenzi that it was nouveau, déclassé, or just silly. Because her client was a *stah*, the woman would tell her whatever she wanted to hear. And that made Kipenzi sad.

"Fame is a motherfucker," Kipenzi whispered.

"Excuse me?"

"Do you play an instrument?" Kipenzi asked.

"Took piano and violin lessons for years."

"Do you still play?"

"I can plink out a few things."

"I think I'd like to teach piano," Kipenzi said.

"Think you'd have time for that?"

"I'm making time. Starting today."

"That's . . . that's great. I think that's a great idea."

Kipenzi leaned over and put her elbows on her knees. "You do? You think it's a good idea to walk away from my career and do what I really want? Teach piano and voice lessons to kids?"

"I'd imagine you might miss . . . your fans?"

Kipenzi shuddered. "When I do a show, I look out in the audience and I see people with their mouths gaping open. They all look like reflections in a fun house mirror. Wearing those masks from *Scream*."

"That doesn't seem like fun."

"It's not. I mean it used to be. But it hasn't been for a long time."

The designer put her hands down in her lap and looked up at Kipenzi. "I'm sorry to hear that."

"I have a bunion," Kipenzi said, holding up her foot to show the swollen bone area on the side of her left big toe. "It bleeds after I dance on it for an hour. I've had surgery twice. Still all screwed up."

The designer winced when she looked at Kipenzi's toe, bulbous and purple from years of abuse. "That looks like it hurts."

Kipenzi shrugged. "I'm used to it now. Thanks for coming by and thanks for waiting for me. I slept in today."

"Oh. You were . . . sleeping."

"Yes. I am very, very tired. What's your name again?"

"Denise. Denise McMillian."

"Denise, I am tired down to the marrow of my bones. I could sleep for three weeks."

"I understand."

Ian showed the designer out and dismissed the others.

"Anything else?" Ian asked, as he watched his client crawl onto the loveseat in her bedroom and pick up her Hello Kitty telephone.

"One more cup of mint tea would be awesome," Kipenzi said. Ian nodded and left the room as she picked up the phone.

"Jake. Do you love me for who I am or for what I represent to you?"

"You. I love you. I gotta go."

Her boyfriend hung up before she could say another word. Kipenzi used a pencil to stab the keys on her phone once again.

"Beth, are you busy?"

Beth yawned. "Just taking a nap. You feel better today? Had me worried last night."

"I'm thinking of doing my office over in a SpongeBob theme. What do you think?"

"That's the stupidest shit I've ever heard in my life."

"But I like SpongeBob."

"Hell, so does Zach. Doesn't mean it makes sense. Kipenzi, what are you smoking?"

"Love you," Kipenzi said.

"Call you later."

"Zander's on his way over there," said Beth. "Wants to know what you think of his new music."

"The stuff he's doing with his little girlfriend?"

"Yeah."

"Okay. I gotta make a few more calls."

Kipenzi took a deep breath and stabbed the keypad once again.

"Mommy? It's Penzi. Is Daddy there? Tell him to pick up."

"Peaches, how you feeling?" Kipenzi's father's deep voice boomed out and she had to hold the phone away from her ear a bit.

"Mom, Dad, I'm thinking of doing a cartoon theme in my home office. SpongeBob. What do you think?"

"I think if you say you want to do it, then it must be hot," John Hill said with a laugh. "You could probably do a spread in *People* and get a licensing deal with the show!"

"Always thinking business, right, Daddy?"

"You better believe it, Peaches. Speaking of, I need to go over some contracts with you. When can you—"

"I'm taking a day off, Daddy. Call you tomorrow!" Kipenzi made kissing noises into the phone over his protests and then hung up.

An hour later Kipenzi's beloved godson, oldest son of her best friend, Beth, appeared in the door of her study. Zander had an ear-to-ear grin, and his smooth, ebony skin made his smile seem even brighter. It was the same kind of smile he used to give her when she would pick him up from Fresh Meadows for a day in the park.

"Zander, get in here."

Zander glanced behind him and then looked at Kipenzi. "I brought someone with me . . ."

Kipenzi rolled her eyes. "Bring her in, Zander!"

Zander slinked his way across the room, clutching his girlfriend's hand tight. He managed to lead them both to a loveseat and sank down, his eyes on the floor.

"A proper introduction, please," Kipenzi said.

"Auntie, this is Bunny Clifton. Bunny, this is my aunt Kipenzi."

Kipenzi reached over the coffee table with an outstretched hand. Bunny was light brown, with a blond weave styled almost identically to Kipenzi's. She grabbed Kipenzi's hand with both of hers.

"Is that your real name?"

Bunny smiled. "Yes. I'm from Jamaica. Named after Bunny Wailer."

Kipenzi nodded. "Nice."

"It's so nice to meet you, Ms. Hill. I love everything you've ever done."

"Really? You heard my first album? It was a piece of crap."

"I don't agree," Bunny said, shaking her head. "I loved your first album."

"It's not even worth using as a coaster. But thank you. I like what you're doing too."

"You've heard my stuff?" Bunny asked, her voice near squealing.

"Yo, chill," Zander said, rolling his eyes.

"Yes, I have. I heard the stuff you and Zan put up on YouTube."

Zander put his head in his lap. "You hate it," he said, his voice muffled.

"I don't hate it," Kipenzi said.

"You don't love it."

"No, I don't love it. But I *could* love it. It needs work. First of all, you guys need a better engineer."

Zander lifted his head. "I used my dad's engineer."

"And he's fine," said Kipenzi. "For that little rinky-dink studio at Electric Lady lined with egg crates. Your father refuses to let them update his studio. But it works for him."

"So how come it can't work for us?"

"Z's music is about rawness and aggression. But your voice—and Bunny's too—is different."

Kipenzi stood up and motioned for Zander and Bunny to do the same. Zander was a full head taller than Kipenzi but she still seemed to tower over them both.

"You guys know 'Gentle' by Frederick?"

"How's it go?" Bunny asked.

"I'm in a daze, I'm so confused," Kipenzi belted out.

Zander and Bunny both nodded. "We know it," Zander said.

"Let me hear it," Kipenzi said.

Zander wrinkled his nose. "Too hard. The chord changes are crazy."

Kipenzi glanced over at Bunny.

"I can do it," the young lady said, her chin jutting out.

Zander inhaled sharply, closed his eyes, and began to sing.

Bunny took in a deep breath, pulled her fists up to her chest, and harmonized with Zander on the chorus. *"'Cause I know you'll be coming."*

The hair on Kipenzi's arms stood up. The girl's voice was crystal clear and flawless. She was loud enough to be heard without a microphone. But her voice was light enough to ripple through the air like a kite on a windy day.

Kipenzi continued to conduct them, keeping one eye on the way their lips formed every word and using a pointer finger to direct how high or low each note should go. Her eyebrows creased when Zander missed a note—which was only once. She smiled brightly when they finished the verse with a strong vibrato.

"Calling, calling, calling your name . . ."

They sang facing each other, staring into each other's eyes. The intensity of both their performance and their emotion made Kipenzi feel light-headed and dizzy. She had looked that way once. She had sounded that way once.

"You've both got such great breath control!" Kipenzi said, squeezing Zander's shoulders and winking at Bunny.

"Feels like we sing old-school stuff better than the stuff we're writing now," Zander said.

Kipenzi shrugged. "Doesn't matter. I used to perform En Vogue for every audition. Slinky black dress, red lipstick, and all. It showcased what I could do. You'll have time to get your own sound."

Zander nodded and slumped back down on the sofa. Bunny remained standing, staring openly at Kipenzi.

"Ms. Hill? Are you working on new music?"

"No, not right now. I'm actually thinking of taking a break."

Zander popped his head up.

"So I can't get a hook or two from you for my album?"

"No. You couldn't afford me anyway."

"Why would you want to take a break?" Zander asked.

Kipenzi rubbed the back of her neck. "Because I'm tired."

"You take a break and you're giving the new girls a chance to take over," Zander said.

"New girls like who? Like this one here?" she said, gesturing to Bunny.

Zander bowed his head but Kipenzi could still see his smile.

"I like her," Kipenzi said. "She's got a great voice. Good look."

She let her smile fade and then looked directly at Bunny. "We'll see if she can sell twenty million records . . ."

Zander laughed out loud.

"Yeah, we'll see," Bunny said, poking out her chest and clenching her jaw tight.

"Somebody probably said that about my dad once," said Zander.

"True," Kipenzi said.

"And someone probably said that about you too."

"Touché."

Kipenzi walked Zander and Bunny to the foyer, where Ian was waiting to see them out. Just before they reached the front door, Bunny stopped Kipenzi by tapping her on the back. Kipenzi turned around.

"I plan to break every record you ever set."

Kipenzi pulled her head back without moving the rest of her body. "Really?"

"Really."

"Do you even know what records I—"

"Most albums to debut at number one—twelve, one more than Jay-Z. I probably won't pass the Beatles though. But your record for most number one singles on the Billboard Hot One Hundred and most weeks at number one? All mine. Mark my words."

Kipenzi smiled with her mouth closed. "Good to have goals," she said. "I'm pulling for you."

"I think you should take a break," Bunny said, running her hands over her spiral curls then letting them flop back over her eyes. "Sometimes people your age don't know when to give it up and let the new blood take over."

"It was nice meeting you, Bunny," Kipenzi said in a loud voice. It was Ian's signal to get her out.

When Ian closed the door behind them, he turned to look at his employer.

"The first day of the rest of your life, Ms. Hill. Looking forward to it?"

Kipenzi glided over to her living room sofa, sat down, pulled her legs up, and crossed them.

"I'm going to fire people left and right, ditch all professional obligations, and nurture my godson's career. Though I don't like that little hellion he's running with." Kipenzi scratched the tracks sewn into the cornrows on the top of her head. "And tomorrow I'm getting my weave taken out. For the last time. Yes, Ian. I'm happy. Deliriously so."

Ian smiled and went to his office on the other side of Kipenzi's apartment. Kipenzi sat on her sofa, still. In five minutes, she was fast asleep. When Ian let himself out of the apartment, Kipenzi was still sitting up straight, her legs still crossed, her back as straight as a Buddha's. She eventually fell over.

And for the first time in twenty years, she slept for twelve hours straight.

three

ALEX WAS AWAKE BUT KEPT HER EYES CLOSED. AS ALWAYS, HER REAL life was turning into a story idea in her head. At some point, she thought to herself, an argument between a man and a woman becomes less about the content and more about the roles they play in the relationship.

Alex opened her eyes, rolled over, and grabbed the black leatherbound journal on her nightstand. It was embossed with the word IDEAS. Birdie had given it to her for her birthday last year. She sat up in bed, resting her back on the headboard, picked up a pen, and began to scribble.

When voices are raised and indignities are hurled, it's not just because the dishes are piled high and the garbage hasn't been taken out for a week. It's because of the ex-girlfriend that he slept with when he said he was at his mother's retirement party. Even if that happened five years ago.

Alex stopped writing, tapping the pen on the notebook. She knew of three magazines she could pitch that story to. But she hadn't read *Cosmopolitan* or *Details* in the past three months. They might have done something similar. She circled the sentences she wrote and then made a note to herself to go to the library and check out the back issues of a few magazines to see if that story idea could work.

With the notebook still in her lap, Alex looked over at Birdie, who was lying on his left side, facing her. His breathing was even and measured. He'd gotten a haircut the day before, including a tight shape-up on his full beard. This meant that when Alex took him in, her heart flipped over once. Five years and he could still make her lose her breath. Alex leaned over and kissed Birdie's forehead. The room was hot and they'd already put away the air conditioner in preparation for autumn. He tasted salty. But he smelled sweet—like Nag Champa incense, marijuana, and gingerroot tea.

Like most of Alex's story ideas, what she scribbled that morning was ripped from her own life. In five years, Alex and Birdie had managed to have at least one minor argument per week.

Birdie: *But if you use these dainty little white trash bags just because they fit nicely, it defeats the purpose if they fall apart when it's time to take the trash out.*
Alex: *Perhaps we need to redefine when it's time to take the trash out. I say some time before there are seven bags stinking up the foyer.*

They usually managed to keep the major blowups to no more than one a month. But by late September they were already on their third. Alex put the ideas book back on the nightstand and picked up her journal. She looked back a few days and noticed the angry red marks underlining her words, signifying that she went to bed angry. Last week it had been Tweet's mother, who'd stopped by unannounced. Alex asked Birdie to talk to her and he refused. Then, just a day later, while Alex was in her office, she heard Birdie come into the house with seven members of his loosely organized rap collective. They settled into the living room—not even the basement!—and didn't leave for hours, smoking weed, listening to instrumentals, and freestyling. As soon as the last dude left, Alex came downstairs and cursed Birdie out for twenty minutes. He never said a word.

It was with these two arguments in mind that Alex decided to tread lightly around Birdie when he woke up.

"If I get a remix from Ras Bennett, I'm guaranteed to get on the radio."

Alex snapped her head to the side and noticed that Birdie had awakened and changed position. He was on his back, with his hands behind his head. She thought she'd be up, washed, and dressed before she would have to deal. He'd caught her off guard on purpose.

"Good morning, Birdie," Alex said, throwing back the sheets and putting her feet on the floor.

"I could probably even get a deal on a major label."

Alex got up and went to her walk-in closet without looking back. "Since when do you want to be on a major label?" she asked. "I thought it was all about keeping the music pure."

"It's all about having more than two sticks in my pocket to rub together too."

Shrugged into her robe and with a towel draped over her shoulder, Alex went toward the bathroom. A cold shower would help her center her mind and come up with better reasons why Birdie wasn't going to get his way. Again. But before she could make it to the door, Birdie leapt out of bed and blocked her path.

"Baby. I don't ask for much, do I?"

No, not much. Just to take care of your daughter. Front you cash when you need it. Pretend I don't know you at industry events. Lie to your manager about where you are. Rub your back after a show. Cook for you. Clean up after you. Tell you that your music is wonderful . . .

"No," Alex said, keeping her eyes on the floor. If she looked up at him, she'd melt. When he was shirtless, wearing just his boxers and a pair of socks, she just wanted to be held by him, close to his chest.

And when his eyes—wide, glassy, and hazel green—were locked onto hers, she turned into a robot that would follow his every command.

"Then why won't you do this for me?"

"It's unethical," she said, for the fifth time since the argument had begun the night before.

Birdie rolled his eyes. "You can't be serious about that. What's unethical about writing a story on this dude's wife?"

"Listen to what you're asking me and try to put yourself in my shoes," Alex said. She leaned against their bedroom door and began ticking off talking points on her fingers. "You want Ras Bennett to produce a record for you."

"Yes, I do."

"And in order to make that happen, his manager wants me to write a cover story on Ras's wife for a local Caribbean magazine."

"You got it."

"And you don't see how that would make me uncomfortable?"

"I don't see the problem at all."

"How does his manager know your girlfriend is a writer?"

"It may have come up in conversation."

"I'm not even dealing with you, Birdie. This is all kinds of wrong."

"Do you care that I'm ready to make some money with my music?"

"If that's what you want, I fully support that. But not at the expense of my own credibility. I'm a journalist. Not a publicist."

"I'm trying to get money to pay for this expensive-ass wedding you want and now you want to play moral police?"

And with that, Alex and Birdie were off to the races. While Birdie's daughter, Tweet, continued to sleep in the bedroom adjacent to theirs, they pointed fingers, hurled insults, and threw their hands up. Alex stomped off in one direction and then turned sharply on her heels and said, "Ex*cuse* me?" Birdie sucked his teeth and laughed (not a real laugh but an indignant *Ha!*). They both rolled their eyes considerably. Neither would back down.

Birdie and Alex had issues. After ten years as a critical darling in hip-hop, Birdie wanted a platinum plaque. He was tired of opening for people like Jake and Z. He was tired of borrowing money from the owner of his record label, a Jewish kid from Harvard who lived two doors down from him and Alex. And he was tired of being respected but not recognized. He was ready to sell out, get a song on Hot 97, make a big-budget video and tape a making-the-video segment for BET. The first step would be a song produced by Ras Bennett. Like T-Pain had his run back in '08, it was Ras Bennett's year and everything he produced, rapped on, sang on, or even contributed a few guitar licks to had stratospheric success. But he charged $90,000 for a track, more money than Birdie made in a full year of rapping, touring, and performing.

Birdie had run into Ras's manager on Fulton two weeks before. The manager told Birdie he'd been trying to get press for Ras's wife, who had opened a bridal boutique on Madison Avenue. Birdie read between the lines and went to work—begging Alex to pitch a story on Josephine Bennett to *Sounds of Caribbean America*. The founder of the magazine was a good friend of Alex's. He knew she had the power to get Ras's wife on the cover.

He wanted to get Alex to do the story so he could manage to bump into Ras and get his music popping before it was too late. Birdie knew Ras wouldn't be hot for much longer. He wanted his piece of the action before the industry tossed him away.

"I understand all of this," Alex said. She was standing in her usual argument spot, at the window facing their backyard. Birdie leaned against the bedroom door, so that they could be warned if Tweet woke up and tried to come in.

"So you'll do it."

"I always said that after, you know, our situation, I'd never blur the lines again."

Birdie's face softened. "It's been five years, baby. You're still tripping over that?"

"I was supposed to interview you. Not have sex with you. Yes, I'm still tripping over that."

Birdie stepped away from the door and came up to Alex until he was a half inch away from her. He stood as close as he could without actually touching her. She could feel his breath on her forehead. And there were certain parts of his body that were skimming hers.

"But you couldn't resist me. You had sex with me. And we lived happily ever after. And that's okay."

"I think it will be okay, eventually. But I still struggle with it. I broke the rules. And now you want me to get this woman on the cover of a magazine to help your career?"

Birdie ran his hands up and down Alex's arms. A warm flush immediately traveled down her body and she had to take a deep breath to keep her composure and not tackle him onto their bed.

"So you're going to seduce me to get what you want?"

"I'm not above it."

Birdie kissed her shoulder, where an unfinished tattoo of a daisy was etched into her skin. The daisy had a long green stem that snaked down her shoulder blade. But the flower only had four petals with room for many more.

"Is it time to get this updated?" Birdie asked.

"Almost," Alex whispered, her eyes closed.

"Is this part of the reason why you feel weird about writing the story?"

"Yes."

Birdie pulled Alex to the bed and sat her down beside him. He kept her hand in his. "Can I say something?"

"Whenever people say that, it usually means you don't want to hear whatever they're about to say. So, no."

"I'll say it anyway. You're a drunk."

"A former drunk."

"A former drunk. Who made some bad decisions once upon a time."

"That's an understatement."

"It doesn't mean that for the rest of your life you have to be perfect. You can still bend the rules sometimes."

"Especially when it's for you, right?"

"Well, yeah. Especially when it's for your man."

"When it comes to my work, I don't ever want to put myself in the position of being less than one hundred percent honorable again. Ever. And I'm pissed off that you keep on pushing this."

"And I'm pissed off that you don't see how important this is to me." The heavy cherrywood door to the bedroom opened with a creak. Alex and Birdie both looked back as Tweet appeared in the doorway, her thumb stuck in her mouth. She had Birdie's cocoa brown skin and her mother's wide brown eyes. Her big, fluffy pony-tails looked like cumulus clouds.

"No fight," she said, pointing at Birdie.

She had such a soft, high-pitched voice that Birdie said she sounded like Tweety Bird. The nickname Tweet stuck.

The little girl looked at Birdie and then Alex and then back to Birdie again.

"She started it," Birdie said, jerking a thumb in Alex's direction.

Alex went to the door and picked up Tweet, cradling her on her hip and carrying her to the bed.

"We're not fighting, sweetie," she said, kissing her forehead. "We're just having a discussion." Alex sat on the bed, still holding Tweet, and looked over at Birdie. "And I think this discussion is over."

"No. It's not. You're making a big deal out of nothing. It's not that deep."

"Did I tell you I'm starting a new ghostwriting project this week? I don't have time to write a fluff piece for a local magazine that can't even afford to pay me."

"They will pay your rate. I told you that."

"That's worse!" Alex said. "*Sounds of Caribbean America* doesn't pay their writers. But they'll pay me a dollar fifty a word? That's payola!"

"Who are you ghostwriting for?"

"That girl who's writing a tell-all about her life as a dancer in rap videos."

"What kind of book is that?"

"I have no clue. But she got six figures for it. And I'm getting fifty grand. So I'm not arguing."

"So it's okay to get fifty thousand dollars to ghostwrite a book about a topic you care nothing about. But you won't take three thousand and write a story that will help your man's career."

Alex laid Tweet on the bed and undid the snaps on her pajamas.

"Fine, Birdie. You win. I'll write the story." She eased Tweet out of her pajamas and picked her back up.

"Just like that? You'll do it?"

Alex snuggled into Tweet's neck and kissed her. "Just like that. See how easy it is to get me to do whatever you want?"

The doorbell buzzed and Birdie and Alex looked at each other.

"You expecting someone?" Alex asked.

"Shoot. It might be Jennifer."

Alex forced herself not to groan since she was still holding Tweet in her arms. But she wasn't prepared to deal with Tweet's mother.

"Are you expecting her?" Alex asked through clenched teeth, as she carried Alex down the stairs, behind Birdie.

"I think she might be taking Tweet out today. I forgot to tell you." Birdie looked through the peephole and then began to turn the locks on the heavy door and opened it slowly.

"Morning, Jen."

Tweet's mother stepped into the foyer and reached out her hands for her daughter.

"Mommy!" Tweet yelled, scrambling to get out of Alex's arms. Alex tried to smile as she handed the girl over.

No matter how many times they did a parental transfer, it never got easier. Alex always felt like a nanny when Jennifer came to pick up her daughter. Not like a person who was about to become Tweet's stepmother.

"Alex, always good to see you," Jennifer said, nuzzling Tweet's neck.

"Of course. Same here."

Alex touched her hair, hoping it wasn't the wild mess it usually was at this hour. Jennifer, as always, was perfectly put together—a linen skirt suit, sling-back Louboutins, a double strand of pearls, and her hair pulled back in a sleek, jet-black chignon.

"Peter, I hope you didn't forget that I was taking Anais to the Jack and Jill brunch this morning?"

"No, I didn't forget. We just . . . we were running a little late."

"As usual," Jennifer said. "Luckily I brought an outfit for her. Has she been washed?"

"I was just on my way to give her a bath," Alex said.

Jennifer smiled with her mouth closed and stepped closer to Alex to hand the baby over to her.

"Would you mind?" Jennifer asked, handing Tweet over. "I would do it myself but I'm already dressed."

"No problem. We'll be right back."

"Thanks a million," Jennifer called out, as Alex turned to leave the room. "But, uh, don't worry about her hair. I can take care of that."

Alex's stomach was boiling. Birdie was always conveniently forgetting whatever plans he'd made with his ex-wife concerning Tweet. And Alex ended up feeling like an idiot, undressed and unkempt in front of his always perfect ex.

As she made her way upstairs, she looked back for a moment and saw Birdie and Jennifer sitting in the living room talking.

Alex bathed Tweet, dressed her in the sailor dress, frilly white socks, and white patent leather Mary Janes her mother provided, and brought her back downstairs.

"There's my baby girl! Thanks so much, Alex."

"Not a problem," Alex said, shooting Birdie an evil look.

"I'll have her back by three," Jennifer said to Birdie. "And I know this is your weekend. Thanks for understanding."

"Bye, baby girl," Birdie said to his daughter.

"Bye, Daddy," Tweet said.

Before he could get all the locks turned, Alex exploded.

"I really don't think it's too much to ask for you to remember when she's coming over here!"

"I know. I'm sorry."

"That's what you say every time. But it never changes. I can't stand it."

"You can't stand it? Or you can't stand *her*?"

"Both. Whatever. What difference does it make?"

"I'm just saying. She's Tweet's mother. Technically, she can come over unannounced if she wants to."

"No. She can't."

"Yeah. She can. Tweet's her child."

"I still feel like I should know when she's coming up to my house."

"Right. Your house. I see."

Alex began to shake her head. "No. Birdie. That's not what I meant."

"Yeah. I know. I'm living with you in *your* house, so I better remember that. What was the name of the story you wrote? 'Keeping His Ex in Check.'"

"I didn't mean that this is only my house."

"But that's what you said."

"I just feel like you could do a better job of keeping me in the loop."

"I forgot. I said I was sorry. I have a meeting in ten minutes. Can we pick up this argument later?"

Alex made breakfast for Birdie and he went into his office in the basement for a meeting with his manager and a tour promoter. Alex made herself a smoothie with frozen fruit and yogurt and then went up to her office on the top floor of the brownstone.

ALEX'S FATHER WOULD NOT TAKE NO FOR AN ANSWER WHEN IT CAME TO buying her the brownstone in Fort Greene, Brooklyn. She begged and pleaded for him to just buy it for himself and rent it out. At one point, she even told him flat out that she would not live in it, no matter what. She was living with two roommates in a three-bedroom apartment in Williamsburg. The apartment was a piece of crap but

Alex felt like she belonged there. She got a thrill out of leaving her four one-hundred-dollar bills on the kitchen counter for Debbie to send off with the rest of the rent. Spoiled beyond belief by her father, an entertainment attorney who had money to burn, Alex woke up one morning in his apartment in the Time Warner Center and decided she wanted to make her own way. Her father said it was like she caught some kind of viral work ethic infection. She knew he was proud of her. In six years, she'd established herself as a music critic and investigative reporter. But he'd worked his way from carrying Quincy Jones's bags to being Mariah Carey's manager. Alex's daddy wanted his only child to enjoy the fruits of his labor.

And so, the house. The minute Alex walked in, with her father and the agent, she knew he had her right where he wanted her.

The wood-burning fireplace. The three huge bedrooms on the second floor. The deck. But she was still tight-lipped and smiling politely while her father showed her the chef's kitchen with the stainless steel appliances. And she just nodded when the agent pulled up the curtains and the view of Manhattan hit her like a sledgehammer to the chest. Her resistance dissolved when they went to the third floor. Alex expected a dingy, musty attic, like the one in her grandmother's North Carolina farmhouse. But the attic was a sanctuary.

There were two small rooms, decorated as guest rooms by the current tenants, each with stained glass windows, beamed ceilings, and glossy hardwood floors. A huge bathroom with a massive porcelain clawfoot tub connected them. On the other side of the hallway was the Room. It was twice as big as the master bedroom. Alex could have run up, done a cartwheel and three back handsprings before making it to the other side (which is exactly what she wanted to do when she walked in). Her father and the agent had stayed behind, in one of the small rooms, checking out the architectural details. Alex stood in the doorway of the Room, her breath ragged.

The Room had floor-to-ceiling windows along one side, showing off water views of the East River. The owners had completely converted it into a pristine workspace. There were built-in book-shelves on one wall and cherrywood shelving installed behind a wall inside an alcove that was the perfect size for a desk. Alex walked to the center of the Room and turned around in a small circle, ticking off the features. Recessed track lighting. High ceilings. A wide-open floor plan. Dramatic and yet cozy. Alex hadn't even noticed when her father and the agent came into the Room. When her father walked up to her and put his hands on her shoulders, all she could do was exhale and say, "Thank you, Daddy."

So after sending Tweet off with Jen, Alex went up to her room and sat at her desk. Her to-do list, carefully handwritten on a yellow legal pad the night before, was to her right. Her daily planner, black leather and embossed with her name on the front cover, was to her left. She kept on her desk a framed photo of herself and Tweet, a small houseplant, and a silver container of pens, all the same brand and color. Her desk was cool, crisp, and inviting. It made her want to sit down to work.

She had two stories due and three stories she wanted to pitch. She had one story that an editor had sent back with minor changes. She still had to find a caterer for the wedding, a place to actually have the wedding, and a dress to wear. Alex's eyes went to her left hand. She didn't know how Birdie had been able to afford the ring. It was at least two carats. (She hadn't asked. And she'd cursed her step-mother out for trying to take her to get it appraised two days after Birdie proposed.) Alex didn't know much about cut and clarity. But she knew that whenever she waved at someone or took her wallet out of her bag at a store, people's eyes lingered on her hand. She was ashamed to be so in love with a material object. Especially something as superficial as a diamond. She'd once prided herself on being bigger than that. But at thirty, she knew her ring was exactly what it was supposed to be, a symbol. Someone was claiming her. And he was willing to go into debt to do it.

Alex twirled the ring around her finger a few times while she waited for her computer to boot up. The ring was a full size too big but she refused to take it off even for an hour to have it resized.

She was still seething about Jennifer's showing up. But she knew it wasn't healthy to dwell on it. She went to her desk drawer and picked up her daily affirmations book. She hadn't been to an AA meeting in years, not since she got her chip marking a year of sobriety.

Thought of the day: *Get a grip on letting go.*

It was like magic. Every time she picked up the book, every few months or so, she'd let the page fall randomly, and it always matched whatever she was feeling. She knew that she had to do exactly that: let go. She was marrying Birdie. His ex and their child would always be a constant presence. She was crazy about Tweet, lukewarm on her mother. She needed to let go.

Alex put the book back and turned to a new page in her notebook. She wrote "Get a grip on letting go" over and over in fancy script until her wrist began to cramp.

four

At the corner of Madison Avenue and Thirty-sixth Street, Josephine's dog, a bichon frise named Mink, jumped into her arms. She pulled him up over her cleavage and kissed the top of his well-groomed head. When the driver stopped in front of her building, she put Mink down next to her and adjusted her clothing. The ride in from Jersey was close to an hour with traffic, so she always felt a bit rumpled by the time she got out of the Bentley. She smoothed down her pencil skirt, which hit her legs exactly two inches above the knee. After checking to make sure the driver wasn't looking, she reached into her suit jacket (she was not wearing a blouse underneath), gave her breasts a quick heave, and refastened the jacket.

When the driver opened the door she looked both ways, up the street and then back down. Ras always said she was silly to be so cautious. He said that no one knew who she was. And if they did, they weren't interested in harming her. Josephine didn't care. Her husband was from a country where people could be kidnapped for a five-thousand-dollar ransom. The address to the showroom was listed in the phone book. What was to stop some lunatic from hatching a plan to get money out of Ras? Josephine was private; only her closest friends and family even knew where she and Ras lived. But her husband. Well, he was different. He was a weakling. He craved attention. Which led him to make some dumb decisions. Decisions that Josephine felt could put her at risk.

With Mink in the crook of one arm, Josephine gathered her packages and exited the car. In the lobby she had duties to perform before she could get to her office on the seventh floor. She dropped off a box of children's clothing with the security guard. His wife was expecting triplets, and Josephine's nephew was growing out of his clothes as fast as Josephine could buy them. Some of the clothes still had the price tags on them. She had homemade *mofongo* and *tipili*, her Dominican grandmother's specialty, for the young lady who worked in the mail room. She had still-warm *tarte au pistou*, her French grandmother's recipe, for the super of the building, who had a tiny office in the basement.

By the time Josephine got on the elevator, she felt warm and content inside. She'd made people happy and genuinely so. The nuns at the Convent of the Daughters of Mary Queen Immaculate of the Dominican Republic always insisted that she begin each day with charity. Sister Ana turned out to be wrong on many things, but she was absolutely right about starting out the day bringing happiness to others. When Josephine stepped off the elevator, she felt like she could conquer the world.

She drank in everything she loved about the office of J. Bennett Designs. She pulled open the large glass door, loving the way the brass handle felt in her hand. She clicked her five-inch Giuseppe stilettos across the hardwood floors, taking in the sound they made. She loved the space she was renting for her line. But she really wanted a back entrance. She knew Donna Karan and Ralph Lauren didn't have to walk past their surly receptionist (and any waiting clients) to get to their offices. As she rounded the corner, she could see Mali sitting at her desk, flipping through the *New York Post*.

Josephine gave her a smile and a quick "Good morning" and kept moving past the front desk, through the double doors, and into the showroom. To the right of the showroom was her office, a tiny space she'd had built just after signing the lease. The day's papers were stacked on her desk and ready for her to flip through, her computer was already on, and her mug was filled with coffee, black with no sugar and piping hot. Josephine put Mink in his doggie bed and sat down at her desk.

In front of her was an inspiration wall: she had tear sheets of colors, patterns, and fabrics that inspired her to sketch. She also had quotes she loved ("Your dresses should be tight enough to show you're a woman and loose enough to show you're a lady," Edith Head) and a few pictures thumbtacked on the wall as well—Ras at the Grammys, standing between rapper Jake and singer Kipenzi Hill; a wedding picture of Ras and Josephine; and a baby picture of Ras, taken two weeks before he left Kingston for Newark.

Josephine wiggled her butt in her seat, took a sip of coffee, and began to brainstorm. There was that fabric she wanted to buy, a beautiful point de Venise lace with a touch of Lycra that would be perfect for a casual cocktail bridal dress. She needed to check on the progress the seamstresses were making on a beaded gown she'd sketched out two weeks ago. And there were all the phone calls to make, including a follow-up call about showing her new bridal line on *The View*. She'd met the producer backstage at one of Ras's shows. She'd sent her all the press clippings on J. Bennett Designs, and they'd been playing phone tag ever since.

There was a knock on Josephine's office door. She ignored it. Five thousand dollars for a state-of-the-art intercom system and Mali still wanted to get up from her chair and knock on her door? Josephine rolled her eyes and waited. She ignored the second knock and swiveled her chair around to go online and check her emails. Ten seconds later, the intercom's buzzer went off. She turned her chair back around and clicked it on.

"Yes, Mali."

Josephine could practically hear Mali sucking her teeth; her assistant usually managed to fume only in her head.

"I have Marasa Wright here to see you."

Josephine sat up straight and looked down at her desk calendar. It was empty for the day. It was empty for the whole week.

"Mali, can you please come back here?"

Mali opened the door and just stuck her head into the office. Josephine waved her in and pointed to the chair.

"Does this person have an appointment?"

"Yes, ma'am. She called last week and I scheduled her for today."

Josephine clenched her teeth, kept her eyes on Mali, and jabbed a finger on the page of her desk calendar. "Then why isn't it on the calendar?"

"You weren't here and the office was locked. I couldn't get in to put it there."

"So when is her wedding?"

Mali looked down at her clipboard. "April first."

"How'd she hear about J. Bennett?"

"She said she saw the segment on summer bridal dresses on *Good Day New York.*"

"But they didn't even say who the designer was!" Josephine was still salty that the newswoman was cut off before she could tell the world that the gowns had been designed by J. Bennett. She'd been sitting on the edge of her sofa, shaking her fists at the television, cursing the news anchor out in French, Spanish, and English.

"She said she called the station to find out the name of the designer and they told her."

Josephine smiled. This woman really wanted a J. Bennett dress! She'd *researched* to get the information.

"Take Mink into the front with you," said Josephine. "And then you can send Ms. Wright back here."

Mali took Mink out of his bed and walked toward the door.

"Mali?"

"Ma'am."

Josephine kept her eyes on her calendar. "How is your sister?"

Mali didn't turn around. "Good. Big. Getting bigger every day."

Josephine felt her stomach flip over and then settle. "My love to her," she said to Mali in a whisper.

Mali nodded and left the office.

JOSEPHINE PUT ONE HAND ON THE WOMAN'S SHOULDERS AND TOOK IN her body, from the tiny feet all the way up to her small, round head.

"You trying to put some weight on before the wedding?"

The woman laughed. "I couldn't if I wanted to. This is as big as I get."

"Hair up or down?" Josephine said. She scooped up the mass of hair that hung down the woman's back and placed it in a handheld bun on the top of her head.

"I haven't even thought about it."

Josephine clucked her tongue and scanned the back of the woman's body. "Lord, if I had a body like yours, you'd have to pay me not to show it off!"

"You're not doing so bad yourself," the woman said. "I'll bet your husband loves your curves."

Josephine laughed and then stopped abruptly. Her eyebrows creased. "What did you say your name was?"

"Marasa Wright."

"Yes, Ms. Wright. Come with me," said Josephine, motioning for her to follow her into the office. Josephine stood behind her desk and waited for her to come inside and take a seat before she sat down. The young lady had the perfect body for a wedding dress, lean, slim, and sleek. She reminded Josephine of the white girl who used to do the print work for Calvin Klein, the one with the boyish shape, no hips or breasts but a nice backside.

"You are going to make a beautiful bride. I already have some ideas," said Josephine, taking out a sketch pad. "You want something that is form-fitting, show off that body of yours." Josephine looked up for a second and then back down at her pad. "You want a fabric that has a little give."

Her new client nodded and leaned over to watch Josephine's hands sketch out a gown.

"See, you want something dramatic in the back," said Josephine. She drew a new sketch, next to the first one, showing the back of a gown. There was a deep V in the back and a long train.

"I definitely want something that is very simple," the woman said.

Josephine nodded. "I have the perfect fabric too! I just found it."

She went into her desk drawer and pulled out a swatch of the white lace fabric she was planning to order that very day. She laid it out on her desk and exhaled.

"It's point d'Angleterre, handmade in Belgium." Josephine looked up at the woman, still smoothing out the lace with her hand. "City called Bruges. Just about every woman there makes lace. I go myself twice a year."

"You fly out there specifically for the lace?"

"I do," Josephine said.

The woman nodded her head slowly. "You're very dedicated to your work."

Josephine smiled and looked down at her sample fabric square.

The woman leaned over Josephine's desk and dropped her voice down to a whisper. "Are you just as dedicated to your marriage?"

Josephine froze. She kept her eyes on the fabric. And she kept her smile on her face. Her heart started to thump in her chest but she didn't move a single muscle. She focused on breathing in and out, still smiling, still holding her lace.

"Do I know you, Ms. Wright?"

The woman leaned back in her chair and looked around the tiny office. "No. But I know you."

Josephine's chest was heaving, her nostrils flaring. And her teeth were clenched tight. She closed her eyes briefly and then sat up straight in her chair.

"You must be Cleo."

"Your husband calls me Marasa. Some kind of Jamaican patois nickname. Not sure what it means." The woman bit down on her bottom lip and extended a hand. When it was clear that Josephine wouldn't touch her, the woman dropped her hand and shrugged.

Josephine leaned back in her chair and crossed her arms over her chest. "What do you want?"

"I'm writing a book. About my life."

"Autobiography of a whore. Should fly off the shelves."

The woman shrugged her shoulders. "Maybe. Maybe not. I just thought you should know that Ras will be in the book."

"And we will sue you."

"You can't sue me. I'm not telling lies."

"Let me get this straight," Josephine said, standing up and putting her hands behind her back. "You came to my office this morning pretending to be a client so that you could let me know that you are writing a book about your pathetic, disgusting life as a whore. And that you will be talking about my life in this book of yours?"

"That is correct."

Josephine put her palms down on her desk and stared Cleo down. "I don't think you want to do that."

"I didn't come here for permission."

"How much do you want?"

The woman shook her head. "I've never loved any man before in my life. I've fucked half of the rappers on the East Coast. Never felt a thing. For anyone."

Josephine stared at Cleo.

"But I love Ras," Cleo said. "And he loves me too," Cleo said. "He *told* me."

Tears began to stream down Josephine's face. But her expression didn't change.

"I want him," Cleo said, closing her eyes tight. "I want him for myself. I can't even explain how deep it is. It's like—"

"What. Do. You. Want," Josephine asked through clenched teeth.

"He won't leave you," Cleo said. "So I need to get my shit together. I'm cleaning out my closets, purging my demons. Getting a fresh start on my life. I'm starting by telling my story."

Josephine thought about the .38 pistol in her top drawer. Sometimes when she had nothing to do in the office, she took it out and pointed it at the door, pretending an attacker had somehow made his way inside. The coolness of the frame always felt foreign in her hand for the first minute. But then, as her hand warmed the weapon, she would get used to it. Ras had taught her to shoot at the Tenafly Rifle and Pistol Club, just a few miles from their home in Saddle River. She always wondered if she'd really be able to pull the trigger and shoot someone if she had to. As she looked at the woman in the chair across from her desk, she knew she could and would absolutely blow Cleo's head off her shoulders if she thought she could get away with it.

"So you want to punish Ras because he won't leave me for you," Josephine said.

Cleo shuddered. "Absolutely not. I want him to be happy. If he wants to be with you, so be it."

"I had a miscarriage," Josephine said.

"He told me."

"I was knocked out on painkillers while you were fucking my husband in my backyard."

Cleo was silent.

"And these are the kinds of things you want to write about. This is how you want to *purge* yourself."

"Yes."

"And you don't want money."

"No."

"You just want to embarrass him. And me."

"That's not my goal . . ."

"I think you just want some attention. That's what you want."

Cleo raised an eyebrow but didn't speak. Josephine pointed at her.

"You have no man, no children, no love in your life. So you want to bring everyone down with you. My husband used you like a hand-kerchief. Blew his snot into you and disposed of you. And now you want him to pay. Well, fuck you, little girl. Fuck you. There. Is that enough attention for you?"

The buzzer rang and Josephine pressed the button without taking her eyes off Cleo. "Yes, Mali," she said into the speaker.

"I have Dylan on the line for you."

"I'll have to call her back."

"She said it's an emergency. About Mr. Bennett's schedule."

"I'll call her back."

Josephine released the button then said to Cleo, "Is there anything else I can do for you?"

"Josephine, I just want you to know that with Ras, it was different."

"Different than what exactly?"

"I can't explain it. But we have this connection . . ."

Josephine rolled her eyes.

Cleo stood up and brushed off the back of her skirt. "I'm going to go," she said.

"Don't you ever, ever come near me or my husband again."

"I can't promise you that, Josephine. If Ras calls me, I will go to wherever he tells me to. You should get all your promises from your husband."

Cleo turned her back to Josephine and put a hand on the door. "I apologize for any inconvenience."

"Are you making the rounds with all the wives?" Josephine asked.

"No. I don't care about any of them. But I want Ras to know what's coming. He's the one who told me I should write my story down."

"Did he really?"

"Yes, when we were in France."

"You went to France with my husband?"

"He took me to Peau de Ville. It's very beautiful there. I told him everything about my life. Everything. And he hugged me tight and told me I could redeem myself. He gave me permission to tell my story and start over. I don't think Ras really believes I'm going to do this. So I needed to tell you myself."

"Did you say he took you to Peau de Ville?" Josephine asked, her voice a whisper.

"Last spring," said Cleo. "You were in Bruges."

"He told me he was doing a food drive in the capital."

"He was. I helped him. But after, we went out to Peau de Ville."

"Where'd you stay?"

"La Chambre de L'amour."

"I see," Josephine said.

"I better go."

"Why?" Josephine whispered. "Why you?"

"I don't know," Cleo said. "I was hoping you could tell me."

Cleo left the office, closing the door softly behind her. As soon as the outer door clicked, Mali's face popped in Josephine's doorway.

"I heard everything," Mali said, one hand on her chest. "Should I call the police?"

Josephine shook her head from side to side.

"But she pretended to be someone else to gain access to you," Mali said. "That's a crime."

"No, Mali. We're not calling the police. We're calling my husband. Tell him to meet me at home. Now."

"Yes, ma'am."

When Josephine was a freshman at NYU, she lived upstairs from a boy named Joseph McCallister, a white boy from Closter, New Jersey, who'd never gone to school with anyone but white folks. The night before the first day of classes, he invited her and her roommate, Luciana, down to his room for beers. Joseph had one too many beers. He tried to grab Luciana and pull her in for a wet and sloppy kiss on the mouth. Josephine grabbed Luciana, smacked Joseph away from her, and hauled ass out of his room.

"Fine. Get out," Joseph screamed, his lips twisted in an ugly sneer. "Fuck both of you. You ugly nigger bitches!"

Josephine and Luciana had frozen in place, their jaws slack. Josephine had been unable to speak. The only sound that came out of her mouth was a gurgle, a soft sputter that sounded like she was choking.

And as Mali closed the door behind her, Josephine felt herself once again struggling to speak. The enormity of the visit from Cleo hit her all at once. It was like when your plane lands and speeds down the runway and in that moment you realize how fast you were going in the sky.

All she could do was sputter, like she did that night in Joseph's room, as she imagined her husband, the only man she'd ever loved, sleeping with a random woman in her father's hometown, in the very hotel where they had spent their wedding night.

five

$\mathcal{C}$LEO GOT OUT OF THE TUB AND RUBBED HER BODY DOWN WITH BABY oil from her shoulders to her toes. In a clockwise pattern, she made slow circles with her hand, massaging the oil into her skin. Every minute or so, she would stop and refill her palm with oil, close her eyes, and return to her body. She took slow and steady breaths.

"Fuck you doing in there?"

The man's voice made her jump. She'd almost forgotten she hadn't come to this hotel alone. For five minutes her mind had allowed her to believe she was on vacation—Cleo went to the door, pulled it open a half inch, and brought her face close to the small opening.

"Be out in two seconds," she whispered.

Before she could close the door, he was there, ripping open the door and grabbing her wrist.

"Fuck that," he said, his voice a low growl. "Come. Now."

He was naked. Cleo didn't like that. She liked to undress her men. It was a powerful feeling to reduce them from construction boots and stiff jeans to a caramel or vanilla cream or plum purple body, vulnerable and nude before her. But he had undressed himself. His penis was flaccid and swinging between his legs as he half dragged her to the bed.

"Baby, slow down, take your time."

He glared at Cleo for three seconds and then let go of her hand. He picked up a crack pipe from the bedside table, lit it, and inhaled deeply. Cleo discreetly covered her mouth and nose with one hand. She could take the smell of just about anything—except crack smoke. It made her stomach do somersaults. She rolled her eyes. Who did crack anymore, anyway? Even Bobby Brown had only smoked weed all three times she'd slept with him.

The man inhaled again, shuddered, and dropped the pipe. Then he pushed her down into a seated position on the bed. He put one hand on the top of her head and with the other he held his penis and began to rub it across her lips.

Cleo didn't like his smell, musky and sweet, like the Obsession cologne her high school boyfriend used to wear. Ras always smelled like freshly laundered T-shirts hung out on a line to dry. She tried to pretend this man was Ras.

"Why don't we just take our—"

He stuffed his penis inside Cleo's mouth until she gagged. She rolled her eyes, though it was dark enough that he couldn't see, and forced herself up.

"Lie down," she said, pushing his shoulders until he was on his back.

She was familiar with his type. They wanted to just fuck her and kick her out. And although they wanted to do it right away, their bodies wouldn't always cooperate. He couldn't get hard for the same reason she couldn't get wet: he needed to be turned on. Most men felt it was a sign of weakness or a lack of virility if they couldn't get it up immediately. But Cleo knew different. Some men, like Ras, were sensitive and needed affection. Even from jump-offs.

"You are beautiful," Cleo said, before kissing his nipples and then his belly. She looked up at him. He was still glowering at her.

He wanted to hate her. But he didn't. And they both knew that. He tried to push her head down between his legs with his hand again but Cleo pushed his hand away and then held it down.

"Don't do that," she spat. "I'm not a blow-up doll."

He relaxed, putting his hands behind his thick, bushy afro and closing his eyes, waiting. Cleo bent down between his legs and took him into her mouth. He started to groan and shifted his buttocks, trying to manipulate himself deeper into her mouth.

As soon as he started to pant rhythmically, Cleo quickly nudged his legs apart, took him out of her mouth, and slipped lower, putting her tongue inside him.

"What the fuck you doing!" he yelled, reaching out to stop her and trying to scramble higher up in the bed to escape her.

Cleo held his arms fast and licked faster, until his protests became a slow, furtive whine.

"Aw sheeeeeiiiiit," he moaned. He spread his legs wider and allowed Cleo to cup her hands under his buttocks.

"Say you like it," Cleo said, using one finger, and then two, instead of her tongue. "Say you like that shit, nasty motherfucker."

"I like that shit, I like that shit, I like that shit," he sputtered, one hand covering his face in shame.

Cleo climbed on top of him, keeping her fingers inside him.

"I know you do," she said. She bent down and kissed him on the mouth. He arched his back and legs up in the air to keep her fingers in the forbidden place. Cleo pulled out of him abruptly and scrambled to position her lower body over his mouth.

"Eat me," she said, lowering herself down to his waiting tongue. He began to lick her.

Cleo planted both feet on either side of his head and leaned over to grab the headboard. She turned to look behind her. On the table a few feet across from her, there was an alarm clock radio facing both of them. She saw the tiny red light and smiled for the camera hidden inside the radio, then turned back to her lover and continued grinding her hips on top of his face.

◆ ◆ ◆

CLEO STIRRED HER COFFEE SLOWLY, TOOK A SIP, WINCED, AND ADDED AN-other packet of Splenda. She stirred, sipped, and winced until she got the flavor just right.

"Nothing like a hot cup of coffee," she said to Alex, before breaking into a wide smile.

"You still haven't told me why you're writing this book," Alex said.

"Because I want to. And because I can."

"Is that a reason to ruin marriages?"

Cleo laughed. "Who's ruining marriages? Me? I did not steal anyone's husband. They all came willingly."

Alex looked down into her coffee cup. "So you don't take any responsibility for your role in any of this?"

"You're not writing a story on me for *Vibe*. You're ghostwriting my book. Why are you giving me the third degree?"

"I can't ask your motivation?"

"You can. But you can't be judgmental about it."

"How will you prove any of your stories? Everyone you talk about is going to want to sue you."

Cleo smiled and took her laptop out of an oversized leather car-ryall. She turned it around so that the back of the monitor faced the restaurant and both she and Alex could see the screen. She looked behind her before she turned on her computer. She clicked on a file on her desktop and a screen popped up. She was naked, her back to the camera, on top of a brown-skinned man.

"Holy shit!" Alex said, covering her face with one hand and then peeking through her fingers. "Is that—"

"Yes, it is. He likes it up the ass. Started with fingers. Within a week, he let me put vibrators and dildos up there."

Alex wiped her brow and sat back in her seat so that she couldn't see the monitor.

"That can't be legal. Did he know you were taping him?"

"Yes. He likes to be taped. And he likes to watch afterward."

Alex let out a long, low whistle. "And you're using real names in this book."

"I'm sparing a few. But yeah, real names."

Alex's face was lined. She put her fingers on her temples and rubbed them slowly. "You really want to do this?"

"Yes."

"I just wish I could understand *why*."

"There was only one I wanted for myself," Cleo said. "The rest of them were just for fun. I only wanted one to claim me."

"And he won't."

"He can't."

"So now everyone has to pay."

"No, now I need a paycheck so I can move on."

"Do you consider yourself a prostitute?" Alex asked.

"Sure, if you want to call me that."

"Do you get money for sex?"

"It's never that simple."

"But your relationships with rappers, producers, executives—it's been profitable for you."

"It's been profitable for all involved."

"How so?"

"I'm a benchmark. Like going platinum."

Alex rubbed the back of her neck. "I feel weird about this."

Cleo sucked her teeth and pulled a magazine out of her bag. "Did you write this story?" she asked, holding up a glossy magazine with a close-up shot of Mariah Carey on the cover.

"I did," Alex said. "So what?"

"She'd never really talked about her marriage to Tommy Mottola before this story. You got her to talk about it. It was a big deal."

"It was a juicy story. But it didn't ruin anyone's marriage."

"How do you know who was affected by it? Your job was to get Mariah's story across. Did you talk to Tommy Mottola?"

"There's no way I could have—"

"Did you even reach out to his people? His new wife?"

"No."

"No, you didn't. You had your own agenda. So did Mariah. You got a story that got picked up by all the blogs and I'm sure your editor was thrilled. Yes?"

"Yes, but—"

"So save your moral-high-road shit. You're getting twenty percent of the royalties on this book. And I promise you it will put your children and maybe your grandchildren through college."

"I don't work just for the money."

"Is Alex your real name?"

"Alexandria. But I write under the name Alex. Why? Is Cleo your real name?"

"No. It's Patricia. But I fuck under the name Cleo."

Alex rolled her eyes and shook her head. "Nice. Real nice."

"Let's meet here tomorrow at ten," said Cleo. "Bring your recorder."

$\mathcal{B}$UNNY COULDN'T STOP TOUCHING THE BACK OF HER NECK. EVERY five seconds, her right hand flew up to her neck, caressing the exposed skin.

Bunny's stylist took two steps back and then circled the chair, looking at her client's hair from every angle.

"It's hot, Bunny. It's very, very short. But it's hot."

"Gimme a mirror."

Mirror in hand, Bunny smiled slowly. For the first time since she had left Port Antonio, she felt free.

"Did Robert say it was okay to cut your hair?"

"No. He's going to have a heart attack." Bunny looked up at her stylist and grinned. "I can't wait."

ALTHOUGH SHE HAD BEEN GIVEN KEYS TO THE SEVEN-BEDROOM MANSION in Greenwich, Bunny never used them. She always knocked on the door and waited for someone to let her in. Every time, Robert and his wife, Sal, would shake their heads and say, "Bunny, you *live* here. Use your key!"

But no matter how many times they tried to make her feel at home, it didn't work. Port Antonio was home. A two-room house she shared with her parents and three sisters. A patch of dirt outside, a clothesline with her father's clothes pinned up. That was home. Walking out to the Blue Hole, where her father was a boatman and gave rides to tourists. Eating saltfish and ackee stew with her sisters and her father during his lunch break. That was home.

Greenwich was not home.

Six months ago her father had taken Robert, a record producer, and his wife on a boat ride. As usual, he sang for the entire trip. And like most tourists, Robert told him he had a beautiful voice. Robert said that if the boatman were twenty years younger, he'd bring him to the States and make him a star.

Derryn Clifton looked at the producer and told him he knew someone twenty years younger whom he could make into a star. The very next day Bunny sang for Robert and his wife in the lobby of their hotel. Two days later she was in New York City, in a real studio, with headphones on her ears, listening to her own voice being played back.

When Robert asked Bunny's mom if Bunny could stay in Greenwich and finish her demo, the young girl's heart sank. She knew there was no way her mother would return to Port Antonio and leave her with this white couple who walked around barefoot and smoked weed on their patio at night. But Mrs. Clifton agreed, quickly, and flew back to Jamaica two days later. She told her youngest daughter to mind her keepers and keep her legs closed.

Bunny had opened her legs two days after she met Zander. But she'd managed to mind her keepers until the night she decided to cut all her hair off.

BUNNY KNOCKED ON THE DOOR OF THE MANSION WITH HER LEFT HAND, her right hand on the nape of her neck. She'd never realized how soft the skin was on the back of her neck. Or how intriguing her natural curl pattern was. She waited at the door, twisting and twisting the short curls.

"Bunny, is that you?" she heard Robert say from the other side of the door. "Use your key!"

Bunny waited. And the twelve-foot-high door opened.

Robert, Bunny's producer and caretaker, took in a sharp breath and grabbed Bunny by the shoulder. "In the living room—*now*."

Bunny slunk into the living room and settled back on the white leather sofa.

"Sally," Robert yelled. "You need to get down here right now!"

He sat across from Bunny. "Why would you do this? Why would you cut your hair?"

"You don't like it?"

Before he could answer, his wife was in the doorway. She gasped and then clapped her hands over her mouth. "Bunny! What did you do!"

Bunny rolled her eyes and her hand went to the back of her neck. "It's just hair. It grows back."

"Robert, don't panic," Sally said, holding out both hands. "She can get a hair weave before the photo shoot."

Robert just stared at Bunny, shaking his head back and forth. "How much did we pay for the hair that was in there this morning?"

"Five thousand dollars," Sally said.

Bunny swallowed. "I know you all think that I should have the traditional long-hair look," she said. "But this haircut makes me feel more confident. It feels like me."

"Does it make you confident that you're going to sell records?" Robert said, looking down on the floor. "'Cause I don't really give a fuck about your self-esteem."

Bunny sucked her teeth. "Obviously."

"Look, you're here because we're investing in you, Bunny," Robert said.

"I know that."

"You don't act like you know that. We have a responsibility to your record label to deliver a certain look. And this is not it."

"I met Kipenzi Hill recently," Bunny said. "I had the exact same weave she has. Why do we all have to look the same?"

"You have to look like whoever the hell is selling records. That's why we sent you to the same woman who does Kipenzi Hill's hair. There's no reinventing the wheel in the music industry."

"There should be."

"You can take your ass back to Jamaica and reinvent the industry. You're not doing it on my dime."

Robert stood up and walked out of the room. Sally lit a cigarette, inhaled, and exhaled.

"I'm not getting my hair done over," Bunny said. "I'm wearing it short like this."

Sally nodded and inhaled again.

"Robert needs to trust me. This cut is hot. It will set me apart."

Sally shrugged and blew out three perfect smoke rings.

"Do you like it?" Bunny asked.

Sally leaned against the wall, narrowed her eyes, and inhaled again. "No," she said. "I love it."

Bunny stood up and looked at her reflection in the full-length mirror in the foyer. "You think Robert will let me keep it like this?"

Sally shook her head. "Second album. You can go dark and edgy and adopt a whole new persona. First album? Long hair. Weave. Get over it."

Bunny put her hand to her neck once more and rubbed. "We'll see," she said.

She left the living room and climbed the steps to the attic.

In the suite in the attic of the Greenwich home, Bunny sang into her mirror, shaking her bangs out of her face. The short cut could work, she was sure of it. But she was also sure that Robert wasn't having it.

Bunny hurled herself onto her bed and took out her cell phone. She sent a text message to Zander. When he didn't respond immediately, she called him. When it went straight to voice mail, her heartbeat started to quicken. They always called each other when their batteries went low. It was common courtesy to give a heads-up if your phone was about to die. But Zander often forgot. Which meant there were times when Bunny could not reach him. And this was unacceptable.

Bunny went into her email server, erased her own information, and put in Zander's user name and password. Immediately all his emails popped up on her phone. She scrolled through, skipping her own name and looking for any addresses she didn't recognize. She found one. From a girl who'd sent a picture of herself bending over at the waist and looking back at the camera.

"I hope you come back soon," the girl wrote, in a scripted pink font. "So I can come again. ;)"

Blood dripped onto Bunny's tongue. While looking through Zander's emails, she'd been biting down hard on the inside of her cheek without even realizing it. She broke the skin when she saw the girl in the picture, and the taste was salty and bitter in her mouth. She went to the bathroom, spit, rinsed, and spit again.

Zander was the first young person Bunny had met when she moved from Port Antonio. They shared a tutor who traveled to both their homes. Once a week, the tutor had them both meet her at the main branch of the New York Public Library to do research. The first time Bunny saw Zander, she knew immediately that she wanted to stand closer to him. And she did. She wrote her number in his spiral notebook and he sang for her over the phone that night. She sang for him. And they immediately began plotting how they could take over the world together.

But Zander was a boy. A teenager. At 16, Bunny was actually younger than him by a year. But she felt much older. He played boyish games. And Bunny found herself chasing him when it should have been the other way around.

And when Zander started playing games, the other Bunny came out. The one who once who smacked her own mother in the face and silently dared her to say something about it. The one who put her boot on her sister's neck and tried to crush her before being pulled off by their father. Bunny was a sweetheart. Until she wasn't. And then she was just trouble.

Sally appeared in the doorway to the attic, cigarette dangling from her lips. "You okay?" she asked Bunny.

"I need to go find Zander," Bunny said, standing up and going to the closet for shoes.

"Don't get yourself in any trouble. You have a hair appointment first thing in the morning. And we're flying to Atlanta straight from the salon. Dallas Austin session starts at two. Interviews scheduled after that."

Bunny nodded and brushed past Sally, heading down the stairs and out the door.

"I do like your hair, Bunny," Sally called out to her. "Next album, I promise. You can wear it short."

seven

"*Y*OU REMEMBER WHEN THIS WAS THE OMNI?" Z THREW HIS ARM around Beth's shoulders and stretched out his legs in front of him. Beth turned to him and smiled. She couldn't nod or she would throw up.

"Zander was six," Beth said. She put a hand on Z's knee. "Zakee was five and I was pregnant with the twins."

On hearing the word *twins*, Zachary climbed over his brothers and stuck his head between his parents' shoulders.

"You came here when you were pregnant with me and Zaire? Did we kick a lot? Could you feel us in your stomach?"

Z's nostrils flared and he turned to face his nine-year-old son.

"Sit your ass down and shut up," he spat. Even though Z never had a kind word to say to his next-to-youngest son, Zachary seemed to experience his father's hatred anew each day. He stared at his father with his mouth open and then turned his head slightly to the right, fully expecting his mother to step in and berate Z for being cruel. And as always, Beth was silent.

For a few minutes, the entire car was silent. The driver, oblivious to anything but the fact that he was driving a celebrity, kept up a steady stream of small talk with Boo, Z's personal assistant, who sat in the passenger seat of the Suburban. Beth and Z sat in the row behind the driver. Their four sons were all sitting side by side in the next row back.

"We came down here and tore the ATL *down*," Z said, more to himself than to his wife.

It was in Atlanta, all those years ago, that Beth first realized that something might be wrong in her third pregnancy. As soon as she'd boarded the plane, she'd felt a strange emptiness in her belly. It was like when something stops humming or buzzing and you realize for the first time that the sound had even been there in the first place. She had reached over to strap in Zander and Zakee and then noticed that something had stopped communicating from her belly to her brain.

For that entire summer, she'd traveled with Z and the kids while he crisscrossed the country with Jake on the Take No Prisoners tour. And she had greeted each city by throwing up in the car on the way to the hotel. In Seattle, she had a blinding headache at her right temple. In Cincinnati, she'd gone to the emergency room because she bled through the entire show. But when they landed at the airport in Atlanta, nothing. She'd had no nausea, no movement, and no headaches. Her belly felt like a prosthetic limb. She didn't even feel like she'd overeaten on Thanksgiving. She just felt fat.

"Mommy, I want to sit with you!"

Beth turned around. Her youngest son, two-year-old Zeke, sat in her oldest son's lap. Beth extracted herself from Z's arms and reached back. Zander handed Zeke over, rolled his eyes, and continued staring out the car window. He had been trying to grow his hair into dreadlocks, so he constantly had his long, thin fingers in his hair, twisting and twisting the short braids.

"Look," Beth said, taking her son's chubby hand and using it to point out the window. "That's where Daddy's going to perform tonight."

Zeke looked out at the Philips Arena and his eyes widened. "Daddy? You play basketball?"

Beth smiled and looked over at Z. He had his head thrown back with his eyes closed. He wasn't asleep but he pretended to be.

"You know Daddy doesn't play basketball," Beth said, tickling her son under his chin. Beth's youngest child was too beautiful for his father to love. With his café au lait skin, soft curls, long eyelashes, and light brown eyes, he looked too much like the girl Z wanted so desperately. And because he wasn't a girl, Z just pretended he didn't exist. Beth and Z's first two sons were carbon copies of their father: temperamental and mean. Their third son, Zachary, who'd lost his brother while still in Beth's womb, tried too hard to matter to Z, who had no use for him because he was sickly. He didn't play sports, suffered from asthma, and had a slight speech impediment. Beth didn't think Z had ever said a word to his two youngest sons after they were potty-trained. She cradled Zeke in her lap, which was getting smaller and smaller, although only her two oldest boys had even noticed she was pregnant again.

"Daddy's sleeping," Zeke said. He held up his hand to his mother's lips and she pretended to bite him. He giggled and Beth leaned in and smothered him with kisses. It wasn't until she brought her head up to move her hair back behind her ear that she noticed Zander staring at her with more hatred than usual. Zakee, his shadow, both physically and mentally, kept his eyes darting from Zander to Beth.

"Zander," Beth said. "You okay?"

"I want to go the fuck *home.*"

Only the driver of the car was surprised to hear a teenager use the f-word not just in front of his mother but directed to her specifically. Beth just turned back around slowly, keeping Zeke on her lap and her eyes on the road. If she didn't move, blink, address Zander, curse him out, or acknowledge his behavior in any way, if she could keep baby Zeke from realizing anything was wrong with his family, if she could keep still for a few minutes, she could make it to the hotel without smacking the shit out of Zander and then throwing up.

Ever since the online videos of Zander and Bunny singing in his bedroom had taken off, he'd been insufferable around the house. It was a simple setup. He sat on his bed with his guitar; Bunny was off camera, playing piano and harmonizing. And they sang classics: "A House Is Not a Home" by Luther Vandross and "Time After Time" by Cyndi Lauper. At first he got attention because he was Z's son. Ten million views later, he was a minicelebrity in his own right. When they'd landed in Atlanta, three giggling teenage girls approached Zander for an autograph while Z was in the bathroom. Beth saw the look on Zander's face and knew she was in trouble.

And then there was Bunny. They were attached at the hip. Every time Zander left her presence, he was tense and wound up, brooding and unruly. Always. Z said it was just blue balls. But Beth was pretty sure they were actually having sex. It was something else.

In the lobby of the Ritz-Carlton, Beth asked for a room service menu. The menu came with a separate list just for the different brands of water. Beth sucked her teeth and readjusted Zeke on her hip. Who the hell needed thirty choices for bottled water? It was yet another rich-folks thing that she just couldn't understand. Kipenzi swore up and down that she could tell the difference between Perrier and Evian, but Beth didn't believe her. They were supposed to have a taste test, with blindfolds and little paper cups. But they hadn't been able to find the time.

"Boo, can you go get the boys something to eat?" Beth held up the menu in front of Z's assistant. "They can't eat anything off here."

Boo nodded his head slowly and began to rise from the comfortable couch in front of the check-in counter, where Z was gathering keys and hotel maps from a pretty woman with two long braids on either side of her head. "Where you want me to go?"

Beth bit the inside of her lip and scanned the faces of her four boys. Zander, standing next to his father and openly gawking at the hotel employee's breasts, would eat anything. Zakee would eat anything Zander ate. Burgers and fries and sodas for them. Zach was lactose-intolerant and allergic to everything from shellfish to peanuts. And baby Zeke was in a chicken-fingers phase; he'd eaten nothing else for the past three weeks.

Beth made a list on hotel stationery, gave it to Boo, and then headed up to the adjoining suites booked by Z's record label. The four boys would share two bedrooms in one suite. She and Z would have the other suite to themselves.

As soon as she got settled into her room, she noticed the red message light blinking on the hotel phone. She thought about not checking it. Who would call the hotel room instead of her cell phone or Z's cell phone? She checked the message anyway.

"Beth. It's Kipenzi. Room three-twelve. I'm coming by around seven so we can eat in the Cheater's Booth. I know your fat ass is hungry. Love you. Bye."

Beth smiled. It had been a tradition since Z and Jake first started rapping that the first person settled into the hotel (or, as was more likely back in the day, the motel) found a spot for dinner and left a message with the other couple. The first time Kipenzi had ever left Beth a message, they were at a Holiday Inn on the New Jersey Turnpike. Jake and Z were doing a ten-minute set at Rutgers University and they'd all met up the night before at a Fuddruckers on Route 9.

Boo returned with the food for the boys. When he went in, they nearly attacked him. Beth closed the door joining their suites and then swept aside the draperies and took in the lights of nighttime Atlanta. She saw the NationsBank Plaza and realized it was the tower that Usher used for the "U Don't Have to Call" video.

She'd never liked Atlanta. It was where her son had died inside her, risking her life and Zach's. Dr. Hamilton said they would never know for sure when Zaire passed away or how. But Beth knew that it had been in this city, where every street, diner, and park was named after a freaking fruit. She'd sworn she would never come to Atlanta again. Especially not if she was pregnant. But somehow Z had convinced her.

Beth opened her suitcase to find something to wear to dinner. Z was at his sound check, and when he returned, he'd be ravenous. Beth was grateful that Kipenzi had made arrangements. She barely had enough energy to put a comb through her hair and check on Zeke to make sure he'd eaten.

Three sharp knocks brought Beth to the door of her suite. They were staying in the Club Level, an ultraexclusive hotel within the hotel, so she knew it had to be someone legitimate. She looked out the peephole and saw Kipenzi sticking her middle finger up in the air.

"Get in here, girl," Beth said, pulling her friend in for a hug.

"Damn! You are huge," Kipenzi said. She held Beth's hand and twirled her around once.

"And I'm only four months. They say when you carry low, it's usually a girl."

Kipenzi rolled her eyes and went to the sofa. She wasted no time digging into the fruit basket that had been waiting for them.

"Who's going on first?" Kipenzi asked, her mouth full of melon.

"Z, right? Doesn't he always?"

Kipenzi kicked off her shoes and shrugged her shoulders. "I think I heard they were changing it up. Just for tonight."

Beth cocked her head to one side. "They who?"

Kipenzi froze with a piece of pineapple still in her hand, the end of it sticking out of her mouth. She looked at Beth and then finished the fruit.

"Don't listen to me. I'm retired."

"So you're not going to do your part on any of Jake's songs?"

"How come no one believes me? I'm done. Not singing. For real."

"Is it gonna be hard for you? Don't you think you're going to miss it?"

Kipenzi let out a deep sigh, put her feet on the coffee table, and yawned. "No, and no."

"Did you talk to Zander about his music?"

"Girl, your son is incredible. He just needs to find the right team. Songwriters. Producers. Management."

"Puff wants to manage him."

Kipenzi snorted. "Right. Like Puff managed me. Zander needs a hands-on manager. Don't get me wrong. I love Puff. But not for Zander. He needs someone who is going to do more than just show up in the video and wave his hands around. You think Puff ever actually took a meeting for me? Looked at my budget? Fought for a third single? Um. No."

"I don't even know if I want Zander in this business. He's still young . . ."

"I got his back. Auntie Penzi is officially unemployed and I'm going to be watching him like a hawk. No worries."

"What do you think about Bunny?"

"I think she's going to be huge."

Beth's shoulders slumped. "I do too. Why does that make me feel weird?"

"'Cause she's a bitch, that's why."

Kipenzi and Beth locked arms and went down in the elevator, talking rapidly and hugging spontaneously for no reason except that they were together in person in the same city at the same time, an extremely rare occurrence. They dashed into the restaurant and headed straight back to the Cheater's Booth before anyone recognized Kipenzi.

The Cheater's Booth was a special, oversized seating area at the Atlanta Grill, in the lobby of the Ritz-Carlton. It was a roomy booth with a table large enough for the amounts of food that Z and Jake could put away. It even came with a discreet curtain that could be pulled around the two couples if they wanted to go for ultimate privacy. Beth would not have minded being completely hidden from the other diners in the restaurant. But Kipenzi, Jake, and Z were all famous. And she noticed that famous people needed to check their celebrity recognition gauges at least twice a day.

Z came next, kissing Kipenzi on the cheek and sliding into the booth next to his wife. He looked over the menu, holding it with one hand, and continually stroked Beth's belly with the other. When Jake arrived, he and Z performed an elaborate handshake, complete with loud finger snaps, that lasted for a full fifteen seconds. Kipenzi and Beth sat there, waiting for them to finish, rolling their eyes at each other in solidarity.

They didn't even pretend to be two couples on a double date. Kipenzi and Beth shared one side of the booth, picking off each other's plates and finishing each other's sentences. Jake and Z sat on the other side, trading industry gossip, constantly checking their various gadgets, and going over song selections for the show.

Later a convoy of Navigators and Suburbans pulled up to the restaurant and the two couples met up with their security detail, who led them all outside. The plan was for one truck to take Kipenzi and Beth to the show, along with a few record label executives. Dylan, Jake and Z's publicist, stood outside, speaking into her earpiece and yelling out orders to a few people milling about.

Beth saw Bunny exit a Town Car and tap Zander on the back. He spun around quickly and they immediately started arguing.

"I saw that picture in your email. *Who the hell is Tonya?*" Bunny screamed.

She put her pointer finger in Zander's face, edging it closer and closer to his nose. Zander's hands were at his sides.

Before Beth could reach Z, who was climbing into one of the trucks, Zander and Bunny were a cartoon-style ball of dust rolling around on the ground and Z and Jake were diving in to break them up.

"Yo, what the fuck is wrong with you?" Jake said, dragging Zander to his feet. Zander swatted the air, trying to get another smack in Bunny's direction.

"Bitch is always trying to start some shit," Zander screamed.

"You trying to get locked up?" said Z. "You can't be hitting no girl, yo!"

Kipenzi and Beth stood side by side, staring at the scene. Both were thinking about the five times Beth had ended up in Kipenzi's apartment, bleeding and crying. There had been a bloody nose, a black eye, a dislocated shoulder, a cracked rib, and once her two front teeth had gone missing. But that was a very long time ago. Z hadn't hit Beth in ten years.

Bunny got up, shadowboxing and dancing around, trying to get another shot at Zander. Dylan kept trying to grab her, but she managed to slip away each time.

"You better listen to your daddy, Zander," she taunted. "I know you don't want to go to jail. Punk bitch."

"No, she didn't," Kipenzi said.

"Yes, she did," said Beth.

"Zander, I will see you after the show," Bunny shouted. "You wanna keep fucking with other girls? This shit is not over—asshole!"

Hotel security came out, and Kipenzi and Beth watched the scene. Z had his arms wrapped around his son as they talked to the police officers. Dylan had dragged Bunny back to the Town Car and stuffed her in the back seat. She was moving and squirming, clearly holding up her middle finger to the glass. One of the officers walked over to the car to talk to Dylan.

Beth walked over to Z, as Zander climbed into another Suburban with security.

"I don't like this girl," Beth said to Z. "She's going to get Zander in trouble."

"Let's talk about it after the show," Z said.

"You need anything before I go?" Beth asked.

"I need some ass," Z said. He didn't even bother to whisper.

"Stop it," she said, smiling. "For real. Me and Kipenzi are going to the arena."

Z palmed her behind and squeezed. "I'm serious. I need it. Before the show."

Beth swallowed. He was serious. But she was so tired. So weak. She wanted to go to the show, stay for just his set, and then come back to the hotel and pass out.

"Z. Baby. I'm so—"

Z waved off the first driver. Kipenzi, on her phone and surrounded by other people in the car, didn't even notice that Beth was missing. Z grabbed Beth's wrist and pulled her in the direction of the hotel entrance.

The elevator arrived just as a young white girl recognized Z and began to walk over with a paper and a pen. Z shoved Beth into the elevator and jabbed at the button for the door to close. He turned Beth around so that she faced the wall.

"I love you, Beth," Z said and pulled her pants down just enough on one side. "You know that, right?" He grabbed Beth's hair and wrapped her blond ponytail around his right hand. He yanked it just a bit and Beth obeyed, bending over at the waist. Random thoughts filled her head: *Are there cameras on this elevator? Are my pants wet? Do the black girls let him do it like this?*

She opened her legs, put her hands on her belly, and waited. By the time they reached the top floor of the hotel and the doors opened, Z was done. He didn't come into the room with her. There was no need to. He zipped himself up, then pressed the button for the first floor.

"Take a shower," Z said. "I'll send a car to come get you in ten minutes."

eight

*B*ETH HAD NOT WANTED TO BRING HER YOUNGEST SON TO Z'S SHOW. She wasn't ready to lose him yet. With her three older boys, the moment they saw their father onstage, their love affair with the woman who washed, fed, and dressed them was over. Zander had sat in the wings of the Apollo Theater in Harlem and watched, mesmerized, as his father stood in one spot and preached a sermon through a rap song. The energy from the frenzied crowd seeped backstage and washed over Zander like water at a baptism. When the show was over, Beth noticed her oldest son was different. He understood that people worshipped his father. And so, he began to worship him as well.

And now that he was beginning to amass his own following, Zander had only enough room in his heart for his father and himself.

Zakee had followed the next year. Zachary, though he knew his father hated him, had still become a convert after a sold-out show at Madison Square Garden. The only one left was Zeke, nearly three years old. She kept him behind at hotels or backstage any time Z performed. When he fully understood who he was related to and how that man was perceived, Beth would be childless again.

Boo came to pick her up. They were waved through three security checkpoints in the Philips Arena parking lot and driven all the way up to a nondescript door. A few of Z's friends from home milled about the backstage door, along with oversized bodyguards keeping a few women from entering.

Beth kept her head down and walked right through the crowd. Someone on the other side of the door opened it and pointed her to the right, in the direction of Z's dressing room. She heard the usual whispers: *That's Z's girl right there. Yup. Is she white? Nah, I think she Puerto Rican. No, she white.*

Beth only darted her eyes as she read the handwritten signs on each door: Lighting, Sound, Crafts Services, Talent No. 2, and then, finally, Talent No. 1. Again, the door swung open before she had to knock.

The chemistry of the room changed as soon as Beth entered. She recognized most of the men in the room; half of them were on Z's payroll. But as always, the women were all strangers. The only woman she recognized was Dylan.

Dylan winked and waved, holding tight to her clipboard and then returning to a rapid-fire conversation with a member of Z's crew. Dylan was a different kind of white girl, and she reminded Beth of it as often as she could. Her father was a judge. Her mother was in the House of Representatives. Dylan had gone to Spence and then Harvard. She carried herself like she was better than Beth. Because she was. Like the three publicists before her, Beth knew she'd leave and take a proper job. She was slumming in hip-hop because it was cool to be a white girl who could boss around rappers, telling them what to do and where to be.

Beth's four sons were playing video games in a corner of the loft-like room. She scanned the room for her husband.

"Boo, where's Z?"

"Just stepped out for a minute," Boo said. "He's on in fifteen." Beth looked at her watch. "Jake already went on?"

"Z's on first."

Beth felt a prickly sensation up and down her arms. For ten years, Jake had always opened for Z. Why would that change tonight?

"Don't worry, it's no big deal," said Dylan, sidling up to Beth. She looked down at her clipboard, and Beth stared at the three inches of jet-black roots Dylan had coming out of her scalp. The rest of her hair was white blond, something that fascinated Beth, a natural blonde who'd never touched a bottle of dye.

"The fucking guitarist for Jake's acoustic set totally missed his flight," said Dylan, her voice musky and deep. "He's on his way now from the airport, but we totally don't wanna hold up, like, the whole show, so the promoters are gonna put Z on first. That's cool, right?"

Dylan gave Beth a quick, plastic grin that translated to *Deal with it.*

Beth resented that Dylan had a better command of her husband's schedule than she did. If he missed a birthday party, here was Dylan: "We had a shot at an Oprah interview, so he had to fly out to this event. *That's cool, right?*" And then when Beth was suffering from postpartum depression and needed Z to come home and help her with just one of the kids, here was Dylan, on speakerphone. "He just got two hundred fifty grand—cash—to perform for five minutes at a bat mitzvah. I'm sending him home as soon as he's done. *That's cool, right?*"

No, Dylan. It's not cool. It's never cool, Beth thought to herself as she made her way to the stage.

When Boo helped her and the boys up the steps to watch the show, Beth got a look at the crowd gathered at the Philips Arena to see Z perform a decade of hits. Her jaw dropped. The place was barely half full. Beth could not remember the last time she'd seen him perform before a noncapacity crowd. And this was Atlanta, not New York, where everyone was jaded and too cool for live shows. She turned around and looked back at Z's people. They were lip-synching to his songs, waving their hands in the air and rhyming back and forth, their faces inches apart and contorted like Z's. Either they didn't notice that the place wasn't full or they were pretending not to notice.

Beth heard the opening chords of her favorite song, "Die Tonight." She had been sitting next to a fifteen-year-old Z when he wrote it. She'd just given birth to Zander and they were all living with Z's grandmother Zena in the Bronx. It was the song that got him signed to the label. It was the song that got him on the radio. It was the song that writers always asked him about. They couldn't get enough of the story: Z holding his two-day-old son and a crack pipe in one hand, scribbling lyrics on the back of an envelope at Grandma Z's kitchen table with the other hand.

A year after the song went to number one, a fourteen-year-old girl in Compton killed her mother, who had abused her for years. In court, she said she had listened to "Die Tonight" on repeat for six hours until she got the courage to shoot her mother in the head at point-blank range. And there was the white boy in Houston, blasting the song in his car when he got pulled over by the police. He shot them both dead.

While politicians and do-gooders insisted that Z's lyrics and sentiments, *Kill them before they kill you*, were responsible for the crimes, Beth knew better. Z just wrote down what he felt. And it turned out that other people could relate, fifteen million times over.

The music came to an abrupt halt and Beth noticed Boo standing just offstage with Zeke in his arms. Her youngest looked confused and tearful and reached his hands out toward his mother. She didn't want him to see the show, but it was too late to ask Boo to take him back. She reached out for him and adjusted Zeke on her hip.

Zeke craned his neck, looked back at Beth, smiled, and then looked back at his father. Beth could see Zander, Zakee, and Zachary on the other side of the stage, nearly visible to the crowd. She knew it was just a matter of time before Zander would be actually onstage with Z, serving as his hype man.

Z stood at center stage and held his arms out wide. He dropped the microphone and remained still and silent. Then, without warning, he began to yell out the lyrics to "Die Tonight," sending the crowd into screams. When he got to the chorus and the music began to slowly build up, an intense rhythmic bass line and a creepy piano riff, Beth instinctively put a hand over Zeke's ear to protect him from the wave of screams that always poured out from the crowd.

But this time something was different. No screams. Beth looked around the stadium, wondering if the lighting was bad. She couldn't understand why Z's performance didn't seem as awe-inspiring as usual. He had the same amount of energy. He performed with the same vigor. So why did it seem like this was a dress rehearsal for the real show? Beth peered out into the crowd, trying to fix and focus her eyes on individual people. When she did, she realized: the people in the crowd were young. Zander's age. They didn't know Z. For them, "Die Tonight" was the theme song to a movie that they'd seen on DVD or a video game that featured one of his songs.

It wasn't the anthem of their angst years. They didn't learn how to drive with that song banging in the speakers of their parents' cars. Z was a relic, at least in this room. And when he threw his arms out in his faux-Jesus pose and they clapped, they weren't worshipping him, they were tolerating him.

Back in the dressing room, Beth stayed in a corner with the boys, making them snacks and talking to them about the show. Z played a dice game with his boys in another corner of the room. They were waiting for Boo to return with the money from the promoter. Normally, when Z was done, the whole show was done. But this time Jake was getting ready to go on. Z told Beth they were going to a skybox in the arena to watch Jake perform.

As soon as Boo walked back in, Beth noticed how everyone in the room except Z looked up with expectancy in their eyes. Boo had everyone's lives in the front pocket of his jeans. The manager, the bodyguard, even the man whose only job was to hold Z's jewelry, they all knew they had to get paid off the cash Boo had just gotten from the promoter. Beth never liked to be around when the men got those glassy, furtive looks in their eyes. It seemed pathetic, living off a man like Z, who rapped for a living. Boo crossed the room and whispered something in Z's ear. Z was standing in a half squat; he was just about to throw his dice, which were still in his cupped hand. He listened intently, moved back to look at Boo, and then laughed, long and hard. The whole room seemed to exhale and Boo began his walk around the room, passing out wads of cash to different people there.

"What the fuck was that?" Z asked, looking around the room.

Beth had felt it too. It was like thunder. It sounded as if it was coming from the walls and the ceiling but she could only feel it under her feet. She picked up Zeke from the couch and walked to the door of the dressing room. As soon as she opened the door, a wave of sound forced its way into the room. It was piercing and all-encompassing and Beth was frightened. She thought of the concert at CUNY, one of Z's first, where there had been a stampede. Seven people had been trampled to death.

"They oversold the show?" Z asked no one in particular.

Z's best friend, Donald, clapped him on the back. "Nah, son. They want you back for an encore!"

Z smiled and stepped out into the hallway to ask one of the promoters what was going on. He closed the door behind him and everyone waited. When he opened the door again, Beth knew something was wrong. His jaw was tight and his eyes were wild.

"Let's pack this shit up," Z barked, pointing at the mess. "My set is done. We got the money. Fuck we sitting around here for? Let's go."

Beth had to move double-time to keep up with Z, who was striding backstage toward the back door like he was about to break into a jog. She kept the three older boys in between them so no one would get left behind and she carried Zeke. Right before they got to the stage, Beth stopped walking.

"Mommy, they're leaving us. Come on," Zeke said, pointing to his father.

Beth took Zeke's hand and placed it on her belly. Zeke looked down at his mother's stomach.

"What's in there?"

"A baby," she said, looking Zeke in the eyes and checking for his reaction.

"A baby for me?"

"Yes, for you. And your brothers too."

Zeke clapped his hands together. Beth knew he'd be thrilled, unlike Zander, who had greeted each of his brothers with increasing levels of disdain. Zeke was different. He was a happy baby.

"Is it a girl baby or a boy baby?"

Beth began to walk again. Z was standing at the door, waving her forward. His face was tight.

"It's a girl baby," she said to Zeke. "A little sister for you."

Zeke put his thumb in his mouth and his head on her shoulder. "Good. I like girl babies."

"Me too," Beth said.

There was a commotion at the back exit, where Beth had come in. For some reason, the security guard at the door wouldn't let Z out. Beth caught up to him and saw that the guard was trying to get a crowd of people away from the door so that Z could get to the waiting car. There was a small group trying to force their way in. And behind her, Beth could still feel that pulsing thunder. Finally, police officers showed up and dispersed the crowd to either side of the doorway so that Z could leave. Beth watched her husband take a deep breath before he walked out. But when she followed him out, she noticed that the crowd, all craning necks and waving hands and arms, barely noticed him. A few people reached out and touched his arm. And two young ladies actually stopped Zander for a picture. But Beth was absolutely sure that everyone else's eyes continued past Z, back at the door. They were waiting for someone else.

As they sat in the car for the short ride to the hotel, everyone took nonverbal cues from Z and stayed quiet. Beth, in the back with the boys, kept her eyes on the back of Z's head. She slid her phone out of her bag with one hand and sent a text message to Kipenzi. "Atlanta is not live like it used to be. Crowd is kind of weak, right?"

Two seconds later, her phone buzzed. "Are you kidding me? I think this place is about to explode. You know it's sold out, right? KP."

Beth shut her phone off and rubbed her belly. She wondered when Jake had surpassed Z in popularity and how she hadn't noticed.

nine

"*W*AIT. SO YOU'RE REALLY SERIOUS ABOUT THIS."

Kipenzi smiled wide and threw her arms around Jake's neck. After ten years, Jake was still the only person Kipenzi felt truly comfortable with. And while she was prepared for all the hangers-on from the music industry to disappear, she knew Jake had her back.

"Serious as a heart attack," Kipenzi said.

"How are you gonna get out of your contract, the endorsements . . ."

"My lawyers are working all that out right now," said Kipenzi. She nuzzled Jake's neck.

"And you're willing to pay for the privilege of not working?"

Kipenzi stepped back and looked Jake in the eye. "You don't think I should do this?"

"I'm not saying that. Necessarily. I just wonder if you realize—"

"What a big deal this is? Of course I do. Have you seen my bunions?"

Jake laughed. "You have the ugliest feet on the planet."

"And my voice. It's changing, Jake." Kipenzi put her hand up to her throat. "I'm just not loving this anymore. I heard Zander and Bunny sing a song me and Usher recorded years ago. They did it better! It's time for me to go quietly."

"Why not go out fighting?" Jake asked.

"Like you and Puff and Jay? Forty years old and still rapping? Putting out a farewell album every other year like it makes sense? No thank you."

"I'm thirty-seven," Jake said.

"That's not what your birth certificate says."

"You remember what you said a few years ago?" Jake asked. "About what you would do when your career was over?"

"I would sleep late every day."

"No. You said you would marry me and have a bunch of babies."

Kipenzi smiled. "I did say that."

"So let's go. Now."

"Wha—?"

"You serious about leaving the business? I fully support that. So let's do the damn thing. Right now. Today. You're retired. Ready for the next phase of your life. Let's do it."

Jake clapped his hands together and then folded them behind his head. He had his long legs stretched out on the sofa, one foot crossing the other on the teak coffee table.

"I love you, Kipenzi. And I want you to be my wife."

"Wait. Jake, you can't say it like that!"

"Like what?"

"Like . . . that. With your feet up and your hands behind your head."

"What's wrong with this?"

"You know, in certain cultures it's considered disrespectful to put your hands behind your head like that."

"I just told you I want you to be my wife. And you're tripping on my posture?"

"It's not your posture. It's your body language."

Jake grabbed his crotch. "Body language this."

"You are awful."

"Come on. Let's get this going. Call your little assistant man and tell him to make it happen."

"His name is Ian," Kipenzi said. "You should call him Ian."

Jake rolled his eyes. "I don't fuck with that dude."

"That's 'cause he doesn't fuck with you."

"He's weird."

"He's indispensable."

Kipenzi flipped open her cell phone and typed a text message. "He just hit me back. He's coming over in ten minutes. Please be nice."

"I need a piece of paper and a pen," Jake said, sitting up straight.

"Here," Kipenzi said, digging out both from her purse.

"You take a piece too. Sit right here."

"What are we doing?" Kipenzi asked, sitting on the floor at Jake's feet.

"Pro and con list. I'm making one for you. You make one for me."

"And then what?"

"I just want us both to be aware of what we're getting."

"Or not getting."

"What do you mean by that?"

Kipenzi shielded her paper with one hand and began to write. Jake leaned over her shoulder.

"No peeking," Kipenzi said. "Write your own list. Here's an extra sheet of paper for the pro side. You'll probably need room for all my wonderful qualities."

"Yeah. You too. Might want to write small."

"I'm almost done already," Kipenzi said, rolling her eyes.

"I know everything on your list already anyway."

"No, you don't. You have no idea."

"Kipenzi, I always know."

Kipenzi lifted her head to look up at Jake. Before she could stop herself, she reached up and put her hands on Jake's cheeks and then kissed him. He was right. He always knew. From day one.

Kipenzi and Jake had met at Electric Lady Studios in the Village, the place where Jimi Hendrix had recorded "Slow Blues" just a month before he died. The year before they met, Kipenzi's father had brought her to New York for a studio session. He'd cashed in his 401(k). When his wife found out, she told him to prepare for a divorce when he returned. The studio session fell on Kipenzi's eighteenth birthday. Kipenzi's father had a meeting scheduled at Atlantic Records with an A&R. Kipenzi stayed behind at the studio, recording all the parts on a ballad that would close out her demo. Her father had only hesitated briefly about leaving her in the studio alone. She'd shooed him off, telling him she was more than capable of taking a taxi to their hotel in Midtown.

The last time she slipped into the booth to sing over the backing track, she looked up from the microphone and saw Jake standing next to the engineer with his arms crossed over his chest. Kipenzi was grateful that her father wasn't there. He would not have been able to keep his cool around a rapper he'd only seen in music videos. And Kipenzi hated it when he asked for autographs or to take pictures with celebrities.

She knew better than to give anyone more props than she'd give herself. Jake was all right, but at that point he'd never even had a platinum record.

She gave him a brief head nod, closed her eyes, and launched into the song she had written the night before. When she was done, she opened her eyes and Jake was gone. She packed up to go and then called her father, letting him know she was leaving the studio and getting in a cab.

But as she talked to her father on the phone, Kipenzi knew that upstairs Jake was waiting for her in the lobby of the studio. She'd never been introduced to him. She hadn't known him from a hole in the wall. She'd only glimpsed him briefly before singing her song.

And somehow, that was all the time it took.

She knew that if she walked upstairs to the lobby and Jake said he was taking her to Redondo Beach or Malaysia or Tuscany, she was going, no questions asked.

She came up the stairs of the studio and saw Jake standing at the front door with his back to Kipenzi. Without looking, he held out an open hand behind him. Without hesitating, Kipenzi put her hand in his. He walked out of the building, holding Kipenzi's hand tight, and led her into the parking lot across the street, where his Benz was idling. They drove in silence. Jake pulled up at a diner in Brooklyn. The owner, who'd known Jake since he was eight, sat them down and locked the door behind them.

Kipenzi remembered Jake looking at her—straight *through* her. She couldn't find her voice.

"When we getting married?" Jake asked.

"I'm busy right now," Kipenzi said, her face buried in her menu. "Working."

"For how long?"

"At least ten years. Few million records. Stuff like that."

"Then?"

Kipenzi put her menu down and smiled at this man she'd only seen on television. He was taller than he seemed in videos. And his smile was wider and brighter. His first words to her had been a marriage proposal. And in that moment, it made perfect sense.

"As soon as I retire, we can get married."

"Cool," Jake said, signaling to the owner that he was ready to order.

"Don't you want to know my name?" Kipenzi asked.

"Nah," Jake said. "I'm thinking it'll come up at some point."

In the ten years since that night, as Kipenzi's career soared and Jake racked up multiplatinum plaques, they had never been apart for more than one week. And they had never publicly or explicitly acknowledged that they were a couple—not even to each other. Somehow, they managed to be engaged but not officially dating.

The first year made sense. Kipenzi was only eighteen. Jake was thirty. It took a year of sneaking around for her to even get up the nerve to tell her father. She thought he would be upset because Jake was so much older. Her father *was* upset, but only because she hadn't told him sooner so that he could have hit Jake up for a verse on a remix for her first album.

But the last three years had been a battle. Kipenzi hated

staggering their entrances into movie premieres and concerts. They went to basketball games and sat far away from each other. The last straw had been the American Music Awards. He came late—on purpose, she believed—and she ended up sitting between her parents while Jake sat *behind* them. She was seething the entire night, even as she took the stage when she won for Best R&B Album.

That night, she'd given him an ultimatum. They came out openly as a couple or it was over. He said it was over. They got back together the next day and continued to keep their relationship out of the press.

"Why'd you start with your Con list?" Jake asked.

Kipenzi shielded her paper with her hand and hunched her back. "Stop looking!"

"Yo. That's foul! Starting with the bad stuff? What's number one?"

Kipenzi held her paper to her chest, peeled it down an inch to peek at it, and then pressed the paper back to her chest. "I'll give you number five: you want us to remain undercover."

"Interesting. That sounds very similar to my number seventeen."

"Seventeen?"

Jake and Kipenzi both broke out into laughter until they were out of breath and holding their sides. There was one sharp knock on the front door of Kipenzi's apartment.

"Come in, Ian," Kipenzi said, still chuckling and trying to hit Jake with one of the pillows from her sofa.

Ian, dressed in a silk paisley smoking jacket and an ascot, breezed into the living room with several binders and two cell phones.

"Do you want a nonsectarian ceremony or a Baptist minister?"

"I want to step on a glass," Jake said.

"I didn't know you were Jewish," Ian said. He didn't look at Jake. He sat on his usual perch, on a high stool next to Kipenzi's wet bar.

"I'm not," Jake said. "We can borrow it."

"Ian, where does that tradition come from?" Kipenzi asked.

"In the Talmud there is a story of a man named Mar who

smashed expensive glassware at his son's wedding to put an end to the celebration at the end of the night."

Jake rolled his eyes and jerked a thumb in Ian's direction. "How the hell does he know that?"

Kipenzi put her hands under her chin and fluttered her eyelashes. "Ian knows everything."

"You Jewish?" Jake asked.

Ian rolled his eyes. "I stay away from anything that I can't do well without becoming completely consumed."

"What's wrong with being consumed by something?" Jake asked, looking up at Ian. "You don't have any conviction about anything?"

"Men never do evil so completely and cheerfully as when they do it from religious conviction," Ian said.

"Blaise Pascal," Kipenzi said.

"Good girl." Ian nodded and then tapped his binder again. "So Jake will stomp on a glass and we will yell out mazel tov. Any guests? Witnesses? If you want this to happen today, we need to get moving."

"Just my parents. And Jake's."

"And Z and Beth," Jake added.

"Are you sure? After the show, I thought . . ."

Kipenzi hadn't been able to get Beth on the phone after the show in Atlanta. It had been an overwhelming success for Jake; one of those shows where every guest appearance brought more and more screams from the crowd. He brought everyone from Drake and Lil Wayne for the young folks and Eric B. & Rakim for the purists. He'd dusted off his entire catalog of number one records and performed with such vigor that Kipenzi watched the show through her fingers, worried that he would pass out.

Z's show hadn't gone nearly as well. And Kipenzi knew that Beth probably didn't know how to handle it. But she didn't understand why that would influence their friendship. For years, they'd weathered Z's and Jake's hot and cold streaks. So Z had a bad show. Big deal. Why would that make Beth stop answering her calls?

"They gotta be there, Kipenzi," Jake said, opening up his phone.

"We can tell them. But they might not show up."

"They'll be here."

"Ms. Hill, would you like me to retrieve an item of clothing from storage?"

"I'm gonna wear something here. Thanks, Ian."

"I'm booking the travel for your officiate. You two need to get up to Rockland County immediately to get a license. Your driver is downstairs. He has the address. The paperwork is in the back seat. Probably a good idea to have it filled out when you get there. Save yourself some time."

Kipenzi stood in front of the large mirror next to her front door and smoothed down her cowlick.

"Jake, you ready?"

"Just finishing up my list."

"Whatever."

Jake maneuvered himself out of the squishy sofa and threw a long, gangly arm over Kipenzi's neck. "A'ight, Ian. We'll be back."

"Enjoy your outing. Both of you." Ian bowed his head just slightly and opened the front door for Jake and Kipenzi. "Ms. Hill? Mr. Giles?"

Jake, his arm still around Kipenzi, spun them both around to face him.

"Congratulations," Ian said.

Six hours later, Kipenzi's mother came into her room, her face long and sad.

"Penzi, I can't believe you all are doing it this way. I wanted to see you in a beautiful gown. Have the whole family here. But if this is what you all want . . ."

Kipenzi's mom began smoothing her daughter's hair into a bun at the nape of her neck. Kipenzi put a hand up to where her mother's hands were and squeezed.

"This is the right way for us, Mommy. The only way."

"Not even your aunt Pam? My own sister can't be at her niece's wedding?"

"Especially not Aunt Pam," Kipenzi said through clenched teeth. "She'd sell me out to *Us Weekly* in a New York minute."

"She would do no such thing."

"She would. And I believe she has."

"You won't even give me a few days to make something for you to wear?" her mother asked. "I've been dreaming about making your wedding dress since I gave birth to you."

Kipenzi hesitated. Her mother had been her only stylist—in the beginning because she couldn't afford anyone else. And now, in the end, because it had become her mother's identity. Kipenzi had grinned and borne it with several of her over-the-top sequin-covered creations. Not today. She turned to face her mother and kissed her cheek.

"Ma. Please. Don't. I'm marrying Jake in five minutes, in my living room, in front of our parents. Wearing a dress that Josephine Bennett made for me last year. And that's it."

"I saw Z and Beth down there."

"Really? Why didn't you tell me?" Kipenzi asked, jumping up from her bed. Her mother pushed her back down.

"Let me finish this bun, chile."

Kipenzi grabbed her hair where her mother left off and dashed to her bedroom door and flung the door open. Without stepping into the hallway, she threw her head back and yelled.

"Beth Saddlebrook, get up here right now!"

Kipenzi could hear laughter from downstairs and then the sound of heavy footsteps and Beth's slow gait coming down the hallway. As soon as Beth approached the door, Kipenzi grabbed her and hugged her tight.

"You came! I didn't know if you would. I miss you, girl."

"Of course I came. I didn't have a choice! Y'all barely have any guests."

Beth leaned in to kiss Kipenzi's mother on the cheek and then sat gingerly on the bed while Kipenzi sat back down at her vanity so that her mother could finish her hair.

"So what made y'all decide to do this today?" Beth asked, her hands on her belly and her back propped against the twenty pillows the cleaning woman used to make up Kipenzi's bed.

"I'm retired." At this, Kipenzi's mother closed her eyes and groaned. "And I'm ready to move on to the next phase of my life: marriage and babies."

"You can't sing and have marriage and babies?"

"I could. But I don't want to."

"You ready?"

"For what?"

"For marriage."

"I've been with Jake since I was eighteen."

Kipenzi's mother closed her eyes and groaned again.

"That means nothing," Beth said. "After tonight, he'll be your husband. Not your boyfriend. It's different."

"I'm ready."

"Y'all sign a prenup?"

Kipenzi smiled. "What do you think?"

Beth looked up at the ceiling. "I'm gonna say no."

"You're wrong."

Beth struggled to sit up straight. "He made you sign a prenup?"

"Please. I've got more assets than he does." Kipenzi cackled. Her mother and then Beth joined in.

"But that can change at any time," Beth said. "This industry is very unpredictable . . ."

Kipenzi caught Beth's eye. "You wouldn't call me back, Beth. Because of the show."

"It was just weird," Beth said. "Z was saying Jake purposely told the promoter to let him close out the show—"

"He wouldn't do that!"

"But do you know for a fact that he didn't?"

Ian appeared in the doorway and rapped on the door with just his fingertips.

"Ms. Hill? Your betrothed awaits."

"What are you going to call me tomorrow, Ian?"

"I assumed that professionally you would still use Ms. Hill."

"I'm retired. I don't have a profession."

"I'm sure when Madonna retires, she'll still be referred to as such."

"I'll bet her assistant calls her Ms. Ciccone."

"I'll bet she hasn't had the same assistant for seven years."

"Point well taken. Call me whatever. Are you here to walk me down the aisle?"

"Your father is downstairs. I can bring him up."

"Is the air on?" Kipenzi asked, wiping her brow. "I'm so hot all of a sudden."

"Kipenzi, get down here and marry me!" Jake yelled from downstairs. Kipenzi, her mom, and Beth all laughed.

"Come on, y'all," Kipenzi said. "Let's go together."

As soon as Kipenzi hit the top step and looked down into her living room, she felt her eyes welling up. There was Jake, wearing the custom-made suit he'd worn to the Grammy Awards, his hands entwined and resting comfortably in front of him. His head was held high and he was looking up at Kipenzi with a serious but somehow still relaxed look of pure determination. It was the same look and posture she'd observed whenever he waited just offstage before a big performance. It was the same look and posture he had when he gave his mother away at her wedding in the Bahamas to her longtime boyfriend. It was the same way he stood before the judge when he was on trial for assault three years before. It was Jake at his most earnest and his most serious. It was when Kipenzi loved him most—when she felt like he would take a bullet for her without unfolding his hands. Jake watched her walk down the spiral staircase, behind Beth, her mother, and Ian, who held her hand and helped her navigate the steps.

It was warm for early November, but Ian still had the fireplace going, which gave the room a wintry vibe. Kipenzi dabbed at her eye with the side of her pointer finger and looked down as she walked so that she wouldn't fall apart before the ceremony even started.

On one side of Jake, her father stood, tears in his own eyes, his chest puffed out and his hands behind his back. Next to her father was Z, who winked at Beth. He was wearing dark blue jeans (his version of dress pants) and new Timberland construction boots. In a true nod to the seriousness of the occasion, Z had his usually wild afro neatly edged up. Kipenzi made a brief mental note of Z's body language. He was still and calm, not twitchy or weird. Hopefully, he wasn't back on drugs.

Standing just behind them were Jake's mother and stepfather, former Black Panthers from Brooklyn who were now animal rights activists. Both had lithe, tight bodies and slim faces from their vegan diets.

On the other side of Jake was Ona, Kipenzi's yoga instructor and spiritual guide. Ian had found out that she was licensed to officiate at marriage ceremonies and had gotten her to take an earlier flight home from a conference in Atlanta.

When Kipenzi reached Jake, he took her hands into his and they both turned to face Ona.

"Jacob and Kipenzi have decided to become a union today," Ona said, opening up a Bible and flipping to a marked page. "And we are honored to be here to witness this intimate act. The Bible says, 'Therefore shall a man leave his father and his mother, and shall cleave unto his wife and they shall be one flesh . . .'"

Jake squeezed Kipenzi's hand and she squeezed back.

"Excuse me, Ona," Jake said. "Are we allowed to talk right now?"

Kipenzi yanked Jake's hand and gave him a look.

"Well, not really," Ona said. "But it must be important. Speak your mind."

"I want to kiss her now."

A ripple of laughs went around Kipenzi's living room.

"I'm not planning on the ceremony lasting more than ten minutes, Jacob."

"I can't wait that long."

"Then by all means . . ."

Jake placed his hands on either side of Kipenzi's face and pulled her in close. He whispered something in her ear that made her body rock with sobs. He held her steady until she was composed and then kissed her on the cheek and took her hands.

When the vows were exchanged, Kipenzi and Jake stared straight into each other's eyes for every word.

"By the power invested in me by the State of New York, I now pronounce you husband and wife. Jacob, you may now kiss the bride."

"Do I have to?" Jake said, as Kipenzi threw her head back and laughed out loud.

"I mean, I kissed her earlier and I think she had onions for breakfast."

Kipenzi continued laughing as Jake wrapped her up in a tight hug and she pretended to try to get away from him. The parents came over and for a moment all the women and Ian were hugging each other and crying while the men gave each other pounds and slapped Jake on the back.

They all had dinner in the living room. Ian had ordered five large pizzas, Caesar salads, and sweet tea. It was four a.m. before Jake wrapped a glass in a linen dishcloth and stomped on it, signaling the end of the party. The sun was coming up over the Hudson River by the time Kipenzi and Jake had the apartment to themselves.

"Hello, husband," Kipenzi said, as she broke down pizza boxes and wiped off the counters in her sleek kitchen stuffed with stainless steel appliances that she never used.

"What up, wife," Jake said, pulling a chair to the island in the center of the kitchen.

"Now what?" Kipenzi said, leaning on the island and stroking his arm.

"Now we make babies."

Out of habit, Kipenzi crossed the room to check the bench in Central Park. Jackson Figueroa, her personal paparazzo, was there fiddling with his camera. Waiting.

"How long will it take for this dude to move on to someone else?"

"A long time. Especially when I start knocking you up. Let's go make some babies."

"Now. Like tonight?"

"No better time than the present."

"Where are we gonna live?"

Jake looked around Kipenzi's kitchen and then out into her living room, where the fireplace was still blazing.

"This place is a little low-budget for me." Jake shrugged. "But if you're okay with slumming, we can live here."

"You're not into the whole triplex-penthouse-at-the-top-of-Trump-Tower thing?"

"Eh. It's so *Diff'rent Strokes*," Jake said, wrinkling up his nose in disapproval.

"Read me your pro and con list," Kipenzi said, her arms crossed.

"Nah. We're on our honeymoon." Jake sidled up to Kipenzi and kissed her neck.

"Read," said Kipenzi. "Now."

Kipenzi grabbed Jake by the hand and led him up the spiral staircase to her bedroom suite on the top floor of the triplex. They got in bed together, with their lists, but they never got around to reading them.

ten

$\mathcal{O}$N THE Q TRAIN FROM DEKALB TO THIRTY-FOURTH STREET, ALEX began to transform. While the train chugged through Brooklyn, she was still Lexi, as Birdie's daughter called her. She was a woman planning a wedding. She was a soon-to-be stepmother, helping her boyfriend raise his child. She was the daughter of a man who spoiled her. By the time the train stopped at Union Square, Tweet and Birdie were slipping further and further from her mind. She stopped looking at children on the train and comparing their outfits and hairstyles to Tweet's.

Her mind was revisiting all the stories she had to do. A Chrisette Michele review for soul.com. A short profile on Jake for the *New York Times,* a Q&A with Quincy Jones's son for *People*; a Q&A for *Teen Vogue* on Bunny Clifton, a new pop act from Jamaica who had serious buzz. And, of course, she was ghostwriting the memoirs of Cleo Wright, who was outing every man (and a few women) in the industry whom she'd slept with in a two-year career as a video model.

Chrisette's ballad was swimming in her head on repeat, Cleo's quotes were typing themselves out on the inside of her eyelids, and in another corner of her mind, she was coming up with questions for Bunny Clifton. She opened her cell and looked up Port Antonio, the city in Jamaica where Bunny Clifton was from. Scanning news articles, she came up with a few questions and then scribbled them in her notebook.

Alex mumbled to herself as she followed the herd off the train, through the station, up the elevator, and outside into the world. As always, Alex stopped and stood on the sidewalk, facing Macy's, and took a deep breath. It was late fall, her favorite season, when the air smelled like football games and first-day-of-school outfits. She mentally ticked off the things she was grateful for: *I'm getting married. I love Bird and Tweet. I have a wonderful house and I fucking love my job.* She opened her eyes, adjusted her messenger bag across her chest, and marched down Thirty-fourth Street.

At least once every six months, Alex did what she called the pop-in. As a full-time freelancer, she got most of her assignments by emails and phone calls. There were many editors she wrote for consistently whom she'd never met in person. And then there were some magazines, like *Vibe*, that were like satellite offices for Alex. She wrote for the magazine so often, and for so many different editors, that she could get away with pretending that she was in the area and just wanted to say hello. Any number of staffers would buzz her in, and after making small talk, she'd prowl the floor, popping into a few offices and getting some face time. Every time she went to a magazine for the pop-in, she left with an assignment.

After print journalism became a contact sport in '06, it became more and more important for Alex to get her face seen if she wanted to get work. She couldn't sit on the third floor of her brownstone and wait for the phone to ring. When *Blaze* and *XXL* and *The Source* were all fighting to have the hottest cover on the newsstand, Alex's phone rang off the hook. Then *King* came out, a splashy men's magazine with half-naked women on the cover. Even though a good friend had founded the magazine, she sniffed past it each month on the newsstand, vowing not to support the T&A publication. And then the editor called her, offering to double her usual rate and let her do investigative pieces for the magazine. Those were the good old days. She made nearly six figures in 2003—solely from freelancing.

Those days had ended with a heavy thud.

Blaze: gone. *The Source*: a shell of its former self. (Alex had even stopped listing it on her resume.) *King*: shut down abruptly while she was on the phone with the editor in chief, outlining an investigative story into the suicide of Shakir Stewart. *XXL* was still standing. And *Vibe* was in its fourth incarnation. It had shut down in 2009 only to resurface and then shutter again. An Italian conglomerate owned the new version. They contracted a group of former *Vibe* staffers to run it.

Alex could barely keep up with any of the print entertainment magazines. Many times she handed in a story and the magazine went out of business before it could be published. And trying to get a kill fee was laughable.

As Alex walked, she pulled her bag closer to her chest and thought about Cleopatra Wright. Fifty thousand dollars? How could she turn that down when the magazine business was so shaky?

She'd been meeting with Cleo twice a week to get her story down. And every time she left the woman's presence, she had to rush home and take a thirty-minute shower to get rid of the heebie-jeebies. Alex had never met anyone like Cleo—someone who seemed hell-bent on ruining every man she'd ever encountered.

She tried to keep a straight face as Cleo ran down a story about the ménage à trois with the NBA player and the player's father, the tryst in a synagogue with a rapper and his Jewish mother-in-law. It was all unbelievable. But Cleo always had proof: audio, video, still photos, mementos.

The last time they'd met, Cleo had told Alex about the welterweight boxer's jockstrap she'd stolen and had framed. Cleo had gotten pregnant by him. He had told her to get an abortion and she had. He then abruptly stopped calling her. So now she was planning to send the framed jockstrap to his wife.

Alex shuddered as she pulled open the door to an office building on Lexington Avenue. On the elevator to the fourth floor, she shook her head back and forth a few times in the hopes of clearing Cleo from her mind, at least temporarily.

"Alex Sampson Maxwell. I'm here to see Celeste Marchado."

The receptionist at *Vibe*, stereotypically surly, grunted and used a letter opener to stab the numbers on her keypad. She listened and then hung up.

"She's on vacation."

"Right. Okay, then can you let Julie Donovan know I'm here?"

"Do you have an appointment?"

"Not exactly. But it's fine because—"

The receptionist took the headset off and swirled her chair around so that her back was facing Alex.

"Can't help you," she said, sorting through mail on her desk.

Just as Alex went to her cell phone to call Julie, the editorial director of *Vibe*, a noisy group of women stepped off the elevator and into the lobby. Alex turned to see Maria, the editor in chief of *Vibe*, flanked by Lorena and Erika, the features editor and the music editor. They were weighed down with cardboard cup holders from Starbucks, loaded with coffee and pastries.

"Hey, girl," said Maria, a striking Latina with wide eyes and an easy smile. She held her coffee to one side and kissed Alex on the cheek. "I would have gotten a coffee for you if I knew you were coming through."

Alex followed the ladies in, sticking her tongue out at the receptionist as she did.

"I was just in the area, thought I'd stop in."

"Good. Just in time for an idea meeting," Erika said, holding the door open for Alex.

Alex followed the women through the maze of cubicles on the

fourth floor of the building where what used to be the number one music magazine in the country was published. These days, *Vibe* had to compete with every zine, website, blog, and mainstream magazine that also covered urban culture. If Jay could be in Oprah's magazine, did he need to be on the cover of *Vibe*?

None of that mattered to Alex. She loved the feel of print magazines in her hands and continued to write for *Vibe* in all its incarnations. Even though she'd been writing for the magazine for five years, she still felt like a newcomer whenever she stepped into the office. All the women were polished and trendy, wearing miniskirts and legwarmers and other combinations Alex would feel silly in.

Several people popped up when they saw Maria heading toward the back of the office and began grabbing notes and papers from their desks and dashing to the conference room. By the time they all arrived, the conference room was filling up quickly. Alex scanned the room, waving at familiar faces and looking for new ones. It was so difficult to keep track of who was who at a place like *Vibe*. The turnover was high. People were promoted—and demoted—often. And for Alex, knowing who did what was essential.

Maria—who had been the editor in chief for five years—was the kind of chief who prided herself on democratic rule. She met with the interns at *Vibe* once a month and encouraged them to be honest about their thoughts on the magazine. Her assistants were always groomed from the start to move up on the masthead, and she very often used majority rule to determine what image to use on the cover of the magazine. During idea meetings, she was silent. She sipped a macchiato and just nodded her head as she listened to the staff throwing out ideas. Alex looked down to get a glance at Maria's sneakers. In five years, she'd never seen her wear the same pair twice. Alex kept a clean pair of low-top white Converses in her closet but that was the extent of her sneaker fetish. Maria was famous nationwide for her kicks. She had limited editions, throwbacks, and collector items. Years ago, Birdie had been interviewed by Maria and he came home telling Alex about how he wasn't able to take his eyes off her Nike Air Jordan 4 Undefeated production sample sneakers. "Them shits are worth at least five thousand!" he'd said to Alex, his eyes wide. Alex stared at him, clueless.

Alex stayed quiet in the meeting. She knew better than to throw out ideas here. Every person at the meeting was gunning to write a story. No matter what they actually did at the magazine, they all wanted the glory of seeing their names in print. Alex was the only person who was solely a writer. If she spoke up, Maria might assign the story to her on the spot, which might anger the other editors, who all hoped to get one. Her job was just to pay attention, take notes, and give her opinion if asked. While an intern talked about a new Ras Bennett song that seemed to have potential, Alex went to her bag to find her ideas book. As she moved things around, she saw a copy of *Sounds of Carribean America* peeking out. It was the issue with Josephine Bennett on the cover. The story Birdie had begged her to write had just been published and he'd given her a copy that morning. Alex looked around the room while she stuffed the magazine back into her bag. It wasn't like she was on contract with *Vibe*. And *S.O.C.A.* had a tiny print run. But she still didn't want to take any chances on anyone seeing her with the story and asking her how she had ended up writing it. She found her notebook and starting flipping through it.

"Does anyone know anything about Ras Bennett's wife?" an editor asked the room. "I think her name is Josephine?"

Alex looked around. For a split second she thought she'd somehow said something about Josephine aloud during the brief moment when she spaced out. But she replayed the conversation that had been taking place and realized the staffers were discussing women who were married to rappers.

"I don't know anything about her," said Julie. "But I do know Beth Saddlebrook; she's married to Z."

The conference room dissolved into a chorus of groans and tongue clucking.

"I feel so sorry for that girl," said an Asian girl with a platinum buzz cut. "How many kids does he have by other women?"

"Like, four!" said an intern.

Maria shook her head and took another sip of her coffee. "Think she'd talk to us?"

Henry, the art director, raised his hand. "If you do a story on women in relationships with rappers, you'd have to talk to Kipenzi Hill."

Julie snorted. "She and Jake won't even admit they're a couple."

"Exactly," said Henry. "And I'd like to know why."

"I heard she doesn't want to alienate her fan base by being associated with a hard-core rapper," said a young woman seated next to Alex.

"Bullshit," Henry said. "She's a woman. Women want to be claimed."

Alex instinctively used her thumb to rub the heavy platinum circling her ring finger. The women in the office sucked their teeth and rolled their eyes at Henry. But they all knew he was right.

"I like this idea," said Maria, looking down at her sneakers. She wiped a speck away and then sat up. "We get a writer to spend some time getting to know these women behind the scenes . . ."

Alex felt a few eyes dart her way.

"Alex's getting married soon; she should do it," said Julie.

Maria squinted in Alex's direction.

"She could give her perspective, as a woman who is about to get married herself . . ." said Julie.

Maria started biting the inside of her cheek, which she always did when she was deep in thought. "Alex, when are you getting married?"

Alex cleared her throat. "June."

"We could do this for the May issue. You could hand it in right before you get married."

Ana, the managing editor, pointed at Alex. "So she'd write it in the first person, right? And reflect on how their lives as girlfriends and wives differ from her own."

The fashion editor raised her hand from the back of the room. Ana nodded in her direction.

"She could maybe get relationship advice from the women and use their tips as a sidebar to the story."

"Yeah," said Julie. "I'd love to know just what to do when my husband comes home and tells me he's having a set of twins by a woman he met at a concert."

There was a ripple of laughter and people jotted notes and talked among themselves. Alex sat, frozen. She thought that if she didn't move at all, she could melt into the office chair and seep into the carpeting. And somehow they would forget Alex Sampson Maxwell ever existed and she wouldn't have to take on a story that was just a little too close to her own life. She had successfully kept her relationship with Birdie a secret to everyone in her professional circle, and though she knew people would find out eventually, she wasn't ready to deal with it at the moment.

But the Cleo factor was even more distressing. She was in the middle of ghostwriting a book for a woman who was making a living by sleeping with married rappers, athletes, and entertainers. That book plus this story were just too close together.

"Let's come up with a wish list," said Maria. "Who would we love to have in this story?"

Alex tried to keep her breath from coming in too ragged. She kept her eyes on her notebook.

"Beth Saddlebrook," said Ana. "I gotta know why she stays with that crackhead."

"What about Beth and Z's son, the one who does the YouTube videos with his girlfriend?"

"Zander," said Maria, clicking her pen in and out. "He's dating Bunny Clifton, next big thing. They're both dope."

"What about Fatin and Aja from Kindred," someone said.

Ana shook her head. "Not sexy. A happily married couple with kids who make great music? Pass."

"It would give us a balance from some of the crazy stuff," said Maria.

"Why would we want that?" Ana asked. "We want *all* crazy stuff."

Maria turned to Alex and pointed.

"Chante Moore and Kenny Lattimore?" Alex offered, looking down at her notebook.

Maria looked over at Ana.

"Um, no," Ana said.

Henry raised his hand and Maria pointed at him.

"What about Snoop and Shante?"

Maria and Ana both nodded, signaling to Alex to write it down.

There was a lull for a moment, as the staffers mumbled to each other and tossed out names quietly. Jessica, a designer in the art department, raised her hand.

"What about Birdie? I think I heard he's married."

Alex felt the contents of her stomach shift and come up to her throat. She willed herself to relax. Instead of throwing up, she sneezed. She stood up, covered her mouth with her hand, and signaled to the group that she needed to be excused.

In the bathroom, she washed her hands and then splashed a handful of water over her face. She stood at the mirror, her hands still on her face, and slowly slid them down.

"You knew it had to happen eventually," she said to her reflection.

Alex liked to pretend that she met Birdie at the supermarket. She'd lied so much that the story about seeing him squeeze an apple to check its freshness actually felt like it had really happened. Birdie went along with it. And they never talked about the night at the House of Blues. Alex with her tape recorder and her notebook, sitting next to Birdie backstage, interviewing him after he opened for Erykah Badu. They never discussed the way he leaned in close so that he could hear her questions over the din of the crowd chanting Erykah's name or the way she showed him how she could pop the cap off a beer bottle on the side of a table. They never reminisced over rolling a fat blunt in the car on the way to her hotel room, a waterfront deluxe with a patio, and splitting a six-pack while the sun came up over Lake Buena Vista.

The fact that they had sex—four times in a row—on that very first night was absolutely not up for discussion.

Alex had never forgiven herself for breaking the cardinal rule of journalism. Five years later she and Birdie were committed to each other, engaged, raising Tweet. But still, it was wrong, tainted. And Alex was ashamed. Hiding the relationship was difficult. Only her closest confidantes knew about Birdie. And she was skittish about making new friends because of it. She never wanted anyone to think that Birdie got press from any magazine because of her. Or that she got access to any of his rapper friends because of him. Somehow she'd never been assigned a story on Birdie. (During the first six months that they were dating, she was asked twice to interview him. She was able to turn the assignments down on the basis that she'd recently covered him for *Vibe*. Neither editor knew she turned the stories down from Birdie's bed.)

They were able to stagger their entrances and exits to parties and concerts. She smiled and nodded her head while rappers dissed Birdie as she interviewed them. She played dumb in editorial meetings when his name came up for possible stories. And her face always managed to go blank whenever anyone asked her if they knew who he was dating. Alex pulled herself together and repeated the words *Breathe deep* in her head. She walked back into the conference room just as the meeting was ending and everyone was streaming out into the workspace. Julie grabbed her elbow and guided her to the back of the room.

"You're on, Alex," she said with a wide grin. " 'The Secret Lives of Rappers' Wives.' It's going to be incredible!"

Alex managed a smile. "Who do you want me to get?"

"We narrowed it down to four," said Julie, flipping through a notebook. If Birdie was one of the four, Alex was ready. She had an arsenal of responses on her lips. *I don't think he's in the country. I heard he's not doing press right now. Didn't you hear? He's gay.*

"Here it is," said Julie. She turned around to stand next to Alex so that she could see the page as well. "We want Z's wife, Beth Saddlebrook; Jake's girlfriend, Kipenzi Hill; and Ras Bennett's wife, Josephine Bennett. And then see what Bunny Clifton has to say about dating Zander. She's not a wife and she's really young. But it's a unique perspective."

Alex nodded and smiled. "Sounds awesome," she said, hoping her face made it seem like she believed it.

"Someone on the staff has a contact for Beth," said Julie. "To get to Kipenzi, we'll have to pull some major strings. And Josephine, I think you should be able to get in touch with her."

Julie took out a copy of *S.O.C.A.* from her bag and held it up.

Alex's eyes widened and she gave Julie a sheepish smile. "Oh. You saw that?"

"Yeah. But don't worry about it. It's not like they're a direct competitor."

"Where'd you find it anyway? I haven't seen it on the news-stands."

"My mother's house," Julie said. "She subscribes. Like I said, not quite our competitor. Start setting up your interviews. I'll send you a word count and an assignment letter next week."

"I'm on it."

"Oh, Alex," Julie called out as Alex began walking away. Alex stopped and turned around. She knew exactly what Julie was going to say.

"There's a rumor going around that some chick named Cleo is writing a book about all the rappers she's slept with. Find her. I'll bet there's some overlap between her book and this story."

Alex smiled with her mouth closed, nodded once, and pushed the button for the elevator, her eyes on the ceiling.

Overlap. Nice, simple way to put it. She was now writing a feature on the wives and girlfriends of rappers. And simultaneously ghostwriting a book for a woman who was most likely fucking all their husbands. Yes. *Overlap* was a perfect word for it.

On the subway ride back home, Alex did not transform. She did not begin to relax as the train emptied at the Chambers Street station. She did not start thinking about making dinner or picking up Tweet from day care. She did not make a note to remind herself to get Birdie's clothes from the dry cleaners. She did not slip her feet out of her shoes the way she usually did for the ride. She stared straight ahead, barely paying attention to each stop. She thought about how her worlds were about to collide. And she wondered if she'd be able to get the story on the life of a rapper's wife without revealing that she was on the verge of becoming one herself.

eleven

𝓘N THE SUMMER OF 1989, RAS AND JOSEPHINE'S FIRST DATE TOOK place in Montclair, New Jersey. Ras was an immigrant from the slums of Denham Town, Kingston. He had crooked front teeth and a wicked smile.

He rode his sister's scooter bike from his parents' crowded two-bedroom apartment on New Street, where the poor folks in Montclair lived, to the front door of the well-kept brick-front colonial where Josephine Beauchamp lived with her parents and two younger brothers in upper Montclair.

Josephine had no idea who Ras was. On her way to a meeting with a modeling agency in Nutley, her keys jingling in her hand, her mind moving a mile a minute, when Ras parked his scooter in front of the house. She looked out the front window and then called out for her youngest brother, assuming Ras was there to see him.

"No, ma'am, I'm here to see you," Ras said, coming up the front walkway but stopping two steps away from the porch.

Josephine rolled her eyes and smiled. "Little boy, you are not here to see me. I promise you that."

"Can I show you the house I'm going to buy for you?"

Josephine turned around to see if there was someone else in the doorway that this young boy with the dusty hair may have been talking to. She turned back to look at him and shook her head.

"Are you friends with Pierre? You want me to call him for you?"

"He's in my algebra class," Ras said. He came up one step, keeping his hand on the railing. "But I'm here to see you, Josephine."

"See me for what?"

"I'm going to marry you." Ras didn't seem to notice that Josephine recoiled in horror. "And I wanted to know if you could take a walk with me to come look for a house."

"Where are you from?" Josephine asked.

"Denham Town, Kingston."

Josephine winced and nodded once. Five generations of understanding were exchanged in a millisecond-long glance. Josephine's mother had taken her to Jamaica as a child, to accompany her as she did some missionary and nursing work in the poverty-stricken neighborhood on the island that was just an hour-long plane ride from the Dominican Republic.

Josephine was only eight. But she'd never been able to forget what she saw in the slums of Denham Town. Children in diapers and nothing else wandering the streets, crying and begging for milk. Mothers with blank eyes, nursing babies in doorways of leaning shacks. It was in Denham Town that Josephine first realized the difference between light and dark. She could see the people casting long glances at her ivory skin and bone-straight hair, features she'd never paid attention to at home. And she'd realized that her mother was dark. Like the people in Denham Town. The dawning was immediate: this was why her father's relatives sniffed at his choice in women. Her father, part French, was a light-skinned Dominican man. And the line was supposed to be kept light.

"Your family's from Boca Chica," Ras said.

"Who told you that?"

"My mother said your parents have a big house on La Matica, right on the water. Why are you all here?"

"My father's teaching at Montclair State for the semester," said Josephine, tossing her jet-black, shoulder-length curls back. "I have an appointment. You'll have to excuse me."

Ras extended a hand up to Josephine. She would have to take just one step down to place her hand in his. She did not.

"I've seen pictures of the house in Boca Chica," Ras said. "I will provide you with something just as beautiful here in New Jersey. Or more so. I stake my life on that."

Josephine stifled a laugh. Among other things, he was on some kind of self-propelled motorless scooter. He was still in the throes of puberty. At eighteen, she was probably only three years older. But it felt like they were worlds apart. He had lint in his hair. He was Pierre's age. He was riding a *scooter*. His family was from the slums.

But, most important, Josephine was Dominican, with the ivory skin color of the *peninsulares* who'd come to the island from Spain in the 1500s. Her father had already broken custom and married a *negra* Dominican woman, one who refused to straighten her hair or lighten her skin. Her father's parents prayed that their child would not be dark. Their prayers were answered when Josephine was born, just as pale as her father. Her paternal grandfather gave her a French name as a constant reminder of her special blend. Her grandparents never missed an opportunity to remind her how lucky she was to be born with her father's coloring.

Josephine knew her grandparents would die if she married someone from Jamaica. The country was a hundred percent black. And the people were not just black. They were blue-black. Purple almost. Hair like nests.

So although Ras seemed very confident for such a young man, and he was handsome, despite his blue-black skin, Josephine knew it would be a cold day in hell before she'd ever date someone like him.

She wouldn't dream of risking a dark child with a *noir* like Ras. It just wasn't done. And she was sorry that it was so. He was a lovely boy and had obviously endured a lot to get from Denham Town to Montclair. And if he was a classmate of Pierre's, at a private school like MKA, then surely he must be intelligent. Smart enough to understand how silly it was to step up on her front step, hand out-stretched, as if she would ever even think of—

And then Ras spoke. And when he was done, Josephine went back into the house, rescheduled her appointment, found a heavier sweater in the front hall closet, and locked the door behind her.

Seven years later, they were married at The Manor in West Orange. There were eight hundred guests, fifty people in their wedding party, and the celebration lasted for a full three days. She lost her virginity on her wedding night in Peau de Ville, France, at her grandmother's chateau.

She waited on her husband hand and foot for the first five years of the marriage, as he moved from being a studio session musician for local artists in New Jersey, to being an in-demand producer who charged six figures for a studio session. She looked up to him, admired him, and worshipped the ground he walked on.

Until she found out about Cleo.

The realization that her husband was being unfaithful knocked the wind out of her. And it had been a slow dawning. There were no whispers. No rumors. No hard evidence. Just a nagging feeling that her husband was disappearing right in front of her.

She had friends with cheating husbands. They talked about the phone numbers and photos found in pockets. But Josephine never saw any proof. Her husband never rushed into the shower when he came home. He stalked around the house, smelling like another woman and daring Josephine to question him. Rough and unyielding, he made love to her nightly. He didn't make sure to bring her to orgasm and often left the bedroom to watch television alone for hours afterward.

He took no meals with his wife. Josephine was convinced that he couldn't see her at all.

Every night, she crawled into bed with him and curled up against his chest. And every morning, she woke up to find her husband facing the wall, curled in a ball away from her. It killed her. Knowing that even in his sleep he was somewhere else. He never spent the night away from home unless he was on tour. That would be too blatantly disrespectful. But though she struggled to embrace him at night, she always woke up to find him turned away, hugging the wall.

This went on for a full year. Josephine prayed. She flew alone to Pedernales to ask her maternal grandmother for help. Her grandmother shrugged and told her she would have to wait it out. She cried on the entire flight home. She begged Ras to talk to her, to tell her what was going on, to explain. He looked straight through her. Stepped over her when she fell to his feet. Closed the door behind him and turned the lock. Started the car and sped off. Came home hours later, his eyes wild, smelling like sex.

And then it was over. One day he came through the door whistling. And Josephine knew her husband had returned to her. She also knew she would never forgive him.

She hadn't left him. Her religion would not allow her to do that. But she would never, ever forgive him, though she wanted to. Hours, days, weeks, months would go by. And then she'd feel it all over again.

By the time Cleo came to her office, it had been a year since he had seemed to return to normal. There had been the one night when he broke down and admitted the affair, telling Josephine every detail. And he refused to discuss it again. Josephine let it go. Until Cleo came to her office to tell her about the book.

After that visit, Josephine made Ras's life a hell. He couldn't leave the house without incurring his wife's wrath. She called him constantly at the studio and showed up unannounced if he didn't call her back. She rifled through his pockets when he came home, and he'd even caught her sniffing his boxers after he'd thrown them into the hamper in their dressing closet.

On the thirty-fifth morning after the visit from Cleo, Josephine woke up, staring at the ceiling, an icy rage filling her chest once again.

"She came to my office," Josephine whispered into her husband's ear. "She was six inches away from me. I touched her. Had no idea who she was. What kind of woman would do that?"

Ras had been pretending to be asleep for thirty minutes. He made sure his lips were parted just so and kept his breath even and measured. He'd been praying that she would leave him be, for just one morning. If she took a shower first, he'd have a few minutes to dash out to the guest bedroom and use the shower and get dressed. If he could make it to the kitchen before she started in, he'd be free for the day. In his mind, he kept hearing the opening chords of a ballad. He hadn't written it yet. But he knew it was special. He needed to get to the studio and work it out on his keyboard. Felt like something that could work for Bunny Clifton, the girl from Port Antonio he was working with that afternoon.

But Ras couldn't move. Not yet. He could feel his wife's hot breath on his neck. She was so close he could smell the evening cream she smoothed all over her body before bed each night and the mint oil she rubbed on her hair. She was too close. Hovering. Although his eyes were closed, he knew she was seething.

"Baby, she's a dirty whore," Ras finally said to his wife, keeping his eyes shut. "She's a dirty fucking whore. I should have never gone anywhere near her. I will snap her neck in two if you let me."

Josephine snorted and moved away from her husband.

"Snap her in two. You did that already. She told me how you loved to hold her legs open and do all those things to her that you would never do to your own wife."

Ras's eyes popped open. "I told you she was lying about that!"

That had continued to be a sticking point for Josephine. She knew that all Carribean men were known for not performing such acts. But who knew for sure? Maybe they did different things with black American girls.

"How should I know what you did with her? Everything that comes out of your mouth is a lie!"

"No. Not true. I came clean. I admitted my mistakes. I told you what I did."

"Tell me."

Ras groaned and pulled the covers over his head. Josephine

whipped them back and punched Ras in his shoulder. He winced although she hadn't hurt him at all. To Josephine, her knuckles felt like they were on fire.

"Josephine. Love. We're not doing this again. I have to get to the studio." Ras sat up and tied his locks into a knot.

"You tell me right now. Everything. I want to know."

"You don't need to hear this again!"

"I will hear it for as long as I need to!"

Ras took in a deep breath and let it out through his nose. "You'd had a miscarriage. You were on pain pills after having the procedure to . . ." He pinched the bridge of his nose. "It was a stressful day for both of us. I brought you home, took care of you. We cried together. You went to sleep."

Ras looked over at his wife. She was wearing a cream silk dressing gown that was seamless with her skin. Her hair was piled on top of her head in a messy bun and each facet of her hazel eyes shone bright like a diamond. She had not a drop of makeup on her face and she was ten times more beautiful than any of the video girls he'd fucked. And most definitely more beautiful than Cleo Wright.

Josephine beckoned him to continue.

"After you were asleep, a few people came over."

"Men. You had strange men in our home."

"Not strange men. Friends that you don't know."

"That makes them strangers as far as I can tell."

"We met up in the garage. Started drinking and smoking. She came over with some girlfriends. They were supposed to be picking up one of my boys."

"She. She who?"

"Josephine, you know—"

"I said who. Say her name, you fucking bastard!" Josephine's face was contorted and she pointed one long finger in Ras's face.

"Her name is Cleo. She sucked my dick in the bathroom of the guesthouse."

It was at this point that Josephine always broke down and cried.

An ugly cry, heaving like a three-year-old with snot coming out of her nose. As she slid from the bed down to the bedroom floor, a sob choked in her throat, Ras jumped out of bed to catch his wife and hold her in his arms.

"Why do you make me do this? Why do you want to know?"

"Tell me," Josephine said. "Were there others?"

"No," Ras said firmly. "No others."

"Why her?"

"I was drunk. I was high. I was grieving."

Josephine just stared at him.

"I have no excuses," Ras said. "I am a man. I am sinful. I did something wrong. And I have been trying to make it right."

"She's writing a book."

"I know."

"She said she loves you. And that you love her."

"I'm not dignifying that."

"She said you told her to write this book."

"She *told* me she was writing it. Wanted me to beg her not to. Fuck that. Let her write it. I've come clean to my wife and we can make it through this. It will be fine."

Josephine was lying on her side on the floor next to the bed. Ras was in a half-kneeling position crouched awkwardly beside her, half trying to pick her up. Josephine looked up at him and drew her hand across his face. The sound of the smack was piercing.

"It will *not* be fine. It will *never* be fine."

Ras stuck his tongue inside his mouth, soothing the area where she'd hit him. Two seconds away from smacking her back, he held strong. He closed his eyes, swallowed hard, and calmed himself.

"What you wanna do, big man?" Josephine taunted. "You wanna hit me back? Divorce me? File the papers. I'll sign."

Ras stood up and sat on the bed, his head in his hands.

"I don't want none of your stinking money either," Josephine said, a sneer twisting her pretty face. "I will go back to Boca Chica. I can teach. I have property there or I could go back to selling real estate. You can turn this house into your own private harem. Let all your lovers live here with you. They'll take good care of you."

"Divorce me," Ras said softly.

Josephine looked up at him from the floor where she was still in a heap. "What did you say?"

"Divorce me, Josephine. File the papers. We have no prenup. Take me for everything I have. Take the house."

"Is that what you want?"

Ras grabbed Josephine by one arm and pulled her to a standing position. She wouldn't look him in the eye, so he used his other hand to hold her chin and force her to face him.

"What I want is my wife's forgiveness."

"I can't give you that."

"You can work on it. You can try."

"It sounds like you'd rather I leave."

"You can do that. And then I will go into that guesthouse, load my pistol, and blow my brains out."

Ras leveled his eyes at his wife. "And you know I would do it. I told you I was going to marry you. I told you I would never live in this life or the next without you as my wife."

"Ras . . . Ras . . . I love you. I just . . . She . . . she came to my office . . ."

"I know, baby, I know," Ras said, wrapping his arms around his wife's waist and rubbing her back as he hugged her.

"I'm so sorry, Ras. You must hate me."

Ras was silent. Josephine whipped her head up to search his eyes. He was smiling.

"You do hate me!"

"I do not. I love you."

"I should have had sex with other men before you."

"But you didn't."

"I could still," Josephine said, holding her chin up.

"You could."

"And you couldn't stop me."

"I could not."

"But I don't want to."

Josephine felt light-headed and dizzy, the way she always did after a good long cry. No matter how many times she tested her husband, he passed. He withstood her agony, her abuse. He never wavered. Not even an ounce.

"Josephine, sit with me," Ras said, patting the bed next to her.

Josephine sat down and Ras reached for the glossy brochure they kept at their bedside. It detailed the various months of a woman's pregnancy and how the fetus was growing at each step. Ras flipped the pages to the section marked "Five Months."

"This is how far along Marie is, right? Five months?" Ras asked. Josephine nodded.

Ras smoothed out the page and read aloud to Josephine about the size of the fetus at that point and what it was able to do. "How do you feel?" Ras asked.

"Afraid. Something could go wrong. It's not my baby."

"It is your baby. This girl got accepted to Harvard. We're paying her college tuition, paying off her parents' debts, sponsoring her brother's immigration, giving him a job. You gave her sister a job . . . We're practically buying this child."

"Ras," Josephine whispered, a hand over her mouth. "Don't say such things. Adoption is not buying."

"All I'm telling you is not to worry."

Josephine made a guttural sound and leaned her head back onto her husband's chest. She had majored in worrying. It was what she did best. She'd worried about not being able to conceive a child since she was fifteen years old and found out her mother had been unable to conceive until she was forty-one. She had no reason to suspect the same thing would happen to her, but alas, it had. After three miscarriages and seven failed rounds of IVF, she'd given up hope.

And then, just before the visit from Cleo, Ras got a call from an uncle in Jamaica. Marie Josef, a young girl attending a prestigious boarding school in Manchester Parish, had been accepted to

Harvard. The entire town was celebrating—until her mother found out she was pregnant and too far along to terminate. Calls to the States were quickly made. Ras agreed to finance the girl's pregnancy if she and her family moved to New York to have the baby. Her older sister, Mali, had been hired as Josephine's assistant, primarily so that Josephine could have constant contact with someone in the girl's family. She'd never met the young woman and didn't want to.

The plan was for Josephine to come to the hospital within twenty-four hours of the child's birth, sign all the paperwork, and take the baby home to the nursery she'd been decorating, bit by bit, in her mind's eye, since she was eleven.

"What made you think I would come with you that day?"

Ras and Josephine had returned to bed. Josephine brought her right thigh up to Ras's stomach and he grabbed it instinctively, rubbing the soft skin and kneading the thick, ivory flesh. After the brutal confrontation, the quiet was heavy in the Bennett residence. On Monday mornings there were no staffers in the five-thousand-square-foot house. Josephine didn't like to start off the workweek with a lot of strangers in her home. So Monday was a day off for the two full-time housekeepers, three gardeners, full-time chef, and handyman. It was the only morning that she could have a few minutes of uninterrupted time with her husband. Usually it was also when she lost her marbles and cursed him out nine ways to Sunday. But the "bad time," as Ras called it, had passed, swept away like clouds in a fast-moving storm. Ras shifted his weight to pull his wife's leg closer to him.

"I just knew," Ras said, closing his eyes and yawning. "Every time I took the bus home from school with Pierre, I would see you coming and going, and I just knew I was going to marry you."

"Ras, are we going to be good parents?"

"Let's stay right here in the present, Josephine. You are forever trying to get grief on credit."

Josephine smiled and nodded, sitting up in bed. "I have an interview with Alex this morning," she said.

Ras frowned. "That story's already out," he said, nodding his head toward the copy of *Sounds of Caribbean America*.

"This is for *Vibe*. It's about what it's like to be married to a rapper."

"I don't know if that's a good idea, *mon amour*."

"It's more publicity for J. Bennett Designs . . ."

"But at what cost?"

"What could happen?"

Ras was silent. He got up from the bed and crossed the room, going into the bathroom and closing the door.

Josephine stayed on her stomach, listening to the shower run. Usually Ras sang in the shower. She waited to hear his deep baritone seep through the bathroom door. Nothing. She rolled over onto her back and ran her hands over her flat, tight stomach. She closed her eyes and tried to concentrate on the child she was preparing to raise. Five months along. The baby would be kicking by now. She couldn't even imagine what that would feel like, a human life stretching and reaching, making its presence known. Did the young girl feel movement? Josephine held her breath and prayed.

twelve

HE WAS FUCKING HER AS IF HE THOUGHT THEY COULD BE CAUGHT AT any time. She was up against the wall; he was behind her, cupping her breasts and thrusting very quickly. Then he would stop, as if listening out for any sounds, and then start pumping again. With the married men, sex was like a fourth-grade cop-and-feel in the coat-room. The lovemaking was always furtive and rushed, even when they were thousands of miles away from their wives. They always fucked her like the wife was standing right there and she had just turned her head away for a second. Annoying.

He pulled her away from the wall a bit and then pressed on her back so she could bend down. She hated it when they tried to bend her in unnatural ways. She widened her stance so that she could bend from the waist, and he held her fast, pushing hard until the front of his thick thighs were completely pressed against her backside.

"I'm about to bust . . . ," he said in a soft, strained voice.

Cleo pulled away from him, dropped to her knees, and took him in her mouth just in time.

"Oh God. Oh shit. *Ma chérie, ma chérie,*" he whispered, standing on tiptoe and shaking his head back and forth.

When he was done, he collapsed onto the bed nearby and tried to catch his breath. Cleo went to him and tried to lie down next to him. But he pushed her away as soon as she sat down.

"Go," he said firmly.

Cleo opened her mouth to protest.

"Go now," he said, turning away from her.

Cleo stood up and exhaled.

"You want me to go home?" she asked.

"No. Go next door. Will and Rich are over there. Come back when you're done."

Cleo nodded, reaching for a towel draped over the chair next to the bed. She wrapped it around herself and started for the bathroom.

"What are you doing?" he asked, when he heard the bathroom door open.

"I gotta take a shower," Cleo said, one hand on the doorknob.

He stood up and led Cleo to the door of the hotel room.

"Go like that," he said. "Fuck both of them just like that. Then come back." Cleo looked him in the eye.

"Okay."

"Okay what?"

"Okay, daddy."

He put a hand between her legs, massaged for a few seconds, and then brought his hand to her mouth. He put two fingers inside her mouth and she licked them, keeping eye contact, the way he liked her to, the whole time. He finally opened the door and looked out into the empty hallway.

"Go."

Cleo walked across the hallway, barefoot and wearing just the towel wrapped under her arms. Her hair was in a windswept disarray from the few minutes she'd spent on the patio giving him a blow job while the salt air from the ocean whipped into her nose and mouth. There was a shiny layer of sweat covering her entire body and she could still taste his semen in her mouth. She was numb, both mentally and physically.

The door opened and a short Latino man wearing dark shades looked over her shoulder to see where she'd come from.

"Happy birthday," Cleo's lover said, holding his dreadlocks back with one hand. "Enjoy your present."

Cleo dropped her towel, right there in the hallway. The man with the shades grabbed her arm and brought her inside.

"Thanks, yo," he said, smiling wide. "Good looking."

"Can you describe the first man for me?"

"The first man ever? Back home?"

"No, the first industry guy."

"He was a producer. Pretty well known. About six feet tall. Light brown. Great physique."

"We need more qualifiers if you're not going to use his name."

"Raps sometimes, widely known as faithful to his wife. He and his wife were once on the cover of a popular magazine together."

"Right. And that same night, after the photo shoot . . ."

"We had sex for the first time in his DeLorean."

"How did you feel about him?"

"I liked him a lot actually."

"Why aren't you revealing his name? You're giving up everyone else's."

"He helped me out at a time when I really needed it. I'm not blowing his spot up."

"Who was the next one?"

"Ras. Someone I'm still involved with to this day. I feel like I'm his soul mate. Like we were meant to be together."

"Except for the fact that he's married."

"In spite of that."

"So why aren't you with him?"

"That's not the purpose he needs me to serve in his life right now."

"Didn't you tell me he passed you off to his manager and some other random guy?"

"Yes. I hate him for that."

"You could have said no."

"I could have."

"But you didn't."

Cleo smiled with her mouth closed and shrugged her shoulders. And then, for the first time since she started telling Alex her story, her eyes welled up. The tears did not overflow. Instead, they seemed to retreat back into her tear ducts and her face became stony once more.

"You love him?"

"Yes. And he loves me too."

"So he shares you with his boys?"

"Yes."

"Can you tell me what you remember from that day in the hotel with Ras? I need details."

Cleo leaned back in the diner booth and closed her eyes.

"Ras has an irregular heartbeat. Two small moles behind his left ear. Penis curves to the right. Small patch of scaly skin behind his left knee. Minor scar from a knife wound at the small of his back. Minor scar on right big toe. No toenail on left pinkie toe. Has both ears pierced but they are both about halfway closed."

Cleo's eyes popped open and she looked at Alex and smiled. "And he has my initials tattooed on his ring finger."

"Get the fuck out of here," Alex said.

"True story. We were both high as hell. It was after a show in, like, Akron, Ohio, or something. His wife was in New York at Fashion Week. I flew home with him. But first we smoked with some of his people. They must have laced it with something, 'cause we were freaking out."

"And so you got tattoos?"

Cleo pulled a thick silver band off her ring finger. There, in script, were the initials *RB*. The letters repeated around her finger three times.

"So he has your initials under his wedding band?"

"It's crazy, right? I think he really gets off on that. Having this double life."

"You looked like you were in a trance when you were running down everything you know about him," said Alex.

"I can see him in my mind's eye on that balcony as if he's standing right here, butt-ass naked."

"Photographic memory doesn't really exist."

Cleo shrugged. "I just know I can tell you about the small patch of gray hair he has in the back of his head and the little wiry hairs that grow out of his earlobe and the three freckles shaped like a pyramid on his inner thigh."

Alex just nodded and scribbled.

"You have tattoos?" Cleo asked.

Alex moved up the sleeve of her T-shirt without looking up.

"It's a flower," Cleo said. "But it's not finished."

"I get it updated every year," Alex said, still keeping her head in her notebook.

"You can't just do the whole flower at once?"

"Each petal represents another year of sobriety."

"How'd you know you had a problem?"

Alex finally looked up. "I woke up in a strange man's bed. Had no idea how I got there. And wasn't sure if I'd had sex with him or not."

Cleo snorted. "You call it a problem. I call it Tuesday."

Alex laughed, loud enough for a few patrons to look over at their booth.

"I guess we just see things differently when it comes to that kind of thing," she said.

Cleo's face fell and she clenched her teeth and gave Alex a severe look. "I'll bet we don't. I'll bet we're a lot more similar than you'd ever like to admit."

Alex clicked off her recorder and stood up to leave. "I doubt it."

$\mathcal{F}$OR THREE STRAIGHT MORNINGS, BETH FOUND BRIGHT RED BLOOD IN her panties. She should have been in a panic. But she was not. Dr. Hamilton sent her for a battery of tests. And the look on her doctor's face—worn lines and furrowed eyebrows—should have worried Beth even more. It did not.

Beth did not know what the future held for her. And her mission in life was to make it through one day at a time. She had tunnel vision. And because of Z's lifestyle, she felt like she was always one phone call away from her life being completely turned upside down. So she put little faith in planning. And she never looked for the bright side in anything.

But she knew without a shadow of a doubt that her child was fine, safe and warm in her belly. And no amount of bright red blood would change that. She thought about telling Dr. Hamilton about how rough Z had been with her for the past few nights. But she didn't. The look on Dr. Hamilton's face whenever Beth came into the office let her know that the doctor was two seconds away from calling the authorities to investigate the entire family.

Beth gripped the steering wheel of the Navigator tighter as she turned out of the parking lot of Dr. Hamilton's office. As soon as she got to the first traffic light, her cell phone began to vibrate.

"Yeah," she barked into the phone.

"Beth. Please remember, I want you to rest. No exercise. No sex."

"I know. I'm on my way home right now," Beth said. She looked in her rearview mirror. For a brief second she thought the doctor was standing in the parking lot, watching to see which way her car was heading.

"Your tests are fine. But I'm worried about the blood. Take it easy, okay?"

"Mm-hm."

Another call was coming through. Beth rushed the doctor off the phone and switched to the other line.

"Turn to Power 105 and call me back," Kipenzi whispered. She hung up before Beth could say a word. She punched the dial on the dashboard until the radio tuner settled onto Power 105. She turned up the volume and tried to make out the two women who were talking. She knew one was Angela Rodriguez, the afternoon DJ. And she was obviously interviewing someone, but Beth couldn't tell who it was.

"So, was it a one-night stand? Or did you two have a relationship?"

Beth felt goose bumps forming on her arm. A woman's high-pitched voice answered the DJ.

"We were together for, like, an entire week. He was in my hometown for a show and he wouldn't leave. He stayed at my house for a while."

Beth recognized the voice instantly now. It was a girl from Philly she'd spoken to on the phone about a year ago. She'd called to let Beth know that she was pregnant and she claimed the baby was Z's. Beth had just told her the number to their attorney and hung up on her. She'd never heard anything else about it.

Beth got the SUV up to seventy and set the cruise control. As she flew up the West Side Highway, she listened to the radio, her hands gripping the steering wheel although she didn't need to.

The woman on the phone would only say her first name was Tasha. She was from Philly and she was claiming that Z was the father of her eight-month-old son.

Obviously, she was looking for more than the usual child support amount. If not, she would have been filing her grievances in court, not on a nationally syndicated radio show. During the next break, Beth grabbed her cell phone and dialed the warm line to the station. She identified herself to the person who answered the phone, and within seconds she was talking to Angela Rodriguez.

"Put that bitch on the phone," she said to Angela, as she turned off the highway at her exit.

"We're about to come back from a break, Beth. You want me to give her your number?"

"Put her on the phone now."

"Beth. Look, she called. I had to let her come up here and speak her piece."

"I'm not mad at you, Angela," Beth said in a flat voice. "Just put her on the phone. Only take a second."

There was a shuffling sound and some muffled whispering. Beth slowed the SUV down. She was only a few blocks away from the house and she planned to be done with this conversation before she went inside. She knew the woman was on the phone because she could hear her breathing. Beth didn't bother with formalities.

"You're not getting more than two thousand a month," Beth said. "So there's no need to go on the radio or do any magazine interviews."

The young woman coughed and sputtered. They were always surprised that Beth got to the heart of the matter, never bothering to question paternity.

"Z told me that he wanted to make sure me and my child would be able to maintain the same lifestyle that his other children have," the girl said. "And I just want to make sure he stands by that." She sounded steely and rehearsed, as if she were speaking to a jury.

"Well, I hope you were making at least six figures a month be-fore you fucked him," Beth said. "'Cause you're only getting two thousand a month from my checkbook. And I pay all the bills. Where you live?"

"Hoboken."

Beth took in a sharp breath. This chick was crafty. She'd moved into one of the most expensive cities in New Jersey. She would file for child support there so that the payments would automatically be higher than they would be in whatever housing project she came from.

"Just curious," said Beth. "Why Hoboken?"

The girl cleared her throat. "I need to be close to New York, where I'm pursuing my career. And also, I . . . I think it's important that, I mean, I think . . ."

Beth sighed. "You want your son to be close to his father."

"Of course. Z said he was going to be a part of—"

"Look, girl. Let me explain to you how this works. Z will take care of this child, financially, for the next eighteen years. I'll make sure of that. Your payments will never be late. The child will have health insurance, and if there is ever any financial emergency, you can contact our lawyer at any time, day or night. If the child gets into college, Z—or his estate—will pay for it. You can have the money directly deposited into an account, you can have it go through the courts, or you can have a check sent to you overnight each month. Your choice."

Beth could hear the girl struggling to compose herself on the end of the line. She probably thought she was going to have a neck-swiveling argument with Beth. Maybe even a physical fight so that she could press charges and sue for even more money. That's the way it had gone down years ago with the first one—a Puerto Rican girl from Miami. But these days Beth was too busy and too pregnant to chase girls down and fight them for violating the sanctity of her marriage.

"I think my lawyer should probably call your—"

Beth interrupted her. "Now let me tell you what will *not*

happen," she said. "You will not contact Z. And you will not contact me. Z will not be in this child's life. There will be no visitation."

"I didn't have any intentions on—"

"You think right now that the money will be enough," Beth spat. "But it won't. When that child starts asking questions about Daddy, you'll start feeling it. And you'll feel that pull. You will want Z to be a father to this child you decided to bring into the world. Won't happen. And that's your cross to bear. He will have nothing to do with that little boy. Deal with it."

"I have to go. They're coming back from commercial."

"My lawyer is Sal Sheffield in Manhattan. He'll handle all the arrangements."

"Z came out to my spot a few months ago," the girl said. There was fear in her voice.

Beth had pulled into the cul-de-sac in front of the house. None of the cars were parked haphazardly across the front drive, which meant everyone was still out for the day. She had an hour before Boo and the nanny would be bringing the kids home from school.

"You fucked him again. And?"

"I'm pregnant. Again."

Beth tapped her front tooth with a fingernail and stared out the window. What looked like rain turned out to be snowflakes, the first of the season.

For once she was stumped. He'd never had more than one child with another woman. She thought she felt something like sadness gripping her chest, but she released it before it could take hold.

"You'll get another fifteen hundred a month for this one," she said. "It won't be double, so don't even think about it."

"I think this one is a girl. That's what Z said he wanted. A girl." The woman's voice was barely above a whisper and Beth could hear someone urging her off the phone.

"Sorry, sweetheart," Beth said with a sigh. She rubbed her belly and then turned off the car, with the cell phone still tucked under her ear. "I beat you to that one."

Beth got out of the car, closed her coat tight against the chill, and tried to walk fast up the driveway and to the front door. Now that she was truly showing, it was easy to start wobbling. Some days, like today, she fought against the wobble, making it a point to stand straight and put one foot in front of the other the same way she did when she wasn't thirty pounds heavier.

She entered the security code next to the doorbell and pushed the door open. Out of habit, she listened first before walking into the foyer. If the cleaning service was in the house, she'd go straight upstairs. Years after moving from Queens, she still felt weird having people inside her home who worked for her. She usually liked to remain out of sight until they were done. She saw a woman sweeping the kitchen floor and she headed for the staircase in the center of the hallway. She pulled off her coat with one hand and dialed Kipenzi's number on her cell phone with the other.

Kipenzi picked up after the first ring. "Is she telling the truth?" she asked Beth.

"No reason to believe she's not."

Kipenzi sighed. "I am so sorry. That shit is fucked up."

"You know how these girls are."

"Did you hear about the other chick?" Kipenzi asked. "The one who's supposed to be writing a book about all the industry men she's been with?"

"I know Z's dumb ass will be all up in that book."

"So you know the chick I'm talking about? Her name is Cleo or something?"

"Never heard of her. But if she's making a business out of fucking rappers, I'm sure my husband's got his own chapter." Beth turned down the hallway toward her bedroom, instinctively looking in the kids' bedrooms as she made her way. "This chick from the radio says she's pregnant again."

"What?" Kipenzi yelled.

Kipenzi's response made Beth feel that sharp pain in her chest again. It was one thing to let Z's affairs roll off her back when no one else knew about them. But Kipenzi's reaction reminded her once again that hers was not a normal marriage.

"You gonna say something to him?" Kipenzi asked.

Beth had just walked by Zander's room. The door was closed and she thought she heard some movement coming from inside. She looked at her watch. He was still in school. She opened the door to see if the dog had been locked inside during the morning rush again. Instead of seeing the dog sitting on Zander's bed, she saw Zander himself. He was in the center of his bed, his back against the wall. His legs were spread wide. Beth was surprised to see that his legs were long enough to be wide open and still reach down to the floor. His baggy jeans, unzipped, hung around his ankles like a puddle covering his construction boots.

A young black girl was on her knees between his thighs. She was completely naked, her brown spiral curls whirling around as she bobbed her head back and forth over Zander's penis. Beth took in the scene completely. Both of the teenagers were oblivious, Zander because he was seconds away from having an orgasm and the young girl because she was seconds away from throwing up.

"Kipenzi, can I call you right back?"

Beth said this just a bit louder than necessary. Zander's eyes flew open and he pushed the girl away with his knees and pulled his pants up in one rapid motion. The girl had flipped onto her stomach and was now facing Beth, her face wet and her eyes wild with embarrassment and fear.

"You should use the bathroom down the hall to clean yourself up," Beth said to the girl.

Beth turned to leave and then turned back to speak to Zander. But the look on his face stopped her. He pulled a shirt over his head and then stepped over the girl, still on the floor. He bumped Beth's shoulder on his way out of the room, went down the stairs two at a time and out the front door, slamming it behind him. Beth brought a towel to the young girl, who was now crying. She heard Zander starting one of his father's cars and peeling out of the driveway.

Beth went to her bedroom, still clutching her cell phone. She sat on the bed and took deep breaths until she heard the girl scurrying down the hall and out the front door. Then she pressed redial on her cell phone. Once again, Kipenzi answered immediately.

"What happened, you okay?"

"Yeah, I'm fine."

Kipenzi and Beth both sighed heavily into the phone. For a second, they didn't say anything—at least not verbally.

"So how's your little one doing?" Kipenzi finally asked.

"Zander's fine," Beth said.

"Zander?" Kipenzi laughed. "I said how's your *little* one!"

Beth shook her head. "Did I say Zander? The baby's fine. Moving around like crazy," she said, rubbing her belly.

Kipenzi chuckled. "Zander hasn't been a baby in a long time," she said.

Beth rolled over in bed and looked out into the backyard. Zander had returned. He was walking toward the cabana near the pool. The snow had begun to come down harder, heavy fluffy flakes covering the walkway. As soon as he turned the doorknob and went inside, she saw the girl with the spiral curls, walking fast behind him, looking back occasionally to see if they'd been seen. The girl opened the door to the cabana and closed it behind her.

"You're right," Beth said to Kipenzi, getting up to head to the grocery store. "Zander hasn't been a baby for a very long time."

"Z? Are you here?"

Beth cocked her head to the side and waited for the sound of her husband's voice. She stood in the kitchen, the door to the basement flung wide open. She rubbed her lower back and then moved her hand around to her bulging belly and rubbed it.

"Z, you down there?"

There was someone in the basement, Beth was sure of that. She was pretty sure Zander was still out back with the Girl Who Was

Not Bunny. And all the younger boys were at school. But she was not about to go downstairs to find out who was in her basement. Since they had moved into the sprawling seven-bedroom house, Beth had been in the basement just once. She'd come down the steps to bring Z a snack. He had recording equipment in one of the three small bedrooms that made up the basement. She had balanced a plate of macaroni and cheese and candied yams in one hand and a glass of Henny and Coke in the other as she looked through the doors to see which room he was in.

She saw him from the back, one elbow bent with a lighter in his hand. He leaned down and inhaled from something. Beth hadn't been able to see what. And then he exhaled, throwing his head back and blowing white plumes of smoke into the air.

Years ago Z had sworn to Beth that he would never smoke crack again. Beth had convinced herself that he'd stopped. As long as she didn't physically see any of the paraphernalia—ever, at any time— she could pretend he only smoked weed, like every other rapper.

But in order to make sure she could keep deluding herself, she had never gone into the basement again. There was an entrance that led outside and Beth knew that men and women came in at all hours of the night. Sometimes, late at night, she'd be in bed, alone. And from far away she'd hear the loud sounds of cackling laughter, music being played at high volume, and sometimes yelling and screaming. Beth usually checked on the boys, who always slept through what- ever happened in the basement, and then put in her earphones and plugged them directly into the television.

Z needed his outlets. And Beth respected that. The only time she even asked him about what happened in the basement was when she went into the kitchen one night and distinctly heard the sounds of a woman moaning and groaning. And a man's deep voice murmur- ing, "Yeah, baby. Do that shit . . ." Z told her it was a producer he was working with. He was in one of the spare rooms with a groupie he'd met on the set of a music video. Beth told him not to have those kinds of chicks in her house and Z agreed.

So when she came home from the grocery store and saw Z's car in the circular driveway, she immediately went to the door of the basement to see if he was there. That morning he'd left early for a studio session in Manhattan. And he had said he was going to stay in the city that night. So she was surprised to see his car.

"Z, if you're down there, let me know!" Beth yelled once more. She was hoping he was there so she could talk to him about Zander and the girl in the cabana. She finally closed the door and locked it. If it wasn't Z, whoever it was wouldn't be able to get into the main house.

Beth began unpacking the groceries and putting them away, stopping every so often to listen for any signs of life in the house. After what she'd seen with Zander and the Girl Who Was Not Bunny, she was on edge. When Boo came through the back door, laden with backpacks and lunchboxes, she breathed a sigh of relief.

Boo had to bend down to get under the doorjamb without knocking his head. He came through and then pressed his back against the door. He waved his hand theatrically with a weary look on his face and smiled weakly at Beth. "Your army has arrived," he said.

Zakee, Zach, and Zeke blew into the kitchen, followed by Mrs. Jacob, their nanny. They dashed off in three directions. Zakee barely breathed a word to Beth, grabbed an apple off the counter, and ran up the back staircase to the second floor in search of his older brother. Zach copied his movements exactly, except he stopped at the bathroom behind the kitchen before heading upstairs. And as always, little Zeke ran straight into his mother's arms.

"How is my little sister?" Zeke asked, as Beth smothered his cheek with wet kisses.

"We don't know for sure that it's a girl."

"It is a girl, Mommy," Zeke said, giggling and trying to break free from Beth's grasp.

Beth lifted Zeke up and sat him down on the island in the center of the kitchen. She pulled his chin up to look him straight in the eye.

"Zeke, how much does Mommy love you?"

"Lots and lots," he said, his face solemn.

Boo cleared his throat and stepped forward with Zeke's bag.

"A'ight, little man," he said. "Go upstairs with Mrs. Jacobs."

As soon as the nanny picked up Zeke and started up the staircase, Beth turned toward Boo, who had his massive frame bent down to look into the refrigerator.

"When did Z start smoking again?"

Beth could tell that Boo was no longer looking for something to eat. He was just stalling. He closed the door and turned to her.

"Is he here?" Boo asked.

"No. He's not here. But someone is in my basement."

"Oh, that must be Donald. Yeah, he was at the studio last night. Must've needed a place to stay."

"Boo. You didn't answer me. Is Z smoking?"

"Beth. How long has it been since he stopped?"

"Three years. But that doesn't mean—"

"You gotta trust him then. Can't be running around seeing smoke when there ain't none."

"He's just been off lately. The show in Atlanta . . . Some chick's on the radio talking 'bout she's got a baby by Z and she's pregnant *again*. Z *must* be smoking if he's getting bitches pregnant *twice*."

Boo sucked his teeth and shook his head. "You know that girl's probably lying her ass off."

Boo had his back up against the entryway of the kitchen that led to the foyer. One of the tiny gelatin snacks that the nanny packed in the boys' lunches looked like pretend food for a doll baby in Boo's massive hands. He dug into the confection with a plastic spoon, looking vulnerable and helpless, like a bear with oversized claws trying to extract honey from a pot.

"Boo, I know you work for Z, not me."

Boo nodded but didn't look up from his snack.

"But you need to know this."

Something in Beth's voice made Boo look up. Her eyes were wide but not glassy like they were when she was upset. They were clear and vibrant.

"You are a part of this family. Not just a part of Z's entourage. Maybe it shouldn't be that way, but it is." Beth looked down at her belly and then back up at Boo. "If my husband is on that shit again, I don't know what I'm gonna do."

Despite the fact that she clenched her back teeth hard, tears still sprouted out of Beth's eyes. "You need to find a way to let me know without betraying Z's confidence," Beth said. "Because I have to know."

Boo froze. A lot was riding on his ability not to give away anything. Whether he knew if Z was back on drugs or not wasn't important. Either way, he couldn't give her a single clue. He'd be out of a job before Beth even approached Z about it.

Boo stared at Beth, his face completely blank. She searched his eyes, willing him to break his gaze or scratch his forehead—anything. Any kind of movement would tell her something.

Boo didn't budge. There was a silent standoff for one long minute. Finally Beth exhaled and looked away. Boo immediately went back to eating his snack.

"Where is he now?" Beth asked, turning to put a pot of water on the stove for spaghetti.

"Studio."

Beth reached over for the cordless phone and began to dial Z's cell number. She heard his phone begin to ring and looked around the kitchen to see where it was coming from.

"I have his cell phone," Boo said, patting his pocket.

Beth's shoulders slumped. She dialed the number to the studio. When the receptionist answered, she asked to be put through to the engineer.

"Electric Lady Studios. How can I help you?"

"This is Beth. Who is this?"

The engineer covered the earpiece for a few seconds before answering. "Mrs. Saddlebrook, Z is not here."

"Does he have a session there tonight?"

"Hold, please."

Beth got on tiptoe and leaned over to get a jar of spaghetti sauce out of the cabinet.

"Hey, Beth, it's Dylan."

"Put my husband on the phone."

"He's in the booth with Kanye. We're paying him an ungodly amount of money. If I move Z, God only knows what will happen."

"I will say this again in plain English. Put my fucking husband on the phone."

"Hold on."

Beth had the phone in the crook of her neck as she opened the jar. She stopped as soon as the safety seal popped up and turned around to look at Boo, who was pretending to be on his cell phone.

"Beth? I was wrong," Dylan said. "Z's actually done. He shut down his session already. I was up here doing paperwork and I thought he was still working."

"He shut down his session? As of when?"

"Engineer said an hour ago. And that he was headed to the airport."

"Where is he going? Did you make travel arrangements for him?"

"He just took my card, he didn't tell me where he was—"

Beth hung up the phone without saying another word and put the sauce in the refrigerator. "He left," she said, wiping her hands on her track pants. "And you know it."

Boo took his cell phone down from his ear and closed it. "Beth, I gotta get back into the city," he said. "If you need anything—"

"Where is he?"

Boo opened his mouth to speak just as Zander came through the door at the rear of the kitchen.

"My dude Boo, what it do?" Zander asked in a playful, high-pitched voice.

"You heard from your father?" Beth asked.

Zander ignored Beth, lifting up the pants leg of Boo's jeans and letting out a whistle. "Damn, son. Them shits is nice. You stay rocking the hot shit!"

Boo shrugged and then stole a look at Beth.

"Zander, did you hear me talking to you?"

Zander sucked his teeth and twisted his lips up in that way that made Beth want to knock him down to the ground. If she weren't pregnant, she would have.

"Whatever, yo."

"Whatever? Who do you think you're talking to?"

Zander stopped and turned around. He took two large steps toward Beth and stopped. Beth realized in that moment that she did not remember when exactly he'd grown taller than her.

"I'm talking to you," he said. He dragged his eyes from Beth's feet to her eyes very slowly, with a disgusted smirk on his face the entire time.

"No, little boy," Beth said, "you are *not* talking to me. I will smack the shit out of you."

"Do it!" Zander screamed, throwing his hands up in the air. "Smack me! I dare you to put your hands on me."

Boo ambled over from the corner of the kitchen. "Zan, chill out. That's your moms."

Zander waved a hand dismissively in the air. "I don't care."

Beth's nostrils flared wide and she shut her eyes tight. Her baby kicked her in the ribs—hard. She winced and took in a sharp breath.

"You a'ight, Beth?" Boo asked, taking one step closer to her.

"I'm fine."

"Ain't nothing wrong with her," Zander spat.

Beth was finding it more and more difficult to breathe. This was her son. Her oldest child. The one she had had when she and Z were flat broke. The one who knew what it was like to go to sleep hungry. The one who actually appreciated having money. Beth could still remember pulling up to the house in Saddle River with Zander on her lap. He was grinning from ear to ear and Beth had to squeeze him tight to keep him from jumping out of the U-Haul before they came to a complete stop.

She'd wiped this boy's ass. Fed him. Clothed him. They were a team. She'd shielded him from his father's abrasiveness and convinced him that Z really did love him. And as soon as he decided he believed her, Zander had turned on her. She didn't understand it. And it didn't just hurt her feelings, it pissed her off. He was a teenager, so being a pain in the ass was to be expected. But for Beth, being disloyal was unforgivable at any age.

Beth looked Zander up and down and then reached for the phone. "You need to spend a few days with your grandmother," she said.

"Please," said Zander. "I'm outta here."

He bounded up the stairs, two at a time, with Beth behind him, moving as quickly as she could.

"Where do you think you're going?"

Zander went into his room, Beth following. He dug into his closet, throwing clothes on his bed. Zakee was sitting on the top bunk of Zander's bunk beds, watching with wide eyes.

"Zan, where you going?" Zakee asked, trying to hide the panic he felt.

"That's what I want to know," said Beth, leaning her frame into the doorway with her arms across her chest.

Zander took a duffel bag from under his bed and began throwing his clothes into it.

"I'm going away for the weekend."

Beth rolled her eyes. "Please. Did you talk to your father about this?"

Zander stopped packing and turned around to face Beth. "I'm going to Anguilla. That's where Daddy is right now."

Beth opened her mouth but didn't say anything.

"Yeah. Don't you feel stupid? You always trying to ride me. Tell me what to do. You ain't even know Daddy was going."

Zander zipped his bag, looked around his room, and then threw the bag over his shoulder and started walking toward Beth in the doorway. Beth didn't move. Zander stopped just a few inches away from her.

"Excuse me."

"Your father went to Anguilla?" Beth seemed to be talking to herself.

Zander's upper lip curled up in disgust. "You are pathetic."

Beth just looked past her son and up at Zakee on the bed. "How could he just leave for Anguilla and not tell me?"

"Could you move? Daddy sent a car to take me to the airport. Got a ticket waiting for me."

"We have things to talk about."

"Like what."

"Like the girl I saw in your room earlier today."

"Nothing to talk about."

"What about Bunny? Are you still seeing her?"

"Yeah. She knows what's up."

"And you're okay with that?"

"The important thing is *Bunny*'s okay with it," Zander said, his lips twisted in a sarcastic smile. "You know how that is. Don't you, Ma? What's the big deal if your man cheats? As long as *you* get what *you* want out of the deal. Isn't that the way that works?"

Zander brushed past Beth and headed down the stairs. Something snapped inside Beth and she hauled ass into the hallway, past Zander, down the staircase, and out the front door, where there was a Town Car idling in front. She dashed around to the driver's side and rapped on the window. The driver looked up, startled, from his newspaper and pressed the button.

"Don't move this car," she said, pointing at him.

The driver threw his hands up. "Look, lady. I'm just picking the kid up and taking him to the airport. Orders from Mr. Saddlebrook—"

"*I said don't move this motherfucking car!*" Beth screamed. She stomped her left foot twice, made a fist, and slammed it on the hood of the car.

"Ten minutes," she said, her voice suddenly calm. "You can leave in ten minutes."

Beth backed away from the car and went back toward the house. She walked directly into a group of men and women holding cameras and lighting equipment and giving each other directions.

"What the fuck is this?" Beth screamed, one eye on the Town Car.

"We're shooting the first episode of *The Z Files*," said a tall, lanky man with spectacles and long, thin dreadlocks.

"Not today, you're not."

"Dylan told us to be here at two. And that we could shoot you and the kids for an hour."

"Dylan told you wrong. Get the fuck off my property."

Beth turned to her front door, where Boo was holding Zeke, who leaned out of his arms in Beth's direction.

"What's wrong, Mommy?" he cried out.

"Nothing," Beth said, taking him out of Boo's arms and going back upstairs.

"We're going on a trip," she said, as they went into Zeke's tidy room.

Zeke's eyes lit up as Beth plopped him on his bed and began opening up his drawers and taking out the neatly folded T-shirts and jeans. She looked out the window and saw the television crew still surrounding her front yard, talking on cell phones and giving each other confused looks.

Boo appeared in the doorway, his cell phone outstretched.

"Dylan wants to talk to you."

· Beth snatched the phone out of Boo's hand. "What."

"Beth, just listen to me," Dylan said. "Z signed a contract for this show. For a lot of money. That you have already spent. MTV's gonna sue if they don't tape something today. This is the seventh time they've rescheduled."

"How the hell could he sign off on a reality show without my permission?"

"I don't know all the details," Dylan said. "But I know they need to get some interiors and brief interviews with you and the boys today. That's cool, right?"

Beth breathed hard through her nose. "I don't have time for this shit."

"They said they just need an hour. That's cool, right?"

"No, Dylan. It's not cool. I'm leaving."

"Wait. Don't forget about the piece for *Vibe*. I promised them you'd talk about your life with Z. I'm hoping to get a joint cover for Z and Zander."

Beth just gave the phone back to Boo and finished packing. He left and returned a few minutes later.

"And now there's some chick named Alex downstairs to see you. She said Dylan told her to come by today to do an interview."

Beth stomped downstairs and flung open the front door. Alex stood there, her eyes wide, surrounded by three cameramen and a producer watching her every move.

"What do you want?"

"Dylan said we could talk today."

"Today is not a good day," Beth said, and closed the door in Alex's face.

Before she could turn away, she could hear Alex's muffled voice through the door.

"I can just be a fly on the wall."

Despite herself, Beth snickered. She went back to the door and opened it. "A fly on the wall . . ."

"We don't have to talk today," Alex said. "I just want to see what a typical day is like in your life."

Beth laughed long and hard. Just long enough for Alex to take one step back and consider leaving the property.

"A typical day in the Saddlebrook home," Beth said. "Come."

She marched down the front walkway and back over to the Lincoln Town Car with Alex practically running to keep up.

"This is the car my husband sent to pick up my son to take him to Anguilla," she said, her hand sweeping in the direction of the car.

"Ma'am, I have to get him to the airport by—"

"Don't fucking move," Beth said.

The driver scowled and went back to his paper.

"See, my husband is trying to get to Anguilla without me. Don't know why. But I can't imagine that would be a good thing. So I'm packing up the boys and flying down there myself."

Beth strode back to the house, again with Alex close at her side. She opened the front door and saw Alex's eyes widen. "Rapping about killing cops makes a nice living, eh?"

"Obviously," Alex said, sweeping her eyes around the spacious mansion.

"Upstairs we go! To prepare for our impromptu trip."

Alex followed Beth up a spiral staircase made of hand-carved mahogany. Beth stopped in the foyer.

"Boys, let's go. Bags packed in ten minutes."

She went to Zeke's bedroom and directed Alex to a small chair near a window overlooking the backyard. She saw Alex look toward the doorway and turned around. Zakee was standing there, his brother Zach's profile barely visible behind him.

"What are we doing?" Zakee asked.

"Have a bag packed in ten minutes," Beth said, rolling up Zeke's clothes and stuffing them in an overnight bag.

"Why are we—"

Beth dropped her head and held up the palm of her hand. "So help me God, Zakee, if you don't have a fucking bag packed in ten minutes . . ."

Zakee turned away quickly, Zach on his heels.

Zeke, looking at Alex with curiosity, took his thumb out of his mouth. "Mommy, you said a bad word."

"I can say bad words. I'm the mommy. But you can't."

"I can't?" Zeke asked. "Shit. That sucks."

Beth's eyes widened. She traded a look with Alex, who dropped her head to mask her smile.

"Zeke Saddlebrook!" she said. " 'Shit' is a curse, you know. You're not supposed to say that."

"Can I say dammit?"

Beth carried Zeke's bag in one hand and scooped him up in the other. It was a struggle to stand upright without feeling like she was going to topple forward. But she took a second to steady herself and then scrambled for her own bedroom.

"You want me to hold something?" Alex asked.

"No."

On her way down the hall, she passed Zakee and Zach's bedroom. "Five minutes and you are at that car!" she yelled out.

She put Zeke on her bed and he immediately ripped the covers down and snuggled in.

"This bed smells like my daddy," Zeke said, his eyes closed.

Beth pointed at a desk in the corner of the bedroom and Alex sat.

"Smells like Daddy?" Beth whispered under her breath. "You mean it smells like a random groupie slut?"

Zeke opened his eyes. "What'd you say, Mommy?"

"Nothing," Beth muttered. She opened her closet and grabbed the suitcase she'd packed for the hospital and dragged Zeke out of her bed and back downstairs.

"Let's go! Let's go! Let's go!"

Zakee and Zach were already outside, rubbing their arms to stay warm and whispering to each other. Alex fell in line with them at the rear door of the car like she was one of the kids and stayed quiet.

"Where's Zander?"

"He's talking to Boo in the kitchen," said Zakee.

"Here," Beth said, putting Zeke's gloved hand in his.

She turned toward the house and took a few steps. "Zander, let's *move*."

Zander appeared at the doorway. "I'm not going."

Beth let out a yell that sounded like a war cry and charged toward Zander. He actually cowered and threw his arms over his head to protect himself as soon as she got close enough to hit him. But before she could cuff him in the face, Zakee and Zach were on her back, grabbing her arms and stopping her from punching Zander out.

"Get in the fucking car before I kick your ass."

Zander gritted his teeth, picked up his duffel bag, and stomped off to the car.

Boo came out the door. "Beth, I don't think this is a good—"

"Mind your business, Boo. You want to protect yourself by protecting Z? Fine. Collect your paycheck. But nobody cares about my husband except me. I am not going to let his ass OD in Anguilla while you sit here babysitting me."

Beth went to the back door of the car, where the driver was standing, and waited for him to open the door. Her four boys stood behind her—Zander right behind her, then Zakee, and Zach holding baby Zeke in his arms. Alex stood a few feet away, trying to blend in with the scenery.

"Ma'am, I wasn't told that you were—"

"LaGuardia Airport," Beth spat.

"Yes, well, the thing is—"

"Excuse me," Beth said, using her right hand to push the driver to the side and her left hand to open the door and usher Zander in. He started to climb in and then immediately stopped, his butt in midair.

"Zander, get in the car!" Beth yelled.

"Ma, I . . . I can't . . ."

Beth pulled Zander back out. "Why the hell not?" she asked.

Zander's eyes were wide and glassy. Beth looked inside the car. There was a young woman, no more than nineteen, wearing a black fur coat, fishnet stockings, and black ankle-strap stilettos. She was clearly not wearing anything else.

"Who the hell are you?"

"I'm here for Zander," the young woman said. "I was supposed to . . . accompany him to the airport. I'm a present."

Beth climbed into the car and closed the door, leaving the boys and Alex with their faces pressed to the windows.

"You're what?"

The young girl edged back toward the opposite door, wrapping her coat tight around her.

"Look, lady, I'm not trying to cause any trouble. The guy paid me a thousand dollars up front. Told me I'd get the rest when I got to the airport."

"To do what?" Beth said slowly.

The girl shrugged. "Whatever the boy wanted to do."

"Who gave you the money?" Beth asked.

"I don't know the guy's name. Tall, light-skinned, gold tooth right here," the girl said, pointing to her incisor.

"Donald," Beth said, rolling her eyes.

"I'm sorry," the girl said, shrugging her shoulders. "They gave me the money and sent the car to my house."

Beth nodded and rubbed her temples. "Not your fault that my husband wants my son to fuck hookers in limos on his way to the airport for a trip he didn't clear with me."

The young girl just kept her eyes at her feet.

"I mean, what do you expect? I'm sure he's smoking again. Which means he's liable to do anything. Can you imagine? I'm pregnant and he leaves for Anguilla without even telling me?" Beth shook her head. "That's fucked up, right? Right?"

The girl nodded slowly, looking past Beth at the boys who were still looking in the windows. "Were you . . . on your way . . . somewhere?"

Beth just stared at her for a second and then shook her head slightly and came back to life. "Yes, I'm on my way to Anguilla to save my husband from himself. Again. You have to get out."

"Excuse me?"

Beth shoulders slumped. "Get out. I am taking this car to the airport."

"But what about me? What am I supposed to do?"

"How old are you?"

The girl lifted her chin and looked Beth in the eye. "I'll be nineteen in three months."

"So you're what? Fifteen? Sixteen?"

The girl looked away. Beth shook her head and looked for her cell phone. She pressed one button and held the phone to her ear.

"Boo, close the house down. Set the alarm system." Beth snapped the phone shut and opened the car door. "Let's go, boys," she said, ushering her sons into the car.

They all got in, stealing looks at the half-naked girl sitting in the back seat next to their mother. Zeke sat on his mother's lap. The three older boys sat across from them. Everyone in the car looked mortally embarrassed, except for Beth and Zeke. Beth rolled down the car window and looked right at Alex, who stood with her notebook in hand, speechless.

"Alex, you think you got enough of a day in my life?"

Alex just nodded. Beth gave her a fake smile.

"I thought so."

She rolled up the window and exhaled as she sat back and placed her hands on her belly. She opened one eye and saw a cameraman peering into the window. Next to him, a man held a microphone high over his head.

Beth rolled the window down again. *"Get the fuck off my property!"*

The cameraman lowered his equipment and stepped back quickly. "We can shoot tomorrow."

"Shoot your momma tomorrow. Fuck off."

The driver brought the divider down and looked at Beth through the rearview mirror.

"Where to, ma'am?"

Beth looked at the young girl. "Let me guess. You from Queens, right?"

The girl nodded. "Southside," she said to the driver. "Francis Lewis Boulevard."

The driver nodded and pulled out of the driveway and down the tree-lined path to the security gates.

Zeke leaned over to get a better look at the young girl.

"Hey, cutie," the young girl said, smiling at Zeke.

Zeke smiled and then looked over at Beth. "Mommy," he said in a loud whisper, "is she a random groupie slut?"

Across from Beth, Zander groaned, covered his hands with his eyes, and sank as deep into his seat as he could. Zakee and Zach were both stifling giggles unsuccessfully. Zeke just continued to gaze at the young girl with a curious look on his face. Beth let out a breath and leaned her head back in the seat.

"No, she's not, Zeke." She buried her mouth in her son's neck and kissed him as the driver pulled onto the highway. "She's not random at all."

ON Z's FIRST INTERNATIONAL TOUR, HE PERFORMED AT THE ANGUILLA Music Festival. Z fell in love with the island and vowed that he'd buy property there one day. Within a year, he'd purchased the three-bedroom oceanfront villa in Mead's Bay. Beth loved Anguilla immediately. Not for the beauty of the island, but because it always brought her back to a simpler time with Z. In Anguilla Z was relaxed and calm. He never used drugs there except for smoking a blunt on the deck after all the kids had gone to bed or possibly having a few drinks with Boo. It was all about riding Jet Skis and hanging out at the local bars and clubs.

Beth felt safer in Anguilla, like she could keep a sharper eye on Z. She knew he wasn't completely an angel out there. There was a woman she knew Z saw every time he came. But now that Beth was six months pregnant, she didn't even care about the girl. She knew Z was going to get it from somewhere. For the moment, she was glad it wasn't going to be from her.

The flight was four hours. All the boys slept for the entire flight but Beth was too nervous to sleep. She was sure that by now Z knew she was on her way. Boo had probably called Z before the car pulled out of the driveway.

But she didn't care if he cursed her out. There was no way he was going to fly out there without telling her. Not a chance in hell. Beth didn't know for sure that Z was slipping back into drugs. But she was losing him to something. And the more she was in his face, the better the chance she had for bringing him back.

She leaned her seat back and slowly lifted up the shade on her window. It was pitch-black outside and she could see nothing but twinkling lights down below. As the plane dipped low to begin preparing for landing, Zeke began to stir. Beth drew him into her lap and stroked his back.

"I want my daddy," Zeke mumbled.

"So do I," Beth said.

fourteen

"*W*HY ARE YOU IN ANGUILLA? I NEED YOU TO HELP ME WRITE THIS song!"

"Bunny, my mom was wilding."

"Yeah, right. You're down there with some girl."

Bunny rolled over onto her back and looked up at the beamed ceiling of the Greenwich attic. Hot tears sprang from the corners of her eyes and slid backward down her face to her neck.

"Bunny, how come you don't trust me? I told you nothing's happening. You my girl. And that's it."

"Like when I saw those pictures of that girl in your email?"

"You still didn't tell me how you hacked into my account."

"She said she couldn't wait for you to come back to see her."

"Do you know how many emails I get like that every day? I don't know half the chicks who hit up my email."

Robert appeared in the doorway and motioned toward his watch. Bunny sat up quickly and nodded.

"I'm about to go to the studio," Bunny said. "When are you coming back home?"

"I have no idea. My mom's out here looking for my dad. I think he's on that shit again."

"I need you to come back."

"I'm trying."

"Is your dad gonna be okay?"

"I don't know. Probably not. Do people ever stop smoking crack?"

Bunny tried to comfort Zander and then hung up the phone.

"Let's go," Robert said. "Ras wants a few ad-libs for the last song you worked on."

"Robert, can I go down to Anguilla after this session?"

"No."

"Why not!"

"Because you need to go to the gym, you missed two sessions with your tutor, and you need to meet with your media training coach."

"Did you schedule any downtime for me?"

"This weekend. Saturday and Sunday."

"So how come I can't go then?"

"Do you have a thousand dollars for a last-minute round-trip ticket? If so, knock yourself out. I'll be in the car."

"You give me five hundred dollars a month for an allowance," Bunny said. "How would I have money for a plane ticket?"

"Exactly," said Robert.

Robert closed the door at the same time that Bunny threw a shoe. The shoe hit the door just as it shut, so Robert didn't hear it. Until she signed a contract, she was on her own for any real money. She picked up her cell phone and dialed.

"Hey, girl, what you got?" said a voice on the line.

"Z is smoking crack again."

"Oh, really. How do we get pictures?"

"You have my account number?"

"Yes. We'll wire as soon as we get some pictures."

"He's in Anguilla. They usually stay in Mead's Bay, so he should be somewhere around there."

"And what do sources say about Z's drug use?"

Bunny looked down at the notepad she'd scribbled on while Zander was talking to her. "Family members don't think he'll ever stop smoking crack."

"Family members. You're sure?"

"Positive."

"You work for them or what?"

"I'm just a very close family friend."

"Well, everything you tell me always checks out, so I know you're in there."

Bunny hung up and went to the window. Robert was standing at the car door, scribbling something on a clipboard and talking into a cell phone. He looked up and saw Bunny. He put a pointer finger in her direction and then jabbed it toward the car.

Bunny dashed down all three flights of stairs, grabbing her heavy coat from the front hall closet before going out the front door.

During the ride from Greenwich to Electric Lady, she tried to convince herself that selling Zander's story was a necessary evil. She'd have the money she needed to see Zander. And it wasn't a real betrayal. Everyone knew Z was on drugs. And it was just a matter of time before the media found out. She'd learned the trick from watching Zander earn extra money. He'd call the paps and tell them where any of his father's famous friends were going to be. He overheard his dad talking to Puffy, who invited him to an ultra-exclusive private party at the Borgata. Zander called the *Enquirer*, which got the first pictures of Puffy and his brand-new, barely legal girlfriend.

By the time Bunny arrived at the studio, she'd checked her bank account: she was two thousand dollars richer. She texted Zander and told him she was flying down to Anguilla to see him that weekend. Then she downed a cup of mint tea with lemon, prayed, and stepped into the booth with Ras.

fifteen

$\mathcal{K}$IPENZI WOKE UP WITH A START AND SAT UP STRAIGHT. SHE FRANTI-cally patted the bed next to her until she remembered that Jake had left for the studio soon after they had made love the night before.

She moved her hand up to her throat, closed her eyes, and took in a deep breath, held it for as long as she could, and then exhaled slowly. Her hands were clammy and shaking and her head was pounding.

She couldn't remember what her dream had been about. But she just saw herself in the back office of some kind of supermarket, wearing a blue smock over her outfit and a name tag over her right breast.

Kipenzi tried to shake the visual out of her head and twisted her body around to plant her feet on the hardwood floors. She stretched out and walked over to the windows and opened the curtains. New York City took her breath away—as it did every morning. The view from her apartment showed Manhattan in its best light.

She yawned, then leaned her forehead against the glass. Kipenzi Hill was tired.

When Kipenzi got tired, it wasn't a normal level of exhaustion. It wasn't the weariness of a new mom who is up around the clock with a screaming baby. It wasn't even the sheer fatigue of a night-shift nurse on hour twelve. It was even deeper. Kipenzi moved on hyper-speed. Nine countries in eight days and eyes still bright. She popped off international flights looking more refreshed than some people do after a ten-hour makeover.

But when it did catch up to her, exhaustion hit her hard. Kipenzi pulled her head back from the window just enough to catch her image in the reflection. There were dark circles beneath her eyes, her lower lip was swollen (she had a habit of biting it in her sleep— particularly if she was having a bad dream), and her hair, free of any kind of weave, was a curly mess, knotted and twisted in limp ringlets hanging just to her chin.

Kipenzi looked out at the area where Jackson usually hung out in the park. He was there and she wondered, as she always did when she stood at the window, what people would do or say if she walked out of her bedroom just as she was right now, in a robe and slippers, and walked out of her apartment, onto the elevator, through the lobby, into the sunshine and sat next to him on that park bench.

Would Jackson know it was her if she wasn't wearing oversized shades and being hustled into the back seat of a stretch Hummer? Would he just assume since she wasn't dressed up that she couldn't be Kipenzi Hill? Would anyone approach her? Ask for an auto-graph? Sit down next to her?

At her most recent show, a sold-out event at the Continental Air-lines Arena, Kipenzi was blown away by the crowds. People were in the aisles, laughing, cheering, crying—singing along to every last line. And each time she came close to the edge of the stage, bodies would lean in and hands would rise up. People wanted her to touch them.

She'd lean down, mic in hand, and slap a few palms as she worked the stage. But it made her very uncomfortable. She some-times wanted to stop singing and bend down and say, "I'm just a per-son. My name is Kipenzi. I took a shit right before I came onstage. Do you really want to shake my hand?"

But her fans always had that faraway look in their eyes. And in some ways it was depressing, because she knew it wasn't her they loved, it was what she represented: money, glamour, excitement. In reality, Kipenzi knew she was flighty, unreliable, and spacey.

Driven only when it came to her own career, she couldn't remember the birthdays of her friends and family to save her life. She could be mean when she was recording. And a straight-up bitch on tour. She was absolutely sure that ninety percent of her fans would not like her one bit in real life.

Kipenzi let the curtain fall and sat down on her bed, reaching for the special edition Hello Kitty phone she'd designed on the nightstand. She pressed speed dial and turned on the speakerphone as she fell backward on the bed.

"Hi, this is Beth. Leave a message."

"Hey, Beth," Kipenzi said, turning to the side to be sure the speakerphone picked up her voice. "I haven't heard from you. I heard you went out to Anguilla. Hope you're having a good time. Um, call me. Okay? I want to know how the baby's doing. And I need to talk to you about—"

The intercom rang and startled Kipenzi. She hung up the phone and picked up the receiver.

"Ms. Hill, Melinda Davis is here to see you."

"Send her up. Thank you."

Kipenzi went into the bathroom and splashed water on her face. She pulled her hair back and secured it with a rubber band and then slipped into yoga pants and a T-shirt.

Melinda Davis was the youngest executive at MusicTown. And she was coming to talk business. Everyone from Kipenzi's new husband to her parents to her friends—everyone except Beth—was trying to convince Kipenzi that she didn't want to walk away from it all. And now the president of MusicTown was sending Melinda to be the voice of reason. Officially Melinda was the head of the A&R Department. But in reality, she was everything.

In the offices at MusicTown, they called her Mrs. Fix-It. Did Z need one more line of coke in order to finish a $50,000 shoot for

Playboy? Melinda would fix it. An executive's sidepiece gets pregnant? Melinda befriends her just long enough to get her to the clinic. But what really cemented Melinda's status was an incident five years before. Jake stabbed an associate he believed had bootlegged his album. He was already on probation. Mandatory jail time was on the horizon, just as he was about to release his best work yet. Melinda told the cops she did it. With her clean record and a few phone calls from her father, she ended up doing thirty days in prison and serving one year of probation.

That a white girl from Upper Montclair would take the rap for Jake was absurd. And it made her untouchable and powerful. Some of the rappers she worked for weren't sure if their own wives would go to jail for them.

As Kipenzi waited for Melinda to get to her door, she wondered if the woman who had helped mold her career for over a decade would play good cop or bad cop.

Kipenzi went to the door and cracked it, peering down the hallway to see Melinda step off the elevator.

"Good morning," Melinda said, leaning in to peck Kipenzi's cheek before breezing into her cavernous living room. She walked straight over to the dining room table and set down a sheaf of paperwork.

"Kipenzi, you are out of your damn mind if you think you're not giving MusicTown at least one more album. At least."

"Ah. So he told you to play bad cop."

Melinda wrinkled her brow. "I'm playing common sense. That's what I'm playing. You want to quit the business? Fine. But you received a twenty-million-dollar advance. You have that money just sitting around? 'Cause I'll take a check and keep it moving."

"I got an advance for twenty million for five albums. I've done four. I shouldn't have to pay back the whole advance."

"You can be sued for what your last album would have sold. Future earnings included. Tell your husband that and see what he says."

"Who says I got married?"

Melinda rolled her eyes. "Anyway. You can put out a compilation to satisfy your last album requirement."

"Really? I could? That would be easy!"

"But they want you to do a DVD of videos for each song and update a daily blog up until the release of the farewell album."

"Done. I can do that with my eyes closed."

"And you have to promote the compilation. Magazine covers, national late-night talk shows, morning shows, whatever they ask."

"I'll do it."

Melinda sat down at the table and pulled out the sheaf of papers. "Well, that's it. When you're done with that, I think your dad will be able to get them to let you go."

Kipenzi nodded slowly. She hadn't expected it to be that easy. From the very first morning when she woke up and knew that her career as a singer was over, she'd been dreading all the steps it would take to be fully free. Jake needled her to give it more thought. Her father outright begged her to reconsider. And now Melinda was telling her that it was really over.

"What if I didn't want to walk away?" Kipenzi asked. "How much would they pay to keep me?"

"You could get a hundred million for a three-sixty deal. You know what that means: tours, albums, endorsements. Everything."

Kipenzi's eyes crossed and she held on to the back of a dining room chair to steady herself. "That's fuck-you money."

Melinda chuckled. "Yeah. It would be a good retirement plan." She got up from the dining room table and walked over to the floor-to-ceiling windows, the way everyone did when they came to Kipenzi's house.

"Sometimes I really wish I could sing."

Kipenzi snorted. "And sometimes I wish I could manage my own life as well as you have."

Melinda put her hands on her waist and looked down at Kipenzi, who had moved to her sofa. "Please."

Kipenzi tried to look surprised. "What?"

Melinda dropped her chin and looked at Kipenzi from a side angle. "You trying to bullshit *me*? You forget I've been working with you since your father drove you to my office in a damn Chevy Nova?"

Kipenzi smiled on one side of her mouth.

"You looked me up and down and asked me why none of my artists had been on the cover of *Vibe*," Melinda said.

"I was just curious . . ."

"Hey, heads up. The Happy Hair folks called. They are pissed."

Kipenzi groaned and sank into her seat. She took a throw pillow and covered her face with it. "What now?" she asked, her voice muffled.

"Your hair color is wrong. You took the weave out and now it's too dark."

Kipenzi kept the pillow over her face and didn't move.

"Your contract explicitly states that your hair color will never be lighter than James Blonde or darker than Berry Bonds or it invalidates the agreement. According to their people, you are now a half shade darker than the Berry Bonds color."

Kipenzi took the pillow off her face but didn't sit up. "Are you serious?"

Melinda threw up her hands. "And the contract says you'll seek permission before deviating from the preapproved styles. All of the preapproved styles involved hairpieces. And you're sitting here with six-inch corkscrew curls. Is that the hair that actually grows out of your head? Um, no. You knew what you were getting into when you signed the deal. They own you. They pay you for wearing your hair a certain shade and length and shooting two commercials a season." Melinda shot a meaningful glance around Kipenzi's apartment. "And it looks to me like it's worth it."

Kipenzi rolled her tongue around in her mouth for a half second. What she wanted to say curled up and died just before she could spit it out. "I am very blessed," she said instead. "I'll have Ian make an appointment for me to get my hair done."

Melinda nodded, and scribbled in her notebook.

"And when is this contract up?"

Melinda flipped through the papers. "Looks like it's year to year. So you're just about done. But you know, they'd probably still bring you on for another year even if you don't have an album to promote . . ."

Kipenzi didn't look in Melinda's direction. "No, thank you."

Melinda shuffled some papers and started to put them in her bag. "How could you just throw this all away?"

Kipenzi's eyes grew wide. "I've worked my ass off since I was three."

"And that's it. You're done. At your peak? You've got film offers on the table, your last album could go diamond if you would support a rerelease. Your dad could get you overseas endorsements that would put your great-great-great-grandchildren through college."

Kipenzi closed her eyes and shook her head firmly. "No."

"You don't even know what the real world is like," said Melinda. "You have no idea. Even with all the money you have. You don't even know what it's like to spend it. It goes fast."

"Thank you for the advice."

"You owe your father better than this."

"What?"

"He quit his job, took night classes in economics. This man turned his whole life over to making your success. Both of your parents. They sacrificed a lot for you—"

"And I haven't repaid them?" Kipenzi asked. "They have to eat off me until I'm dead?"

"They're not eating off you now—"

"My father earns ten percent of my income. That's how he eats. I'm not mad at him. But, seriously, it's a job. He's being downsized. Company's folding. I have a right to do this."

"Of course you do," Melinda said. "I just want to make sure you're ready to deal with life on the other side. Without me to buffer you from the real world."

"I'm a big girl."

"Did you hear about the book? The video girl who's been with all the rappers?"

"What about it?"

"Her attorney sent a chapter to Jake's attorney. Sounds like either Jake or at the very least someone close to him may make an appearance in that book."

Kipenzi looked up at Melinda. "Did you read it?"

"No. They sent it via messenger. And the messenger was instructed to stand there as the attorney read the chapter to make sure no copies were made and no written notes were taken."

"Does Jake know?"

"I hear he was in the office. So, yeah."

Kipenzi turned around, stood up, stretched her arms out, and stood on tiptoe. "Would you mind if we finish up over the phone this afternoon? I've got a few meetings and I still need to jump in the shower."

"Of course, of course. I totally understand," Melinda said, sweeping her things into her bag and standing up.

Kipenzi walked her to the door and opened it.

Melinda turned back as soon as she crossed the threshold. "Have you spoken to Beth recently?"

Kipenzi's heart flipped over and she searched Melinda's face while trying to appear calm. "Why?"

Melinda looked both ways down the hallway and then leaned in the doorway. "Look. Z's my client, not Beth. So I'm not really supposed to tell her anything. But there's a warrant out for his arrest."

Kipenzi let out a breath of air and rolled her eyes. "What now?"

"Possession of crack cocaine. Trying to board a flight to Anguilla with it. Boo bailed him out and he went to Anguilla. If he's not back in time for his court date . . ."

Kipenzi's shoulders slumped.

"I don't know how much Beth knows, but . . ." Melinda trailed off.

"Thanks, Melinda."

"All right, sweetie, you might want to check in on Beth if you can catch up to her. I know she's pregnant. This can't be easy for her."

Kipenzi nodded, gave Melinda an air kiss, and closed the door.

She called Ian.

"I need to get out to Anguilla by this evening. Call Mead's Bay and tell them I want the oceanfront villa. And can you please book the other three villas? One for security, the rest empty."

"Yes, ma'am. Your favorite threader is in Mead's Bay. Should I have her come by to do your eyebrows in the morning?"

"That would be perfect. And also make an appointment for both me and Beth for a full day of services at the spa at Cap Juluca. And please send a car to pick me up in one hour. Tell the driver we'll be making two stops. First stop: the label. And then the airport."

Kipenzi climbed into her unmade bed for a quick minute to collect her thoughts. Somewhere far away, she was worried about Beth. But knowing that she was flying out there temporarily pacified her. Two percent of her mental capacity was focused on getting out of her contract and endorsements.

At the forefront of her mind was Cleo Wright. When she'd first heard rumors and whispers about the book, she'd instantly felt sorry for Beth. She knew Z would be in that book. But Jake?

"Hell fucking no," Kipenzi said out loud to her empty apartment. "Hell motherfucking no."

Kipenzi had already asked Jake a few nights ago. And he'd sworn he'd never slept with her.

Kipenzi pulled her knees up to her chest and held them there, keeping her eyes closed tight.

Jake had been rough with her the night before, so much so that she was still throbbing between her legs seven hours later. It always concerned her when he was like that. Most times, Jake moved slow with her, usually bringing her to orgasm twice before even entering her. Last year, after a show in Prague, he spent twenty minutes kissing the inside of her left thigh until she forced him inside her.

But last night was one of the other nights. He came into her apartment tipsy and just slightly disheveled. No conversation. He twisted her arm and broke her gold bangle as he pushed her down onto the floor.

Kipenzi loved it. But it also let her know something was brewing. The last time he went all *Animal Planet* on her, he'd lost a million dollars playing a game of horse with a player from the New York Knicks. She couldn't walk straight for two days.

So Kipenzi had a feeling when she woke up that morning that something was going down. She just didn't know what. She'd assumed that it had something to do with Z, and maybe it did. But maybe it had something to do with this book that was now surfacing. Kipenzi rolled over to her stomach, buried her face in her sheets, let out of a muffled scream, and then quickly got out of bed and started running in place. She stopped, looking at herself in the mirror above her dressing table.

"All right, Jake," Kipenzi said to her reflection. "I married you. Don't let me down." She threw a one-two punch and pretended to dodge a blow. She crossed the room and hopped on her treadmill. She set it for a sprint without even warming up and did a mile in five minutes.

"Please, baby," she said, out of breath but still running. "Don't let me be wrong about you."

Kipenzi stopped running abruptly, jumping onto the sides. She turned off the machine, stepped down, and went to her dresser. She peered into the mirror over the dresser, her breath coming in ragged gasps.

"Please."

As Kipenzi's heels clicked through the lobby of Jake's label, she left a wave of people whispering behind their backs and pointing. She moved quickly, one security guard on either side of her. She held her hands up to the collar of her white chinchilla coat, keeping her oversized shades on in the building.

Before she'd left her apartment, she had her hairstylist come over and do a quick weave, getting her back to the appropriate Berry Bonds shade and unbelievable length in case the paparazzi got a few shots en route to the label. She cried as the stylist put the weave back into her hair.

Her hair was now halfway down her back, shimmering and silky. A long bang swept over one eye and feathered down past her shoulders. It was as demure as a waist-length lace front weave could be.

The new receptionist at the label, an older white woman with a severe snow white bun, had been in the business for years. When her hair was dark, she'd ushered a young Whitney Houston into Clive Davis's office after he'd started Arista in the seventies. It was getting harder and harder to recognize when she was in the presence of stardom. She wasn't watching much MTV.

"Can I help you?" she asked Kipenzi's bodyguard.

The bodyguard ignored her, speaking into the wireless cell phone receiver attached to his ear.

"Front lobby," he barked.

Within seconds Jake's assistant, a tiny young woman with an afro and black horn-rimmed glasses, came into the lobby.

"Kipenzi? Come on back," she said, holding the door open.

The guards stayed close as Kipenzi glided down the hall behind Jake's assistant.

"How's your daughter?" Kipenzi asked.

The young lady blushed. "She's great," she said, looking in Kipenzi's general direction but not making eye contact. "She really loved the show. Can't stop talking about how she touched your hand."

Kipenzi smiled as the assistant opened the door to Jake's office and stuck her head in.

"Kipenzi's here," she said.

The bodyguards turned around and took a glance at the cubicles surrounding Jake's office. Their looks made it clear: no one was to hang around for a glance at Kipenzi or call a friend in another department to conveniently drop by. Kipenzi closed Jake's office door and leaned against it, keeping both hands behind her, clasped around the doorknob. She crossed one leg over the other, showing the bare leg beneath her full-length white chinchilla fur.

Jake's brown leather executive chair was facing the window behind his desk. He was on the phone, with his back to Kipenzi. He ended the call but didn't turn around right away. He waited for what he knew was coming.

"Did you fuck her?" Kipenzi asked.

Jake took a deep breath and slowly swiveled his chair around to face his new wife.

"Love the boots, ma," Jake said, slowly taking in Kipenzi's all-white ensemble.

"Are you in this woman's book?"

"The skirt is hot. Shows off the legs," Jake said, standing up. He walked in front of his desk and leaned back on it. He opened a humidor, took a cigar out, and used the double-bladed guillotine Kipenzi had bought him years ago to clip the end of the cigar. He stuck the unlit stogie in the side of his mouth and smiled wide at Kipenzi.

"Jake, I'm not playing."

"The hair's a little over the top," Jake said, taking the cigar out of his mouth and gesturing to her hair with it.

"Is that why you were so rough with me last night? Are you worried about what's in this book?"

"Don't like the shades either," Jake said, twisting his lips to one side.

"Can you pay her off?"

Jake pushed himself off the desk with his hands and took a few steps toward Kipenzi. "How you feeling today?" he asked. "Seemed a little weak when I left this morning."

He put an arm around Kipenzi's waist and pulled her to him.

"I want to know the truth about this chick," Kipenzi said through clenched teeth.

Jake bit her neck and pushed her firmly against the door of his office. "You know the truth."

Kipenzi wriggled out of his grasp and walked to the seating area on the other side of the office.

"I only know what you tell me."

Jake's shoulders slumped slightly. "That's the only version of the story I can give you—mine. And it's the truth."

"This chick Cleo is saying something different."

"You want Cleo's truth? Ask her."

"So your truth is that you never had sex with her?"

"That's my truth."

There was a brief and silent standoff. Kipenzi stared Jake down. Her eyes filled up but she didn't break her gaze. Jake froze his face and just stared at her. She clenched her teeth and raised her head slightly to keep the tears from falling down. Jake's eyes were pools of cement.

Kipenzi broke Jake's gaze and melted into the sofa. "I'm going to Anguilla tonight."

Jake nodded, returning to his desk. "Good idea. Beth needs you."

"Where's Z?"

Jake sucked his teeth and rolled his eyes. "Somewhere being incredibly stupid. Three rocks of crack cocaine in the back pocket of his jeans. At the airport. I heard he's trying to say it wasn't his. But whatever." He rubbed a hand over his smooth head. "Penzi, I can't carry him anymore. I can't walk into a conference room with a promoter, talking about I'm on tour with this dude."

"Jake, you can't drop him from the tour. And I know you're not even thinking of dropping him from the label."

"I'm not dropping him! *He's* dropping him. Penzi, he's the one fucking shit up. You know what the plan has always been."

Kipenzi nodded.

"Tell me," Jake said. "What's the plan?"

"Five albums. Five international tours. Five points on at least five albums. Then cash out."

"I'm at the 'cash out' part," Jake said. "And this company needs to actually be worth something in order for me to cash out."

"What about Beth? You drop Z and they're gonna fall apart. What's going to happen to Beth and the boys?"

"I'm a businessman, Penzi, not a welfare agency. Beth got family, don't she?"

"Yes, she does. She has Z. And she has me and you."

Jake looked temporarily shaken. He knew what she was saying was true. But he could not internalize it.

"Life is hard," Jake said. "She's a grown woman. And she made a decision to marry a crackhead and have ten babies by him."

"You made a decision to go into business with a crackhead. When he was hot."

Jake shrugged. "Exactly. When he was hot. Now he's wack. That little dog your mom carries around in her purse can bark a better verse than he can write at this point."

There was a knock on the door and Jake's assistant poked her head in. "Alex Sampson Maxwell is here—the writer from the *New York Times*."

"Two minutes," Jake said.

"I gotta catch my flight," Kipenzi said, rising from the couch.

"Chill out for a second," Jake said, motioning for her to sit. "Let me finish up this interview and I'll take a ride to the airport with you."

"I'm not in the mood for any reporters," Kipenzi said.

"So don't say anything," Jake said. "Just look cute. That's all you good at anyway."

Kipenzi flung a throw pillow from the sofa in the direction of Jake's head. He caught it and threw it back, barely missing her. They both laughed out loud and then stopped abruptly when they heard the knock at the door.

Kipenzi stood up in front of Jake, put her hands on her hips, and turned around in a circle.

"I'm good?" she asked, gesturing toward her body.

Jake looked over at his wife and did not smile. "Better than good."

sixteen

 $\mathscr{A}$ LEX'S FIRST WRITING ASSIGNMENT FROM A MAJOR MAGAZINE WAS A story on Prince. By then she'd interviewed lots of celebrities for her school newspaper and for various websites. But it was usually a brief Q&A over the telephone. For the story on Prince, she'd actually traveled to Minneapolis for the weekend and conducted the interview at the indoor basketball court in Prince's infamous Paisley Park Studios.

It was one of the few times she'd actually been starstruck. The moment he slipped into the chair next to hers and motioned for her to turn on her recorder, her tongue grew thick and her mouth went dry and she had to cough out her first words.

And then, within five minutes, Alex realized that Prince was human. He was a person, just like she was. Except much shorter. Yes, he was a musical genius and the subject of all her seventh-grade fantasies. But ultimately he was a wee man with a strange hairstyle who smelled like gardenias and polyester.

From that moment on, Alex never felt any particular excitement when she interviewed a celebrity. They were all flawed in their own ways, and seeing them up close always took away some of their mystique. There was the time she interviewed Sisqó at the height of the "Thong Song" mania. He had dried mucus in the corner of his eye that made her stomach churn for the entire interview.

Two years before, she'd broken a rule and smoked a blunt with Common during an interview. She was disappointed to discover that he didn't adhere to the puff-puff-pass rule. And his blunts were rolled with way too much spit. How do you look up to anyone after you see him use too much spit to roll a blunt?

Years before, she'd fallen in love with Mariah as they bonded over their mutual crushes on Tupac. And she once cried in Cee-Lo's arms after a vicious breakup that went down right before she had to interview him. He gave her advice on getting over it. And he still called her every year on her birthday and told her she was beautiful.

There were horror stories too. The superproducer in LA who made her wait seventeen hours for an interview and talked to her for seven minutes. There was the rapper who promised to sit still for the interview if she came with him to a strip club. She went. He disappeared. She had to pay a cab $150 to get back to her hotel.

Then there was the time she almost came to blows with a female rapper who was pissed off that Alex wrote about watching her get her hair weave tightened. They crossed paths in a bar the same day the story came out. Fortunately they were both too drunk to land any punches.

She liked several celebrities. And she hated a few. But she was never starstruck.

Still, as she followed Jake's assistant down the corridor toward his office, she noticed an unfamiliar thumping in her chest. She'd interviewed Jake twice before. But he wasn't nearly as famous then as he was now.

Jake's assistant gave Alex a sharp look. "He's not discussing his personal life for this piece. We really want to stick to the music."

"I've been told," Alex said, making sure not to catch her eye.

Every artist had the same instructions. Alex always asked whatever questions she wanted to anyway. Let them tell her they had no comment—which was itself a comment.

"How much time do you need?" the assistant asked.

"I was going to just see how things go."

The assistant looked Alex up and down. "Twenty minutes," she said, then knocked and walked away.

Alex thought she heard a woman laugh before Jake's voice boomed out.

"Come in!"

Alex twisted the doorknob and leaned the top half of her body into the office while keeping her feet outside. She saw Jake sitting at his desk, an unlit cigar dangling out of his mouth. To his right, Kipenzi Hill sat with her feet up on a metallic leather couch, her head in a magazine.

Alex felt her stomach drop and her underarms go clammy. Kipenzi—the holy grail of her *Vibe* story—was now less than two feet away from her.

Jake stood up and waved her inside. "It's Alex, right? Nice to see you."

Alex came all the way inside and crossed the office to shake Jake's hand.

Jake motioned to the sofa. "This is my assistant, Kipenzi," he said with a sly smile.

Alex felt her cheeks grow warm as she held in a chuckle. Kipenzi looked up from her magazine, smiled at Alex, and then went back to reading.

"Does your assistant always sit down on the job and read magazines?" Alex said.

"Yeah, she does," Jake said. "I'm about to fire her."

He pointed to the chair across from his desk and then sat down. "Did you hear the new music?"

"I did."

Jake nodded. "Where's the flattery? It'll make me open up and tell you something good."

Alex made direct eye contact with Jake and held it for a second. "You're going to open up to me whether I flatter you or not."

Jake leaned back and smiled. "Word?"

He looked over at Kipenzi, raised one eyebrow, and jerked a thumb in Alex's direction. "You hear this? She's pretty bold. I think I might have to make her my new assistant after I fire you."

Kipenzi swung her legs around and placed the magazine next to her. She stood and then turned back to scoop up her coat. "Jake, I'll be in the car."

Jake nodded and Kipenzi gave Alex a tight-lipped smile as she made her way to the door.

"Wait. Ms. Hill?" Alex asked.

Kipenzi turned around. "Yes?"

"What do you think the future holds for Jake? Can he make it as an executive?"

Kipenzi smiled with her mouth closed. "I think Jake's making a natural progression from the studio to the boardroom. I'm sure he'll be fine as long as he continues to surround himself with good people who are not afraid of taking chances."

"Does that include you?"

"We've always enjoyed a healthy working relationship."

"Your biggest hits have featured him—"

"He complements my songs well."

"Ms. Hill, I'm writing a story on celebrity wives for *Vibe*."

"I know."

"I recently met your friend Beth—"

"I'm aware."

Alex closed her notebook and made sure they both saw her turn off her recorder. "I know that the media shouldn't care about whether or not you two are a couple . . ."

Kipenzi bristled. Jake didn't move.

"And I know I'm way out of line. But I can't waste an opportunity like this." Alex forced herself to look directly at Kipenzi. "A lot of people look at you two as the perfect love story," Alex said. "Are you two ever going to publicly state that you're an item?"

Alex looked from Kipenzi to Jake and back to Kipenzi. Kipenzi looked directly at Jake and raised one eyebrow. Jake turned his head to the ceiling and smiled. Neither of them said a word. Alex's shoulders dropped. She pulled her chair closer to Jake's desk and switched her recorder back on. She turned around to look at Kipenzi, who had one hand on the door to Jake's office.

"I'm sorry that I asked. I respect that you guys don't talk about it."

Alex turned back to face Jake and flipped through her notebook to find her list of questions.

"Can you tell me a little bit about a typical day for you?" she asked, moving her recorder in his direction.

Jake looked past Alex. "I wake up next to that chick right there."

Alex bent down and scribbled.

"Her breath is usually somewhere between rank and atrocious."

Kipenzi, who had not yet walked out of the office, laughed out loud. "I know you're not talking!" she said. "Everyone's breath stinks in the morning. At least it's not my feet that smell up the whole room!"

"Kipenzi, that was one night—after a show," Jake said. "Your dogs don't smell so fresh when you get off stage either."

Kipenzi walked back to Jake's sofa and sat on the arm. "Who else are you interviewing for this story?" she asked Alex.

"Beth, Josephine Bennett. Hopefully Shante Broadus."

Kipenzi nodded. "What do you want to know?"

"Don't you get tired of hiding? Pretending you're not together?"

"Do you have a boyfriend?"

"Yes."

"And you get to just walk down the street with him whenever you want and no one bothers you. You can go to the movies, out to eat, go shopping. And no one cares."

Alex just looked at Kipenzi. She could tell that Kipenzi wasn't expecting a response.

Kipenzi smiled and looked at Jake. "It must be nice," she said.

"Are you guys still close with Z and Beth?" Alex thought she felt a weird vibe ricochet from Kipenzi to Jake and then to her but she wasn't sure.

"Z—that's my man for life," Jake said, each arm resting on either side of his chair.

"Even though he's not . . ."

"Not what?"

Alex rolled her tongue in her mouth for a moment. She knew exactly what she wanted to say. But she wanted Jake to think she was struggling with it.

"There are rumors that he's back on drugs," said Alex. "His recent performances have been lackluster. People are saying you're carrying him right now. And that it's just a matter of time before you have him dropped from the label."

Jake shrugged. "People always talk."

"So you're not dropping him from the label."

"Me and Z have a long history of working together. If we were ever going to make any changes, it's not something that would be worked out through the media."

Alex stopped writing and looked up. "You're not saying no."

"Is this story about me or Z?"

"It's about you. And Z." Alex looked to her right. "And it's about Kipenzi too. It's about all of the people in your life who are influencing you." She sat back in her chair and gestured just slightly in Kipenzi's direction. "So, when are you two getting married?"

Jake laughed. Kipenzi did not. She cleared her throat and shrugged into her coat.

"Jake," she said, lifting an eyebrow but saying no more. She walked past Alex's chair and stopped, offering her hand. "It was nice meeting you, Alex."

Alex stood up.

Kipenzi kept her eyes closed and tapped at the side of her head with a perfectly manicured index finger. "Few years ago, in *XXL*, you wrote, and I quote: 'When Kipenzi Hill finds her voice, it will be an event. Until then, we'll be forced to listen to her scream out the notes to petty pop songs that are unworthy of her time. For now, she's full of all style and no substance. Hopefully she'll learn that a true artist does it vice versa.'"

"I wrote that years ago . . ."

Kipenzi nodded. "Probably why I remember it so well. I barely keep up with what's written now. But back then?" Kipenzi held her hand to her stomach. "Lines like that had me depressed for weeks."

"I don't know what to say."

"Say you're welcome!" Kipenzi said. "I just buckled down and worked harder after I read that review. And by the way, you were right."

She opened the door and her two bodyguards quickly enveloped her and led her down the hallway.

Jake's assistant came into the office with a coffee cup. She placed it on Jake's desk and then walked away. "Ten more minutes, Alex," she said, before closing the door.

Alex exhaled and looked at Jake. "That's not enough time."

"Let me ask you something," Jake said.

"I'm supposed to be asking the questions."

"What does your editor want from you?"

"Perspective. They want me to give them a side of you they've never seen."

A knock on the door. A tall young man with long, shiny corn-rows came in with a stack of CDs and sat on the couch, sorting them into small piles. Jake raised his chin in greeting to the young man and then turned back to Alex.

"Give me an example," Jake said.

"I ask you about the dad you never knew and then you start cry-ing . . ."

Jake's face went blank and he dropped his chin.

"Well, you asked!" Alex said.

Jake took a sip of his coffee and gagged. "What if I cursed out some chick who screwed up my coffee order?"

Alex shrugged. "Rapper with a temper? Nah, they know that side already."

"That's not how I get down."

"I know. But that's how they assume all rappers get down. Bor-ing story."

"My job is to give you something without giving you everything."

"Exactly."

"And the best-case scenario is for me to give you something without giving you anything."

Alex smiled. "What's your earliest memory?"

Jake rolled his eyes. "You can't be serious."

"You're living in the Brevoort Projects with your mom and your two little sisters. What can you remember?"

"My mom coming home from work in the middle of the night. I always woke up when I heard the key in the lock. I would go into the kitchen while she warmed up her dinner. And she would keep telling me to go back to bed. But she knew I wouldn't. So she'd tell me about her day but keep saying, 'Go on to bed, boy.'"

Alex nodded, dropping her head to make sure her recorder was still running.

"That became our thing. Even when I was much older. Anytime I'd see her, she'd say, 'Go on to bed, boy.' And that meant, like, get out of here. Even though she didn't really want me to."

Alex looked up when she realized Jake wasn't saying anything else. She opened her mouth to speak when the assistant opened the door again.

"Time's up, Jake. Car's waiting downstairs."

"And before you go, I need to talk to you about these beats," said the young guy with the braids.

"I know. Just chill for a second," said Jake, who seemed to come out of a trance. He stood up and shook it off and then extended a hand to Alex.

"Thanks for coming through. Hope I was helpful."

Alex stood up and shook his hand. "I've written about you before. Twice."

"You used to work for *The Source*. You gave my second album four and a half mics."

Alex gave Jake a weak smile and shrugged her shoulders. "The whole staff voted. I didn't decide that by myself."

"It was your name on that review."

"It wasn't a five-mic album," Alex said.

Jake made a face like he'd gotten a whiff of spoiled milk. "You must be crazy."

"The beats were hot," Alex said. "But you got lazy toward the end. That one song? With the hook where you're, like, singing or whatever? That was horrible."

Jake sat back down and looked Alex over as if seeing her for the first time. "You thought so?"

"Yeah. I did. And it's so annoying the way you always explain your obscure metaphors. You'll say, 'Get it, I'm always leaning . . .' You need to trust your audience. We'll figure it out."

Jake nodded and smiled. "I'll take that into consideration. You ever think about doing A&R?"

"Nah. I like what I do."

"What else would you like to do? Write a book?"

Alex swallowed. "Maybe one day. I love trivia. I could do some kind of trivia book."

Jake and the guy with the cornrows exchanged a look and they both chuckled. "Me and Damon have been arguing about the theme song to *Good Times* all week," Jake said. "He swears they're saying 'hanging in and jiving.' Which makes no sense. They're talking about hard times. They're saying 'hanging in a chow line.'"

"But the show is called *Good Times*," Damon said. "Hanging in and jiving is good times!"

"I'm telling you," Jake said. "The line is hanging in a chow line. The show was set in the projects in Chicago. Chow lines. Trust me."

"You're wrong," Damon said, still separating his pile of CDs.

Jake made a show of standing up from his desk, walking into the middle of his office, and digging his hands into the pockets of his oversized jeans. He lifted his chin high and leveled his eyes at Damon. "How much you putting on that?"

"Everything you got in your pockets right now—times five."

Jake threw his head back and laughed out loud until he started to cough. He then abruptly stopped laughing and caught his breath. He pulled out a wad of neatly folded bills and began to peel them off the roll, slapping them onto his desk.

". . . seventeen, eighteen, nineteen, twenty."

Damon pretended to yawn and checked his phone for a new text message.

". . . seventy-three, seventy-four, seventy-five."

Damon looked up. "Why the fuck do you need seventy-five hundred dollars in your pocket?"

"You never know."

"Don't you got an ATM card?"

Jake laughed. "When the stock market crashes, I ain't trying to fuck with no banks."

Damon rolled his eyes. "If the stock market crashes, what the hell you gonna do with seventy-five hundred dollars?"

"Stop stalling. It's 'hanging in a chow line.' I want thirty-seven thousand, five hundred dollars from you—today."

"Whatever. Prove that shit."

Alex cleared her throat. "It was a husband-and-wife team that wrote it. The Bergmans."

Jake snorted. "How do you know?"

"I wrote a story about them last year." Alex sat down on the arm of Jake's chair and opened her laptop. "Norman Lear, the creator of the show, hired them to do the theme song. The show didn't even have a name yet."

Jake smiled. "So they got the name of the show from the song they wrote?"

"Yeah," Alex said, swinging the screen around to the story she'd written so Jake and Damon could see it. "And it's 'hanging in and jiving.' Not 'hanging in a chow line.'"

Jake and Damon looked at each other. Then they both started screaming at the same time.

"Ah, I told you! I told you!" Damon said, laughing at Jake.

"You said you wasn't listening to this chick!" Jake said, laughing.

He slammed the money down on the table in front of Damon and sucked his teeth in mock disgust.

"I changed my mind," Damon said, licking his pointer finger and theatrically counting out the bills. "She's a genius! She's a trivia queen!"

"It was nice meeting you, Alex," Jake said, shaking his head and still chuckling as he walked Alex to the door.

"You know," Alex said, "four and a half mics is almost perfect."

"*Almost* only counts when you're throwing hand grenades."

Before Alex could respond, Jake had closed the door.

"And that was it! That was the whole interview!"

Alex was sitting across from Birdie, Tweet sitting in her lap. They were on the parlor floor of the brownstone, Birdie on a barstool, getting a haircut from Richard, his best friend.

"You got enough to write the story?" Birdie asked, holding up a hand mirror to inspect his hairline.

"Just barely," Alex said.

"He say anything about the song I did with Talib Kweli?"

Alex hesitated. "No, he didn't mention it."

Birdie twisted his lips in disappointment.

"But that doesn't mean anything," Alex said quickly. "I told you I didn't get much time with him."

"Y'all talked about the music he's listening to. If he was really feeling my verse, he probably would have mentioned something about it."

Alex put Tweet down and directed her to a play area in the corner of the room. "When did this suddenly become about you?"

"I can't ask a question?"

"While I'm trying to tell you about my day?"

"You interviewed a hip-hop celebrity," Birdie said with a sneer. "So what else is new?"

"What's new is your attitude. You can't get a song on the radio, so you're taking it out on me?"

"Yo, I'm done. I'll see y'all later," said Richard, throwing his equipment into his backpack. Alex and Birdie ignored him.

"You going way too far now," Birdie said.

"You started with me! Why? Why can't you just talk to me? Tell me what's on your mind. The only time I know you're feeling uneasy or nervous about something is when you start shit with me. It's so unnecessary."

Alex and Birdie were quiet. Richard closed the front door and they still didn't speak. The only sound was Tweet, playing with a train set.

Birdie got off the stool and walked toward Alex. He put his arms around her waist and brought her close. "You're right."

Alex didn't move. She was still keyed up from the interview. The last thing she needed was Birdie's mess.

"I'm going into the studio with Ras Bennett tonight. I think I'm just nervous."

Alex's eyes widened. She put her hands on Birdie's shoulders and moved him back so she could look him in the eye. "Tonight? Seriously? Shit, Birdie, that's awesome."

Birdie smiled. "Well, it's not like he just decided that I'm the best thing ever. He's only doing it 'cause of the story you did on his wife."

"Whatever! It's getting done. This is what you wanted!"

"I know. And what if it doesn't work? What if I still can't get radio to play it?"

"That's not possible. Everything Ras Bennett does gets constant airplay, no question, and you know it. Baby, I am so happy for you!"

Alex nuzzled Birdie's neck, soaking in his musky smell.

He rubbed the small of her back and sighed. "Why you want to marry me?"

Alex looked up at him. "I have no idea."

Birdie tickled her on one side, holding her close as she laughed and tried to get away.

"*Nooo*, Birdie, stop," she said between laughs. "You're going to make me pee on myself."

Tweet appeared near Birdie's legs. She tapped him on the knee with a toy train.

"Let Lexi go to the potty, Daddy," she said, which just made Alex and Birdie laugh louder.

"Nope, I won't," Birdie said to Tweet, while still tickling Alex. "She's gonna have an accident right here."

"Daddy, that's not nice."

Alex got out of Birdie's grasp and dashed to the other side of the room.

"I gotta get my questions ready for my interview with Josephine," she said, out of breath.

"For *Vibe*?"

"Yeah. The whole story is giving me a stomachache."

"Well, you got something on Kipenzi from seeing her in Jake's office."

"Right. That's a good thing. But I didn't exactly get any quotes from Beth."

"You will. You always do."

"It's not this story that's bothering me. It's the book."

"The Cleo chick."

Alex nodded. "I feel weird. I talk to her three times a week about all this crazy stuff she's done with all these industry dudes. Some she names. Some she doesn't. Drives me crazy."

"So ask her."

Alex grimaced. "I don't even want to know. Just from researching these women for the *Vibe* story, I can't even imagine how they would feel knowing their men are in this book. It's horrible."

"I think they know. It's part of the business."

"Sleeping with whores is part of being a rapper? Is that what you're telling me?"

Birdie threw his hands up in the air. "Hey, I'm barely a rapper! Cleo wouldn't even give me a second glance," he said. "Don't look at me like that."

"Oh. But once you get a song on the radio and you do become popular and she comes looking for you . . ."

"She's dirty. And nasty. I wouldn't touch her with a ten-foot pole."

Birdie put one hand on Alex's cheek. He kissed her forehead. "I would never do no shit like that. Ever."

Alex sighed. "Why do you want to marry me?" she asked.

Birdie grinned. "I have no idea. I gotta go to the studio. See you in the morning."

Alex put Tweet to bed and then took her recorder into her office to download her Jake interview and start transcribing. She turned the recorder on and listened to Jake and Kipenzi. But before long, she'd drifted away. Her body was buzzing from head to toe and she felt light-headed and dizzy. With writing the Cleo book, researching the *Vibe* story, and seeing Kipenzi and Jake together, she'd had more excitement in a day than she usually had in a month.

But that night, as she prepared for bed, there was something else buzzing around her brain. This woman. Cleo. She claimed she'd slept with ninety percent of all the rappers with record deals in the tristate area. Did that number include Birdie? Birdie made it seem like it was absolutely impossible. But didn't they all?

seventeen

JOSEPHINE'S HOME OFFICE, ON THE FIRST FLOOR OF HER SPACIOUS home, offered a fantastic view of the backyard. When she was deep in thought, she often spun her leather office chair around so that she could look out at the kidney-shaped pool, lined all the way around with mature walnut trees and several well-kept gardens and koi ponds. The floor-to-ceiling windows behind her desk stretched across the entire wall, allowing warm sunshine to fill the space. Natural sunlight was always best for creating new ideas in her sketchbook or making the finishing touches on a gown.

The holidays had been difficult. She wasn't up to traveling. So she and Ras ate dinner alone. There were more staffers in their house on Christmas day than family members.

Today, now that New Year's celebrations were over, she was ready to get back to work. Beginning with another interview with Alex.

The original plan was to meet Alex at the office, but then Josephine and Ras found out that Marie Josef, the young woman carrying their child, had been having contractions and could go into labor at any time.

Which meant that Josephine would soon be a mother. For three hours that morning, she'd stared out into the backyard, envisioning her feeding her infant child, walking the grounds with the baby in a sling. She saw a child playing in the pool, arms wide and splashing . . .

"Ma chérie . . ."

Josephine jumped. She turned to see her husband in the doorway, his waist-length dreadlocks tied in an intricate knot.

"My love . . . I was so deep in thought," Josephine said, holding a hand to her heart.

"You are a nervous wreck," Ras said, leaning into the doorway. "You need a drink."

Josephine giggled. "Ras, it's eight in the morning!"

Ras walked completely into the room, his hands behind his back. "What time is acceptable to start drinking?"

"At least five p.m. And even then, just a glass of wine or champagne."

Ras brought two glasses from behind his back. The stemware was a gift from his great-grandmother in Jamaica. The glasses were hand blown in France, sixteen inches high, with an elaborate pattern of roses with thorns snaking around the stem. Each glass had champagne with a splash of orange juice and a split strawberry perched on the lip.

"It's five o'clock somewhere," Ras said.

Josephine was normally ultracomposed. She always looked as though she were being held up by an imaginary thread coming out of the very top of her head. But when Ras handed her the glass, she slumped in her chair, pulled her bun down from the top of her head, and shook her hair out. She rolled her eyes at Ras, took the glass, and drained it.

"That's what I'm talking about!" Ras said, taking a sip from his own glass and then holding it up to toast Josephine's empty one. Josephine held hers up, clinked it, and then let out a loud belch.

"Oh my!" she said, holding her hand up to her lips. Ras laughed out loud and Josephine joined him. As their laughter subsided, a light tension rose up between them.

"Is there anything you need me to do?" Ras asked.

"Promise me everything will be okay."

"You know I only promise when I know I can deliver."

Josephine nodded. "I know. That's why I need you to promise."

"Let's think this through," Ras said. "What could happen?"

"She could change her mind and keep the baby."

"She could. But not likely."

"Something could go wrong while she's in labor."

Ras nodded. "True. But again, not likely."

Josephine sucked her teeth and sank back in her chair. "I don't want to be fucking rational right now, Ras. I want you to just tell me everything will be fine."

"Everything will be fine, *ma chérie*. Breathe deep and prepare for motherhood."

Josephine stared at Ras for a long moment. He held her gaze and continued to nod. They were still staring at each other when Mali, Josephine's assistant, came to the door of her office.

"Alex's here. Should I send her back?"

"Alex? From *Vibe*?" Ras asked.

"Yes, why?"

"I just don't like it. And this is not a good time."

"I want to do it now. Before . . . the baby comes. I'll be too busy later."

"What's her angle? What kind of questions has she been asking you? And why do you need to talk to her so much? I've been on the cover of *Vibe*—twice. And I never talked to a reporter for more than an hour."

"Wait," Josephine said, holding up her hand. "Are you worried about *me*? Or are you worried about what I'll say about *you*? You don't have to worry. Your secrets are safe with me."

"That's not what this is about . . ."

Mali slipped out of the room and closed the door behind her.

"Then what is it about?" Josephine whispered, her eyes narrowed. "That woman can write a book. And talk about having sex with you. But I can't speak to the press and make my own name? I have to be only Ras Bennett's wife?"

"This just doesn't seem like the right time. That's all I'm saying," Ras said.

"I'm going crazy. Can't stop thinking about the baby. It'll be good to focus on something else."

"If you say so."

"I say so."

Mali came back to the door. "Just let me know when I should bring Ms. Maxwell in," she said.

"In two minutes," Ras said, ushering Mali inside and closing the door behind her. "Any further news about your sister?"

Josephine forced herself not to comb Mali's face for any signs. She tried to look concerned but not frantic.

"Good," Mali said. "She's two centimeters dilated."

Ras nodded slowly. "And they'll call us when it's time . . ."

"Of course," Mali said. "Everyone's prepared."

Ras gave Mali a quick hug and then began to walk with her out of the office. Mali turned back before she walked away.

"Are you coming? When she goes into labor?" Mali asked Josephine.

"I'm not sure," Josephine said. "What do you think?"

Mali shrugged. "It's completely up to you. I'll bring Alex back for you."

Josephine opened the center drawer of her desk, where she kept a sterling silver hand mirror that had belonged to her great-great-grandmother, a Frenchwoman from Luxembourg for whom Josephine was named. She took out the mirror and held her chin up high, inspecting her face for any visible imperfections. She wore one layer of makeup more than she should. Which always seemed like half of what she needed. She checked each nostril, flashed a grin, and inspected her teeth. She placed the mirror back in the desk and closed it just as Mali was bringing Alex into her office.

"Alex, so good to see you!" Josephine said, standing up behind her desk and leaning over to hug her.

Alex shrugged out of her heavy winter coat, leaned over, and pecked Josephine's cheek. "I love your house," she said.

"It's home. Nothing special."

Alex snorted. "Right. The angels in the fountain on the front lawn? Nothing special about that."

Josephine giggled. "Okay, I'll admit that's a bit over the top."

"A little?"

"Yes, just a little."

"Let me ask you this," said Alex. "Does this property have a name?"

Josephine smiled and looked down at her desk.

"What is it?" Alex asked.

Josephine rolled her eyes. "Come on. Cut me a break. Ras and I have worked hard . . ."

"What's it called?" Alex asked.

Josephine mumbled something that Alex couldn't hear.

"What was that?"

"Duarte."

"After Juan Pablo Duarte?"

"You know your Dominican history."

"I love it," Alex said. She clicked on her recorder and turned it toward Josephine. "So is it worth it?"

Josephine pretended she didn't understand the question. "Worth what?"

"You have everything," Alex said, pointing behind Josephine's desk toward the pool and patio area. "You have money, power, and respect. But your husband is rarely home. Is it worth it?"

"I often daydream about snapping my fingers and going back to Ras's parents' house in Montclair—flat broke but happy."

"But in reality, you'd never trade this. Not for anything. Would you?"

Josephine looked down at her desk and adjusted some paper-work. She cleared her throat and then stood up and walked over to the rolling racks, where several of her gowns were hanging in various stages of completion.

"When Ras first began to sell records and make real money, I went shopping every day. It became a religion. I'd wake up, call a friend, my driver would take me from one mall to the next. I kept binders of everything I purchased. I had a stylist call me when some-thing I wanted was available. It was like having a full-time job!"

Josephine took a dress off the rack, a black satin evening gown that swept the floor. "And I would come home and try on my new clothes. And then lie on the sofa waiting for Ras to come home."

"You could travel too," Alex said.

Josephine rolled her eyes. "Travel. Please. Do you know how bor-ing the islands can be when you're alone? No fun in that. Trust me."

"Is that why you started your bridal line?"

"No husband wants to leave the house in the morning, kiss his wife on the cheek, and then come home and see her in the same spot where he left her. That just won't work."

Alex nodded slowly.

"I have to contribute to this household," Josephine said, turning her back to Alex and hanging up the dress. "I don't care that I only bring in one percent of the money. I have to do something."

"Why clothing?"

"Always I've designed clothes. Growing up in D.R. and spend-ing time in France, I dreamt of designing wedding dresses. I love rich fabrics, the tactile feeling of selecting the right brocade or the perfect handmade lace."

"You didn't have the same experience growing up in the Carib-bean that your husband did."

"You mean eating dirt cakes and selling tainted meat? No, I did not. Very different. Boarding school. Servants. Summer homes. The works."

"I know that in your culture, a woman of your . . . complexion wouldn't ordinarily—"

Josephine interrupted Alex. "My mother was five shades darker than Ras. My father's parents were horrified that he would marry someone so dark. My paternal grandmother raised me after my grandma died. And she got down on her hands and knees and begged me not to marry a *negro*."

"The color thing is that deep . . ." Alex whispered.

"No, it's deeper," Josephine said. "Can you imagine. My grandmother begging me not to marry someone black? The shame of having a child ruining all chances to continue lightening the line was more than she could bear."

Alex nodded. "I read a study that although ninety percent of the Dominican population has African roots, only eleven percent identify as black."

"I call that the Sammy Sosa effect," Josephine said, rolling her eyes.

Alex smiled and grimaced.

"Well, you and Ras have been together for a while," said Alex. "Is your grandmother over it now?"

"I'd imagine so. She's dead."

"I'm sorry."

"Don't be. I think she wanted to make sure I wouldn't have any babies at all. We've been trying since our wedding night and—" Josephine threw up her hands.

Alex shifted in her seat. "Josephine, I have to ask you about Cleo Wright. It's rumored that—"

Josephine raised a hand to stop Alex from speaking. "I don't talk about her. She doesn't exist to me."

"I just need to know if you ever—"

"Alex, have I not shared my story with you? I've told you everything you've asked. And more. Just don't ask me about her."

"But I'm trying to tell your story. People want to know about—"

"About what, Alex? They want to know that my husband cheated on me. Fine. Tell them. She's telling the whole goddamned world anyway." Josephine waved an arm like she was shooing Alex away. "Go on. Tell them about dumb Josephine."

"Why did you stay?"

"Would you stay with your man under the same circumstances?"

Alex looked down at the floor and shook her head. "No, I wouldn't. Maybe if only a few people knew about it. But not if—"

"Not if the woman was writing a book about it."

"Right. I don't know if we could live that down."

"I don't know if I can live it down either. He had a nickname for this girl. A *nickname*."

"What was it?"

"Marasa," Josephine said.

Alex wrinkled her eyebrows. "Marasa?"

"You know the name?"

"I did some work in Jamaica for my senior thesis."

"And?"

"And in Jamaican voodoo culture, everyone has a twin," Alex said. "It's called *marasa*. The former president of Jamaica said his successor was his twin. Something about one can't live on earth—or in the underworld—without the other."

Josephine nodded, tears welling up in her eyes. "You can imagine how it feels to find out your husband thinks of his mistress as his twin."

Alex turned a page in her notebook and began to scribble while talking. "So do you believe in this theory of twinship? Do you believe that Ras was drawn to Cleo because they shared a kinship?"

Josephine shrugged. "Ras could not resist her. That is all I know. I knelt on this floor at my husband's feet. I was bent from the waist, heaving and sobbing. Begging my husband not to walk out the door. He stepped over me and into Marasa's arms. I know my husband. I know him like I know myself. That man—during that time? That was not my husband."

"And so you feel like you can be with him today because . . ."

"Because that was not him, don't you understand? If he was in love with another woman, I would have left and not looked back. You can't come back from falling in love with someone else. But this was different."

Alex looked confused.

Josephine smiled. "My husband was unwell."

"And how did he recover?"

"I don't know for sure that he has."

Alex opened her mouth to ask a question just as Mali opened the door to Josephine's office.

"Mrs. Bennett," she said. "I need to speak to you in private."

Josephine was up from her desk before Mali finished speaking. "Excuse me," she said to Alex, without looking in her direction or waiting for a response.

Mali led Josephine to the kitchen, then turned to face her boss. Josephine put both hands on Mali's shoulders and leaned down a bit to look her directly in the eye.

"You heard from Marie? What's going on? Is she okay?"

"She's fine. Her water just broke."

Josephine put a hand to her mouth. All she could manage to say was "Oh."

"Now, Mrs. Bennett, they don't know how long it will take at this point. It could be hours."

"Right. I understand."

"My mother thought you might want to stay put and wait until things got moving before driving to the hospital."

Josephine nodded slowly. "Makes sense. Did you tell my husband?"

"Yes, he's on a conference call in his office. He said he's ready to go whenever you are."

Josephine tried to focus on breathing in and out. She was so anxious that she was two seconds away from wetting herself.

"Breathe, Mrs. Bennett."

"Thank you. I'm going to go upstairs for a moment. Can you please let Alex know that I've had an emergency?"

"Of course. I'll schedule another appointment."

"I forgot to tell you, Marie didn't go to Good Samaritan Hospital. She went to Valley instead."

Josephine froze. "Why?"

Mali shrugged. "I have no idea. Maybe she was afraid she wouldn't make it in time."

"But what about her obstetrician? Are we sure he has privileges there?"

"I'm sure it's fine," Mali said. "Don't worry."

"Don't worry. Don't worry. Don't worry," Josephine said. She brought her fingers to her mouth and chewed on the thick skin on the side of her thumb—a nasty habit that had been beaten out of her years earlier by the nuns at the Convent of the Daughters of Mary Queen Immaculate.

"I'll go speak with Ms. Maxwell."

"You know what? I will tell her. Thank you."

Josephine went down the hall to her office. Alex had her head buried in her notebook, scribbling furiously, when she walked in.

"Alex, my apologies. A lot of excitement happening here today."

"Good things, I hope?"

"What kind of story are you writing about me?"

"An honest one."

Josephine tossed her hair and grimaced. "The worst kind. Listen. You must be gentle with me."

"My kind aren't known for that," Alex said with a smile.

"I'm going to become a mother very soon," Josephine said. "And it's been quite a journey."

Just hearing herself say the sentence made her heart stretch out to fill her chest. Josephine had never given herself the luxury of saying it out loud: *I'm going to become a mother*. But after hearing that the young girl was in labor, she began to give herself some breathing room.

"Congratulations!" Alex said, scanning Josephine's midsection. "I thought you said—"

"Not from my body," Josephine said. "I've had some trouble. But a young girl from my hometown . . ."

Alex nodded. "Still a time to celebrate."

"Indeed. It's the only thing I have not been able to share with my husband. I know it's not politically correct to say this, but I don't feel like we're really a family without a child to complete us."

"Boy or girl?" Alex asked.

Josephine closed her eyes and turned her head toward the ceiling. "We didn't want to know. We'll take what we get."

"But secretly . . . ," Alex said in a soft voice.

Josephine whipped her head down to look at Alex. She bit her bottom lip and swooned. "Oh, a little girl would be so heavenly." She sighed.

"I can see you with a little girl," said Alex. "Decked out in couture on the way home from the hospital."

Josephine went to her desk, opened a cabinet on the right side, and pulled out a white leather box. She placed the box on her desk, lifted the lid, and moved aside some white tissue paper. She pulled out a tiny all-white dress in plush velvet with satin trim and a full crinoline underneath.

"Oh, Josephine," Alex gasped. "It's beautiful."

Josephine shrugged. "I had some leftover velvet. I was going to make it for a doll. But then it started to make sense as an outfit. If it's a boy . . ."

"You'll save it for the next one."

"From your lips to God's ears," Josephine whispered. "Alex, I hope I've given you enough for your story."

"More than enough. I didn't expect you to be so open with me."

"I figured this might be my only place to defend myself."

"What do you mean?"

"Well, once your book comes out . . ."

"My book?"

"Alex, you're ghostwriting that whore's book."

"How'd you know that?"

Josephine's eyes twinkled. She leaned back on her desk, crossed her arms, and smirked. "Same way I know I only got the cover of *S.O.C.A.* so that your man could get some time in the studio with my husband."

Alex's eyes widened and she attempted to think of something to blurt out that would make sense.

"Oh? You thought I was dumb? You don't think I know where most of my business comes from? You don't think I know that Kipenzi models for me every year so Jake can get a hit record from my husband?"

"That doesn't bother you?" Alex managed to ask, her eyes on the floor.

Josephine let a *pfft* fly out of her mouth. "It would only bother me if the checks didn't clear."

"Why'd you agree to let me interview you," Alex asked, "if you knew I was the one writing the book about Cleo?"

"I want you to know *me*. Understand *me*. I don't want to be a nameless, faceless victim in this *Vibe* story or in this woman's book."

Alex nodded.

"I have to go now. On my way to the hospital," Josephine said. "Thanks for coming."

"Good luck," Alex said. "I'll be thinking about you."

"Don't just think," Josephine said, holding out her arms and bringing in Alex for a hug. "Pray for me too."

eighteen

"Yo. Why are you here?" the man asked.

Cleo sat up, pushed her hair back out of her eyes, and exhaled. "What do you mean?"

"Why? Why do you do it? Mess around with men like this."

Cleo yawned. It was way too early for one of these conversations. "It's fun. I'm one of those women who just love sex." Cleo smiled hard. "It's a gift."

"That's a lie."

"Yeah, it is. What do you want? My whole sob story?"

"Who molested you?"

"Not a single soul."

"No woman does this for fun."

"I'm different."

"You make money off this?"

"I'm keeping my head above water."

"Making waves when you can?"

Cleo swung her body around to straddle the man in her bed. "You could say that," she said.

Cleo licked the man's neck and then leaned in to nibble at the salty skin behind his ear. She could feel his body relax beneath her. He put both his hands on her back and sighed.

He shifted, inserting himself in her and then moving swiftly. In five minutes he was done. She crawled off and lay beside him, listening to his breath begin to even out.

"What do you think they're saying in that song," he whispered to Cleo. He was half asleep and his voice was low and soft.

"What are you talking about?"

"*Good Times*. The song. You think they're saying 'hanging in and jiving' or 'hanging in a chow line'?"

Cleo knew the man was more asleep than awake. She wasn't sure if he was actually talking in his sleep or expecting an answer.

"I never really thought about it," she said.

The man's eyes fluttered open and then closed again. "It's 'hanging in and jiving,'" he said.

"How do you know?" Cleo asked.

The man began to snore softly. Cleo rolled her eyes and got up and dressed. She took out her camera phone, leaned in next to his face, and snapped a photo of herself kissing him on the cheek. Then she helped herself to a handful of the hundred-dollar bills he always kept in a knot in his pocket and let herself out.

KIPENZI HAD THE ENTIRE SPA AT CAP JULUCA SHUT DOWN FOR THE AFternoon. Seven of the fourteen full-time employees were given the day off, with pay. The other seven, all handpicked by Ian, were on deck to administer facials, manicures, pedicures, and deep-tissue massages to Kipenzi and Beth. They were all older than sixty, trained professionals who spoke not a single word of English, so the women could speak freely.

In the salon, the two women were swathed in monogrammed terry cloth robes, their heads wrapped in towels. They sat side by side at a manicurist's station. Kipenzi had landed the night before and called Beth from the back seat of the car service taking her to the private villa. Beth was staying with the boys at their home nearby. They'd made plans to meet the next morning, when the sitter arrived.

"It's been a week, Kipenzi. And I have no idea where Z is."

Beth looked over at her friend. The woman doing Kipenzi's nails was applying the clear top coat. Kipenzi was leaning over, watching each stroke.

"He's out here," said Kipenzi, her eyes on her nails. "You'd know if he wasn't."

"I think he's with this chick over in Saint Thomas. I know he messes with her sometimes when he comes out here. But I lost her number."

Kipenzi looked up from her nails. She wrinkled her eyebrows and blinked at Beth as if she didn't recognize her. "Why would you ever have some side chick's number?"

Beth shrugged. "She called me once or twice."

"And you talked to her? And kept her number? I swear I love you. But I just don't understand you." Kipenzi shook her head and then leaned over to look at her nails once more.

"You really think Jake is faithful to you, Kipenzi?"

Kipenzi's lips set into a thin line. She didn't turn her head in Beth's direction. "I'm pretty sure," she said.

"But he might be cheating. Right? He very well could be, right?" Beth knew she should just leave it alone. But she couldn't help it. She hated it when Kipenzi got judgmental.

"The truth is," Beth said, "Jake could be cheating on you. I know that Z's not always faithful to me. But I do know he's completely honest with me. I don't like the other women. But I hate crack more than I hate groupies."

"Actually, I'm thinking both should be equally offensive."

"I want Z to love me. That's all I've ever wanted. I want him to love me and only me. He doesn't love any of the other women he's ever been with."

"But he's had other children, affected your health . . . Isn't there another chick pregnant right now?"

"Now she's denying it's his baby."

"Um, good?" Kipenzi asked.

"Did you hear about the book, Kipenzi?"

Kipenzi clenched her teeth and turned to look at Beth. "Is Jake in it?"

"I have no idea."

"Don't lie to me."

"I swear. I don't know. I know Z's in it. I don't even have to ask."

"How do you know?"

"I've seen them photographed together before. And one of the engineers at the studio told me that a girl named Cleo did some interlude on his last album. Pretending like she was fucking him. Except she really was."

Kipenzi just nodded. "But you haven't heard anything about Jake . . ."

"No. I haven't. But God forbid your perfect husband was slumming with a groupie."

Kipenzi's eyes widened. "Yes, Beth. God forbid. Jake's not perfect. But I'm wrong to be worried about him being in this chick's book?"

"Are you concerned about him being in the book or knowing that he cheated?"

"Both."

"I think you could get over it if there was no book. You don't want your reputation tarnished. Don't want your business on Front Street."

"Can you blame me?"

Beth shrugged. "You knew what you were getting when you married him."

"I'm not like you," Kipenzi spat. "I'm not going to sit back and give my husband tacit permission to fuck other women." She shook her head. "No. I won't."

"I don't think Jake's in the book," Beth said. "He's not as stupid as my husband. But that doesn't mean he doesn't cheat on you. Jake gets pussy thrown at him on an hourly basis. I haven't met a man yet who consistently resists."

"Beth, I trust Jake. I wouldn't be with him if I didn't."

Beth nodded. "I know. Don't listen to me. I'm tripping. Z's got me all screwed up in the head. I got the kids here. No one knows where the hell he is."

"Beth. Do you think he's back on . . ."

Beth gave Kipenzi a stony look. She knew exactly what she was trying to ask but she wasn't going to make it easy for her. "On what?"

"Is he using again?"

"Why would you ask me that?"

Kipenzi rolled her eyes and spoke in a heavy whisper. "Oh for God's sake, Beth. You follow him to Anguilla while you're pregnant. The boys should be in school. Why else would you come chasing him out here if you weren't worried about that?"

"He left without telling me and I just thought it was weird."

"And now it's been a week and you still haven't seen him and you're not sure if he's back on that shit?"

"Why do you want to know? So you can tell Jake? He's still using you to spy on my husband?"

"Still? What do you mean, still? When did he ever do that?"

"Whatever. In Atlanta. He switched the order of the show and made Z open up for him."

"Beth. The promoters decided to alternate. Jake had no control over that. You know this."

"Whatever."

"Whatever?"

"You heard me. What-fucking-ever!"

Beth scraped her chair back, leaned forward to steady herself on the manicurist's station, and then stood up straight. "I didn't ask you to come out here and check on me."

Kipenzi looked down at her hands. "I know you didn't."

"So don't act like I owe you something."

"I'm your friend, Beth. I came out here because I'm your—"

Beth looked up, past Kipenzi, through the glass window of the spa. Z was standing there, watching them both. She felt rooted to her spot. He was standing on the grass, just off the walkway leading from the main building of the hotel down to the spa. Beth wondered how long he'd been standing there. His hair was long and matted, gray strands rippling through from the crown to his ears. His face had three deep cuts caked with blood and pus, under his left eye. He stood with both hands pressed flat against the window. He looked like he was under arrest and being patted down by police officers. Except he was alone, his eyes dead, his lips white, and the pinks of his palms pressed into the window.

"Baby?"

As soon as Beth whispered the word, Z began to slide down the window, his body crumpling. He slid farther, keeping his hands pressed against the window until his knees were on the ground.

"Baby!" Beth yelled out. She shuffled out of the spa and hurried around to the window. She bent down to grab Z just before he was completely in the grass.

"Fuck her," Z said. His voice was thick and his breath was hot and rancid.

Beth looked around the resort and saw the manager standing a few feet away, asking wordlessly if she needed help. Beth shook her head and held up a hand. The manager backed away, shooing away a few employees who were leaning in to get a look at Z and Beth. Beth leaned down as far as she could and tried to pull Z up.

"Yo. Fuck that bitch!" Z screamed, pointing through the window at Kipenzi, who sat watching in horror. The employees in the salon began to get nervous, whispering in Russian about leaving by the back door.

"Z, you're sick, baby," Beth pleaded. "Let's get you well."

"No."

Beth nodded and tried to pull Z's dead weight. "Yes, baby. You want me to get you some medicine?"

"I want you to leave me the fuck alone!"

Z grabbed the tiny metal ledge surrounding the building and hoisted himself up to a squat. He turned away from Beth, vomited in the grass, wiped his mouth with his hands, and then wiped them on his pants.

"I'm outta here."

"Yes, let's go."

"No. Not you. Go home."

"Listen, Z. You have to—"

Z's skinny arm shot out and he throttled Beth, slamming her back against the salon window. All the women in the salon screamed at once. All except Kipenzi, who just watched. The resort manager stepped over to Beth and Z.

"Sir, I'm going to have to ask you to leave the property."

"Z, please," Beth sobbed, and then began to gag.

"Go the fuck home, Beth. Take the kids. I don't need them to see me all fucked up and shit."

"Okay," Beth managed to choke out. "Just . . . le . . . Let. Me. Go . . ."

Z leaned in close and bared his teeth at his wife. "Stop fucking following me, Beth. I gotta do what I gotta do."

Beth didn't answer. She had no more breath in her throat to do so. She tried to use her eyes to say yes. He was gripping her neck so tight that she couldn't nod.

"You and your little friend get the fuck outta here." Z slid Beth's head over a few inches so he could see Kipenzi. "And you, ugly bitch, you can tell Jake I said *fuck him*!"

Kipenzi sat in the chair, nostrils flared, chest heaving. But the rest of her body was still. She didn't dare move. Z loosened his grip on his wife's neck but didn't completely let go.

"Go back to New York, Beth," he muttered under his breath. "You hear me?"

"No."

"Take the boys home," Z said, panic rising in his voice.

Beth's voice was flat and even. "No, Z. I'm not leaving."

Z dropped his hand from her neck and it hung at his side, as if he could no longer use it. He looked Beth in her eyes, then turned away and began to cry.

"I don't want to be here, Beth," he said, sobbing. He put his hands on his knees to steady himself as his cries racked his body, causing his back to spasm. "Oh Jesus, I don't want to do this to you . . . to the baby, to the boys . . . I just can't stop. Why can't I stop, Beth?"

Beth turned her head just an inch to the left. In her peripheral vision she could see Kipenzi, her arms still crossed, her eyes still fixed on Z. Beth knew Kipenzi had to see her glance over, but her friend did not move.

Z continued to cry until he began to heave and catch ragged breaths instead. As Beth continued to offer him words of comfort and occasional back pats, the manager approached.

"Mrs. Saddlebrook, I've called the authorities and they are on the way. I'm sorry. But we need to remove your husband from the property. There are photographers on the property as well. I'm trying to have them removed."

"Baby, we gotta get outta here," Beth said. "Did you drive here?"

Z looked up at Beth as if he'd never seen her before in his life. "I want to see my mom," he moaned.

"Your mom is not here," Beth said, lifting him up. She walked Z over to a bar near the pool and sat him down.

"He's okay," she said to the young girl behind the bar, who was supposed to be preparing a piña colada. But she simply stared at Z with her mouth open.

"He just needs something to eat. Do you have a piece of fruit?"

The bartender reached under the counter without taking her eyes off Z and produced a banana.

"Eat this," Beth said. "I'll be right back."

She went back into the spa, holding her head high, and walked over to where Kipenzi was sitting. Neither of them said a word. Kipenzi was still staring at the spot where Z had slammed Beth against the window. She narrowed her eyes and gritted her teeth, as if the scene from two minutes before was playing on a loop in her mind. Without moving her head or averting her gaze, Kipenzi reached into her bag and took out a pair of car keys.

"Here's the key to my rental," she said. "You can leave it at your house and I'll have someone pick it up and bring it back."

Kipenzi held the keys in the air. After a half-second pause, Beth took them and closed her hands around them.

Beth opened her mouth and then shut it.

"It's fine. Just go."

Beth's nostrils flared. She kept her head high as she walked slowly out of the salon. But she quickened her step back to the bar, where Z was slumped over the counter. Just as she got to where Z was sitting, she saw the manager leading two uninformed officers along the walkway leading to the spa.

"They tryin' to lock me up?" Z asked, his mouth thick with phlegm.

Beth did not answer him. She noticed an employees' entrance to the hotel's main restaurant.

"This way," she said, pulling him up and draping his arm across her shoulders.

"Excuse me, miss," said the young woman at the bar. "You can't go in—"

Beth turned to look at her. And the girl couldn't even complete her thought. Beth knew the girl was taking them in—her swollen belly, the kerchief covering her hair, and the crackhead, whose head kept lolling back, forcing her to readjust his body weight so he didn't fall.

Beth turned back around and walked through the back entrance to the kitchen. They walked straight across and out an exit that led to the main parking lot and came around to the front of the building, where Kipenzi had parked her car, right behind where the Anguillan police sedan now sat.

She clicked the alarm on the roadster and eased Z into the front seat. As soon as he was adjusted, he began coughing hard. Beth found a tissue in the glove compartment. He spat into it and the phlegm was tinged with blood.

"I'm so sorry, baby," Z whispered.

"We're going to take care of you," Beth said.

"I'm not even worth it. I promised you I was gonna take care of you. I'm all fucked up."

"When did you start using again?" Beth asked, as she steered the car onto the main road that circled the island.

"Don't remember."

"When's the last time?"

Z pulled the lever to let his seat go back and then winced and covered his eyes with his hands. "A week ago."

Beth took her eyes off the road just long enough to look at her husband. "You haven't used out here?"

He shook his head. "I came down here to try to detox, baby. I'm fucking dying right now."

Z cried softly and leaned against the window. Beth carefully pulled to the side of the road and turned the car off. She leaned over as much as her belly would allow and cradled her husband's head.

"Why didn't you tell me?"

"I'm just tired, Beth. I'm tired of using. Tired of needing that shit."

Z dug into the pockets of his filthy jeans and pulled out a crumpled piece of paper. Beth smoothed it out. There was an Anguillan address written in Z's graffitilike script, the name of a D. Smith, and a four-digit number.

"What is this?"

"Just take me there. Now."

Beth plugged the address into the GPS system and followed the directions. They led her to a hilltop a few miles inland. A white gate with the name SMITH etched inside was closed and locked. There was a keypad at window level. She looked over at Z, who pointed to the crumpled paper again. She punched in the four-digit number under the address and the white gates swung open slowly.

"Z, what is this?"

Z kept his eyes half closed and just waved a hand at his wife. "Drive."

When Beth pulled up to a circular driveway, there was a tall, elderly, dark-skinned black man with curly white hair standing at the entrance with a clipboard. He looked as if he was expecting Beth—or someone. He stepped to the driver's side of the car as soon as Beth put the car in park.

"Mrs. Saddlebrook?"

Beth looked over at Z again. His eyes were still shut tight.

"Yes, I'm Beth."

The man opened the door and beckoned Beth to get out. A young man who looked like he could be the older man's son appeared on Z's side and eased him out of the car and into the large white house.

"This is Eden."

"Rehab?"

"You can call it that."

"Was Z ordered to come here?"

"We don't accept court-appointed rehab patients," the man said. "We only accept people who are ready. They have to get here on their own and check themselves in."

"My husband came to Anguilla to go to rehab?"

"Yes, ma'am. I found him passed out on the front steps a week ago. I put him in one of our rooms and prepared for him to detox. The next morning he told me he wanted to detox on his own and that he would be back when the drugs were out of his system."

"And he left."

"He did. And now he's back. You should be very proud of your husband. I'm not sure how he did it, but he did the worst part on his own."

Beth squinted in the bright sunshine and looked up at the house. "Now what?"

"Now we work on repairing him. Making him ready to deal with the demons that led him to drugs in the first place." The man smiled and offered his hand. "I'm Dr. Smith."

Beth shook his hand. "Thank you."

"Thank your husband." The doctor gestured to Beth's belly. "He told me the child you are carrying would never know him as a drug addict. He came here on his own. I think he wanted to do this without burdening you. I believe his goal was to get himself cleaned up in time for your delivery and not let you see him until then."

"My husband has been sick for a long time. And it's not just drugs."

The doctor nodded. "Your husband has a lot to recover from."

"And you think he can be saved?"

"*Saved* is not the right word."

"He can be helped?"

The doctor led Beth back to the door of her car. "He can help himself."

BETH STAYED IN ANGUILLA, TAKING THE BOYS TO THE BEACH, SHOPPING downtown, and going to the spa for prenatal massages. A massive snowstorm had hit New York and she was in no hurry to get out of the sun.

She'd had the boys' teachers send assignments and hired a local woman to tutor them. Bunny popped up. And though she had her own room at a local bed and breakfast, she was up under Zander whenever he wasn't being tutored. They spent hours together in the only studio on the island. Beth rolled her eyes whenever the girl came around but stayed silent. She was losing her hold on Zander.

And if she told him not to see this chick, it would be World War III. Beth could only deal with one catastrophe at a time.

She wasn't sure Kipenzi had left the island until she saw her on BET's *106 & Park* a few days after Z's breakdown. She put the television on mute and simply watched her friend's movements for a few minutes and then turned the set off.

After a month, she knew she had to get back home. She began packing their things, sending most of them ahead of her so she wouldn't have to deal with luggage. She called Boo back at home and told him to book tickets for everyone and inform the boys' teachers that they would be returning to school on the following Monday morning with all the completed assignments.

On the night before her flight was to leave, she called Eden to leave a message for Z.

"Your husband's not here at the moment," the doctor said.

Beth's heart dropped. "He left? Is he still . . . in treatment?"

"Yes. But he is free to come and go as he pleases. He usually takes a walk after dinner and before bed."

"I'm flying back home tomorrow. I just wanted him to know that. And I want him to know that I love him and that I'm pulling for him."

"You should work on yourself too, Mrs. Saddlebrook."

Before Beth could ask him what he meant by that, there was a knock on the door to the villa. The entrance was heavily guarded and she knew security would never let anyone inside except Kipenzi. Or Z.

Beth dropped the phone and dashed across to the front door. She looked through the peephole and saw her husband. She threw open the door and grabbed him around the neck.

"Damn, girl. Slow down!" Z laughed and rocked his body side to side, holding his wife tight in his arms.

Beth moved back and covered her mouth with both hands. Z smiled and turned in a slow circle.

"I clean up pretty good, right?"

Beth drank in her husband's new look. His skin was shiny and clear. He was wearing stiff, dark denim shorts that actually fit. They weren't sliding off his butt as usual. He was wearing a plain white V-neck T-shirt and had the nerve to even have on leather huaraches. The man who believed that construction boots were perfectly fine beachwear was wearing *sandals*. The bushy afro was gone. His hair was in a tight Caesar and shaped up expertly.

But what made Beth cry was his eyes. For years they'd had a dull lifelessness to them. The whites of his eyes were usually yellow, the pupils often dilated. There was often mucus or other foreign matter in the corners of his eyes. And they were always shifting. He had trouble making direct eye contact and he was always squinting.

As he stood in the living room of the villa, he looked at his wife with wide, clear brown eyes. And a soft, sincere smile that took up his whole face.

"Did you miss me?" Z asked.

"I don't think I've seen this version of you since I was seventeen," Beth said, tears streaming down her face.

"This is the only me you will ever see," Z said, wiping his wife's face with his hand. "I can promise you that."

"Can we go home now?" Beth asked. "We're all packed. The boys are ready too."

"You guys go. I need more time. At least a month. Maybe more."

"But the baby . . ."

"Beth. If you go into labor and I miss the birth of our daughter, so be it. I will be there for her, for you, for all of us, forever. I can't rush this. I can't leave here until I know I'm ready."

Beth nodded and looked at her husband's outfit once again. "I love your outfit. You went shopping?"

Z shook his head. "Kipenzi sent me a new wardrobe."

"Really?"

"Yeah. With a note. Said she loved me. And that she was proud of me."

Beth felt her eyes welling up again.

Z looked down at his feet. "After how I talked to her that day when I was detoxing, I didn't deserve anything from her. She's a good woman."

Beth nodded. "She is."

"She gave me something else," Z said, reaching into a canvas messenger bag. He pulled out a CD. "It's the new single she's putting out on her farewell compilation."

"You're doing a verse?"

"Did it already. Recorded it at the studio out here."

"And she didn't get Jake to do it?"

"She said she wanted me. Thought I might need some work."

"And you're happy with it?"

Z smiled. "Shit is fire."

Beth grabbed the CD and placed it on top of her carry-on bag. "I'll be the judge of that."

"Go home, baby," Z said, pulling Beth in for another hug. "Let me do this."

Beth took both her husband's hands into her own and kissed his fingers. "I'm so proud of you."

"It's because of the baby," Z said. "A girl . . . a girl is different. I just couldn't have my daughter seeing me like that. I feel like I already know her. I feel like I know what she looks like, what she sounds like. I couldn't look this little girl in the eye until I got my shit right."

"Z, you're killing me with this. We don't know if it's a girl!"

"I know," Z said, stroking Beth's hair. "Maybe you don't know. But I do."

nineteen

ON THE FIRST WARM DAY IN MARCH, ZANDER AND BUNNY SAT ON THE bed of her attic bedroom, staring at the stick.

"Why didn't you just get the one that said pregnant or not pregnant?" Bunny said.

"Why didn't you just take the pill like you said you would?"

"Why didn't you just wear a condom anyway like you said you would?"

Zander and Bunny glared at each other and then both looked back down at the stick, resting between them on the bed on a folded paper towel.

"Robert said Universal and Interscope both have firm deals on the table for me," Bunny said, chewing on her thumbnail and staring at the test.

"I know. They both want me too."

"You wanna be on the same label?"

"Makes sense. I guess." Zander didn't move his eyes from the stick.

"You wanna be a father?" Bunny asked.

"No."

Bunny's heartbeat quickened. Of course he didn't want to be a father. They were both teenagers. She didn't want to be a mother either. But Zander didn't say it right. He just said no. He was supposed to say, *Yes, but not right now*.

"I could have this baby and still do my thing," Bunny said. "I'm not even done recording yet. By the time I had a firm deal and a finished album, the baby would be born and I'd be ready to go."

Zander looked at Bunny. "Hell no," he said. "We can't have no fucking baby."

"Why you gotta say it like that?" Bunny jumped off the bed and stood over Zander, her hand pulled back.

"Don't hit me, Bunny. I told you about that shit. I'll be wrong if I—"

Bunny socked Zander in the shoulder as hard as she could. Zander grabbed his arm and fell over on the bed.

"Why the *fuck* are you always doing that shit!" Zander barked. He scrambled off the bed, tackled Bunny onto the floor, and held her neck in his hands.

"Put a mark on me and I'll have you in jail in thirty minutes," Bunny said, her voice smooth and even.

"You love putting your hands on me and then threatening that shit!"

"*Rob!*" Bunny screamed.

Zander put a hand over Bunny's mouth, listening for anyone coming upstairs. When no one came running up, he pulled Bunny to her feet and then shoved her. Bunny smiled.

"Stop hitting me, Bunny."

"Okay."

"I mean it. That shit is not cool."

"Whatever. You know you—"

Bunny's cell phone alarm went off and they both stopped and looked at the pregnancy test again.

"It's two lines," Zander said, picking up the box. "Is that good or bad?"

"I guess that would depend on how you're looking at it," Bunny said.

"But one line is lighter than the other," said Zander. "What the hell does that mean?"

Bunny scanned the box and then threw it on the bed. "I'm pregnant, Zander. Now what?"

"Now we make you an appointment to handle this."

"Just like that? We don't talk about it?"

"What is there to talk about? You're seventeen! We're both about to get signed to major deals. This is not baby time."

"Can you see yourself ever having a baby with me?"

Zander closed his eyes and remembered a story his father had told him about telling a groupie what she wanted to hear so you could get what you wanted. But he'd never thought of Bunny as a groupie.

"Yeah, I can see that. Not right now. But after we both get established. We could make a little superstar." Zander tried to smile.

"Lying ass," Bunny said, pushing past Zander and going into the bathroom. She closed the door behind her and locked it.

"I'm not lying," Zander pleaded. "In a few years, if we're still . . ."

Bunny opened up the bathroom door just enough for Zander to see that she was crying. "Get out of my house, Zander," she said.

"Are we going to . . . make an appointment? I mean, don't wait too long . . ."

"Get *out*."

Bunny slammed the door and Zander could hear her sobbing. He sank down to the floor, his back against Bunny's bathroom door. He dropped his head into his hands, Bunny's cries piercing him. He waited for them to subside. Then, when he heard her calming down and running bathwater, he slipped out of her room and out of the Greenwich home.

◆　◆　◆

"So you're saying I can't be a member because I'm not fifty?" Kipenzi asked Ian.

"AARP is for people over the age of fifty," Ian said. He was sitting at Kipenzi's dining room table, arranging photos of Kipenzi's outfits for a spring museum exhibit at FIT.

"I thought AARP was for retired people," Kipenzi said.

"It is."

"Well, that's me. I'm retired."

"Yes. But you're only thirty."

"Doesn't AARP stand for American Association of *Retired* Persons?"

"Actually, no. It used to. But it's no longer an acronym."

"What are you talking about? What does it stand for now?"

"Well, when I called, they told me it doesn't stand for anything. It's not an acronym now. They're just . . . the AARP."

"That doesn't make any sense. Do they now call it *arp*?"

"No. They still call it A-A-R-P."

"So those letters have to stand for something!"

"I'm just telling you what the woman told me, Ms. Hill," Ian said. "You have to be over fifty, period. Retired or not. I know you think it would be cute to have your little AARP card to show you're really retired. But you can't. Sorry."

Ian didn't even look up from his binder. He was the only person, besides her husband and Beth, who could tell her no without feeling like he was going to lose his place in her life.

"I was totally looking forward to using my AARP card to get a discount at the movie theater."

Ian rolled his eyes. "I know. 'Cause you're on a fixed income now, right?"

"Is Beth back in town?" Kipenzi asked.

"Yes. She's staying close to home. Doing well. I spoke to her nanny this morning. You could call her, you know."

"Not yet. I want to give her some space. It was ugly in Anguilla. Do you know how Z's doing?"

"That I don't know. Have you asked your husband?"

"Not yet."

"I heard your song this morning," Ian said. "The one with Z on it."

"It didn't ship yet!" Kipenzi yelled. "You heard it where?"

Ian waved a hand dismissively. "My dial accidentally ended up on one of those loud rap stations. They were having a call-in contest. Hot or Not or some such nonsense."

"Right. Accidentally landed there."

"You'll be happy to know that the song received a ninety percent 'hot' rating."

Kipenzi climbed onto the bar stool in the kitchen and fiddled with her phone. "I wonder if Beth knows. This could be big for Z."

"I'm sure she knows. And I'm sure she appreciates you taking a chance on her husband when he was at his lowest point."

"I've always loved Z as a rapper. His voice. His lyrics. He's always been dope to me. Even better than Jake in some ways. Though I'd never tell Jake that."

"You don't have to. He knows."

"Can you have a tailor come by the house this afternoon? All my pants are too long."

"Did you shrink?"

"Kinda. I've been wondering why all my pants have been dragging the ground lately. Just realized it's because I'm not wearing stilettos every day! I'm wearing comfortable flat shoes and now all my pants are too long."

Ian flipped through the appropriate binder. "I'll have someone here by six."

Kipenzi's phone buzzed on the counter and she flipped it open. She read a text message and then crinkled her brow.

"It's Zander. He's downstairs. Needs to talk to me. Can you tell security to send him up?"

Kipenzi walked over to the living room and sat down, arranging pillows behind her back. In five minutes Ian was leading Zander into the living room.

"Auntie Penzi, I'm sorry I didn't call you first."

"You don't have to call first, Zander. Give me a hug."

He hugged her stiffly and Kipenzi thought about the day she babysat him when he was eleven. He'd eaten a live goldfish out of her tank on a dare from Jake. She had taken him to the emergency room to get his stomach pumped and the doctor laughed at her. Their picture had been in all the tabloids that week, with captions that got the story all wrong. One magazine said he'd been poisoned. Beth had never let her live it down and even framed one of the stories and hung it up in Zander's room.

"I got followed here by a photographer," Zander said, his eyes wide in amazement.

"Tall, dark curly hair?"

"Yeah."

"Jackson," Kipenzi said. "My own personal paparazzo. That's what happens when you get a million views on YouTube and a bidding war for your debut album."

"How much do you think Jackson's getting for a picture of me?"

"Right now? Probably a thousand dollars."

"Word? I'm gonna start telling him where I am and splitting the profits. Didn't Britney do that?"

Kipenzi laughed. "Why are you here, Zander?"

"It's a few things, actually."

Kipenzi narrowed her eyes and twisted her lips to one side. "How far along is she?" she asked dryly.

Zander hung his head. "I think like six weeks."

Kipenzi shook her head back and forth very slowly. "Bunny?"

"Yeah."

Kipenzi dropped her head in her hands. "What about her career? She's got so much talent. Please don't tell me she's keeping this baby."

"We don't know what to do yet."

"What about *your* career, Zan? You can't remake your image. Once you're a father, you lose an entire fan base."

"I know," Zander said.

"And I'm not a big fan of Bunny," Kipenzi said. "She's dying to get you locked up for hitting her. And you played right into her hands."

"Nah, things are better now. But I have another . . . situation."

"You've gotta be fucking kidding me. Someone else is pregnant too?"

"I don't even know this other chick. She's saying it's mine but I don't know for sure."

"Zander, what has your Uncle Jake been telling you since you were thirteen?"

"Bitches ain't shit but hos and tricks?"

Kipenzi's face was blank.

"Sorry."

"Can you give me a translation for mixed company?"

"Uncle Jake said that no woman can be fully trusted."

"So why on earth would you have unprotected sex with some random girl?"

"I did have a condom on . . . the first time."

"Is this the one your mother caught you with?"

"Yeah."

"Are you ready to be a father?"

"No. Not at all."

"So. Now what?"

"I need three hundred dollars for an abortion for the sidepiece chick. I can't get more than two hundred from my account without my mom's or dad's signature."

"And you came to me. Not Uncle Jake."

"Uncle Jake would kill me. I'm supposed to be smarter than this."

"Indeed," Kipenzi said, rolling her eyes and reaching for her bag. She took out a business card. "Call this doctor and make an appointment." She waved the card in Ian's direction, who nodded and opened his cell phone. "He'll be expecting your call. He can take care of it first thing in the morning. Make sure you go with her, stay with her, and take care of her for a day or two afterward. No need to get her all bitter and blow up your spot."

Zander nodded his head and held the card in his hand.

"And what are you going to do about Bunny?" Kipenzi said.

"I don't know yet. Puff's talking about signing her . . ."

"Does she know this other girl's pregnant?"

"No."

Kipenzi sat up straight on the sofa and leaned over, her hands folded in her lap. "Zander, listen to me. You don't get a second chance to start in this game. Everyone is watching you right now. You know Steve Stoute?"

"Yeah."

"He can get you endorsement deals with any brand you can think of, if you're polished and drama-free. I've made more money from his deals than any note I've ever sung."

"I know, Auntie, it's just that—"

"I'm not saying you can't do dirt. You will. That's a part of growing up. But you don't have the same freedom as your friends. Your every fuckup is being chronicled. If you're serious about your career, you can't ever forget that. You are a brand. Zander, Inc. Every move you make should consider that. Every time you walk out the door, remember you are a walking advertisement for your brand. I know your mom's been telling you this stuff."

"I've been going through some stuff with my mom. We haven't been really getting along."

"Actually, you've been a certified jerk toward your mom for months now."

"She acts like she wants my dad to stay an addict. So she can always come in and save the day. Gets on my nerves."

"What right do you have to judge your mother for how she treats your father? That's none of your business."

"He treats her like sh—crap. And she just takes it."

"How's that your business?"

"I don't respect her."

"Doesn't give you the right to curse her out."

"Auntie Penzie, I heard there's this book coming out."

Kipenzi let out a breath and leaned her head back on the sofa. "Yeah."

"I think my dad might be in it. And I just think it might make things . . . weird."

"I can't tell you all your parents' business," Kipenzi said. "But I don't think you should worry about that book."

Kipenzi cleared a place on her coffee table as Ian brought over a sterling silver tray with tea service for two. He dropped two sugar cubes in each teacup, poured tea, and then went back to the kitchen. Kipenzi took a sip, closing her eyes for a long second before sitting back on the sofa.

"If your dad is in it—and I'm not saying he is or he isn't—I think your parents are both prepared to deal with the fallout."

Zander drummed his fingers on the coffee table and glanced up at the plasma television above the sofa.

"He might start using again over this book," he said, eyes on the television.

"If so, he wasn't really ready to be clean," Kipenzi said. "You can't stay clean just when life is going according to plan. You have to stay clean when everything's fucked up too."

Zander nodded. "Do you care about the book?" he asked. "I mean, you know, do you think . . ."

"Do I think Jake's in there? No. Do I care? Yes. I would be devastated."

"I don't know any men that don't cheat, Auntie Penzi."

"That's beside the point. Cheating is one thing. And cheating with someone like Cleo Wright is something very different."

"Seems the same to me."

"Let me give you a lesson in women right now. Deep inside, we never believe you will be one hundred percent faithful. We want you to. We expect you to. But we know. We know that you are primal, sinful animals who think with your penises. We just don't want to be disrespected. Or embarrassed. Or humiliated. Don't bring us any diseases, outside babies, or unwanted attention."

"My father's done all three to my mom—and more."

"He's starting over, Zander. Let him start over."

Kipenzi put a hand over her chest and exhaled. "I haven't talked to your mom since we were all in Anguilla. And it was . . . tense. I miss her."

"She misses you too."

"You are going to make such a good big brother."

"I haven't done such a good job of it so far."

"You're starting over too, Zander. Give yourself a chance to start over. Hell, we're all starting over."

Kipenzi threw an arm around Zander's shoulders and squeezed him tight. She took the elevator to the lobby with him. They both looked up at the numbers and watched them light up until they reached the first floor.

ALEX LOVED VISITING THE EDITOR IN CHIEF'S OFFICE AT *VIBE*. MARIA had the corner office, with bamboo shades covering the windows that looked out onto midtown Manhattan. Alex felt important and special whenever she had to meet with anyone in person. It was one of the few times she allowed herself to revel in her profession. When she was seven, she'd sit at her kitchen table with a typewriter that didn't work and pretend to have a meeting with an editor about a book she was writing. She thought of those quiet moments and her pretend meetings whenever she had a real meeting.

She waited in the lobby, her bag between her legs, while her back rested against the black leather couch. After a whirlwind month of preparing for her wedding, trying to pin down interviews with the wives, and keeping the home life intact, she was in a perpetual fog. Hours ago she'd woken up to Birdie stroking her thigh and breathing heavily into her neck. She'd brushed him off much more severely than she'd meant to, but she needed to make it clear—it wasn't happening.

With her eyes still closed, Alex made a mental note to

apologize to Birdie as soon as she got home. It wasn't his fault that she was—

"Alex, girl, are you asleep?"

Alex jerked and opened her eyes to see Maria standing on the staircase in front of her.

"Just resting my eyes," Alex said, leaping up from her seat and tripping over her bag. She righted herself, shook her head, and laughed. "It's one of those days."

"Every day is one of those days," Maria said. "Come on up. The magazine is going to the printer in two days, so we're all stressed."

Alex followed Maria up the staircase and waited as the editor held her magnetic card to the reader and pulled the door.

As soon as Alex sat down, Maria looked at her watch and made a face. "Alex, I have seven minutes to talk to you before I have to meet with my photo department. So let's skip the formalities."

"Wait. First, I have a present for you," Alex said, reaching into her bag and pulling out a shoe box.

"What's this?" Maria asked, reaching out for the box.

"I'm writing a story on Jake for the *New York Times.* One of his boys sent me a thank-you note for settling a bet between them."

Maria opened the box and pretended to faint.

"Jake's first shoe?! Original? Never worn? Holy shit!"

Alex nodded her head and smiled. "Enjoy."

"So how's the story coming along?" said Maria, clutching the shoe box to her chest. "Have you interviewed all the wives we talked about?"

Alex cleared her throat. "Almost."

Maria shook her head and frowned. "I don't like that word."

Alex held up her hand. "I'm spending time in their world, which counts for something."

"It does," Maria said. "Who've you actually met?"

"I had a great interview with Josephine Bennett."

Maria nodded. "Well, what's she like? Ras Bennett's got more money than God. Does she just spend it all day?"

"She designs bridal gowns."

Maria grimaced. "Right. I think I saw that. She's not serious, is she?"

Alex felt a twinge of something she could not name. "Yes, she is actually. And she's good."

Maria smiled wide. "Getting close to the subject? Sound a little defensive."

"I met Kipenzi Hill a few weeks ago."

Maria's eyes widened. "You did not."

"I did."

"Her publicist told me there was no chance in hell we could talk to her for this story," said Maria.

"I wasn't doing this story. I went to his office for the *New York Times* interview and—"

"Get outta here," Maria yelled, smacking her hand on her desk. "She was there?"

"Splayed out on his sofa reading a magazine."

"Niiiice. Did she talk to you?"

"A bit."

Maria squinted at Alex. "Enough?"

Alex couldn't help but smile. "I think so."

Maria clapped her hands once and then stood up. "Thanks for coming in, Alex. I'm really looking forward to reading this."

"Me too."

"You've made some headway with Kipenzi. You've interviewed Josephine."

"She has a baby due any day now."

"I didn't know she was pregnant."

"She's not. She's adopting."

"Wow. Nice twist. What about Beth?"

"I've been to the house. I've seen . . . a lot."

"From what I hear, life with Z can be complicated."

"That's an understatment."

"And the son, I'm hearing he's signing with Universal."

"Is that definite?" Alex asked.

"Looks like it. His buzz just from the online videos is through the roof. And he's dating Bunny Clifton, which is adorable. So it's turning into a cute family story."

"Except . . ."

"Except Z is a crackhead, I know. That's what makes it a *juicy* family story, my favorite kind."

Alex nodded.

"Now. Did you ask them all about the Cleo book?"

Alex swallowed hard. "Well, I didn't ask Kipenzi since she was standing right next to Jake when I talked to her."

"What about Beth?"

"She's in denial. About a lot of things."

"And Josephine?"

"She knows. She knows everything." Alex felt light-headed and ran a hand over her face.

"Are you okay?" Maria asked.

"I'm cool. It's a tough story, you know?"

"I can imagine. Especially for you."

Alex's stomach dropped. "Especially for me?"

Maria leaned in even closer. "My sister works for Simonstein Publishing. She told me you're writing the book."

Alex smiled weakly. "You knew all along, didn't you?" she asked.

"Maybe," Maria said. "Now, have you heard about some kind of initiation thing with anyone who wants to work with Ras Bennett? My sister said if you want to work with him, you have to get a blow job from this Cleo chick."

A lump formed in Alex's throat. An initiation? For anyone who worked with him? Her mind raced, trying to remember what Birdie had said about his studio session with Ras. Had he come straight home that night? Had he even played her whatever they had worked on? She couldn't remember. What she did know was that in the canvas tote bag sitting at her feet was Cleo's manuscript. And she knew that Cleo had never mentioned any kind of initiation.

"Alex, can I ask you a question?" Maria asked, her eyes on the floor.

Alex didn't answer. She just put one hand over her eyes and waited.

"Is it true that you're engaged to Birdie?" Maria said.

Alex exhaled. "What happens if I say yes?"

"I knew it! Why didn't you tell us?"

"I wasn't sure if it was really relevant."

Maria laughed out loud. "You're marrying a rapper and you weren't sure if it was relevant? You've gotta be kidding me."

"I don't talk about it—ever. I keep my personal life really private."

"And yet."

"Right. I'm stalking three women to make them open up to me. I'm aware of the irony."

Maria shook her head slowly from side to side. "You've gotta write this story in the first person. I want to know what you've learned from these women. How it relates to your own life. How would you feel if Birdie was in this book?"

"That's hard for me. I'm not sure I really want to—"

A young redhead with silver hoops that brushed her shoulders popped her head into Maria's office. "They need you to sign off on the cover. Ten minutes in Henry's office."

Maria nodded and stood up still clutching her shoebox tight under her arm. She took a PDA out of her purse and began furiously typing while heading out the door of her office. She'd switched gears so suddenly that she didn't even realize she hadn't said good-bye or that Alex was still in her office.

Alex stayed in the chair across from Maria's desk, collecting her thoughts and watching midtown Manhattan in rush hour. She looked down into her bag and glanced at the manuscript she had to give to Cleo later on that day. It was full of every perverted story Cleo told her over the past few months. Cleo had told her flat out that she'd been with ninety percent of all the rappers in the tristate area. And Birdie had looked her in the eye and said he'd never go near her. But this initiation story . . .

Alex stuck her hand into a side pocket of her bag for her cell phone as she took the stairs two at a time out of the offices of *Vibe*.

"Cleo, this is Alex."

"What's up? We're still on for two, right?"

"I need to know if we can meet earlier. I have to talk to you about something."

"What's the problem?"

"I'd like to talk to you in person."

"Alex, do you want to know if I ever fucked your boyfriend?"

Alex stopped at the top of the stairs for the subway platform. "Yeah, as a matter of fact, I would like to know that."

"I'll see you in thirty minutes," Cleo said before hanging up.

By the time Alex got to the diner, Cleo was already there, calmly adding Splenda packets to a cup of coffee, stirring, sipping, and adding more packets.

Alex slid into the booth, stripping off her raincoat and dragging her bag next to her. "You drink way too much coffee," she said.

"I like coffee," Cleo said with a shrug. She leaned away from her coffee to sneeze, then went back to adding more sweetener.

"If you're sick, you should probably drink tea," Alex offered. Her voice was measured and steely.

"I never drink tea. Ever," Cleo said.

"What you got against tea?" Alex asked. She didn't take her eyes off Cleo.

Cleo finally dragged her eyes up to meet Alex's. She inhaled, exhaled, and then looked up at the ceiling.

"Alex, my story is typical. My father's a jerk. Mom left. Blah blah blah."

Alex bit down on the inside of her cheek to keep from speaking.

Cleo hugged herself and smiled. "When I was really young, I'd watch television with my dad. We never watched anything I wanted to see. But I would just sit nearby and watch with him just to be close to him. He loved Angie Dickinson on that show *Police Woman* and he loved the two chicks from *Cagney and Lacey*. Every time they took some bad guy down he would say, 'Damn! That girl don't take no tea for the fever!'"

"What does that mean?" Alex asked.

Cleo shrugged. "He never told me. I never asked. But I think it means, you know, they're so bad-ass that they don't need hot tea when they're sick. They just barrel through it. I so wanted to be that kind of woman in my dad's eyes. I wanted him to look at me and grunt and say, 'My little girl? She's tough as nails. Don't take no tea for the fever.'"

"Some people would say you are like that," Alex said through clenched teeth.

"Nope. I'm not. But I want to be. So I don't drink tea when I'm sick. I just barrel through it."

"So did you?" Alex asked.

Cleo looked up and shook a Splenda packet, ripped it open, and put a few granules in her cup. "Did I what?"

"Bitch, don't play with me."

Cleo opened her mouth wide in mock horror. "Alex, I didn't know you had it in you."

"Answer the question."

"You didn't ask me one."

"Have you ever had sex with Peter 'Birdie' Washington?"

Cleo took a sip of coffee, locking eyes with Alex the entire time. When she was done, she dabbed at her mouth with a napkin and placed it in her lap. "I've never understood that. Why do the women come to me? Why do they ask me? I don't owe them shit. It's the husbands and boyfriends they should ask. Not me."

"Maybe I did ask him."

"If you did and he said yes, you wouldn't be asking me. If he said no and you don't believe him, then you have a problem."

"I want to hear *your* answer out of *your* mouth."

"Did I fuck your man? No."

"What is this initiation story? You never told me about Ras using you as some kind of initiation process."

Cleo waved a hand in the air. "I've been nothing but honest with you. And you're believing random shit? I told you I got passed off to his management. Now it's an initiation process? Like my life is not crazy enough. I guess you believe that I put voodoo on Ras too, right?"

"Did you?"

"I'm not dignifying that."

"So you're not saying no."

"It's the women under spells, not the men."

"What women?"

"The wives, the girlfriends, the baby mamas. They stay. Even when they know about me. I don't understand that. Can you explain it?"

"They're in love."

"That doesn't do it for me. I went to Josephine's showroom and told her that her man ate me out, something he never did to her. And she stayed. Who's under a spell here?"

Alex reached into her bag and placed the manuscript on the table. "Here's your book."

Cleo flipped through the pages, shaking her head. "I don't know how y'all women do it. These men ain't worth shit."

"Y'all women?"

Cleo looked up from the book. "Yeah. Y'all women. Present company included."

Alex stiffened. "Why are you including me?"

Cleo rolled her eyes. "I didn't fuck your man. But I did suck his dick. Ras told me to."

"When was this?"

"Does it matter?"

"No. I guess not."

"I'm like a Cuban cigar or a vintage whiskey. Ras appreciates what I can do to bring pleasure to his associates. At a studio session, he wants them to relax and enjoy themselves before recording. That means fine food, the best spirits—and me. Birdie wouldn't fuck me, though. I wanted to. But he turned me down."

Alex kept her eyes on Cleo and did not let her face reveal a single emotion.

"I didn't know he was your man until much later. Ras told me. It wasn't my place to say anything."

Alex signaled to the waitress for more coffee.

"You shouldn't break up with him."

Alex stared at Cleo, willing the tears in the corners of her eyes to stay put.

"I'm serious. Birdie's a good guy. Technically he cheated. But he only did it 'cause everyone else took a turn. Peer pressure that night, I think. And he was pretty drunk."

"I'm not sure you're the right person to defend him."

"You told me you once woke up in a strange man's bed. And that's when you stopped drinking."

"Yeah. And?"

"Were you with Birdie then?"

"Yes."

"Does he know?"

"Yes."

"And he forgave you and moved on."

"That was a million years ago," Alex said. "Where we are right now is something totally different."

"I'm sorry, Alex."

"No, you're not."

"I am, actually. I really am. Birdie thought I was someone random that night. He didn't know I was the chick taking mental notes to write a book."

"That doesn't do anything for me."

"It's just unfortunate. I appreciate what you've done for me so far. You're getting my words down. Helping me tell my side of the story. I'd rather the lines weren't blurred this way."

"Me too," Alex said. "You're going to have to find another writer for the final revisions. I'm taking myself off this project."

"I can't bring someone else in now. You signed a contract."

"You'll be okay," Alex said, gathering her notebooks and packing her bag.

"I can sue you—"

"Go right ahead."

"I won't sue you. I need you. Look, I'll cut you in on more royalties."

Alex smiled with her mouth closed and shook her head. "Unlike you, Cleo, I'm not for sale."

"Birdie won't be in the book."

"Put him in there. It's your story. I don't care. I just don't want anything more to do with this project. Or you."

"Have you ever been to Caliente's?"

Alex stood up and then looked down at Cleo. "On Seventh Avenue?"

"Yeah."

"I guess. I don't know."

"You have," Cleo said. "It was back in your drinking days, though."

Alex sat back down in the booth. "What are you talking about?"

Cleo pulled out her ever-present laptop and patted it. "It's not just ballplayers and rappers I have dirt on."

Alex blinked. "You're trying to tell me you have something on me . . . something from back in the day."

Cleo smiled.

"So it's not enough to tell me that you fucked my man," Alex said. "It's not enough that I have to go home and break things off with my fiancé because I will never be able to look at him the same knowing that he was with you."

"I told you I didn't have sex with him," Cleo said.

"And now, when I'm ready to walk away from you and this hurtful, hateful project, you want to throw up whatever dirt you have on me. Something I'm sure you dug up long before we met."

"True."

"And something you wanted to make sure you had in your back pocket in case I ever wanted to walk away."

"Yes."

"And you think there is something you can tell me—some photo, some video, some whatever—that will make me crumple up and finish this book, in the hopes that you'll destroy it."

"Right."

"You're wrong. I don't care. Do what you gotta do."

"Even if it means you end up as a chapter in my book?"

Alex's eyes widened. "What?"

"Girl. People know about you. You were wild for the night before you got that daisy tattoo. Isn't it true that you had sex with Birdie when you were supposed to be writing a story on him? What a compromising position to be in—"

"Is this all you've got?"

"Not at all. I think I heard you were pretty adventurous after a few drinks."

Alex stood up and put her bag over her shoulder. "I've waited five years for my past to catch up to me. If that's what you need to do, go for it."

"I get off on people hating me," Cleo said. "That's sick, isn't it? The whole time we've been working together, I couldn't wait to get to the point where you hated me."

"I don't hate you," Alex said, finally letting the hot tears she'd been holding in stream down her face. "I feel sorry for you. And I hope you find whatever it is you're looking for." She turned her back on Cleo and walked out.

twenty

For ten minutes Alex just stared at Birdie. She sat on the floor of her office, her back up against her desk, her legs folded like a pretzel. Birdie stood, leaning against the back window. When she came home, he called out to her from the basement. She didn't answer; she'd been crying ever since she got on the C train and for the entire walk home. She raced upstairs to her office, collapsed on the floor, and cried for ten minutes. By the time Birdie noticed that she wasn't coming down to the basement to say hello as she usually did, she was already slightly composed, sitting on the floor.

As soon as he walked into the office, he knew. And she knew that he knew. He took his spot at the window and waited for her to speak.

"Why didn't you tell me?"

Birdie kept his eyes on the floor. He scratched the back of his head and then looked at Alex. "I can't say anything. I'm so sorry, Alex."

"I went against my own morals. Wrote a story on Josephine just so you could get in the studio with Ras. And you thank me by cheating on me? *With her?*"

Birdie dropped his head in his hands. "It was so crazy. Dude was acting like I had to do it if I wanted to work with him. It was fucking weird as hell."

"But you did it."

"It felt wrong from the very beginning."

"But you still did it!" Alex screamed. She got up from the floor and attacked Birdie, smacking him in the face with one hand and trying to punch him with the other. Birdie shielded himself from Alex's blows and then tried to grab both her hands to stop her.

"Don't hit me, Alex," he said. "I know you're mad at me, but don't—"

"Fuck you, Birdie," Alex said. She pushed him away and then spat on the floor at his feet.

Birdie clenched his teeth and took a deep breath. "Tell me what to do to make it right."

"You watched me go meet with this chick every week." Alex's chest began to heave as she cried harder while still trying to talk. "You swore you'd never touched her and never would."

"I know."

"Birdie. I won't ever forgive you. I can't."

Alex tried to move past Birdie and leave the room but he blocked the doorway.

"Wait, Alex, I know you're pissed off. You have every right to hate me. And maybe you need a break. But don't tell me it's over."

"Fuck you! I don't need a break! I have no respect for you. I could never look at you the same again. Never."

"Don't say that."

"Never," Alex said, shaking her head. "Not ever."

"I didn't have sex with her."

"You just let her suck your dick."

"I barely looked at her."

"Is that supposed to make me feel better?"

"I want to be brutally honest with you. We smoked a blunt. I was tipsy. She came in the room and I didn't even know who she was. She started dancing for all the guys in the studio and I—"

"Spare me, Birdie, please."

"She starts taking her clothes off and I'm, like, okay, whatever. Strippers in the studio is not the craziest thing I've ever seen. But then she comes over to me, and before I can even really process it, this chick is, like—"

"Did you kiss her?"

"Hell fucking no." Birdie began walking toward Alex.

"Move the fuck back. And don't even think you can touch me."

"We can get over this, Alex. Please don't let this ruin what we have."

"What do we have?"

"We have a good life together. We're getting married. We're gonna have babies. I'll go back to working at FedEx and give up rapping if it will make you stay with me."

Alex looked up at Birdie. His eyes were bloodshot red. She hadn't noticed that he was crying.

"Are the tears supposed to represent how sorry you are?"

Birdie stepped closer to Alex. "Please don't leave."

"I don't think I have a choice."

"Yes, you do. I had a choice."

Alex opened her mouth slightly. "This is not the same thing, Birdie. Don't even try it."

"It's not? I get a call from some dude I don't know. And he's telling me *my* girl is at *his* house?"

"Don't you dare turn this on me. That was five years ago!"

"I'm just saying! I forgave you. I moved on!"

Alex shook her head back and forth. "It's not the same. And you know it."

"I'm not saying it is. I just want you to remember that I've been where you are right now. And I know how you feel. And I fucking wish I could take it back. But I can't."

"She said she's not putting you in her book."

"I don't care," Birdie said.

"But I might be in it."

"What?"

"She's got something on me from my days as a drunk slut."

"Oh shit."

Alex smiled. "That bitch knew from the very first day. She set me up. I can't believe I didn't see it coming. The first time we met, she said we probably had more in common than I thought."

"You don't have anything in common with her."

"I was worse. She's always acted sober. And everything she's ever done has been for a purpose. She's evil and spiteful. But she moves with a purpose. I just had a lack of control."

"She's not putting any of your business out there. She's just fucking with you."

"She said you wouldn't have sex with her. Why not?"

Birdie shuddered. "I'm embarrassed. For real. I'm ashamed of myself."

"Have you ever cheated on me before? With anyone else?"

Birdie closed his eyes. "At Richard's bachelor party three years ago. Got a little carried away with a stripper. We had sex in the bathroom. I ended up throwing up all over her."

Alex winced. "Anything else?"

"Five summers ago. When I went on that Vote or Die tour. I had sex with some random girl who drove me to my hotel."

"That was the night I called your room and your boy said you weren't back from the show."

"Yes."

"And I didn't believe it. Kept asking you for months about that night."

"Do you want me to leave?"

"I don't know."

"You now know everything there is to know. We can get married with no secrets. With everything on the up and up."

"What if Cleo does out me? I don't even know what she knows. But it could be embarrassing. For you."

"I don't give a fuck. I'm not marrying Alex Sampson Maxwell

from five years ago, although she was a lot of fun. I'm marrying you. Right now."

"I need a minute, Birdie."

"I'm not going anywhere."

Birdie wrapped Alex up in his arms and rubbed her arms while she cried softly.

"All of this is just too much," Alex said, wiping her face with the bottom of her T-shirt. "This story for *Vibe*. This book. I just can't deal."

Alex's cell phone rang.

"You want it?" Birdie asked.

Alex nodded.

Birdie took the phone out of her bag and passed it. Alex didn't recognize the number but she flipped it open anyway, hoping for a temporary distraction. Before she could even bring the phone to her ear, she heard the screaming—so loud that it made her jump. She brought the phone up slowly, afraid of who it could be and what could be so wrong. The screaming was intense and primal and chilled her to the core. She could hear the beeping sounds of monitors and the intercom system paging a doctor in the background. Whoever had called her was screaming at the top of her lungs. Alex covered the mouthpiece with her hand.

"Listen," she whispered, holding the phone for Birdie to hear too.

"Who's screaming like that?"

Alex shushed him and pressed the phone to her ear again. She could only hear snatches of muffled conversation; it sounded like the cell phone had been dropped.

"Somebody's hurt," Alex said to Birdie, "or in some kind of trouble. Someone with my number in her phone."

She put the phone up to Birdie's ear again. He covered up his other ear with the palm of his hand and was silent. After a moment he gestured for Alex to pass him a pen and paper from her bag. He scribbled something as he listened and then put the phone down.

"Someone hung up the phone," Birdie said, still writing. "Whoever it was is at Valley Hospital. I heard a doctor tell someone to order lorazepam. What's that?"

"A sedative," Alex said.

"Think it was just some random person who called your phone by mistake?"

"Could be," Alex said.

"But you don't think so."

"That screaming," Alex said. "Somebody's going through some serious shit."

Alex reached out her hands. She and Birdie locked hands and pulled each other up to stand.

"You're going to that hospital, aren't you?"

"Yeah."

"We still gotta talk, Alex," Birdie said. "I want to deal with this."

Alex nodded. "Birdie, I can't guarantee you that everything's going to be okay. I need some time to figure out if I can still go through with everything."

"I know."

"I'm stunned right now."

"I know."

"And I'm disappointed."

"I am too."

"I'm gonna go see if I can find out who's at Valley Hospital."

"You're gonna just case the emergency room and see if you see any screaming patients you know?"

"If someone was calling me, I feel like I'm gonna find out right away."

"Call my cell if you need me," Birdie said.

Downstairs, Birdie walked Alex to the front door and tried to turn her around before she could walk out. Alex stiffened so that her body was still facing the door.

He began, "I want you to know that I—"

"I love you too," Alex said, without turning in his direction. She shrugged off his arm and closed the door softly behind her.

twenty-one

"*Ma chérie!*" Ras grabbed his wife by her shoulders and shook her once, hard. "*Ma chérie*, look at me. Stay with me! Right here!"

Josephine's body was limp, her eyes dead and glassy. She opened her mouth to speak, but only a guttural groan came out. Ras and Josephine Bennett were in a hospital room on the first floor of Valley Hospital. Above them, three floors up, the baby they had been planning to adopt had been born the previous evening. This morning the mother had left a note on her bed—"I'm sorry. I want my baby."— and walked out of the hospital with her newborn.

"She . . . she took my baby," Josephine said, collapsing into heavy sobs on Ras's shoulder.

"No, she took *her* baby, *ma chérie*," Ras said softly, stroking his wife's hair. "We knew the risks. That baby was not ours until we took the baby home. She always had the right to change her mind."

"But you said!" Josephine pulled away from Ras, searching his eyes as if he could have been an impostor. "Ras, you swore to me! You said everything would be okay. You promised me!"

"I know. I know, sweetheart," Ras whispered over and over into his wife's ear. Her skin was hot. If he didn't calm her down soon, they were going to have to sedate her before she made herself sick.

Josephine stood up straight, dropping her hands to her sides. The whites of her eyes were bloodred. One side of her face was lined, from pressing into Ras's shirt and crying.

"You explain to me right now how this happened. Where did she go? When? *Why?*"

"Sit down," Ras said.

Josephine put her hands out to balance herself. She didn't trust her body to let her walk across the room to the chair. But she couldn't sit on the bed. If she let her body rest in that position—flat on her back on a hospital bed—she might never get up again. She had to sit in a chair like a normal, healthy person. Although she knew she was neither.

Josephine smoothed down her hair with her hands, sat down in the fake leather club chair, and crossed her legs. Ras sat on the edge of the bed.

"The father . . . her boyfriend . . . ," Ras said.

"I thought he wanted nothing to do with her."

"He had a change of heart."

Josephine stifled a scream and just looked at her hands folded neatly in her lap. Those thin ivory hands, no scars on them, perfectly manicured, understated gold jewelry. They were not the hands that belonged to someone who felt the way Josephine did. She'd never understood until that moment how her great-grandmother had been able to kill a chicken with her bare hands in D.R. Now she knew.

She wanted to slice her skin and make herself bleed, turn herself inside out, rotate her head three hundred and sixty degrees. Anything to frighten people into paying attention to her. Something to make them feel as hollow and empty as she felt inside.

Ras coughed into his hand and then threw his head back, tossing his dreadlocks behind his back with care.

"He got an apartment in Boston, told her to have the baby and go back there."

"What is he doing in Boston?"

"He's going to Boston University in the fall. He got an apartment in between his school and Harvard so they could both go to school and take care of the baby."

"How do you know all of this?"

Ras broke eye contact with his wife. "I spoke to him."

Josephine stood up and took one step toward Ras. "You did what?"

"He called my cell phone right before you got here."

"You let him! You let him take my baby!?"

"There was nothing I could do, Josephine."

Josephine's face crumpled. "I just know I'm heartbroken, Ras. I'm just . . ."

"Don't worry, *ma chérie*, we will have a baby. I promise."

Ras folded her into his arms and hugged his wife as she cried. "I know, *ma chérie*," he said, as his wife's body vibrated from the racking sobs.

"This is your fault," Josephine whispered into the sleeve of Ras's shirt. He didn't hear her clearly and continued to rock her.

"This is your fault, Ras," she said again. Her husband just held her tighter. Finally she pulled back to look him in the eye. She could tell that he knew exactly what she meant.

"Don't, Josephine," Ras pleaded, his patience wearing thin. "Please don't."

"I'm not supposed to have children with you. We're cursed. My grandmother cursed us. And Marasa, your twin, she's cursed us as well."

"Don't start this shit, Josephine! I know you are hurting right now. I am too. Let's be there for each other. Don't bring this up. Not now."

"Fuck you!" Josephine yelled, snatching her arms away from Ras. "You fell in love with her."

"I never loved her."

"You liar. You loved her so much. Your twin. Ever since, we haven't been the same."

The tears coming down Josephine's face were now hot and salty. Josephine put her hand to her throat. Bile crept up her throat and she swallowed it back down. "I have to sit down."

Ras held her side and eased her down into the chair.

"I did love her."

Josephine's jaw dropped. Her eyes widened and then she slowly lifted her hand to her mouth.

Ras closed his eyes and breathed in deep. "Maybe I didn't love her," he said, shaking his head. "But I had some very strong feelings for her. No matter how many times I said I wasn't dealing with her anymore . . . I kept going back. I have no reasons. No excuses. No explanations. It just . . ."

"No, Ras . . . I don't need to hear this."

"Yes. You do. You'll never let this go until I do."

Josephine tried desperately to catch her breath, shaking her head vigorously.

Ras kept speaking, his voice a dull monotone. "At first it was just lust. And the excitement of someone new. We were on the road, far away from home. You didn't want to come out to those rinky-dink cities to see me."

"I tried!" Josephine shouted. "I tried to come—"

"I would never have you backstage at some college student center in Kentucky. My wife? No. I wanted you relaxed. Comfortable and at home."

"So you could do your dirt."

Ras nodded. "So I could do my dirt. And the first time I had sex with her, I cried afterward. There was something there . . . And I will not stand here and deny it to you. I knew I would never ever leave you. Not while I was taking breath on this earth. But for a while . . . I wanted both of you."

Hearing Ras explain this, so simply and straightforwardly, dried Josephine's eyes. She was still dead inside. She could feel the dull thump of her heart inside her chest, ticking like a clock counting down her last seconds of life. The pain of losing her child was still a white-hot membrane pulsing over her body. But the shame of Ras's betrayal had vanished.

"The baby . . . ," she said, looking into her husband's eyes.

"A girl."

She beckoned Ras to her side and he joined her, rubbing her arms and brushing back her hair as Josephine moaned softly and silently shed tears that collected in the crook of his elbow.

There was a firm knock on the door, but they both assumed the door was locked and ignored it. Not until the door began to push open did Ras leave his wife's side and walk over, one hand extended, to keep the person from entering.

"Who's there?" he asked, turning his face toward Josephine, who was staring at the wall and mumbling to herself.

"It's Alex. I'm looking for Josephine."

"No. Not right now."

Josephine heard Alex's voice and stirred. Something about Alex's voice was calm and comforting to her ear.

"It's okay, *mon chéri*," Josephine said. "Let her in."

Ras pointed to a corner of the hospital room and gave Alex a look that meant *Stay right there*. He walked over to his wife and bent down to put his mouth as close to her ear as possible.

"It's not a good time for you to talk to her, my love. We need to get home and you need to rest."

Josephine shook her head. She sat up and turned her head toward Alex.

"You see?" she said. "You see what I mean? All the money in the world does not mean shit. Ras can play for the queen of bloody England. He can tour the world. I can live in a mansion the size of a small town. And where am I right now?"

No one said a word.

"Where am I right now? Losing my sanity in a hospital because a teenager just ran away with my baby. How is that fair?"

Josephine looked at Alex as if she really wanted her to answer. When Alex didn't say anything, Josephine just clucked her tongue and continued. "What do you know? You spend a few weeks in our world? You still don't know anything. It's not glamorous. It's real life! It's real fucking life and it's deep and it's depressing and it's real."

Josephine watched as Alex began to look down at the floor.

"Ask me something," Josephine said, pointing to the notebook poking out of Alex's bag.

Alex looked up. "Josephine, no. I honestly just came here because—"

"Ask me something for your story. Here I am. Big juicy exclusive. Josephine Bennett speaks, on the evening of the most traumatic day of her life!"

Josephine's voice was just high-pitched enough to worry both Ras and Alex.

"My wife is not well," Ras said in a whisper. "I'm going to have to ask you to leave."

Alex stood up.

"You sit," Josephine said. "I want to talk! I want to be interviewed about my awesome, glamorous life. Doesn't it look outrageous!" she screamed. "Doesn't it, Alex? Don't you wish you could be me?"

"I think I should go," Alex said, knowing Josephine wasn't listening to her.

"Wait. Here's a quote for your story: I wish I was flat broke. Living with my husband on the top floor of his parents' home. I wish he still played guitar in Times Square for change. And I wish he'd never met Cleo and never got signed to a major label. I wish we had nothing but each other. I would trade every diamond I own, every home, every article of clothing, and every stupid fucking car to have our simple life back. All I would ask for is to be a mother. That is all. Write that down in your story."

Josephine closed her mouth. She wouldn't speak a single word for three weeks.

twenty-two

D r. HAMILTON SNAPPED HER GLOVES OFF AND SIGHED. "NOT YET, Beth."

"Are you serious?"

"Not one centimeter." Beth's doctor turned her back and scribbled something onto her clipboard. "Any contractions you're feeling are Braxton Hicks. It's false labor. This baby's not fully cooked yet."

"That's impossible. I couldn't even walk. I've been doubled over in pain. I even timed them. It was every six minutes and—"

Dr. Hamilton pointed at the clock. "I've been in here for seventeen minutes and no contractions."

"They slowed down. But I thought—"

Dr. Hamilton's face softened and she put one hand on Beth's leg. "Sweetie, it's stress, plain and simple. Go home. Take a long warm bath and try to relax. Take a Tylenol PM if you need to."

Beth closed her eyes and laced her fingers over her chest. Dr. Hamilton watched her chest heave up and down.

"Where's your husband?" the doctor asked, trying to keep her voice light and noncommittal.

Beth did not open her eyes. "On his way," she said, in a voice that she knew betrayed her.

"Good. He can take you home."

Beth didn't respond.

"You can't go home alone. I won't allow it."

"I told you Z is on his way."

Dr. Hamilton opened her mouth to speak and then changed her mind. Instead, she stabbed at her paperwork with a pen, hung the clipboard on the front of the bed, and walked to the door. "Call the service at any time if you are having timed contractions less than five minutes apart or your water breaks."

She walked out and Beth stayed on her back, her eyes shut tight. She did not want to be pregnant for even one more hour, much less one more day. And she thought for sure this morning when she woke up that today was the day. She'd even called Z and left a message for him at Eden's Nest that he should come home as soon as he could. Dylan had called. She'd said she spoke to him and that he was working out in the clinic's gym. She'd said she told Z to call Beth right away.

A soft knock on the door made Beth open her eyes.

Kipenzi stood in the doorway. "Can I come in?"

Beth nodded as her friend rushed to her side. "How did you know?" she asked, making room on her tiny bed for Kipenzi, who sat down next to her and grabbed her hand.

Kipenzi jerked a thumb toward the door. "The nanny told Ian. Zander's here too. He's waiting outside."

"It was a false alarm."

"A *what*?" Kipenzi stood up and put her hands on her hips. "You sneaky bitch. You just wanted me to come down here and see you."

Beth laughed out loud, then clutched her belly. "Stop, Penzi. Don't play. I can't . . ."

"Can't what? Laugh? Whatever. I can't believe I thought you were really in labor."

"I really thought I was."

"So now what?"

Beth began to sit up and Kipenzi helped pull her to a sitting position. "Now I go home."

"Did Z . . . ?"

Beth locked eyes with Kipenzi. "He's not here yet. But he's coming. He's doing really well, Kipenzi. Really well."

Kipenzi pressed her lips together tight and hugged Beth. "I heard me and Z on the radio on the way over here."

Beth smiled. "Me too. I love that shit. The baby moves like crazy every time it comes on."

"I'm doing a farewell show at the MTV Awards. I'm gonna ask Z to perform with me."

"That would be hot."

"Yeah. Might have my husband do a cut or two as well. Don't want him to feel left out."

"Did you say Zander is here?" Beth asked. "Why didn't he come in?"

"He said he didn't need to see all your business."

"How is Zander?" Beth asked. "I can't get through to him."

"He came by my place a few days ago. Wanted to talk to his auntie Penzi about some things he's going through. It's all good."

"Bunny is knocked up."

"How'd you find out?"

"You just told me."

"Aw, shit. Beth, Zander's gonna kill me if he thinks I told you."

"Is he gonna take care of it?"

"We've got it under control."

"And what else?"

Kipenzi made a dismissive noise. "He's fine, Beth. Worried about that stupid book that girl is writing."

"Dylan told me the chick who is ghostwriting the book is the same chick I've been talking to for the *Vibe* story."

"Who? Alex?"

"Yeah, you know her?"

"I just met her. She's doing a story on Jake for the *Times*. She wanted to talk to me and Jake about Z and the tour and stuff."

"What happened? What did Jake say?"

"Beth," Kipenzi said, patting her friend's leg. "Not now. I definitely don't think you should talk to Alex anymore."

"Why not?"

Kipenzi shrugged. "She's helping to write a book about your husband cheating on you. That's not reason enough?"

"I don't care about Cleo's book. I care about this *Vibe* story."

"But why? Why do you care?"

"Right. 'Cause what do I have to say?"

Kipenzi dropped her shoulders and rolled her eyes. "That's not what I meant and you know it."

"Y'know, I used to manage Z."

"No shit, Beth."

"Jake too. When they were both running around selling crack. And then spending the night in the studio. I was right there. I bagged their shit up in the morning, booked the studio time at night. A white girl from West Virginia was their backseat girl and manager while you were at finishing school or taking ballet or whatever."

"See. This is where it gets fucked up every time, Beth. I don't go there with you. And I don't know what your problem is. But I'm sick of it."

"I'm sick of you thinking that what I go through is not worthy of being discussed. I'm the one who told Z to put Jake on his first song. Without me your man wouldn't have a career. I think people should know that. I want to speak. I know she's gonna write whatever she wants to about me anyway."

"True."

"Might as well give her some facts."

"I haven't found that to be a good strategy for dealing with the media."

"I just feel so . . ."

"Invisible?"

Beth looked up at Kipenzi and nodded.

"I'm supposed to be one of the most recognizable celebrities in the world," Kipenzi said. "There are about fifty people outside the hospital right now who are waiting for me to walk outside so they can take my picture."

Beth looked down at her lap.

"And I can guarantee you there are some nurses giving quotes to some journalist right now, giving out confidential information on who you are and why I came to see you."

"I know."

"And I'm still invisible too."

"You are so not invisible—"

"I'm not? I don't have to come into a restaurant twenty minutes before Jake and leave ten minutes after him? I don't have to vacation with him as far as possible from the States so we can escape photographers with telephoto lenses? I don't have to straight-up deny it when people ask me about him?"

"No," Beth said. "You don't have to do any of those things. You choose to."

"I don't choose to. Jake does. I don't care anymore about who knows. But he thinks it's best to continue the way we always have. Deny, deny, deny. It's fucked up. But what am I supposed to do? Force him to tell Barbara Walters we're married?"

"My husband will tell everyone and anyone who asks that I'm his wife and that he loves me. Even the groupies he sleeps with."

"Which one of us has it better?" Kipenzi asked.

Beth and Kipenzi stared at each other. "You do," they said in unison.

Kipenzi turned her head toward the door, where the sounds of a commotion seeped through. The door cracked open and Zander's brown face poked through.

"Come in here and give your mom a hug," Kipenzi said. "She's not having this late-ass baby yet."

Zander went over to his mother, bent down, and buried his face in her neck. Beth choked back tears and rubbed her oldest son's back.

"You want me to get Dylan to send a car to take us home?"

Zander asked. Beth nodded. Zander took out his cell phone to make the call.

"I better go, girl," Kipenzi said. "They're gonna have a red carpet leading from your door to some movie premiere in two minutes if I don't leave."

"I'll call you tomorrow."

Kipenzi leaned over Beth and kissed her on the forehead. "I love you, girl," she said. "And if you need anything, call me."

Zander, sitting in a chair in the corner of the hospital room, read a text message. He waved his cell phone in his mother's direction. "Daddy's about to call you right now," he said.

As soon as Beth sat up, the phone at her bedside rang. "Z?"

"You okay, baby?" Z asked.

"Yeah. False alarm."

"I think I'm ready, Beth. I think I'm ready to come home."

"Don't rush. I'm not going anywhere."

"Saturday. I'm coming home on Saturday."

Beth smiled, covered up the mouthpiece, and whispered the word *Saturday* to Zander and Kipenzi.

"Tell Dylan to pick me up. I don't want to fly back by myself. I hate flying."

"That's not a problem." Beth said. "You are going to be fine. I'll make sure Dylan's there on Saturday."

"Who's with you now?"

"Kipenzi. And Zander too."

"Put Zander on the phone."

Beth leaned over and Zander jumped up to grab the receiver. He nodded and said "Yes sir" and "No sir" a few times. And finally Beth and Kipenzi heard him say, "Love you too." They all avoided eye contact with each other as Zander cleared his throat and replaced the handset on the receiver.

"You two get ready to get out of here and go back home," Kipenzi said. "I'm leaving." She shrugged into her coat and then typed a message into her phone. "Wish I could escape through this window."

"You can," Beth said. "We're on the first floor."

"No shit," Kipenzi said, crossing the room to peek out the window.

"Parking lot's right there."

"And not a single photographer," Kipenzi said with a smile. She typed for another second and then her bodyguard knocked on the door.

"Come in," Beth and Kipenzi said in unison.

"You want me to do what?" the guard asked when Kipenzi told him.

"I'm going out the window. Make sure I don't kill myself."

"I can't let you—"

"You first. Get out that window. I'm jumping in two minutes. And I want that car right there, engine running, door open."

The guard shook his head and climbed onto the ledge. The ex–football player and former police officer was strong enough to knock an overeager fan to the ground with one hand, but he wasn't agile enough to jump out of a window with ease.

Beth rolled her eyes. "Kipenzi, you're really going out of the window?"

"Do you hear that noise outside your door?"

"Why, Kipenzi? Why do they need to know every detail of your personal life? They want to feel close to you?"

Kipenzi kept her eyes on the parking lot. "I stopped trying to figure it out a long time ago," she said.

"Would you trade it?"

"Would you?"

"I'm not famous."

"What about Z? Would you like him to go back to living with his grandmother? No money. No sold-out shows. None of that."

"Sometimes, yeah." Beth looked up at the ceiling. "Sometimes I wonder if—"

"Love you, girl!" Kipenzi shouted, one leg hanging over the sill. "Call me when you're really having this baby." She swung the other leg over the sill, looked back at Beth one more time, and winked at her. And then jumped.

Beth angled herself out of bed and got over to the window just in time to see Kipenzi's bodyguard reaching out to grab Kipenzi by the waist, although he didn't need to, since her feet were just a half foot off the ground. Kipenzi and her bodyguard looked around quickly as they took two brief steps toward the car. As the car pulled out, Beth could see Kipenzi and the guard in the car. Kipenzi had her head thrown back and her mouth wide. Although Beth couldn't hear a sound, she could tell Kipenzi was laughing.

"Mrs. Saddlebrook, do you need anything?" said a nurse, pushing into the room without knocking. Beth noticed instantly that she had a cell phone in her hand—the kind with a camera attached.

"You're not making any extra money off me today," Beth said. "Kipenzi Hill has left the building."

twenty-three

"**I**'M JUST NOT UP FOR A FAMILY GATHERING," JOSEPHINE WHINED. For the twentieth consecutive day, she'd been wearing an old gym T-shirt from high school that had become a security blanket over the years.

"You don't have a choice," Ras said. "We have to get you out of this. Come. We have people waiting downstairs. They want to see you."

Josephine shrugged. "Nothing to celebrate, if you ask me."

"Can we celebrate a beautiful spring day? Can we celebrate that we're in good health and have each other?"

Ras went to a corner of the room and pulled out a copy of *Billboard* and flipped to the charts section. "Can we celebrate your husband's twenty-fifth number one record?"

Josephine smiled. "The song with Kipenzi and Z?"

Ras shrugged. "I'm a miracle worker, plain and simple. If I can bring Z back from the dead, I can do anything."

"I think Z did that for himself."

"I helped. Gave him a hot record. Now, you. Five minutes," Ras said, holding a pointer finger in her direction. "Not a minute more."

In the weeks since the young lady had left the hospital with the baby, Josephine seemed to have shrunk three inches. For days, she shuffled around her palatial estate, firing and rehiring the help, walking to the gas station in her robe and slippers for chewing gum and diet sodas. Ras sent her to Kingston for two weeks to stay with his great-grandmother, who fed her *ackee* and *saltfish* until she began humming to herself as she walked the grounds of the property, stopping to smell the sandalwood bramble that lined her walkway.

Ras came to pick her up and they cried together in his great-grandmother's front yard. And then Ras straightened his back, wiped his face and then his wife's.

"You will be a mother," Ras said. "I stake my life on that."

And with that, she'd returned home. But she was far from normal. She was twitchy and nervous, jumping out of her skin anytime the phone or the doorbell rang.

Memorial weekend arrived on a Saturday, three weeks after her return from Denham. Josephine begged Ras to postpone the event, or at least have it somewhere else. Ras was gentle but resolute and firm. For twelve years he'd hosted the celebration at his home, even after his mother's death and during his father-in-law's treatment for prostate cancer. No matter what, on Memorial weekend they celebrated the motto emblazoned on the flag: Out of many, one people.

Josephine stood at the full-length mirror in her bedroom and tried to steel herself for the questioning looks, the phony smiles, and the clucking noises she was sure to get from everyone. Not only had she lost her baby, but her husband would very likely be prominently displayed in Cleo's book. Josephine placed a hand over her heart and spoke to her reflection.

"We're heartbroken, of course. But the mother always had the right to change her mind. It's a risk we understood."

She tried on a wan smile, the kind where the eyebrows are raised, and then shrugged her shoulders to make herself look more vulnerable. Josephine tried to soften the edges of her face, unclench her teeth, straighten her eyebrows. She took her hands and physically tried to turn her lips into a pseudo-smile, the way an undertaker does on a corpse.

At the top of the steps, she peered down into the living room and saw all the usual faces: Ras's parent and siblings, a few friends and other family members. Swirls of reggae music and the smells of plantains and pumpkin soup nearly overwhelmed her, but she held it together long enough to slip into the crowd with no fanfare.

She lightly placed her hand on someone's back. Turning, the person jumped a bit and then grabbed her in for a tight hug. The warmth of the bodies of her sisters, nieces, and brothers-in-law made her feel calm and centered. It had only been a few months since she'd seen most of her family, but she was shocked at how different everyone looked. One nephew was now married; a niece was now expecting her second child.

Alex was there. And although she wasn't family, Josephine was happy to see her and grateful that Ras had obviously invited her.

"You look beautiful," Alex said, kissing Josephine on the cheek.

"I feel like shit," Josephine said. "But thank you."

Balancing a plate weighed down with food, Alex gave Josephine a sheepish grin. "Thought I should try everything."

"You're lucky, we're having the best of both worlds. My family sent *rabo encendido* and *sancocho*. The best. And from Ras's side, we have *callalloo, loulla* and *sorrell* and *navarin*. And you have to try some coconut *toto*."

Alex stuffed a forkful of food in her mouth and smiled.

Josephine patted Alex on the back and continued making the rounds. She spotted Ras's great-grandmother, two heavy snow-white braids crisscrossing her head, sitting on the patio beyond the sliding glass doors off the great room. She was holding an infant on her lap, tipping the baby over slightly and patting the back to get a burp out. From the baby's almond-shaped eyes and the lemon drop head, Josephine knew it had to be one of Ras's brothers' new grandchildren.

"Gran' Modda," Josephine said, closing the doors behind her. "How are you?"

"I'm ninety-eight."

"No, I said *how* are you?"

"I heard you," she said, turning the baby to rest on her chest and continuing to pat the baby's back. "I said I'm ninety-eight. How do you think I am?"

Josephine smiled and sat next to Ras's great-grandmother, marveling at how at ease she was with such a tiny newborn. The baby couldn't have been more than two weeks old.

"How many babies have you raised, Gran' Modda?"

"Babies from my body—eleven. Your husband's grandfather, my last child, was the worst. Biggest head. Six days of labor. Thirteen pounds."

"I'm not over it," Josephine said. "It's not getting any easier. You said it would."

"We've been through this," said Ras's great-grandmother. "That girl took her own baby. That one wasn't yours. They got married yesterday. Little ceremony up in Boston."

"That's nice."

"You don't meant it. You want to cause some bodily harm to that girl. Ain't right."

Josephine set her eyes on the water falling through the carefully sculpted rocks that led to a koi pond.

"I'm getting better," she said, believing it for the very first time.

"Here," the woman said, turning the tiny baby into Josephine's arms. Josephine started to get up, trying to give the baby back.

"No, no, no, no," she said, "not yet. I can't hold someone else's—"

"Look, now. I'm ninety-eight years old. And I gotta pee. You gon' hold this baby till I come back," the old woman said, struggling to get out of her chair.

The baby immediately began to screech at the unfamiliarity of the new arms.

"Whose baby is this? Is this Saul's new grandbaby?" Josephine asked over the baby's cries. She looked back toward the house for an answer, but Ras's great-grandmother was gone.

She juggled the crying baby for a bit. And as soon as she turned and began to walk down the path leading toward the pool, the child began to quiet.

"Hey, pumpkin," she whispered. The baby's eyes widened and took Josephine in. "Aren't you the sweetest little thing?"

The baby burped and a bit of milk came out of the tiny pursed mouth. Josephine quickly brought the hem of her shirt up and dabbed at the baby's mouth. She winced, thinking of the many days she'd spent pumping her breasts, preparing to nurse. She'd taken a class with a midwife who specialized in helping adoptive parents. She'd pumped her breasts three times a day and taken twenty milligrams of domperidone before each pumping session to help build up a milk supply. Even now, weeks later, she was still pumping and taking the hormones, though she knew full well there was no need. She pumped her few ounces of milk and bagged them in the neat plastic bags that piled up in the freezer. Ras pretended he didn't notice, but Josephine knew he was concerned.

Josephine felt transported to the moment in the hospital when Ras told her that the young woman had left town with the baby. Again the rage started in her belly and came up, spreading warmth through her body. She got the feeling now that if it came up to her throat, she wouldn't be able to breathe and she would pass out with the baby in her arms.

"Do you want to go away with me?" she said to the caramel brown baby, who yawned. "I would make a very good mother for you. We might not live in a fancy place like this. But I could take care of you."

The baby stretched out and then settled back against Josephine's chest.

I could leave right now, Josephine thought to herself. *I could walk down to the gas station and get a taxi.* She shifted the baby in order to pat her pockets. She felt a few bills there and pulled them out. She had three hundred-dollar bills and couldn't remember where they came from. She walked down to the edge of the walkway and then farther away from the property.

"Do you mind if I just pretend I'm your mom for a few minutes?" Josephine asked the baby, who gurgled.

Josephine took in a sharp, deep breath and exhaled slowly. She closed her eyes and stood in the driveway, matching her breaths to the baby's. Eventually she couldn't hear herself breathe. For the first time, all the tension and anger she'd carried for weeks disappeared. She felt as if she and the baby needed each other to take a breath. She stood under the Hispaniola pine trees, holding the child tight, her hair blowing slightly in the breeze. As she stood in that driveway, she went back in time, saw her husband, a pimply adolescent, holding out his hand to guide her down her parents' front steps. She was a mother. The mother of the child she held in her arms, whose breathing mirrored hers. She felt her belly swell, contract, and release. She understood, as she stood there, how that young girl could run away with the little girl she'd promised to Josephine. She understood. *She must have felt like this,* Josephine thought. It was an undeniable force connecting her with another being. It was what she felt with Ras. It was what Ras felt with her—and probably with Cleo. It was what Josephine felt with the child in her arms. Josephine lived lifetimes, died, returned.

She felt a stinging pain under her arms that ran through her breasts and straight through to her wrists. And then moisture began to drip into her brassiere. The baby stirred and began rooting toward her chest. Without a second thought, Josephine opened her blouse and put the child to her breast. With eyes wide open, the baby nursed, one chubby brown hand resting comfortably on the top of her breast as if it had always been just this way.

When the baby was done and slipped off with a look of self-satisfied drunkenness, Josephine snapped out of her trance, feeling intense shame and fear. She'd just nursed this child as if it were her own. A child whose parents were surely relatives, distant or close, who had to be looking for—

"Josephine?"

It was Alex, standing next to Josephine, her brow furrowed, as if she'd been calling her for some time. "Josephine, are you okay?"

Josephine opened her mouth to speak but no words came out. Alex turned back toward the house and gestured wildly with one hand, holding on to Josephine's shoulder with the other hand. Ras saw her hand and bolted out the back door and hurried across the cement patio.

"Ma chérie," Ras said.

Josephine did not turn to face her husband. "This baby . . . something just happened."

Ras motioned for Alex to leave and she did, moving back toward the house, her eyes on the couple.

"Josephine, I need to tell you something . . ."

"No. Ras, listen to me. Grand-mère asked me to hold the baby while she—"

"I know. Because—"

"And then I suddenly started thinking about taking this baby, leaving you and everyone else behind."

"Josephine, I know."

"What do you know?"

Ras turned to stand at Josephine's side and peered over at the baby. "This is Reina. Reina Josephine Bennett."

"What are you saying?"

"She came here this morning from Denham. Gran' Modda brought her here."

"But we didn't . . . How do you know . . ."

"Her mother couldn't take care of her. She knew Gran' Modda would bring her to us and that we would give her a good life."

Josephine shook her head back and forth. "No. It can't be that easy. Something will go wrong. Some random relative will come and take her."

"Gran' Modda adopted her. She has all the paperwork. She wanted to make sure there was a connection before she told you. Do you feel a connection to this little girl?"

Josephine ran a hand over the little girl's cheek; the child eyed her peacefully. Tears streamed down Josephine's face and she simply nodded her head.

"Josephine, I will say this as many times as you need to hear it. This is Reina Josephine Bennett. This is your daughter."

Ras led Josephine and Reina back to the house, one arm around his wife's waist to keep her legs from buckling.

"Family," Ras said as he brought Josephine inside. "This is my wife, Josephine. And my daughter, Reina Josephine Bennett."

Josephine was swarmed by her aunts, nieces, and female cousins. Her cheeks were kissed, her arms were rubbed. Someone recited a chant over her and the baby while someone else fastened a gold anklet around baby Reina's ankle and then kneeled down to place an identical chain around Josephine's ankle.

Josephine Bennett stood still, drinking in the smell of her daughter's neck as the world bustled around her.

Reina Josephine Bennett slept through it all, her hand clasping her mother's pinky finger, squeezing occasionally as if to let her know, *I'm still here.*

twenty-four

KIPENZI HILL SAT IN A 1997 HYUNDAI EXCEL AND WATCHED THE front window of Mike's coffee shop. It was the same diner Jake had taken her to the night they met. She'd told the owner to call her the next time Cleo came in. At six a.m. that morning, her cell phone buzzed with a text message. Cleo was there. Alone.

Kipenzi watched Cleo. She was flipping through stacks of paper, making notes. Her mouth was moving as she read. Occasionally she winced, crossed things out, and then began reading again. After a few minutes she began stacking her papers and putting them away.

Kipenzi, dressed in a white tank top, skinny jeans, and high-top pink Converses, got out of the car. She pulled her baseball cap low on her head and went into the diner. She nodded at the owner, who was standing at the register. She approached the booth.

"Good morning," Kipenzi said, as she slid in next to Cleo.

"Can I help you?" Cleo asked.

"You don't recognize me? Damn! I should have bought some sneakers years ago."

Cleo stared at Kipenzi. And then her face revealed a mixture of disbelief and fear. Kipenzi took off her baseball cap and shook out her hair, a five-inch fluffy afro of soft curls she'd cut herself after getting released from her contract with Happy Hair and having her weave taken out, again, for the very last time.

"Yup. It's me. Crazy. I'm so loving this! I stopped at a traffic light on the way here and this girl did a triple take. But she didn't think it was me. She just pulled off."

"You'll have to talk to my attorney if you wanna know anything about the book," Cleo said, moving closer to the wall and away from Kipenzi.

"I don't think that will be necessary."

"You want to know if Jake's in the book," Cleo said.

"I believe he has a responsibility to me," said Kipenzi. "To be honest, loyal, and faithful to me. You don't owe me anything."

"Agreed. So why are you here?"

Kipenzi sighed heavily. "Because I'm weak, like most women. And I can't take his word for it."

"That's sad."

"Sadder than targeting rappers so you can write a book about them?"

"I never thought about a book until recently."

Kipenzi propped her chin in her hands. "So what's your motivation?"

Cleo stirred her coffee so hard that drops of liquid began to slosh out. "You know how a man looks right when he's about to come?"

Kipenzi didn't answer.

"I'm talking, like, two seconds before it happens. Maybe one little drop has spurted out. His eyes glass over or he closes them tight or he stares at you . . . I feel like that's the only time you really see a man's soul. How he looks at you then is how he really feels about you."

Kipenzi thought about every time she'd had sex with Jake. Every time, he held her chin in his hands and stared at her, sometimes biting on her bottom lip as he came. He always, always looked her in the eye when he came. Usually whispering her name as he did.

"I love that intimacy," Cleo said. "I love that closeness."

"You can have that with one person," Kipenzi said.

"Maybe. Maybe not. But I love that feeling of control. I love knowing that whoever they're married to or dating or in love with—at that very moment, it's all about me."

"See, that's what I don't understand. Why? What does so much promiscuity do for you?"

Cleo waved a hand in the air. "That's too easy," she said, opening up her laptop and tapping the keyboard. "Let's Google it."

Kipenzi didn't move. She just watched as Cleo typed.

Cleo began to read. "'Causes of promiscuity.' Let's see, we have depression . . ." Cleo dug into her bag and took out a vial of medication. "Fluoxetine. Don't leave home without it."

Kipenzi just stared.

"What else do we have here? Ah, the classic: 'an insecure attachment to father.' Check! Ooh, look. New study says that promiscuity could be caused by a hormonal imbalance."

"So there might be a cure for you," Kipenzi said.

"There's a cure. Unconditional love. That's not likely to happen for me." Cleo shrugged. "So here I am."

"Are you going to tell me if Jake's in your book?"

"Are you going to leave him if he is?"

"I don't know."

"Beth won't leave Z. No matter how many times I sleep with him."

"That's Beth."

"And Josephine wouldn't leave Ras. Even though Ras almost left her for me."

"Almost."

"Jake's known for not fucking with groupies."

Kipenzi locked eyes with Cleo and didn't blink.

"Don't be relieved," Cleo said. "He's just got OCD about fucking random chicks. He's had sex with his exes since y'all have been to-gether. Some girl down south? The one who got pregnant by him and then miscarried? Yeah. He was still hitting that a few months ago."

"And what about you?"

"Why is every woman so obsessed with her man being with *me*? I mean, I'm flattered, but I just don't get it."

"You're the one who's writing a book."

"So you don't care? As long as the affairs are not in print?"

"I didn't say that."

"So what are you saying, Kipenzi?"

"You're right," Kipenzi said, nodding once. "I don't need to know. If Jake's in there, I'll deal with it."

"I need to go now," Cleo said.

Kipenzi slid out of the booth and waved Cleo out.

"Here," Cleo said. "Take a copy of the book. You might recog-nize a few folks in there."

"It was nice meeting you," Kipenzi said.

"Yeah. Whatever," Cleo said.

Kipenzi stayed in the booth, staring at the first page of Cleo's manuscript. The word *Platinum* was spelled out vertically over a black background. Kipenzi rolled her eyes. *Platinum.* Of course Cleo would go for a title that was obvious and over the top. She turned the page, read a few lines about someone who was clearly Z, and then closed it.

Did she really want to know? Would it change anything? The answers were yes and yes. But she still couldn't bring herself to open the manuscript again.

Kipenzi got back in the Hyundai and drove around Brooklyn aimlessly, humming to herself and thinking about the manuscript on the back seat. She felt as if that pile of papers were glowing green, like the little bit of radioactive matter than Homer always brought home in the opening credits of *The Simpsons*. Even when she wasn't looking at it in the rearview, she could see it. She could swear she heard Cleo's voice narrating every word. Her cell phone rang and she pressed the device to her ear.

"Auntie, turn to Hot 97," Zander said.

It was Kipenzi's swan song, featuring Z. Kipenzi felt far removed from the song. As if she'd written it for someone else. Her voice wasn't flawless anymore. But Z sounded as fresh and clean as the eighteen-year-old rappers being discovered on the internet instead of at open mic nights.

"We sound pretty good, right, Zan?"

"For some old folks? Yeah, y'all sound all right."

"Now turn to Power 105," Zander said. "Hurry."

Kipenzi stabbed the dials on the radio a few times and then stopped. It was Zan's latest, a midtempo song with Bunny on the hook.

"I told you I liked that song when you recorded it," Kipenzi said, rolling her eyes. "But if I hear it one more time, I'm going to scream. You're oversaturating the market and you don't even have a deal yet. You've put out two mix tapes! Why would anyone want to spend any money on your actual album?"

"They won't," Zander said. "They'll download it for free. I haven't paid for music since I was in the seventh grade."

"What about *my* last album, Zander?"

"Two words, Auntie. Bit. Torrent."

"Bit what?"

"It's a file-sharing site. C'mon, Auntie. No one buys albums anymore. It's about establishing a brand," Zander said. "I don't care how many records I sell. The way contracts are these days, I'll never see any royalties anyway. The album is just marketing. You gotta get people to love you. If they decide they love you, they might actually spend money to see you in person or join your fan club or download your ringtones. That's how I'm getting my money."

"It used to be the other way around," Kipenzi said. "You sell records and the fans will come."

"I'll bootleg my own music if it will help me go on tour faster."

"And this is why I'm retiring," she said. "I'm on my way to your house now. Tell your mom and I'll see you guys in an hour."

Kipenzi took out her earpiece and got the Hyundai up as fast it would go, humming along to everything on the radio and occasionally still glancing at the manuscript in the back. Maybe she'd give it to Beth, let her be prepared . . .

As soon as Kipenzi's car pulled around Beth's circular driveway, a 4Runner came roaring up the gravel. The driver nearly sideswiped Kipenzi's car and seemed to jump out before it was fully in park.

Kipenzi got out of her car at the same time that Zander came out of the house, throwing up his hands.

"What is *wrong* with you? You drove all the way from Greenwich for what?"

Bunny walked toward Zander, a pointer finger in his face.

"I heard that voice mail some chick left you. She said she's pregnant."

"You still hacking into my shit?"

"You still want to fuck around?" Bunny screamed. Her weave was gone again. Her spiky hair was now dyed blond at the tips, making her every move seem more dramatic than usual. She had acrylic tips on her nails, filed out to V-shaped talons.

Kipenzi went to the front door and began banging on it. "Somebody get out here and separate these two," Kipenzi yelled.

Bunny dashed for Zander, who grabbed her and spun her around, wrapping her arms around her chest like the straps of a straitjacket.

"Stop. Fucking. Playing," Zander said, squeezing Bunny tighter with each word.

"Zan," Kipenzi warned, still banging on the front door. "Let her go."

Zander shoved Bunny, who stumbled but quickly recovered. She ran over to Zander, cocked her fist back, and punched him square in the jaw.

"Oh, girl, you are wildin'," Kipenzi said, coming down the steps and heading straight for Bunny. But it was too late. Zander had lost it. He mushed her face with his entire palm, knocking her to the ground, and then kicked her in the side.

"Fucking bitch," he said, kicking her again in her ribs. He leaned down and pulled his fist back.

"Zan! No!" Kipenzi screamed.

Zander pulled back a few more inches and then punched Bunny in the nose. She screamed. He pulled back his fist, now bloody, and punched her again. Zander got up quickly, his eyes wide. He ran to one of his father's cars, got in, and peeled out of the driveway in reverse.

Bunny sat up in the gravel and put her head down, her hands covering her nose. Kipenzi went over and kneeled down next to her.

"I'm calling the police," Bunny mumbled, holding in the blood pouring out of her nose.

"You hit him first," Kipenzi said.

"So? You won't see any bruises on *his* face."

"What the hell is your problem?"

Bunny stumbled to her feet, keeping one hand over her nose. "Look at this," she said, pushing up the sleeve to her shirt. Her arm was marked with purple bruises. "Zander did this to me in the studio last night. It's even on tape. The surveillance camera caught everything."

"Bunny, what do you want?" Kipenzi asked.

Bunny pulled her T-shirt up to her face and wiped the blood away from her nose. "I don't know," she said.

Finally Beth appeared in the doorway of the house. "What the hell is going on?"

"I've been banging on the door for five minutes!" Kipenzi said.

"I was asleep. The cops just called. Neighbor said someone was . . ." Beth's voice trailed off as she got a look at Bunny, her left eye turning purple, her lip split open, and her nose still dripping blood.

"I expect you'll be pressing charges," Beth said, her voice flat and lifeless.

Bunny smiled, showing off bloody gums. "Hope you guys have a good attorney."

Kipenzi went inside with Beth. Zander returned, slinking into the house and onto the sofa without speaking. Kipenzi watched out the living room window as the cops pulled up. When they knocked on the door, Beth, Kipenzi, and Zander all looked at each other.

"Just tell the truth," Kipenzi said.

Twenty minutes later the police were pushing down Zander's head and guiding him into the back seat of the patrol car. Kipenzi choked back her own tears and concentrated on comforting Beth, who was sobbing.

"I need my husband," Beth said, trying to catch her breath. "I can't deal with this."

"Call Boo," Kipenzi said. "Have him find out when they're setting bail and how much. Then have Boo go get him. Zander won't be there longer than an hour. I promise."

"I told Zan to stay away from her, Kipenzi," said Beth. "She's deranged."

Kipenzi stayed with Beth until the judge set bail and Boo was on his way to pick up Zander.

"I'm going home," Kipenzi said. "Call me."

Beth nodded and walked Kipenzi to the door. They hugged tight and Kipenzi got in the Hyundai and headed for home.

WITHIN AN HOUR, KIPENZI HAD GONE HOME, HAD CHANGED HER clothes, and was on her sofa, dozing. Just as she slipped into a real sleep, her cell phone rang. She was in that halfway world: she knew the phone was ringing but she couldn't bring herself to reach for it. It stopped. Then rang again. Stopped. Then rang again. She reached over and pressed talk.

"Kipenzi, where are you?"

"Who is this?"

"It's Dylan. I'm at Teterboro. Where are you?"

Kipenzi smacked her hand against her forehead. She'd completely forgotten that she had one final shoot to do for Happy Hair. They'd paid ten thousand dollars for a custom hybrid wig with clip-on pieces that matched the last weaved hairstyle she'd worn in their ad campaign. She had to endure one final shoot and then she would be done. She'd scheduled the shoot to take place on Mead's Bay so she could fly back with Dylan and Z. "I can't make it, Dylan," Kipenzi said, sitting up and rubbing her foot, which was throbbing as always. "Just make sure you get Z here in one piece."

"You need to get here now."

"I can't get on a plane right now. I'll reschedule with Happy Hair."

"If you don't come now, they're automatically extending your contract for a year."

"Shit. Send a car to come get me," Kipenzi said.

Jake walked in the door, wrinkling his eyebrows as he heard Kipenzi talking about leaving.

"Where are you going?" he said, as soon as she closed her phone.

"Anguilla. Last shoot for Happy Hair."

"I'm coming with you."

"Fine," Kipenzi said, looking down at her cell phone. "There's a car on the way."

"Bet. I'll be right back."

Kipenzi sat down at her kitchen table and sent a few text messages. She picked up a folder her attorney had left behind and signed a few release forms to dissolve three more of her business ventures.

Jake came downstairs with a leather overnight bag over his shoulder and his cell phone pressed to his ear. "Why does it have to be tonight?" he barked into the phone. "We've been trying to sign her for six months!"

Jake sucked his teeth and closed the phone and threw it on the sofa. Kipenzi could tell that he'd hung up on whoever had called.

"Where do you have to go?" she asked.

"Fucking Harlem. We've been trying to sign Zander's girl Bunny for months. Now she's got an offer from Puffy. His people are up there now with paperwork. She wants to go with them. The manager wants to go with us. Thinks it could tip in our favor if I show up in person."

"Shouldn't she be in a hospital or something?" Kipenzi said. "What is she doing taking business meetings after what happened with Zander?"

"She's fine. Now Zander, on the other hand—no one is gonna sign him after this."

"And you shouldn't sign Bunny!" Kipenzi said. "She's insane. And she's been baiting Zander since the very beginning. Don't sign her at all."

"She's fiery, temperamental, and she can sing her ass off. I'm signing her. And the first thing I'll have her do is refuse to testify against Zander."

"Fine. I'm leaving. Be back in the morning."

Jake kissed Kipenzi on the forehead before unlocking the private elevator and closing it behind him.

Kipenzi sent a text to her driver to make sure he was ready and checked her purse for all her essentials. She had her cell phone and keys. She looked across the room and saw the three-pound makeup bag she used to lug around everywhere she went. She smiled and lifted up her bag. It was light and manageable. No extra tracks for her hair. No makeup bag. No flat shoes for an emergency.

Kipenzi glanced down at the smaller bag she'd taken into the diner that day. Cleo's manuscript stuck out and she bent down to pick it up. She flipped through the first pages with her thumbs and then shoved the whole thing into her bag, threw it on her shoulder, and walked out of the apartment.

She thought about throwing the manuscript out in the lobby

of her building, but she didn't. Someone could find it. She thought about taking it back upstairs and telling Ian to come over and shred it. But she didn't.

Instead, when she boarded the private jet at Teterboro Airport in New Jersey, she peeled off her sneakers, adjusted her seat until she was almost completely horizontal, and began to read.

twenty-five

*B*UNNY OPENED HER EYES AND IMMEDIATELY SQUINTED. THE ROOM was too bright. For a split second, she had no idea where she was. She tried to sit up and her belly cramped. She fell back onto a hard surface and looked to her left.

A nurse appeared at her side. "How do you feel?"

"I'm fine."

"Take it easy for the rest of the day. You'll feel some mild cramping overnight. Anything excessive, give the doctor a call. Robert's waiting for you in the lobby whenever you're ready. Take your time."

The nurse squeezed her shoulder and left the room.

Bunny sat up slowly. Before she could sit all the way up, Robert and Sal were in the doorway.

"Can we come in?"

Bunny shrugged.

"How are you?" Sal asked, rubbing Bunny's shoulders.

"Going to hell," Bunny said.

"No, getting on with your life," Sal said, fluffing Bunny's spiky bangs with her fingers.

"I want to see Zander."

Robert walked over to Bunny's side, cell phone outstretched. He put a finger to his lips and gave the phone to Bunny, mouthing the name *Melinda*.

"Bunny? How are you?"

"I just got my uterus scraped. How do you think I am?"

"The paperwork is almost complete on our end. I just wanted to let you know: you did the right thing. We've got Kanye West, Timbaland, and Mark Ronson on board to produce for you. Cee-Lo loved your demo and is talking it up in the press—"

"Melinda, I'm still cramping and bleeding heavily. Mind if we talk shop later?"

Bunny flipped the phone closed and tossed it to Robert. "I need to talk to Zander."

"No," Robert said. "No more Zander. That's over."

"It's my fault that he's in trouble. I need to talk to him."

"Absolutely not."

"I need to apologize. I was wrong."

Robert shook his head. "We're this close to cementing a deal. I told Melinda there will be no more drama with you two."

"We have to talk about this now? Can I stop bleeding before you start telling me what to do?"

"I just want you to focus, Bunny."

"I'm focused."

"We'll be outside," Robert said, pointing Sal toward the door.

Bunny sat up straight, swung her legs over the table, and began to get dressed. She found her cell phone in the clear plastic bag with all her belongings. She pulled on her jeans and tank top before opening her cell phone. "Where are you?"

"Home," said Zander. "Where are you?"

"At the doctor."

"Are you okay?"

"I'm going to rent a room at the Marriott in Brooklyn tonight. Meet me there."

"You forgot about the restraining order?"

"Zander, I'm sorry. I'm gonna fix all of this."

"You can't just drop the charges. The DA's involved now and I might lose my deal."

Bunny was silent.

"What time you checking in?" Zander asked.

"I'll be there by ten."

"Bet."

Zander hung up. Bunny finished dressing and gathered her things. Robert and Sal stood up when she came out into the waiting area of the doctor's office. Robert draped an arm around Bunny and led her outside to the car.

Jackson Figueroa, Kipenzi's longtime personal paparazzo, stepped out from behind his pickup, pointed his telephoto lens, and shot twenty pictures in quick succession.

twenty-six

Alex had known Chino since high school. She had a crush on him and let him cheat off her in algebra. He repaid her by drawing elaborate tattoos on her arm with a pen during study hall. A brilliant artist, she wasn't at all surprised when she was assigned a story on him for a tattoo magazine. He'd had no idea that she was the reporter, and she didn't tell him. She just waltzed into the tattoo parlor and laughed when she saw how shocked he was that the reporter was his old friend. He'd been the only person to ever tattoo her body. The morning she interviewed him had been her first anniversary—a full year of sobriety. In the course of talking to him about setting up his shop, he told her that he was a recovering alcoholic. Alex blurted out that she was celebrating her first year that very day. He got out of his chair and hugged her tight.

Even after the story came out, he stayed in touch, sending her an occasional clipping about sobriety he came across or just a thinking-of-you card. The following year she flew out to LA to interview Nelly and the St. Lunatics and stopped in his shop to get her daisy tattoo and the first two petals to symbolize her two years of sobriety.

It was now a ritual that every spring she flew out to Los Angeles and had another petal added to her shoulder. Chino had a six-month waiting list even for a consultation. And three months longer to get the artwork done. Alex always walked right in and he would take her on the spot.

"Your tattoo is raised up," Chino said, rubbing alcohol over her skin with a cotton ball.

"I know. It's been that way for a few weeks. Freaks me out when that happens."

"It's normal. Could have irritated it with something."

"Maybe."

"But in my experience, it's usually your body's way of telling you to slow down. Are you under any stress?"

Alex smiled. "I'm supposed to be getting married in two weeks."

"Supposed to be."

"Just found out he cheated on me."

Alex was always surprised at how easy the words flowed from her mouth when she was talking to Chino. She'd never dream of telling even her closest friends about what she was going through. But Chino's eyes were so clear and calm and free of judgment that his voice was like a truth serum.

"He cheated with his body or his heart? Or both?"

"I think just his body."

"What else is going on?" said Chino, packing his needle with bright yellow ink.

"A few disturbing overlapping assignments."

"Letting your subjects get into your head again. I've told you about that. Leave your work at work."

"Right. Couldn't do it this time. Way too close to home."

Chino motioned for Alex to remove her shirt and had her straddle the black leather chair in his booth. There was a round vinyl doughnut-shaped pillow for her to rest her face in as he worked. For a full minute he just rubbed her shoulder, smoothing out the skin under her tattoo and relaxing her at the same time.

"Have you learned anything new in the past year?" Chino asked, turning on his needle and filling his area with a dull hum.

Alex sighed and then winced slightly as the needle hit her skin. "I'm done with collaborating and ghostwriting," she said through clenched teeth.

"Relax," Chino said. He put the needle down and reached down to Alex's hand, which she had clenched into a fist. "Relax your hands, your arms, your shoulders. Just give your body to the chair."

Alex slumped down and exhaled slowly through her mouth.

"What else?" Chino said, bringing the needle back to her skin.

"I love Birdie. No matter what. The blow job he got from that woman doesn't change that."

"What if it happened again?"

"I can't think that way. He swore to me it wouldn't. I have to take that at face value."

"Did you ever cheat on him?"

"Probably. I don't even know for sure."

"Understood. Has he forgiven you?"

"Categorically."

"Do you think it should work both ways?"

"Not necessarily. I mean, I did my dirt five years ago. And I made my peace with it all when I went through the twelve steps. I apologized to him back then for anything I did. What he did was recently, just a few weeks ago. It's different. We're engaged, for God's sake. Or we were."

"Can you move forward?"

"Can I? Yes. Will I? I don't know."

"What else?"

"I'm never going to get used to his ex-wife being a presence in our lives. And I'm never going to get used to the fact that I feel inferior to her."

"Okay. How will you manage it?"

"Not sure. But I know she's a trigger. When she drops off Tweet or picks her up, I want to pick up a drink."

"Why?"

"Take the edge off, I guess. Not deal with the jealousy I feel."

Chino stopped and dabbed her shoulder with a white cloth. "You're bleeding more than usual this time."

"What does that mean?"

"Doesn't have to mean anything. Just interesting. I happen to believe that a bloodletting during this process is a good sign."

"I just wrote a story about women married to rappers."

"Women like yourself."

"Kinda. Birdie's not there yet. Might not ever be there, actually."

"They must lead interesting lives."

"That's not the right word. *Bizarre* is more like it."

"When is it coming out?"

"I'm not sure. I handed it in a few days ago. I should have heard from the editor for changes by now."

"Are you proud of it?"

Alex closed her eyes and thought of a few passages in her story.

"Here's your quote," says Josephine. "I wish I was flat broke. Living with my husband on the top floor of his parents' home. I wish he still played guitar in Times Square for change. And I wish he'd never met Cleo and never got signed to a major label. I wish we had nothing but each other. I would trade every diamond I own, every home, every article of clothing, and every stupid fucking car to have our simple life back. All I would ask for is to be a mother. That is all. Write that down in your story."

"I'll never write another piece like it," Alex said.

"You're all done," said Chino, dabbing her shoulder once more and then slathering it with ointment.

Alex pulled herself up from the chair and backed up to the full-length mirror, covering her chest with her shirt.

"Is it gonna be insane when I have, like, fifty petals all over this thing?"

"I'm thinking we start a new flower in a few years. It can be intertwined with this one. You'll have a bouquet before we're all done."

"I don't know if I'm gonna keep this up when I'm, like, seventy."

"You will. And I'll be right here, looking forward to our annual get-togethers."

"It's always good to see you, Chino."

Chino bent down and embraced Alex in a tight hug. "Are you in town for a few days?"

"Nope. Leaving right now. I need to be home when I get those changes from my editor."

"Godspeed. And good luck."

Alex fumbled for her cell phone as she followed the other passengers off the plane at Newark Airport. She tucked her phone in her ear and dialed the number for her messages.

"You have fifty-six messages."

Alex felt terror ripple through her. She knew she'd cleaned her messages out before she got on the plane. Fifty-six messages in six hours was not a good sign.

As soon as she stepped into the terminal, she sat down on the floor and held the phone to her ear to listen. Before she could hear the first message, her cell phone rang. She quickly pressed talk.

"Alex? It's Maria."

"Hey. I know you want to talk about the story, but can I call you back because I—"

"So you heard?"

"Heard what? I just landed at Newark."

"Oh God, Alex."

"What's wrong? Did something happen with my story?"

"Alex, are you near a television?" Maria's voice trailed off at the same time that Alex glanced up and saw a small crowd gathering around a wall-mounted television in the terminal.

Maria said Alex's name every once in a while for a full minute and got no answer. She could hear Alex breathing steady measured breaths. But there was no response.

Alex finally snapped the phone shut. She pulled her knees up, her back propped against the wall in the airport, and looked around. The crowd of people standing near the television was growing. A few people were shaking their heads slowly and pointing at the screen. Some people were furiously text-messaging on their phones. One woman kept making the sign of the cross over her chest, her head bent low.

Alex couldn't hear the television but she didn't need to. There was a helicopter shooting from directly above a wooded area where a small plane was in a crumpled heap. The fuselage was engulfed in raging flames and Alex could just make out what looked like emergency response people barking orders at each other.

Alex stood up, leaving all her belongings on the floor. She told her brain to take her to the screen but could not feel the sensation of her feet taking actual steps. She glided over to the crowd to get a closer look at the text crawling underneath the image of the flaming mass of twisted metal.

Breaking news . . . private jet believed to belong to superstar singer Kipenzi Joy Hill found just a mile out from the Wallblake Airport . . . not presently known if singer was on board . . . the authorities are confirming four deaths including the pilot and copilot.

Alex looked down at the phone in her hand. It was ringing and she didn't recognize the number. She pressed ignore and collapsed into a chair near the television.

twenty-seven

*B*ETH HAD A FEELING THIS LABOR WAS GOING TO BE HARDER THAN all the rest. Harder than giving birth to Zaire, who'd died in utero, and then having to push Zachary out right afterward. Although this baby was the smallest, Beth struggled to stay on point with her breathing as she sat in her favorite armchair, timing her contractions.

When it was time Zander drove her to the hospital and sat with her as the staff administered the epidural.

Once the pain medicine kicked in, Beth was able to relax. She sat up in bed and chewed ice chips. Dr. Hamilton checked on her, marking how far along she was dilating and reminding her to relax.

"Where is Kipenzi? Did she get back yet?" Beth asked Zander when he came in.

Zander looked down at his cell phone. "She hasn't called me."

"What about your father?"

"He hasn't called either."

"Call Kipenzi again," Beth said. "This is not like her."

Zander looked down at his phone and read a text message. "Ma . . . ," he said, walking toward the television and turning it on.

"What, baby?"

"Auntie Penzi . . ."

Beth stared at the screen. An all-news station had a helicopter view of a plane on fire. Before Beth could scream, two nurses came into the room. One took away the television remote, led Zander out, and turned off the television. The other put her hand inside Beth's gown.

"She's seven centimeters. Almost time to start pushing, Beth."

"Don't fuck with me," Beth said, her breath ragged. "What's going on?"

"Beth, I want you to focus on your breathing. It's almost time to push this baby out."

A contraction overcame Beth and she leaned back and moaned, her head swinging from side to side. "Kipenzi . . ."

Dr. Hamilton came up to Beth's ear. "Her plane went down in Anguilla," she said. Beth began to yell out and Dr. Hamilton squeezed her forearm tight. "Listen to me. Look at me." Dr. Hamilton grabbed Beth's jaw and turned her face around. "I just got off the phone with the hospital in Miami, where she was airlifted. Kipenzi just came out of surgery. And she is going to survive. Do you hear me? Let's focus on getting this baby out, okay? Please, Beth? I have someone here to help you . . ."

Z came into the room with Zander. Seeing him standing in the doorway took Beth's breath away. He was, as his grandmother would say, as clean as the board of health—even more fit, toned, and clear-eyed than the day she had seen him at Eden.

Z took his position on Beth's left side, leaning into her neck to kiss her. They breathed together, screamed together, and when the baby, a seven-pound little girl with a full head of jet-black hair, whooshed out of Beth's body, the doctor placed the baby on Beth's chest and the three of them all clutched each other and sobbed.

Thirty minutes later, after the baby was cleaned up and swaddled tight, Z dropped his head in his hands and cried.

"Baby, what's wrong?" Beth asked.

Z clenched his teeth and raised his head to face his wife, his eyes bloodshot red. "Kipenzi . . ."

"She's okay, right?" Beth looked at Z, who had his mouth open but couldn't speak. She looked at Zander. He had his head down and was crying softly.

Beth dropped her head and cried. There was no need to hear the actual words. When she came home with the baby, Ian was there, holding a black binder in his hands, ready to make arrangements for Kipenzi's funeral.

"She was already gone before the baby got here, wasn't she?" Beth asked Z, as they lay in bed her first night home.

"Yes. She was," Z said, stroking his first daughter's cheek.

"What about Dylan?"

"She survived."

"I want Kipenzi here. Right now."

"She's gone, Beth."

Beth squeezed her eyes tight and forced herself to sit up, bringing the baby up with her. "Z, you don't understand. When I came up here with you, those girls in Fresh Meadows weren't fucking with me. The white girls said I was dirty and trashy. The black girls said I stank. Kipenzi was the first person to really talk to me."

"I know," Z said.

"I can't even imagine living without her."

Z took his new daughter out of Beth's arms and cradled her. "Hey, Kipenzi," he said to the little girl. "Are you going to be a singer too?"

"Z, this wasn't supposed to happen. She was leaving the business. She was going to teach piano and travel."

"While I was in rehab, she wrote me a few letters."

"Really?"

Z smiled and nodded, his eyes filling up. "She told me I had to get it together for you. Told me that you needed me. Kids needed me. Wanted me to really understand that."

Beth nodded. He cradled her head, stroking her hair. He stopped to peek into the blankets and stare at his little girl, whose mouth was pursed into a tiny O.

Beth leaned on him and kissed him. "I love you, Z," she said.

"I know."

Beth leaned over and kissed little Kipenzi. Z motioned toward the television. Beth looked up to see Kipenzi on the screen, in a clip from a performance she'd given at the Grammy Awards the year before.

Z turned the volume up and held his two women as tight as he could. Beth closed her eyes and pretended Kipenzi was in the room with them, singing to little Kipenzi, making her chin quiver so that Beth would laugh. As the song came to an end, Beth whispered a prayer into the top of her daughter's head and hoped that Kipenzi heard her.

twenty-eight

SINGER, SONGWRITER, ACTRESS
KIPENZI JOY HILL BURIED IN HOMETOWN
OF HOPE, ARKANSAS

The New York Times

Monday, May 24, 2009
by Alex Sampson Maxwell

On a rainy Sunday morning in a town called Hope, Grammy Award–winning singer and actress Kipenzi Hill was transported to her final resting place. In accordance with her instructions, her casket was carried by hand from the Hicks Funeral Home, where her body was prepared, to the burial plot owned by the Hill family since the late 1800s.

The service, fiercely guarded by a private security detail, opened with a poem read by Beth Saddlebrook. Mrs. Saddlebrook is married to Isaac "Z" Saddlebrook, a rap singer who is currently enjoying a resurgence in popularity with a verse he contributed to Kipenzi Hill's latest song. Ironically, the song, "So Long," was meant to be a farewell. Ms. Hill recently announced her retirement from the music industry. The single was the first and last from a final album, a greatest-hits collection.

Mrs. Saddlebrook, who recently gave birth, had to be helped up to a small podium by her husband and her oldest son. She cried briefly before unfolding a paper handed to her by Ian Peterson, Ms. Hill's longtime personal assistant, and reading a message left by the deceased: "As you watch me enter this new phase in my life, please treat this show like you would any other. Applaud me! Rejoice! Just because I'm retiring doesn't mean I don't like to make an entrance."

Ms. Hill is survived by her parents, who managed her career since its inception. Ms. Hill recently married her longtime boyfriend, rapper Jacob "Jake" Giles.

Mr. Giles, along with Mr. Saddlebrook, Mr. Peterson, and Ms. Hill's father, John Hill, carried Ms. Hill's white casket to a section at the far right of the burial plot. The foursome dropped to their knees to settle the coffin into the ground. The men, all dressed in white, used their hands to drop mounds of dirt to cover the coffin. After ten minutes, they were joined by the remainder of the guests. For one hour, the ten people in attendance transferred dirt. The rain came down heavier, turning the dirt into a thick, heavy mud. By the time Ms. Hill's casket was completely covered, the attendants were covered in caked-on mud. Just a few feet away from where Ms. Hill was buried, the small group sat on the ground, crying and embracing each other. They left as a group. The groundskeepers followed, finishing the job.

Ms. Hill's gravestone is inscribed with her full name, Kipenzi Joy Hill-Giles, and her date of birth and date of death.

$\mathcal{A}$LEX RAN UP THE STEPS OF BROOKLYN BOROUGH HALL AS FAST AS she could with Tweet on her hip. "How can I be late for my own wedding?" she said to Tweet.

Tweet shrugged and laughed. "What if my dad marries someone else 'cause you're late?"

"Imagine that," Alex said, swinging open the door and dashing over to the elevators leading up to the judge's chambers.

"Alex?"

Alex, having just gotten into the elevator, turned around to see Cleo Wright coming down a staircase surrounded by three men in suits.

"Cleo, I can't talk to you right now," Alex said, stabbing the number seven on the elevator pad.

Cleo nodded at the men, shook hands quickly with one of them, and then ran over to the elevator and put her hand out just before the doors closed. Alex rolled her eyes and stepped as far away from Cleo as possible.

"Why are you here?" Cleo asked.

Alex shifted Tweet's weight on her hips. "I'm getting married today. Want to be my maid of honor?"

"Oh, wow. Congratulations, Alex. I mean that."

"I'm sure."

"The book will be out soon."

Alex looked up at the numbers, waiting for the number seven to light up. "I heard," said Alex. "You're already number three on Amazon for preorders."

"You're still getting royalties, even though you took your name off the book."

Alex smiled with her mouth closed. "Thanks."

"I was wrong, Alex."

Alex kept her eyes on the number pad and raised one eyebrow.

"This book," Cleo said. "It's all wrong."

The elevator doors opened and Alex put Tweet down and held her hand firmly. She looked back at Cleo. "Did you realize that before or after Kipenzi died?"

"After."

"Your sales are going through the roof now," Alex said. "You talk about what you did or didn't do with her husband and her husband's best friend. Even the boyfriend of the reporter writing the book! It's all very salacious."

Cleo took a box out of her carryall and handed it to Alex. "I changed it. A lot. Toned it down. The one in stores next week is softened up a bit. This is the real one. All real names. All true. Only copy that exists."

"Is this the version that they found at Kipenzi's crash site?" Alex said, holding up the box.

Cleo nodded. "The idea that she might have died reading about . . ." She dropped her head and put a hand to her mouth. "It's not right," she said.

"It was never right," Alex said.

"I know."

"Cleo, I have to go get married now. My bridesmaid is getting a bit antsy," Alex said, holding up Tweet's hand. Alex held onto the box with one hand and led Tweet into the judge's chambers with the other.

"The truth is in there," Cleo said as she got back on the elevator. "About me and Birdie. And you too. If you want to know."

Without speaking, Alex let the glass door of the office close behind her.

"AND BY THE POWER VESTED IN ME BY THE STATE OF NEW YORK, I NOW pronounce you husband and wife. Mr. Washington, you may now salute your bride."

Birdie picked Tweet up. They both leaned over and kissed Alex on each cheek at the same time.

"Where's the honeymoon?" the judge asked, going back to his desk.

"On our front stoop in Brooklyn," Birdie said. "We're on a budget."

"You can at least do a nice dinner."

"We have something to take care of first," said Alex, looking at Birdie.

Birdie tilted his head. "What's up?"

Alex turned to the judge. "Do you have a shredder?"

"In the front hall, in the copy room."

Alex grabbed her bag and ushered Birdie and Tweet into the copy room.

"Tweet, have you ever used a shredder?"

The little girl shook her head solemnly.

"It's fun. But you have to be very, very careful. See, look. You put a piece of paper right here at the top."

The dull roar of the shredder made Tweet jump and then laugh. "Let me do it again!" she said.

"We're all gonna do it," Alex said. She handed the top half of the manuscript to Birdie, who scanned the title page and then looked directly at his new wife. "Did you read this?"

"No."

"Do you want to?"

"No."

Birdie looked at Alex for a long moment. "We can talk about this."

"Shred," Alex said.

It took twenty minutes to shred all five hundred pages. When they were done, they emptied the plastic container filled with the confettilike scraps and put them inside a clear plastic garbage bag. Alex held the bag over her shoulder as if she were a hobo. On their way out, Alex tossed the bag into a garbage can on the corner of Joralemon and Court streets.

Birdie and Alex walked to Junior's and shared a slice of cheesecake with Tweet. That night, Tweet's mother picked Tweet up for the weekend. And Birdie and Alex folded themselves into bed and watched television until the sun came peeking through for a sunny May morning. When the sun was completely overhead, Birdie got out of bed to draw all the curtains and returned to his wife.

thirty

*C*LEO SAT ON THE FLOOR OF THE LIVING ROOM OF HER NEW HOME. The movers had brought the last of the boxes inside hours ago.

Seven bedrooms. Six full bathrooms. One half bathroom. An interior designer would be there in the morning to fulfill her vision and cater to her every whim. A full-time housekeeper was scheduled to begin before she'd even have a chance to get the place dirty.

Cleo's new home was nestled at the top of a hill in central Jersey. She'd envisioned a farm with lots of land in northern New Jersey, a place where she could raise livestock and ride horses. Instead she was in a gated community with twenty-four-hour armed security. The death threats had begun pouring in to her publisher as soon as *Platinum* hit number one on the *New York Times* Best Sellers list. She'd gone into hiding for three weeks, hunting for homes online. She'd closed on the house sight unseen and had movers pack up all her belongings.

Cleo flipped through the contacts in her phone and stopped at Ras Bennett. She hit dial.

"Yes?"

"Ras?"

"You have the wrong number."

Cleo pulled back the phone to make sure she had dialed correctly. She had. She hung up and called the studio.

"He doesn't work out of here anymore," the receptionist said, before hanging up.

Cleo called the secret landline Ras had installed in the cabana by the pool. It had been disconnected.

Ras? Where are you?

Cleo went out to her backyard and sat on the steps that led down to the swimming pool. She called every one of Ras's contacts. She either got voice mail or the number was disconnected. Finally Jean, his driver, picked up the phone in his Town Car.

"Where's Ras?"

"Jamaica."

"When is he coming back?"

"He's not. Moved the family there last week."

"That's impossible. I just saw him a few weeks ago. He never said anything to me about moving."

"He's gone."

"Thank you," Cleo said.

Cleo settled herself on the floor of her dining room with a stack of her books and a pen. She scribbled messages in each, stuffed them in padded envelopes, and then set them aside to be mailed out. She reached for a copy and opened it to the title page: "Dear Mommy: Here's how I turned out. Make sure you show everyone at church. Love, Patricia." She inscribed a copy to Ras: "Thank you for encouraging me to tell my story. I love you. Love, Marasa."

The doorbell rang. Cleo grabbed her stack of books and rushed through the kitchen, dining room, recreation room, and sitting room to get to the front door. *He's here.*

It was a deliveryman with an oversized package. "Be careful. It's heavy."

Cleo gave the mailman the books to send out and then signed for her package. She dragged the enormous parcel into her living room and ripped the paper off. It was a ten-by-twelve replication of her book cover, the letters *Platinum* spelled out high. She had to get on tiptoe to touch the raised foil lettering at the very top. At the bottom was a metal plate. A re-creation of the issue of the *New York Times* in which her book was number one was centered. The inscription: "In recognition of your accomplishments. Here's to the sequel! Your friends at Simonstein Publishing."

Cleo went to her bare kitchen. In the refrigerator was just a bag of oranges and a bottle of Veuve Clicquot. She took the bottle and two champagne glasses and walked back to her dining room and slid down to the floor, crossing her legs. She pushed one glass away from her, as if someone were there to take it. She poured each glass to the rim, raised hers to no one, and whispered, "Cheers."

She drained her glass. And then reached over to take the other glass and drank that one as well.

Her head swimming, she sat in silence, pouring and sipping her champagne. She stared at the reproduction of her book cover until her eyes blurred over.

An hour later, she was still sipping and deep in thought. The only sound in the house was her phone opening and clicking closed again as she fiddled with it in her hand.

She went to the last letter in the alphabet and pressed talk. A man's groggy voice answered the phone. In the background she could hear the sound of a baby crying.

"Come over," she said.

"What you got over there?"

"Whatever you want."

"Text me your address and give me an hour."

Cleo hung up. Texted her address. And then went to her bedroom and took out a half ounce of crack cocaine, five ecstasy pills, and a twenty bag of weed from her dresser. That would be enough to get him through the weekend.

Cleo stayed on the floor, pouring and sipping her champagne. She closed her eyes and let her mind drift, waiting for the doorbell to ring.

thirty-one

ALEX SAT ON HER FRONT STOOP, TWEET SITTING ON THE STEP below her. She was making dozens of two-strand twists that she put in Tweet's hair every Sunday. Every so often she'd shield her eyes from the sun and peer down the street, looking for her husband and his modified pimp strut to come down DeKalb Avenue. Birdie was meeting with Jake about signing to the label and her stomach was churning.

"I see Daddy!" Tweet exclaimed, half standing.

"Okay, calm down," said Alex, kissing her on the cheek. "Sit."

Birdie walked down a few steps to the mailbox, gathered the mail, and then came up to the steps.

"My two favorite women," said Birdie, leaning over to kiss Tweet on the cheek.

Alex closed her eyes and lifted her face. Her husband cupped her chin in his hand and kissed her softly on the lips. "Would you still love me if I was rich and famous?" Birdie asked.

"What kind of question is that?"

Birdie pulled a sheaf of papers out of his knapsack.

Alex flipped through the first few pages and then stood up, nearly knocking Tweet off the stoop. "This is a contract. From Jake."

Birdie bowed. "Consider me officially a proud sellout with a six-figure advance."

Alex clasped her hands over her mouth. She leaned in to hug Birdie.

Birdie sat next to Alex as she continued to work on Tweet's hair.

"So when are you gonna start changing?" Alex asked.

"Never."

"You're not gonna wear shades at night, in the club?"

"Absolutely not."

"Who's gonna be in your crew?"

"You and Tweet."

"We don't make much of an entourage."

"I want you to stop writing."

"Yeah, right."

"Just for a little bit. Take yoga. That painting class. You supported us for long enough. Can you please take a year off to do anything you want? No deadlines. No editors. No crazy groupie stories. No travel. Just be with me. Give Tweet a sibling."

Alex smiled. She finished Tweet's last twist and the little girl ran next door to look for a friend. Alex leaned onto Birdie's shoulder.

"What else we got," she said, pointing to the random letters and packages in the pile of mail.

"Bills I can actually pay!" said Birdie, making a pile. "And yet another cover story for Alex Sampson Maxwell." She pulled out a new copy of *Vibe*. A black-and-white picture of Kipenzi graced the cover. There were no cover tags, simply the word *Vibe* behind her and the date of her birth and death at the bottom.

"It was supposed to be about all the wives, not just Kipenzi," Alex said.

"Death changes things."

"Tell me about it."

"Something else for you," Birdie said, handing over a parcel.

Alex frowned as soon as she saw the return address. "It's from Cleo. I don't want it."

"Open it."

Alex moved over, as if the book could bite her. "No."

"I'll open it," Birdie said, peeling back the brown wrapper. "It's the book. Just a copy of the book."

Birdie handed it over and Alex took it. The black background of the cover was striking. Every time she got on the subway, there were at least three or four girls with their heads buried in the book she had written. It was a strange sensation. Even though Cleo was unscrupulous, vindictive, and evil, Alex was still proud of the narrative she had been able to put together.

"How's it start?" Birdie asked, leaning back, his head to the sky, eyes closed.

Alex cleared her throat and turned to the first page:

Being with me is an honor. I'm not a commoner. And contrary to popular belief, I don't have sex with everyone. If you've been with me, you've achieved something. I'm a benchmark. Like going platinum.

Alex rolled her eyes and thumbed through the book. "I can't," she said. "Can't read another word. I'll be sick."

Birdie leaned over. "What's this?" he said, turning the pages to the inside front cover.

"Oh God," Alex said, pressing the book back into Birdie's hands. "She left me a message."

"Want me to read it to you?"

"No."

"Can I read it?"

"Knock yourself out."

Alex tried not to look as Birdie's lips moved. His face was stricken.

"You should probably read this."

Alex took the book, opened it, and placed it on her lap.

Alex, thank you so much for helping me get my story down. Good luck to Birdie with his deal. I talked him up to a few important people so I think that might have helped. ;) Not sure how deep you're going to be in the writing game. But I have a story for you.

You should ask Ras about that baby he adopted. There's a good story there. And if I know you the way I think I do, you won't be able to resist finding out the truth. You can thank me later.

C

Alex looked up at Birdie.

"You're taking a year off," Birdie said. Alex opened her mouth to speak and he shook his head. "No, Alex."

Alex looked back down at the book and read the words again. And then once more. She closed the book, clutched it to her chest, and nestled closer to Birdie.

"A year off?" Alex whispered, leaning into her husband's chest. "Maybe . . ."

Acknowledgments

This novel was born out of a story written for *VIBE* several years ago. Many thanks to Serena Kim for assigning the story to me and always helping me to do my best work.

My agent, Ryan Fischer-Harbage, planted the seed for this novel. I can't thank him enough for the idea and for pushing me to complete it. In ways both professional and personal, Ryan has been in my corner since we sat next to each other at the Radcliffe Publishing Course in 1998. Who knew?

Sulay Hernandez: my editor. I'm in good hands with you. And I'm grateful. I look forward to more books together. And be prepared to let me rock with a thoroughly flowery and literary title. Unless, of course, this book lands on a few best seller lists. If that happens, you can name the next one *Diamond Life* and I won't bat an eye.

I'd like to thank everyone at Touchstone/Fireside and Simon & Schuster for making this book happen.

Faith Evans: you emailed me out of the blue in 2006 and asked me to coauthor your memoir. I'd never had a book published before. And I wasn't sure if I was the right person for the job. You were sure. And you jumped off my career in books. For that I am forever grateful.

I'd be remiss if I didn't acknowledge [Name Redacted]. You swindled me out of $18,000. I wrote a book for you. You never paid me. I have to acknowledge your pure jerkiness. (Is that a word?) From you, I learned how important it is to handle your business (word to Thembisa Mshaka), and never get so caught up in the creative that you don't check your contracts. You also taught me how to forgive. Other people. Not you.

Writing a book is torture. You have to make the time to get the words down. And for me, that means depending on a pit crew who patches me up, fixes my life and makes sure I can get it done. I may have put down all the words in this book but it wasn't written alone.

Without the help of my pit crew, I'd still be in Starbucks trying to outline this thing:

Jasmine Volmar, Myrlove Denestant, Skye Volmar, Rita King, Nicole Green, Erik Parker, Ashanti King, and the staff at Executive Baby made it possible for me to write and know that my baby girl would be well taken care of. Thank you.

Thanks to my father, Robert E. King. You assigned me the most fascinating book of my career: yours.

Much love to Shydel James, my research assistant, faux baby-sitter, ghostwriter, GCH, confidante, wardrobe consultant, stylist, pharmacist and patron saint. Thank you for being my very first reader and for all your constructive criticism. And thank you for funding my writer's retreat (also known as three nights at the West Orange Marriott) when it was time to crank out this novel at the very end. I love you so very much.

My family in general is always a beacon of light and support for me. Much love to the King, Parker, Volmar, Shelbourne, Mbako, Peterson, Cagle, Lee, Johnson Barnes, Siders, Lane, Webb, Dunson and Lockett families. Love to my brother Al-Tariq, and all my nieces, nephews, cousins, aunts and uncles, sisters-in-law, brothers-in-law, and my in-laws, Terry Peterson and Charlotte Parker.

I'm blessed to have a tight knit cheering squad who love me like cooked food: the Honorable Victoria F. Pratt, Maya T. Harris, Portia Chinnery, Paul Chinnery, Anton Lendor, James Hall, Dylan Siegler, Ukachi Arinzeh, Felix Mickens (shout-out to his wife, LaTerra Howard for being one of my first readers), Anita Johnson, and Darron "Chill" Wallace.

I'm also honored to belong to two top-secret online communities: to my Threadren and my Lede-ing ladies, I love you all so much for being a place where I can truly be myself.

A heartfelt thank-you to a variety of folks to whom I'm forever indebted: Lindy Hess, Leslie Hendrickson, Jamilah Barnes Creekmur, Leslie and Jermaine Hall, Malcolm Shabazz, and Gianna Miceli. Y'all know why.

Love and respect to Akiba Solomon, Laini Madhubiti, Selwyn Seyfu Hinds, Carlito Rodriguez and my ENTIRE family at *The Source*. To Sheena "more substance, less style" Lester, The Blackspot, Datwon Thomas, and the whole old-school *XXL* crew. Love to Steven Samuel, Felicia Palmer, Jordan-River and Galilee.

Hugs and kisses to my girl, Elise Wright, who has held me down from day one; Cheo Hodari Coker, for always dispensing advice—fast! Clover Hope and Linda Hobbs, for inspiring me to be a better writer. Tamara Warren, for a kind word just when I needed it. Heather Faison, aka HAFtime, for my kick-ass website and being the best unpaid intern ever.

To everyone at Chill E. D. Management (not to be confused with Ed from accounting): I can't thank you enough for your assistance and advice.

Shout-outs to Emil Wilbekin, Mimi Valdés, Raqiyah, Shani and Norman Parrish, Jamie Katz, Rob Kenner, Celia San Miguel and the ENTIRE staff at *Vibe*, past and present. And many thanks to Joyce Davis, Adenike Olanrewaju, and Reema Mitra for their invaluable book advice.

Thank you to Bevy Smith, Tai Beauchamp, and Naima Brown for helping me find my inner diva.

Thank you to Cynde Watson and Luis Antonio Thompson for showcasing my inner diva.

Thank you to E. Monique Johnson, Kym Backer, Bernard and Sheila Bronner, and the entire UPSCALE team for keeping me with the steady check that allowed me to write this novel.

In the process of writing this book, I've connected with people I've admired from afar for years. They've opened themselves up to me, offering advice and tips (and some awesome blurbs!) I'm forever indebted to Denene Milner, dream hampton, Erica Kennedy, Yanick Rice Lamb, Kierna Mayo, Virginia DeBerry, and Donna Grant.

This has nothing to do with anything. But I remember in *Waiting to Exhale,* in the acknowledgments, Terry McMillian shouted out her hairstylist for always hooking her hair up. I was like, huh? You're thanking your hairstylist? But now I get it. I write better when my hair's cute. So much love to Lynn Miles, at The Shades Hair Studio, for always hooking my 'do up. From a TWA to a Diana Ross–Beyoncé–Wendy Williams hybrid—and everything in between—you keep my strands in check.

TH, TG, Tog, Tati and TB: I love you all more than you could ever know.

Shoot. This acknowledgments mess is an impossible task. I'm at the end now. And someone very important to me is sucking their teeth and saying, "Oh, no, she didn't leave my name off!"

Charge my mind. Not my heart.

Aliya S. King
March 5, 2010